FISHER
OF
SOULS

FISHER OF SOULS

HANNI MÜNZER

Translated by John Brownjohn

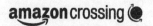

Text copyright © 2013 Hanni Münzer

Translation copyright © 2015 John Brownjohn

Previously published as *Die Seelenfischer (Seelenfischer-Tetralogie, Band 1)* by the author via the Kindle Direct Publishing Platform in Germany in 2013. Translated from German by John Brownjohn. First published in English by AmazonCrossing in 2015.

Published by AmazonCrossing, Seattle

www.apub.com

Amazon, the Amazon logo, and AmazonCrossing are trademarks of Amazon.com, Inc., or its affiliates.

ISBN-13: 9781503949492
ISBN-10: 1503949494

Cover design by David Drummond

Printed in the United States of America

"Man, in his ignorance, takes time to believe in what he cannot see."

—*Giacomo della Marca (Saint James of the Marches), d. 1476*

PROLOGUE

Rome 1773

The man at the window stood with his hands clasped behind his back, looking down at the rapidly emptying courtyard. He eyed the milling crowd with a contemptuous smile that made his chiseled features look even harder. Everyone seemed to be in a hurry to reach a place of safety before nightfall. To him the people were merely drones, simple-minded sheep in need of the guidance of shepherds chosen by God. In other words, men like him. How else would he have attained his eminent position, if not by God's will and his special blessing?

A servant had just lit the candles, and their flickering light cast dark shadows on the lofty walls.

Behind him, he heard the sound of leather sandals. The footsteps betrayed the reluctance with which the newcomer entered the room, and this evoked another cynical smile. He despised people who were afraid of him.

"Well, Brother Domenico, what have you to report?" he asked without turning around. "Do you have the names of the woman and her fellow conspirators?"

"Forgive me, Venerable Father, but we could get nothing out of her." There was an almost imperceptible tremor in the monk's voice.

"Why trouble me, then?"

The man answered hurriedly and with obsequious eagerness. "We may have happened on an indication that the parchment is only a copy and not the original. If so, it is a masterly forgery. I am having it examined by some knowledgeable brothers at this moment."

"Good. I wish to be informed at once of any results, no matter what the hour. Meanwhile, continue to question the woman. She's a weak creature—she'll talk. By tomorrow, I want to know where she obtained the secret ecclesiastical documents she was carrying. Do not return until you can bring me results. You are dismissed."

Impatiently, and still standing with his back to his visitor, he flicked his hand as if shooing away an importunate fly. The gesture caused the fitful candlelight to catch the sparkling ruby on his right hand, intensifying its luminosity and making it gleam like a gout of blood. For one fleeting moment, the room seemed to be bathed in fire.

Brother Domenico, who had briefly raised his eyes from the floor, construed this as a sinister omen. He humbly stood his ground.

Angrily, the man at the window turned to face him at last. "Well," he snapped, "what more do you want?"

"Venerable Father, I regret to inform you that it's impossible for us to comply with your wishes." The monk's head was bowed again, and the tremor in his voice now ran through his whole body.

"Why so?" the harsh voice demanded. The man at the window was accustomed to having his orders carried out at once.

Brother Domenico's cold lips reluctantly shaped the answer he knew would seal his own fate too. "Because the woman is dead."

A TREASURE TROVE
OF KNOWLEDGE

Nuremberg, Germany—present day

Nuremberg is a city rich in history. Founded at the beginning of the first millennium, it enjoyed a heyday at the end of the fifteenth century, when the city was ruled by a council composed of influential merchant families who, after the Roman model, called themselves patricians and became rich and powerful through trade. When the Second World War ended, the victorious powers used the city as a showcase for the settling of accounts with prominent Nazi henchmen like Hermann Göring and Rudolf Hess. The Nuremberg trials were held in the Palace of Justice on Fürther Strasse, which can be visited to this day. Many major industrial concerns originated in Nuremberg, the most famous of them being Siemens.

It was to the home of an owner of one of those well-known firms that the blue delivery van was headed this morning. Its destination was a seventeenth-century mansion surrounded by parklike grounds in the Nuremberg district of Lauf am Holz. A straight drive lined with cypresses led up to the main house, whose façade was picturesquely overgrown with climbing roses and pale-pink wisteria. Running all around the property was a brick wall interrupted only by a wrought-iron gate. There was no need for a nameplate or mailbox. Everyone knew who lived there.

The van pulled up outside the gate, and the sturdy, bespectacled driver stuck his arm out the window and rang the bell.

A woman's voice issued from an intercom. "Yes?"

"It's Fugga, heating engineers."

The big gate purred open, and the van drove up the drive and came to a halt outside the house. The driver and his younger passenger got out, and each unloaded a heavy toolbox.

A stout woman wearing a white apron over her dress was waiting for them. "Good morning, I'm Frau Gabler, the von Stettens' house-keeper. Come in. I'll show you where you can start."

The two Fuggas, father and son, followed her into the entrance hall, which was tiled with black-and-white terrazzo. To the right and left, curving staircases with carved-oak banisters ascended to a gallery on the second floor. Paintings in gilded frames lined the walls. On the left, double doors stood open to reveal a wood-paneled library.

Frau Gabler led the two men purposefully inside. "Please start in here."

"Er, sorry, Frau Gabler," said the elder Fugga, "but Herr von Stetten instructed us to replace the central heating pipes in the bathrooms and bedrooms only."

"That's all right. Frau von Stetten would like them replaced through-out the house, and she wants you to start in the library right away. You can revise your estimate and submit it to her tomorrow. I've got some work to do in the kitchen. If you need anything"—she pointed to an eggshell-colored telephone beside the library door—"there's the house phone. Dial 2."

Although the master of the house, Heinrich von Stetten, wanted the Fuggas to carry out no more than the work agreed upon, the mistress of the house, his wife, Evelyn, had resolved to take advantage of her husband's absence on a ten-day business trip to have the entire system modernized.

The two men surveyed the library. The walls and ceiling were lined with panels of fine mahogany. The room was some twenty-five feet long and fifteen feet in width and height. The surrounding shelves were filled from floor to ceiling with leather-bound volumes. A wrought-iron spiral staircase led to a loft punctuated by two arched windows. Situated between the windows was an early twentieth-century radiator covered with a wooden grille. Below the stairs, in the corner, was another door. The younger Fugga tried the handle. It was locked. Having completed their inspection, father and son exchanged a look of bafflement. They were in trouble and they knew it.

The elder Fugga removed his glasses and polished them on his handkerchief. "*Pff*, talk about counting one's chickens! We thought this was going to be an easy, well-paid job we could use as a reference later on. Not a chance! Now we'll have to drill holes in the ceiling and locate the central heating pipes under all this mahogany. What do we do with the books? They look old, and old means valuable. I don't think our insurance would shell out if one of those old tomes fell to dust in our fingers. I'd better get permission to clear these shelves." Resignedly, he shuffled over to the house phone.

Frau Gabler tersely informed him that they were welcome to stack the books on the Persian carpet. Frau von Stetten would have no objection, she said.

So the two Fuggas set to work. A job was a job, and theirs had just multiplied itself by five.

They chose the shelf above the radiator on the logical assumption that the central heating pipe would not zigzag across the ceiling. When they had stacked the first of the books on the floor behind them and the back wall became visible, they were appalled to find that the shelf did not abut directly against the mahogany paneling. Screwed to the wall behind it was yet another slab of mahogany that would have to be removed.

Once that had been done, the younger Fugga wiped his moist forehead on the sleeve of his coverall and said, "Lucky we're being paid by the hour."

"Yes," sighed his father, "it's our most profitable job in a long time, but how are we going to get it done in just ten days? You go on ahead to the cellar and take a closer look at the heating system. I'll carry on here."

The elder Fugga put his ear to the wall and systematically tapped the exposed paneling until he found a spot that sounded hollow. That had to be where the pipes were located. In search of some place where he could lever off the precious mahogany without damaging it, he carefully inserted his thinnest crowbar into the crack between two panels. When one of them came away, he lifted it out and shone his flashlight into the opening. He was in for a surprise: there was not a central heating pipe to be seen; instead, there was nothing but books! The niche was filled with them. It was strange that they were concealed behind the shelves, so rather than get into trouble, he went again to the house phone and dialed 2.

It was two or three minutes before Frau Gabler appeared, rather out of breath, and took a look at Fugga's discovery. The housekeeper turned pale. She had always dismissed the story as a myth, she told him, but it appeared he'd found precisely what the master of the house had been seeking for decades.

At that moment, the younger Fugga returned, covered in dust and with cobwebs in his hair.

Frau Gabler frowned at the sight of him. "Kindly stay here and don't touch a thing, either of you," she told the two men sternly. "I'll go and see if Frau von Stetten is up yet."

Hurrying up the stairs and along a passage so thickly carpeted it muffled her footsteps, she knocked on the door at the far end.

"Come in, Alma!" called a soft, refined voice.

Although Frau Gabler had been in her employer's bedroom innumerable times, its elegance never failed to captivate her. It was like being immersed in the fairy-tale world of *The Thousand and One Nights*. Evelyn von Stetten's father, Senator Hohenkamp, had lost his wife early on, and Evelyn was his only child. The senator had been German ambassador to various countries in the Middle East. Like most men of his generation, he did not know how to deal with a young child on his own, and he entrusted her upbringing to sundry private tutors and, more particularly, an Arab nanny named Fatima. Although Fatima could scarcely read or write, she was an inexhaustible source of mystical fairy tales. The mysteries of the Orient were irresistibly attractive to a child as fanciful by nature as Evelyn, and this was reflected in her private quarters. The room's showpiece was a four-poster bed. It contained no other furniture apart from a dressing table and chair and two sandalwood tables on each of which a Venus orchid bloomed in a Murano vase. The walls were adorned with trompe-l'œil motifs that created perfectly the illusion of a seraglio.

The baroness was already up and wearing one of her antique kaftans. Seated at her dressing table, she was brushing her fair hair, which fell in soft waves to her shoulders.

"Forgive me for disturbing you so early, but it's about the workmen," said Frau Gabler, coming closer. "They've discovered something— a mass of old books."

"But Alma, what else would they be likely to find in a library more than two hundred years old?" Frau von Stetten said gently, at pains not to sound impatient. Frau Gabler had served the von Stetten family faithfully for over thirty-five years. The baroness blithely ignored the fact that she herself would soon turn sixty. She'd retained her figure by dint of iron discipline, and her reflection in the mirror, which revealed the image of a well-groomed woman with fine features, belied her age. Her youthful appearance was intensified further by her sensitive mouth and the hint of melancholy in her eyes that dated from her eldest son's death in an accident. Sadly, her impressionable soul had struggled with the demons of depression since Alexander's death, and she had already spent two longish periods in an exclusive clinic.

"Forgive, me, Baroness. I meant that the men have removed some of the mahogany paneling. Behind it they found a concealed niche filled with old books."

"Oh!" exclaimed Evelyn, clearly disquieted by this news. The central heating dated from the first decade of the twentieth century, and she had been pestering her husband for years to have it replaced, often complaining over breakfast how badly she had slept because the incessant gurgling of the pipes gave her a headache.

For his part, Heinrich von Stetten was opposed to making any alterations, however small, to the house his family had owned for over two centuries. He liked the familiar nocturnal noises peculiar to the building in which he had grown up.

Not much later, the elder Fugga was eagerly using his flashlight to show off his find to the baroness. On her direction, he removed two more panels to give them an unimpeded view of the opening. It was stacked with books.

Evelyn picked one up. The embossing on the cover indicated that it was a Luther Bible from 1529. Thoughtfully, she handed the book to Frau Gabler, who produced a cloth from her apron and promptly wiped it clean of dust.

Meanwhile, the baroness took out another book, a first edition titled *Cautio Criminalis*. No author's name was given, but she found a dated dedication: in 1632 a Friedrich Spee von Langenfeld had given the book to someone whose name she could not decipher. After examining two more volumes, she knew she had seen enough.

Evelyn von Stetten had spent too long living with a man obsessed with ancient books and manuscripts not to realize that this find was exceptional. It might even be a part of the family treasure reputed to have been hidden long ago. One after another, members of the von Stetten family had gone looking for it on the basis of this rumor. How ironic it would be if the legendary treasure, which the imagination of those who handed down the story from generation to generation had transformed into a mountain of jewels and gold and silver coins, turned out to be no more than a heap of dusty old tomes. However, Evelyn could think of no one who would be less disappointed than her husband. This long-lost library was Heinrich von Stetten's Camelot. She knew if she told him about the find, he would board his executive jet and come home at once.

At almost seventy years old, Heinrich von Stetten served as majority stockholder and chairman of the board for the family firm, which was active in the arms industry and had won numerous government contracts for precision-guided missiles.

Evelyn suddenly had an idea: she knew whom to call. Turning to the Fuggas, she told them, "Gentlemen, we'll discontinue work here for the time being. I suggest you carry on in the rooms upstairs."

The two men packed up their tools and were about to follow the housekeeper when Evelyn detained them. "One more thing. Kindly keep quiet about this find. It concerns the von Stetten family alone. I don't want a word of it to leave this house. I'm sure you wouldn't want to lose such a lucrative job. I hope we understand each other, Herr Fugga?"

Old Fugga's lips were sealed. He understood quite well that the legendary baroness had just, in the most genteel fashion, held a pistol to his head. At the same time, he would have to have a serious talk about the matter with his son. His son was a good lad and not given to shooting his mouth off—when he was sober. Unfortunately, on weekends he tended to have a couple too many with his pals at the Brewer's Drayman.

Frau von Stetten closed the door, picked up the phone, and dialed. A young man's friendly voice answered.

"Hello," she said. "Evelyn von Stetten here. May I have a word with the bishop? It's urgent."

The bishop's office staff knew she was his sister-in-law, and so she was put through at once.

"What's so important, my dear?"

"Hello, Franz. I need your help. Right away!"

Having canceled all his engagements, Bishop Franz von Stetten drove up in his black Mercedes two hours later. His sister-in-law, who had been waiting on the steps, accompanied him to the library.

The bishop shared his elder brother's passion for books and conducted a preliminary examination of the cache. The books' diversity and quality electrified him. He took out one gem after another, among them numerous scientific treatises ranging in date from the eleventh to the eighteenth centuries. Trembling with excitement, he sat there surrounded by ancient tomes. One characteristic about the books had struck him immediately: at the time of their publication, most of them had been on the Vatican's *Index*; their possession had been condemned as heresy. Some of the others, however, were quite unknown to him. Were these the last extant copies of long-lost works—copies that had escaped the flames of ignorance? One thing was certain: all in all, they constituted a treasure trove of inestimable value. Two particularly thick volumes turned out to be dummies. Inside their covers, each contained a twelve-by-eight-inch casket of hammered metal. The contents were heavy and jingled—probably coins. He couldn't immediately find the keys, so he laid them aside. The books interested him far more. He also discarded a leather map of some distant land, which fell out of one of the books.

After reveling in the precious volumes for a while, the bishop told his sister-in-law his idea. Since his brother would turn seventy in less than six weeks' time, he, Franz, would remove all the books from their hiding place and catalog them, and then bring them back on the morning of Heinrich's birthday and display them in the library's air-conditioned chamber reserved for rarities. He hoped Heinrich would be so delighted by the precious find that he would forgive his wife for arbitrarily countermanding his direction.

Evelyn was predictably taken with this plan.

Together, they packed the books in several hurriedly assembled wine cases, which were lined with blankets to protect their precious contents, and stowed them and the map in the trunk of his Mercedes.

Finally, the bishop fetched the two locked metal boxes from the library and put them beside him on the passenger seat. He said goodbye to his sister-in-law, telling her not to worry. He would phone her in the next few days.

Watching with interest from the master bedroom, the younger Fugga saw an unknown clergyman—he had no idea it was the bishop of Bamberg—drive off with the books. He was particularly struck by the two boxes, which were the last things to be loaded. He imagined them as treasure chests filled with gold and jewels. He'd been excited by the discovery of the cache, which represented a highlight in his otherwise uneventful existence, and by the beautiful baroness's injunction to keep quiet about it.

Two days later, in the Brewer's Drayman tavern, the inevitable happened: young Fugga presented a sensational account, laden with half-truths, of the discovery of a treasure trove in the von Stetten mansion.

Since most of those present had known the amiable young workman since he was a boy, none took him very seriously. Like his previous tall tales, this one might also have fallen flat and been dismissed as just another flight of beer-fueled fancy, but for one thing: on this of all evenings, a young reporter was drowning his sorrows in his beer. Abandoning his tankard, which was half-full, he deposited a few bills on the counter and left the pub more sober than he'd planned.

Two days later the *Nürnberger Nachrichten* carried a small article headlined "Hidden Treasure in the von Stetten Family Home?" The story was not worth much, in the news editor's opinion, because it lacked any form of corroboration and was based solely on the statements of a young workman and an old legend, that a member of the von Stetten family had salted away treasure of some kind.

The editor called the von Stetten home, only to be informed by Frau von Stetten that the whole story was ludicrous. She flatly denied it.

The article did, however, have unpleasant consequences for Fugga & Son, Heating Engineers, who were fired within five minutes of the editor's call to Evelyn von Stetten. The baroness always kept her promises.

Far away in Rome, the article about the alleged discovery of treasure in the von Stetten home was also read with interest. The news that the trove had been removed by a priest was given particular attention.

RABBI HOOD

Rome—three months later

Streaming with sweat after the five-mile run with which he began each day, Lukas von Stetten inserted his key into the lock of the front door of his apartment. The building was situated on the Via dei Coronari in the midst of Rome's Centro Storico, where numerous antique dealers had settled around the turn of the century. The Piazza Navona was only a short walk away.

Although it was still early, the narrow streets of Rome were already swelteringly hot. By day the temperature often exceeded ninety-five degrees, and it was little cooler at night.

The apartment was in a palazzo his family had acquired in the middle of the nineteenth century. Renovated several years earlier, the building had been converted into six apartments and updated with modern amenities. No trouble or expense had been spared in order to preserve the charm of times gone by. The other five apartments were leased to well-to-do Romans. All of them, except the old contessa who lived opposite, had fled to the seaside to escape the August heat.

For the first time since his family had sustained yet another stroke of misfortune three months before, Lukas von Stetten had managed to go a night without nightmares. He had even been exempted from the dream that had pursued him since childhood, in which a beautiful young woman was tortured.

With newfound optimism, he hoped that today would bring him the eagerly awaited permission to access the secret Vatican library.

First, however, he tripped over a pair of red high-heeled shoes lying in the entrance hall of the apartment. *Lucie!* He mentally suppressed an oath that would not have befitted a promising young Jesuit priest on the verge of completing his doctoral thesis. Instead, drawing a deep breath to calm himself, he picked them up and put them neatly in the hall closet. This closet contained just three pairs of men's shoes and around thirty pairs of women's shoes of all kinds and colors, the heels of which sometimes reached dizzying heights. Lukas couldn't help grinning indulgently at the sight of this motley assortment, all of which belonged to his twin sister, Lucie.

Some six weeks earlier, she had suddenly turned up at his door with bag and baggage and the words "Don't ask!" As so often had happened with Lucie, a grand passion had turned out to be too small for her. Her brother was not overly concerned, however. It had happened to Lucie at regular intervals ever since puberty.

Filled with enthusiasm, she plunged into one affair of the heart after another, breaking men's hearts and then blundering headlong into her next affair. ("I can't help it, Lukas, honestly . . .") The young Jesuit had not, however, expected his twin sister to select her brother's home in Rome as the springboard for her next adventure.

Before he could even say yes, Lucie had moved into the apartment. It was not so much her numerous shoes as the delivery of her grand piano two days later that had finally alerted him that his musical sister was planning a lengthy stay.

Since then he had made persistent attempts to inculcate concepts such as tidiness, privacy, and peace—for instance, that music could also be enjoyed at a lower volume. But his patient entreaties regularly foundered on his sister's airy unconcern, as they had for twenty-eight years. Lucie was his twin and he adored her, but there were times . . . He shut the closet with a sigh, wondering if there was some kind of a shoe devil that afflicted women only.

There could scarcely have been another pair of fraternal twins who looked more alike and were more temperamentally dissimilar than Lukas and Lucie von Stetten. There are people who cause every head to turn when they enter a room. Lukas was one of those people. Lukas von Stetten was tall, broad shouldered, and well built; his physique spoke of athletic pursuits engaged in from an early age. He wore his fair hair close-cropped and surveyed the world with a pair of aquamarine eyes. All that marred the regularity of his features was a repeatedly broken nose—a legacy from the boxing he had done in his student days. But the whole charm of his personality became manifest when one knew him better. Sure of his destiny in life, he treated everyone with the same natural dignity. Many might have called it charisma, but it was something more: Lukas radiated essential goodness, an aura of decency.

Lucie, his attractive, older twin sister ("five minutes older, Lukas!"), deliberately exerted an effect on people, and the male of the species in particular. When she laughed, her eyes sparkled with happiness; her whole being conveyed undiluted joie de vivre. Lucie might have been described as an inveterate flirt, but one with her heart in the right place.

With the egoism of youth and without the least regard for her parents' anxieties, after finishing school, Lucie had disappeared for six months, heading in the direction of the Middle East with her best friend, Rabea Rosenthal, taking a rucksack but no credit card with her. Thanks to her mother's influence, Lucie had developed a childhood interest in the mysteries of the Orient. She'd returned from her trip with an enhanced predilection for the secrets of ancient civilizations, and had consequently decided to study Egyptology and ancient languages. Now, at the age of twenty-eight, she had enrolled in a ninth semester at a Rome university.

Rabea was her visual opposite: short, petite, and freckled. She was a mathematical genius capable of solving the most complicated problems, and as a child, her teacher had tried to persuade her to move to a school for specially gifted children. However, she had categorically refused to leave the Nuremberg school she attended with her only friends, the twins Lucie and Lukas von Stetten. Besides, she wanted to become a rabbi like her grandfather Josef, whom she idolized. But shortly before her tenth birthday, something happened that ended her wish to become a rabbi. At that point, Rabea announced to her friends that she wanted to become a newspaper reporter instead. It was the profession that suited her best because it involved searching for the truth.

Influenced by the two most important males in her life, Grandfather Rabbi Josef Rosenthal and young Lukas, whose uncle was bishop of Bamberg, Rabea had early grasped that religion was invariably male dominated, and had wondered what was so superior about men. Was it an accident of birth? Was it blameworthy to be born a girl? Her teachers said she was brighter than the other children, so why could she become a mathematician but not a rabbi, when all *rabbi* meant was "teacher"?

Thanks to her keenly analytical mind, which was coupled with inveterate obstinacy, she studied journalism at the University of Munich and soon earned a good reputation as a reporter. Since graduating from university, she had traveled from one crisis area to another as a foreign correspondent.

As far as Lukas knew, Rabea was now in Iraq. He glanced at the answering machine, a relic from which his mother had so far been unable to part. No blinking light, no calls. Beside the phone was a shiny black crocodile-leather purse. It caught his eye because he was familiar with Lucie's love of monstrous, showy handbags, but this one exuded a sheer feminine elegance. The clasp was open, and he saw that the bag was lined with red silk, which somehow conveyed the morbid impression that the purse was bleeding inside. The idea made him shiver, but he couldn't think why it had occurred to him. Lukas sensed there was a reason, but it was too vague to drift to the surface from the depths of his subconscious.

In his stocking feet, he padded into the spacious bathroom, got undressed, and climbed into the old-fashioned claw-foot bathtub, which also served as a shower. Lukas started to pull the shower curtain closed and stopped short: this wasn't the original shower curtain. That seemed to have fallen prey to one of his sister's innovations. This one reeked of plastic and was profusely decorated with frog princes wearing gold crowns. He heaved a sigh of resignation. Since Lucie moved in, the apartment had undergone what she considered some wondrous improvements.

The cold water felt marvelous on his overheated body. He shampooed his hair, humming contentedly.

All at once, the curtain was yanked aside. "Morning, Lukas," said a cheerful female voice. "I've a letter for you from the Vatican. A messenger just delivered it."

"Goddammit, Lucie!" he exclaimed in a wholly unjesuitical tone of voice. "Can't I even take a shower in peace!" Blindly, he groped for the shower attachment and quickly rinsed off the lather. He felt for the towel with his eyes still screwed shut.

It was handed to him with the words, "Shame on you, Father Lukas. That'll cost you at least twenty-five Paternosters. Or isn't that a Jesuit kind of thing?"

In the middle of drying his face and hair on the towel, Lukas suddenly froze like Lot's wife in the Negev desert. It wasn't his sister speaking, but he knew the voice. *Could it be her?*

For a fraction of a second, he hesitated to open his eyes. When he did, he knew he hadn't been wrong: it was the moment he'd been dreading for years. The voice really did belong to Rabea—the Rabea who had

17

been his great and only love. It was six long years since he had spoken with or seen her. Now she was standing in front of him as large as life, grinning the way she had in the old days, with a challenge glinting in her green, feline eyes. Her derisive expression and the thick, auburn braid that dangled over her right shoulder seemed to be the only things about her that hadn't changed since he'd last seen her. What stirred his emotions was neither her pallor nor the slenderness of her figure, which was accentuated by a black T-shirt and tight jeans, but the melancholy that underlay her outward gaiety. Looking down at her bare feet and unvarnished toenails, he suddenly remembered the extravagant handbag and red shoes in the hallway. He knew why the sight of them had disturbed him: they were hers.

His eyes now met her sparkling gaze. All at once, he became conscious of his nakedness. To preserve a vestige of dignity, he tugged rather too hard at the shower curtain and brought it down completely, curtain rod and all. The wet plastic came rustling down and clung unpleasantly to his body. The rod hit him on the head. True to the rule that mishaps always come in threes, he then slipped in the bathtub while attempting to extricate himself and landed on his backside.

"Rabea, what are *you* doing here? I'm having a shower," he growled belatedly. *And where has that goddamned towel gone?*

Rabea was momentarily afraid he may have hurt himself, but then promptly recovered her poise. "I can see you were having a shower," she retorted. "Don't be so bashful—it's not as if I haven't seen it before, is it? How about 'Great to see you again, Rabea. How are you?' Or, better still, a welcome kiss for an old girlfriend?"

Lukas couldn't help blushing at her allusion to their onetime affair. He finally managed to free himself from the clinging shower curtain, found the towel, and wrapped it around his waist. "Would you mind leaving me to get dressed on my own?"

With a parting glance at his bare midriff, she made herself scarce.

A moment later, he heard her messing around in the kitchen. She was obviously preparing breakfast, which wasn't like her. As far as he could recall, Rabea had never done more than stir a cup of instant coffee, and he didn't possess any instant coffee. Before long, he heard his espresso machine gurgling.

He left the bathroom and went into his bedroom. While picking out a pair of jeans and a pale-blue shirt, he contended with the peculiar emotions that had overcome him since Rabea's appearance. Although she must have heard him return to the apartment, she'd postponed her entrance until he was naked under the shower. Typical of her to leave nothing to chance. She hadn't just come to pay old friends a visit; he could sense there was something more to it.

And how could he have forgotten Rabea's thing for red shoes? They were a part of her personal theory. She divided people into two categories: those who looked first at her shoes, and those who ignored them. She had explained that her theory worked best in journalism's premier discipline, the interview.

"My red stilettos are a symbol, Lukas. At first, I wore them to distract attention from my youth, but then I noticed how people reacted to them—like 'Show me your shoes, and I'll know who you are.' People see my shoes and promptly pigeonhole me as frivolous, tasteless, and thoughtless. Now when I conduct interviews, I register the direction of my subjects' gaze. A lot of them never even notice my shoes. Those are the ones I prefer to interview. They make the most difficult interviewees but also the best. However, most of them start by staring at my feet, and that gives me time to observe them. That initial assessment determines whether my work succeeds or fails. As soon as they classify me as a saucy little minx—easy meat, in other words—I pounce. They underestimate me."

Lukas knew from personal experience just how saucy Rabea could be, but it hadn't deterred him from asking her what category he fell into.

Rabea had then said something quite nice. "That's an irrelevant question, Lukas. The first thing you looked into was my heart."

There was something comforting about his recollection of those words. They poured oil on the troubled waters of his soul. He felt the last of his annoyance evaporate and give way to a feeling of melancholy—the kind of sadness only an old and unfulfilled love can evoke.

With a faint smile, the young priest was just returning to the bathroom to hang up the towel when his eye was caught by the envelope bearing the Vatican coat of arms. Rabea had left it next to the sink.

In the interests of his thesis, Lukas had requested from the head of the Archivio Segreto Vaticano permission to examine a number of books inaccessible to the general public. Quickly breaking the seal, he found that the letter contained the permission he had been hoping for. He resolved to pay the Vatican library a visit that very afternoon, after meeting with his best friend, Simone, another Jesuit priest.

His order did not prescribe a particular style of dress except on official occasions. Estimating that his visit to the arcane section of the library entailed formality, he decided despite the hot summer day to wear a clerical suit and dog collar. He wondered for a moment whether his subconscious had played a part in this decision. Could it be he thought his formal dress would demonstrate a certain distance from Rabea?

Before he could pursue this thought any further, the delicious aroma of coffee came drifting through the apartment—a signal that alerted his stomach as well. Feeling all at once like any hungry young man, he strode briskly into the big kitchen, where an ample breakfast was awaiting him on the oak table. Cappuccinos were steaming in two huge cups, slices of toast and *cornetti* gave off a seductive scent, and boiled eggs lay ready in a basket. Rabea hadn't forgotten that he always ate two eggs for breakfast.

She had made herself comfortable at the kitchen table in one of the cane chairs and was reading *Il Messaggero*, the Italian daily, with a cup of coffee in her left hand.

"Where—or rather, why—did you learn to do this sort of thing?" he asked in surprise as he fished a cornetto out of its basket, dunked it in the strawberry jam, and, still without sitting down, hungrily sank his teeth into it.

"I'm afraid hunger and an inability to cook don't go together in the long run." Rabea got up and took a bottle of milk out of the fridge. "As Lucie has probably told you, I've spent much of the last few years in hot spots: Gaza, Iraq, Afghanistan. You can't just pop into the nearest bistro or supermarket, not there. You have to carry supplies in your rucksack, and eating cold food out of cans all the time is . . ." Rabea broke off as if aware that she had given too much away. She eyed him, leaning against the kitchen counter with her arms folded. She had never seen him in clerical garb before. Lukas saw her wrinkle her nose a little and braced himself for some derisive remark, but it remained unspoken.

Instead, Rabea fished another egg out of the saucepan. "I'm sorry I ambushed you before, Lukas. I thought it was an amusing idea. Aren't you just a teensy bit pleased to see me?"

Lukas, still standing because his rump was sore from his fall in the bath, almost got the impression that Rabea was embarrassed. *Rabea embarrassed?* he mused privately. Could she really have changed so much? First the breakfast and now an apology? Looking into the depths of her green eyes, he detected a new and touching hint of vulnerability. He relented and took her in his arms. "Of course I'm pleased you're here. Great to see you again," he said, echoing her words. "How are you? Would you like a welcome kiss?"

Rabea nestled against his chest, her head only just level with his armpit. Then she stood on tiptoe, cupped his head in her hands, and kissed him hard on the lips.

Lukas, who had envisioned a brotherly kiss on the cheek, was momentarily so taken aback, he returned the kiss.

He had overcome his surprise and was about to detach himself from Rabea when a derisive voice broke the silence: "Am I intruding?"

His sister, Lucie, was leaning against the doorpost, looking disheveled. She yawned and stretched her long limbs languorously. She was wearing a perilously short, pale-blue baby-doll nightie and was barefoot, like Rabea.

Lukas and Rabea answered simultaneously; her yes easily drowned out his no.

Unmoved, Lucie went over to Rabea and gave her an affectionate hug. "It's lovely you came, Bea. When did you get here?"

"An hour ago, around seven. You were snoring so nicely I didn't want to wake you. Thanks for leaving the key under the flowerpot, incidentally."

"Snoring, *pah!* How long are you staying? You'll stay here, of course. No question of a hotel." Lucie snatched the last cornetto from her brother. In so doing, she noticed the red mark that had adorned his forehead since its collision with the curtain rod. *When did Lukas start boxing again?* she wondered, but she was distracted by Rabea's reply to her suggestion and Lukas's ensuing, violent reaction.

"Six weeks in Rome will be enough, I guess. At the moment, I'm still negotiating for a series of interviews, but I've also got some interesting articles in the pipeline. Thanks for the offer, Lucie. I'll gladly stay here."

Lukas, who had just taken a mouthful of coffee, choked on it. "Wait a minute! What do you mean? Not here in the apartment, surely?"

Lucie gave him an appraising look. She had always been sensitive to her equable brother's moods, especially as he seldom had any.

Rabea promptly added fuel to the flames. "Why so anxious to get rid of me again, Father Lukas? Are you scared I might lead you astray?"

The young priest flushed scarlet for the second time that morning.

What a beast! Lucie couldn't help thinking of something that had happened on Rabea's sixth birthday. She vividly recalled her friend climbing onto a chair to get closer to the birthday candles alight on the cake in front of her. "Blow them out, blow them out!" yelled the roomful of little guests. "Make a wish, Rabea!"

Afterward, one of the children said, "Go on, Rabea, tell us what you wished for."

And Lukas called, "No, Rabea, don't tell or it won't come true."

"I don't care," she answered defiantly. "I wished that Lukas and I would get married and have babies."

Rabea's sixth birthday was one of Lucie's earliest memories. She, Lukas, and Rabea were inseparable until they left school. Everyone had called Rabea the third twin. Being the same age, they had all matriculated the same year. Then Lucie and Rabea had decamped for six months to the Middle East, where they'd undergone some frightening experiences. Just how frightening, neither of them had ever told him.

Rabea was determined, strong willed, and tough. Lukas was the only nut she'd failed to crack. About six years earlier the two of them seemed to have had a momentous reunion. Then, seemingly overnight, Rabea had gone off to Afghanistan, and Lukas had entered the Jesuit seminary. Neither Rabea nor Lukas had ever told Lucie what happened, although she'd pestered them for the truth.

"What was in your letter from the Vatican, Lukas?" Rabea asked, every inch the brazenly inquisitive journalist.

Lukas had deposited the envelope on the kitchen table when he'd come in. "It's really no business of yours, but since it's no secret: for my thesis, I requested permission to study some publicly inaccessible documents in the Vatican library, and today I got it."

"Congratulations!" Lucie said delightedly. She knew how eagerly he'd been awaiting a reply.

"Tell me something, Lukas," said Rabea. "How well do you know the Jesuit superior general, Ignazio Bentivoglio? The old fart is right at the top of my interview wish list. And incidentally, what about the rumors that he's suffering from old man's curse, a.k.a. prostate trouble? Could you ask him to grant me an interview? Or give me his cell number?"

Lukas, who had just stuffed half a boiled egg into his mouth, had another violent choking fit. "In the first place," he gasped, "kindly don't refer to him as an 'old fart,' and secondly, no, I certainly won't ask him about his prostate or request an interview on your behalf. You must be crazy." His next paroxysm of coughing ejected a morsel of egg the size of a fingernail. It landed, alas, on Rabea's lap.

"*Bon appétit!*" Shrugging her slender shoulders, she picked up the morsel of egg with her fingertips and put it in the waste bin.

Happy to leave the other two to their verbal skirmish, Lucie had taken cover behind the newspaper when the doorbell rang for the second time that morning. "I'll get it," she said, jumping to her feet.

"Good morning," said a voice through the intercom. "I've an envelope for Father von Stetten."

Lucie, quite unembarrassed by her baby-doll nightie, opened the door and took delivery of the envelope.

The messenger gazed at her saucer-eyed. He was probably wondering how a priest came to share his home with such a delectable apparition.

Lucie handed him a small tip from the bowl on the hall table and padded back into the kitchen in her bare feet. She waved the envelope. "Here, Lukas. For you."

Lukas took it. "Funny, there's no sender's name."

"Maybe you'd better open it," said Rabea, coming closer as she pointed to the envelope. "Remind me. What does the SJ after your name stand for? Silver Jubilee, isn't it?" She was winding him up; she knew perfectly well that the initials stood for *Società Jesu* and were appended to the name of every Jesuit priest.

Lukas carefully opened the envelope. He was astonished to see the seal and signature at the foot of the letter: its author was none other than Ignazio Bentivoglio, current superior general of the Jesuit Order, whom Rabea had just called an old fart. The brief communication requested Lukas von Stetten, SJ, to be at the stated address punctually at 3:00 p.m. today. It concluded with a curious postscript: *Maintain the strictest silence about this meeting, and ensure that you are not followed. Ring the bell beside the blank nameplate.* Suddenly aware that Rabea was standing on tiptoe beside him, trying to catch a glimpse of the letter's contents, Lukas swiftly folded it in half.

Rabea assumed a look of unconcern. In her brief but eventful career as a reporter, she had learned to derive maximum information from the minimum of input. In the case of letters and e-mails, therefore, she always began by reading the closing words, which often contained the most profitable information. Although she had managed only to glance at the letter, those few seconds had allowed her to read the postscript and identify the seal. This was genuinely interesting. Lukas was scheduled to have a secret interview with the Jesuits' superior general!

While Rabea was turning these thoughts over in her mind, Lukas was also pondering the unusual nature of the invitation, especially the peculiar postscript. Why wasn't Bentivoglio summoning him to his official residence in Borgo Santo Spirito—why to the Via Condotti not far from the Piazza di Spagna, one of the least private places in Rome? He knew that Rabea's allusion to rumors of Bentivoglio's ill health was well founded. Although it was an open secret within the order, he had never imagined this information had already left the Borgo Santo Spirito. Suddenly sensing Rabea's searching gaze, he threw her a serene smile that abruptly ended in another paroxysm of coughing—an aftereffect of the egg that had gone the wrong way. Between two coughing fits, he announced in dignified tones that he was going to rehang the shower curtain and would then shave.

The sound of Lukas turning the big old iron key in the lock on the bathroom door was audible in the kitchen. The young Jesuit had evidently resolved to preclude any further invasion of his privacy.

The two young women looked at each other and burst out laughing simultaneously. "What on earth did you do to him?" Lucie chuckled.

Rabea described how she had surprised Lukas in the shower. "I'll never forget the sight of him lying there in the bathtub, clinging to the shower curtain," Rabea giggled. "He didn't know what to hide first."

"Ah, that accounts for the bruise on his forehead. Oh, Bea, it's so lovely to see you again. It must be at least six months since the last time."

"Seven months, actually," said Rabea. "That's how long I was in Baghdad. I paid only one brief flying visit to Berlin to prepare some material back at headquarters."

"I admire you. The news here is filled with horror stories—one suicide bombing after another. How did you manage to stick with it there for so long? Forgive me for saying this, Rabea, but as your best friend, I'm entitled to: You look awful. Didn't you eat or sleep?"

"I'll tell you in a moment, but first I need another coffee. You too?"

"Always," Lucie replied.

"How's that horse you were raving about? Abraxas?"

"Abraxas is fine. That stallion is the smartest horse I've ever ridden," Lucie said eagerly, wondering at the same time if Rabea was trying to change the subject. "He tried to bolt again, the dirty devil—you can't afford to let him get away with anything. And the same goes for you, Rabea," Lucie said with mock menace. "I won't allow you to change the subject."

Rabea grinned at her. "I can only try. I know better than anyone that you aren't to be underestimated, blondie."

"No problem, witch. So tell me: You're thinner than a stray cat—didn't you get enough to eat out there, or has war spoiled your appetite?"

"A bit of both. But please, Lucie, let's not talk about it. I'm here to enjoy the luxuries of a Western metropolis. So what shall we do today, launch a raid on the Via Frattina? I badly need some new clothes." Lucie had told Rabea that the Via Frattina was the in place for the young women of Rome to buy smart but affordable clothes.

Lucie watched Rabea closely. Her friend sounded cheerful enough on the surface, but there was something wrong. She leaned toward her. "Okay, smarty-pants, pigs can fly. Enough, already! We're the Thelma and Louise who survived. Second chance, *da capo*?"

Rabea heaved a sigh. "I should have known you wouldn't give up. I'm here because I need your help, Lucie. You know there was no adventure I didn't plunge into with drums beating and trumpets blaring. Fear and self-doubt have always been alien to me. My batteries were always charged, my reserves of energy inexhaustible. Or so I thought. I'm burned out, finished, absolutely done."

Lucie noticed that Rabea's hand was shaking. It was that, far more than her friend's confession, which dismayed her.

Rabea detected the look of concern in Lucie's eyes. "You can see how far gone I am, Lucie. I'm trembling like an old woman. I'm not the person I was."

Lucie looked at her without speaking.

"All right," said Rabea. "But I warn you, it's a depressing story. Tell me, do you remember Master Friedolin?"

"Your goldfish? How could I ever forget my first childhood trauma? We were around seven when I found him floating belly-up in his bowl."

"Yes, and you asked me if goldfish could swim backstroke." Rabea gave a melancholy smile. "Remember how my grandfather comforted us when we burst into his study in tears?"

"Sure, he told us Master Friedolin had spent his whole life swimming belly-down and the goldfish bowl had been his own happy little world. Now he had left it for another, even nicer goldfish world, but everything there was the other way around. He'd had to turn over in order to live there forever."

"Yes, and it's the same with me. I'm drifting on the surface belly-up, but my world feels far more terrible. I know it'll never be a peaceful place, not as long as there are people in it. It's my old conflict, Lucie. I just can't come to terms with the suffering and crime that religious fundamentalists inflict and commit in *his* name. I hate God even though I don't believe in him. I've seen too much over there—the images explode inside my head as if my thoughts were a thousand little bombs. At the same time, I can almost understand the terrorists. They're as much at the mercy of their boundless hatred and anger as I am, except they solve their inner conflict with violence. I combat it with words and articles, and it's cost me my job."

"But Rabea, getting fired isn't the end of the world." Lucie felt almost relieved. She'd been expecting something far worse than a lost job. "Believe me, it won't be long before new offers come pouring in."

"It isn't quite as simple as that. I was arrested and expelled from Iraq."

It took Lucie a couple of seconds to respond. "My God, Rabea," she cried in horror. "What did you do this time, pelt the president with rotten eggs or found an Iraqi women's movement?"

"If only," sighed Rabea. "Since 2008 I've paid numerous visits to Iraq. Last year I went back to Baghdad when the Americans were planning their withdrawal. My channel offered me a chance to broadcast live, and I was keen to capture the Iraqis' reactions. I faded out my heart and soul—neutrality and objectivity became my gospel. I swathed myself in my professional ethos because I wasn't allowed to have an opinion. But something happened to me out there. I *do* have an opinion: End the goddamned war! It's juristically questionable and humanly reprehensible, and—what's far worse—it hasn't achieved a thing except suffering and death."

"Oh, Rabea." Lucie shook her head sympathetically. "If I know you, you publicized your opinion in a loud and unauthorized way."

"I accused the US administration of wrangling a second presidential term by manipulating its own people."

"But no Western journalist would be summarily arrested and expelled for expressing a personal opinion."

"I dropped my producer in it by trotting out my opinion at peak viewing time—during a live broadcast from the center of Baghdad."

"Wow, you don't do things by halves!"

"I confronted the Bush administration with its lie about weapons of mass destruction and stated that ordinary Iraqis believed the only weapon of mass destruction in their country to be the Americans. And that all America cared about was oil. That was when they cut me off and arrested me. On security grounds."

"Ah, that explains why I couldn't reach you and why you weren't at Uncle Franz's funeral. You lied to me, Rabea. What happened after that?"

"I was accused of being an enemy of the American people. I thought they'd issue me a ticket to Guantánamo, but the production company argued my case—young reporter overtaxed by stressful situation, et cetera. I was fortunate in the military police captain who arrested me. Patrick was a very reasonable man. He supervised my interrogations by CIA agents and protected me, which caused him personal issues. In the end, I had to sign a gag order and play the war-damaged young woman for the benefit of two American psychologists. Then I was escorted to the airport and put aboard a plane."

"When was this?"

"Two days ago. I was only in Berlin for a day."

"Well, at least that explains why you're so thin and pale. Don't worry. I'll fatten you up. By the way, will you be seeing him again?"

"Who?"

"This Patrick, of course. I've never heard you speak of a man with more respect since Lukas."

"No," Rabea said curtly.

"Why not? All right, so he's a soldier and you're a pacifist, but that's no bigger a gulf than the one between the sexes. The war will be over someday, and—"

"Drop it!" Rabea cut in. "He won't be coming back. He's dead."

"Oh," Lucie murmured, visibly dismayed. "I'm a jerk. How . . . ?"

"On patrol four days ago. A suicide bomber." What Rabea failed to mention was that she didn't believe it was a random attack. Patrick had been murdered because they had jointly made a lethal discovery in Iraq—one that could not be disclosed to the world at large. It if became known, it might set the whole of the Middle East ablaze. She had managed to get the documents smuggled out of Iraq in the nick of time with the help of a young woman doctor, but the latter seemed to be under suspicion because her Berlin apartment had been ransacked.

"So many good people are dying on both sides," said Rabea. "There's too much suffering."

"And to wage a one-woman campaign against suffering and death, you planted yourself in front of a microphone and ruined your professional career."

"I KO'd myself, but I had to. Not as a journalist, as a human being. They're murdering in the name of God, Lucie. On both sides. It's incomprehensible, how cowardly and contemptuous of humanity they all are. And these suicide bombers—it's we who breed them. These self-appointed divine warriors take no responsibility for their actions; they hide behind the skirts of a God invented by man! Fanatical faith replaces reason—it stupefies people because they no longer have to think for themselves. To them, anyone who believes is right. Just as Christians have always believed good deeds can earn them everlasting life, so the divine warriors in suicide vests are lured by the prospect of doe-eyed virgins awaiting them at the gates of paradise. The hypocrisy of the American Christians who carry their bloated democracy around in front of them like a burning candle and try to force their credo on the whole world! When will they learn that democracy is no more enforceable than religious faith? They keep on making the same stupid mistake, and it's exacerbated the situation over there, especially for Israel. We Jews draw the short straw every time." Furiously, Rabea slung her braid over her shoulder.

"Politics isn't my strong point, as you know," said Lucie, "but my clever brother recently mentioned that terrorist attacks have tripled worldwide since the so-called liberation of Iraq."

"That's true, but I'm talking about Iran. The new president is a Khomeini loyalist Shiite who hates the Jews. He'd never have been elected if the Americans hadn't marched into Iraq. What mobilized conservative voters was the image of a common enemy. Hatred is the finest aid to solidarity."

Rabea came to a halt, verbally as well as physically. It was a good thing. Her impassioned gesticulations and rapid pacing up and down were enough to make one dizzy. She locked eyes with Lucie.

"Oh, Lucie, I know that all this sounds like the ravings of a hysterical atheist. I not only lost my objectivity in Iraq, I lost all hope as well. The most I'll be able to do now is interviews and articles for women's magazines. Amen, as Lukas would say." Disconsolately, Rabea slumped into an armchair.

Lucie rose from her chair and hunkered down in front of her. "No, you silly thing, you didn't lose hope. It has always been there. All you did was bury your heart and soul beneath your professional ethos to protect yourself from the suffering you had to share. If one can't tell the truth, you always said, one can always leave it alone. You're the person you always were, our Rabea, whose dearest wish is to save the whole world and every man and beast in it: our Rabbi Hood. Please don't be so hard on yourself, or on God. I hold no brief for the deity, but I happen to have a brother who's a priest, as you know, and he believes in him as categorically as you deny him. Mathematically, that's an equation that amounts to zero. I admit the whole place has gotten rather out of hand since God created it, but there must be something to be said for him if so many people take comfort in him and there are men like Lukas who do a lot of positive things in his name."

"Oh, Lucie," said Rabea, "I know you mean well, but that's the worst part. *They*, the church authorities, recruit the finest of men, the ones who do good at the grassroots level. They use priests like Lukas as bait for the masses and derive their power from the church as an institution. Vatican City is a profit-making concern. It devours people's money as well as their souls. The more God-fearing donors there are, the higher its income. More money, more power—that's the equation." Rabea squeezed her friend's hand. Then, surprisingly, she caved in. "You're right. As long as pure and decent souls like Lukas exist, there's still hope for humankind. Lukas is a soul whisperer." As she was speaking, the last spark of anger in her eyes died, replaced by a hungry, wistful expression.

Lucie understood. She knew that look, having sometimes detected it on her brother's face over the past few years. The words were out of her mouth before she'd thought about them: "You're still in love with Lukas, aren't you?"

"I've never stopped loving him."

"Oh, you two." Lucie heaved an understanding sigh. She was the more experienced in terms of sex and lovers, but not the first person one would ask for expert advice. "Know what you remind me of? An ancient legend my Dutch professor told me. I'll introduce you to her. We've become good friends. You know the *Gilgamesh Epic*, the earliest-recorded collection of legends in the world? Not long ago, the well-preserved ruins of a house were found in one of the places it mentions. Inside were the remains of a table, and some chairs on which seven skeletons were sitting. The legend states that some clan chieftains had met there to dine together and reach an agreement after many years of sanguinary feuds. However, since all seven mistrusted one another and were afraid of being poisoned, none of them dared to be the first to taste the food."

"And what's the moral of the story—that men would sooner starve than make peace?" Rabea sighed resignedly.

"Exactly. They all starved to death."

"You just made that up—come on, blondie, admit it."

"Maybe, but a person can starve to death for want of something other than food. Did you know that?"

"And did you know you're pretty smart for a blondie?"

"Of course. It's my ploy. Always act dumb. People usually disclose more than they mean to because they think I won't understand. Do suicide bombers truly believe there'll be dozens of virgins waiting for them in paradise when the deed is done?"

"Yes, I think the precise number is seventy-two. It's almost funny, the way that exposes the one-sidedness of male thinking. Men picture paradise with a goodly surplus of virgins."

"Honestly," Lucie said. "Only men could have hit on such a cocka-mamy idea. No woman would fall for it. Imagine being awaited in heaven by seventy-two unknown men. God, or whoever, might have the bad taste to assign you some specimens with mustaches, bad breath, and beer bellies. Ugh!"

"Really, Lucie, that shows a gross lack of respect for religion," said Rabea—of all people.

"Wrong. Not for religion, for men. Imagine what poor Jules would do, being not only a devout Muslim but queer as a two-dollar bill! He'd look pretty silly if he had to face being mobbed by a horde of virgins. Or," said Lucie, embroidering the idea still further, "do you think God knows the sexual predilections of his flock and assigns gays seventy-two male virgins instead? I'll ask Jules the next time we're on the phone." Her eyes twinkled. "He'll give me a roasting, but it'll be worth it." They both giggled. Jules was an old friend of the two, who'd shared some harrowing moments with them. If there was anyone who appreciated gallows humor, it was Jules.

"It's nice you can still laugh, Rabea. There's nothing like men to cheer one up. Which brings me back to the subject at hand. Just now you said you were no longer yourself. Just between the two of us, I don't think Lukas got the impression you'd ceased to be yourself, especially this morning." Lucie had meant this remark to cheer Rabea up even further, but for some reason it had the opposite effect. Rabea abruptly burst into tears.

Lucie stroked her friend's luxuriant auburn hair. "That's right, have a good cry, wash it all out of your head."

Dear Lucie, thought Rabea as her shoulders shook with dry sobs. She had suddenly returned in spirit to that day, nine years earlier, when she'd held Lucie in her arms during their madcap trip to the Middle East. They were in Beirut, and Rabea and her then-new friend Jules had at last tracked down Lucie. For days they'd searched for her after she'd been abducted, conducting a desperate quest for her amid narrow alleyways shimmering with heat. Everything dominated by her fear for Lucie, Rabea had been unable to eat or sleep for three days.

It had been Rabea's zany idea to fly the coop after leaving high school to escape the gloomy atmosphere prevailing after the death of Lucie's older brother, Alexander. She'd had to sweet-talk Lucie into that crazy road trip. Lucie felt obliged to remain with her bereaved mother, but she'd eventually yielded to Rabea's argument that her mother was under sedation in a sanatorium, so she couldn't be of help to her anyway.

The Lucie that Jules and Rabea met after securing her release from captivity was grimy and exhausted but, despite the circumstances, remarkably calm and collected. When they broke down the door of the crude wooden shack in which she'd been imprisoned, she squinted at them and said drily, "About time. What took you so long?"

After that, she treated Lucie to some world literature in modified form: "My kingdom for a bar of soap." Back at their hotel, she showered for a solid two hours, and only then did she cry her eyes out in Rabea's arms.

Rabea's memory of their adventure helped her to regain her composure. "Do you remember your shower orgy at the hotel in Beirut, Lucie? Can I tell you something? You're the soap of my soul."

Lucie gave Rabea another hug and got up to fish out a tissue for her.

"Hey, how is Jules these days?" Rabea asked as she dabbed her eyes. "Have you heard from him lately?"

"Yes, of course, we telephone regularly. He's made it. He opened his hairdressing salon in Munich two years ago. Typical Jules, all oriental whorehouse, lots of red plush. I went to the opening, a regular stampede. Jules is still the same as ever—he casts his nets all over the place. It won't be long before he gives Vidal Sassoon some serious competition."

Jules, thought Rabea. How lucky she'd been to run into him in that little photographic shop in Beirut. The owner had tried to charge her a ridiculous price for a spare part for her camera. She'd been arguing loudly with him, although neither of them could understand what the other was saying, when a voice behind her asked in French-accented German, "May I be of assistance to the young lady?" The man had said only a few words to the suddenly obsequious storekeeper, and the goods had changed hands at an acceptable price.

That was how Rabea had made the acquaintance of Jules Lafitte. Jules, who had introduced himself as a barber, seemed to know everyone and everything. Rabea had noticed that, for a garden-variety barber, he knew how to engender universal and surprisingly deep respect. They immediately became friends, and Jules had taken her and Lucie on long excursions into the desert and shown them long-forgotten archaeological sites. He also took them to restaurants no ordinary tourist ever got to see, where they sampled the most delicious specialties.

One morning, Lucie swathed herself in a veil and told Rabea she was going to the nearby market to buy some fruit. Growing worried when she hadn't returned to the hotel after two hours, Rabea called Jules.

That was the moment Jules revealed his true occupation. His occupation as a barber was a front. In reality, Jules Lafitte was a major in the Lebanese secret police, specializing in arms and drug smuggling. Beirut was the center of a secret but flourishing sexual slavery trade, and Jules immediately sprang to the right conclusion. Lúcie had been abducted for sale into prostitution—the pretty young European blonde would fetch an astronomical sum on the clandestine market. Jules moved heaven and earth, but it still took three days before he traced her to that shack behind a slave trader's house.

Rabea and Lucie recovered from this experience at the home of Jules's mother, Daria, where they stayed for nearly six weeks. While there, Jules taught them some survival tricks, as he called them. Among other things, they learned what could be done with an ordinary hairpin. Picking the locks on handcuffs, car doors, padlocks, and doorknobs was one thing. But it could also be used as a concealed weapon to be plunged into an assailant's eye or ear. Jules made them practice on a dummy until he was satisfied with his training.

Jules's double life was not his only secret—only Rabea and Lucie knew that the Damoclean sword of homosexuality hung over Jules. If his sexuality came to light, it could have serious consequences for him as a Muslim and as a Lebanese public servant. He would lose his job and his reputation, possibly even his life. Jules had confided in them that he was considering emigrating, sooner or later, to a more tolerant country in Europe. He had inherited some money from his father, a wealthy French cloth merchant, and spoke fluent French, English, and German, as well as Arabic.

Rabea, who by then owned a small apartment in the Pankow district of Berlin, sang the German capital's praises to him. "In Berlin," she told him, "even the mayor is gay."

In the end, however, Jules had opted for Munich.

"Incidentally," Lucie giggled, "do you know what he's called his salon? I nearly busted a rib laughing: 'The Bavarian of Seville.'"

"It may not be true, but it suits our linguistic genius," Rabea said, chuckling. She hadn't laughed this much for a long time. In the plane that morning, she had pressed her forehead against the cool window-pane and wondered if she would ever feel carefree again after her experiences in Baghdad. In fact, it had taken just one morning with Lucie to banish some of the ghosts in her head.

A sudden loud "Damn it!" from the bathroom indicated that Lukas's shave wasn't going as planned.

Lucie and Rabea burst out laughing again, and the last of the tension in the kitchen dissolved as quickly as the lather on Lukas's cheeks.

Still chuckling, Rabea stood up. She sauntered over to the kitchen counter to examine her reflection in the shiny metal toaster. The mascara she had applied to her eyelashes that morning had run.

"Know what you look like with your pale face and that smudged mascara?" Lucie asked rather insensitively. "Like the mystical black raven that lurks between the worlds, waiting for the souls of the undead."

"Thanks a lot, *friend*." Rabea pulled a face at her. "Speaking of the souls of the undead, does Lukas still dream about that woman being tortured?" Both had heard about Lukas's recurrent nightmare since their earliest youth.

"Yes, and the dreams have intensified since our uncle Franz was murdered. That's another reason why I'm here. Several times in the last few weeks, I've dreamed of the girl myself. You know how close we are, Lukas and I. I haven't added to his worries by telling him, but I thought it would be a good idea to see if all was well with him. I shouldn't say so, but the pope's death was very convenient. When Lukas came to Rome in February to complete his thesis, the Vatican and all the seminaries and guesthouses were crammed with clerics from all over the world. That was the only reason they gave him permission to stay here instead, where I can look after him—" Lucie broke off. "He'll be out any minute, we'll talk later. Let's go for a stroll through the city center. I'll show you where to get the best ice cream in Rome—ninety-six varieties. Lukas has tried them all. I'm still working on it. He'll be gone soon, and then you can shower and freshen up. Meantime, I'll clear up."

Rabea wasn't averse to making herself scarce. She didn't want to bump into Lukas looking like the raven from the realm of the undead. In the guest room, waiting for her beside the double bed was her only piece of luggage, a black traveling bag. Unlike her extravagant purse, it looked shabby. On her travels in war-ravaged areas, Rabea had often overnighted far from any form of civilized amenity. She was no stranger to flea-infested blankets and moth-eaten mattresses, or to sleeping on bare ground under the open sky. Unfortunately, not everyone around her on the fringes of civilization had a conception of mine and thine, so Rabea had often woken up to find her luggage ransacked or stolen. She'd finally resigned herself to traveling only with the shabby old bag, which never contained more than a few panties and T-shirts and a spare pair of jeans.

Out of habit, Rabea had not packed much this time either. Some jeans, shorts, plain T-shirts, and—her sole concession to Rome—a backless black dress. She had owned this for over three years but never worn it. It was only on impulse that she'd stuck it in the bag. She wondered now if the name of that impulse was Lukas von Stetten. She turned on the spot, and the wardrobe mirror reflected several images of her. The morning sun was timidly filtering through the window behind her. She inspected herself with a critical eye. Her breasts were almost too big for her slight build. She ran her hands over her figure from bosom to hips. Definitely too thin. She'd had no appetite since Baghdad. Everything tasted insipid—she might as well have been eating sand.

She eyed her thin face, smoothed her reddish eyebrows with her fingertips, and came to the conclusion that her best attribute was still her hair. It was a truly regal adornment. "Witch's hair," the other schoolkids used to chant. Lukas had called it "fairy's hair." He'd let it slip through his fingers, stroked it, buried his face in it.

Once, before a mission in Afghanistan, she'd been on the point of cutting it off but had chickened out at the last moment. It had suddenly seemed sacrilegious to part with her hair, as if she would thereby sever her ties with Lukas—as if her hair were a vital artery through which the heart's blood of her love flowed. With an abrupt gesture, she flung her braid over her shoulder and started to unpack her bag.

Meanwhile, in the kitchen, Lucie was worrying about her brother. How would he cope with the next few weeks, living under the same roof as Rabea? She wondered too late if it had really been such a good idea to invite her to stay at the apartment. Lucie knew her brother. He was her twin—she could sense his soothing presence and empathize with him even when they were hundreds of miles apart, so she knew that Rabea's unexpected appearance had unsettled him far more than she would have anticipated. She felt uneasy. Lukas was working on his thesis. He needed peace and concentration, but personal experience of over twenty years' friendship with Rabea had taught Lucie that no one could be more unsettling. Rabea was the antithesis of peace.

Lucie had cautiously broached the subject of Lukas on the phone before Rabea's visit, but Rabea had credibly assured her that she had far more pressing concerns than an adolescent love affair. Although Lucie now knew the nature of Rabea's other concerns, her sensitive antennae had picked up on something else.

"Hey, Sis, why so glum?" The object of her thoughts had suddenly appeared beside her. The bruise on his forehead had been joined by a Band-Aid on his chin, on which a spot of blood expanded.

"Heavens, what have you done to yourself this time?" At least the Band-Aid explained his loud expletive of a few minutes ago.

Lukas felt it with his forefinger. "It simply won't stop bleeding."

Lucie fetched an ice cube from the freezer compartment. She ripped the Band-Aid off his chin and clamped the ice cube to it.

"Ouch," he said indignantly.

"Don't be such a coward. It'll stop the bleeding." Privately, she resolved to have another serious talk with Rabea about the Lukas question. The fact was, her friend had been in the apartment scarcely an hour, and her brother had already bruised and cut himself.

The same thought seemed to have occurred to him. "I've been in Rome for six months, and now that I've an important meeting to attend, what do I look like? Like the victim of a barroom brawl! A fine impression I'll make." Lukas belatedly bit his tongue, having almost disclosed that he was calling on the superior general later that day.

However, it was clear from Lucie's response that she thought he was alluding to his visit to the Vatican. "Oh, go on. If the bookworm-in-chief asks you about it, simply tell him you're training some street urchins in self-defense. It'll earn you brownie points."

Lukas regarded his sister with amusement. "You've just advised me to tell one of my superiors a blatant lie."

"Would you rather tell him the truth? How about, 'Sorry, Your Excellency, but an old girlfriend caught me naked in the shower today. I slipped and the rod of the shower curtain hit me on the head.' Anyway," Lucie added, "Uncle Franz also used to box in his youth, and he became a bishop."

"Must you, Lucie?" Lukas looked pained.

"Sorry," she muttered remorsefully.

As much as he could, Lukas forced himself to banish the memory of their uncle's senseless murder from his thoughts, at least during the day. At night he was at its mercy. Because his uncle had called him the day of his murder, urging him to travel to Bamberg, it was Lukas who had been obliged to make the formal identification of Franz's body. On the telephone, Franz had firmly declined to disclose the reason he was summoning his nephew with such urgency.

Since then, the dead man's image had assailed him every night with apocalyptic force. Franz von Stetten, bishop of Bamberg, had fallen prey to a uniquely barbaric act of cruelty. How could a merciful God have permitted a man like the bishop, who had devoted his life to righteousness, to be killed in such a frightful and undignified manner? But the most agonizing question for Lukas was, Why had the bishop been punished for something he, Lukas, had done?

Lukas's soul had been burdened with a secret for the last six years: he had attempted to deceive the Almighty. When he resolved to enter the Jesuit Order and dedicate his life to Jesus Christ, it had not been his personal wish. Rather, it had been a reckless, impulsive act inspired by feelings of rage and disappointment at being cheated out of the love of his life. He had also done it—he didn't delude himself in that respect—because he knew how much it would hurt *her*. But now he knew God had seen through him. There were no bad debts in God's ledger. He never forgot, and always collected sooner or later—with compound interest.

It was his uncle Franz, bishop of Bamberg, of all people, a man whose heart was so big that it embraced everyone on earth, who had settled his unpaid bill. Franz had been more than just a mentor since Lukas's childhood. He had almost taken the place of a father. Heinrich von Stetten, who headed the family's commercial and industrial empire, saw little of his sons or daughter.

Uncle and nephew had devoted hours to genealogical research. No one had yet solved the mystery of the von Stettens' origins. The first recorded member of the family, Alexander Stetten, had turned up in Nuremberg at the end of 1778, seemingly out of thin air. He was a good-looking man of education and refinement. Above all, he was so fabulously wealthy that he managed to buy his way into the long-established and patrician Haller von Hallerstein family, marrying the daughter of the house. Through the good offices of the von Hallersteins, he acquired a patent of nobility from Emperor Franz II and thereafter styled himself

Alexander *von* Stetten. His connection with the von Hallersteins was probably one of the reasons why speculation about a family treasure had never subsided. When the French revolutionary army occupied Nuremberg on August 9, 1796, it was a Colonel Johann Haller von Hallerstein who conveyed the precious insignia of the German Empire to a place of safety that morning.

Alexander von Stetten, who had shrewdly invested his wealth in mines and shipping, was quick to trade with the new United States of America. What particularly fascinated Franz and his nephew was that, although Nuremberg had proclaimed its allegiance to Luther and Protestantism back in 1529, Alexander clung stubbornly to his Catholicism—quite a risky thing to do at the time. His marriage produced several children of whom only two sons survived. The younger embarked on a successful career in the church, as had one youthful member of every generation of von Stettens.

Uncle and nephew often wondered about the vanished family treasure. It was the bishop himself who had sparked this speculation in 1963, as a young theology student, when he found a military post office letter in a battered old bible in the family library. Written by Major Ferdinand von Stetten, Franz's great-grandfather, to his wife, Edith, during the Battle of Verdun, the letter ended with a postscript: *Deposit this envelope with the notary for Heinrich!* Young Franz was convinced that he had hit on a reference to the family treasure.

Fifty years earlier, Franz also infected his older brother, Heinrich, with treasure fever. Together, they compiled all the recorded data about the family, as well as items of information dating from before and during World War I. Without knowing it, they ended up coming quite close to the truth. They surmised that their great-grandfather Ferdinand, a soldier who died during the horrors of the First World War, had feared he might not come home. Both his parents were already dead, and he had no other close relatives. Was that why he had wanted the envelope deposited with a notary for his sole heir—to prevent it from falling into the hands of a stranger who would reveal the family secret? Unfortunately, further research disclosed that the notary employed by their great-grandfather's family had survived him by only two years, and that the whole office, together with all its documents, had been destroyed by a big fire at the end of 1918. Although the brothers not only combed the library but also turned the entire ancestral house upside down, they were unable to find any further clues.

But their shared interest in family history wasn't the only tie between Lukas and his uncle. They were both keenly interested in ancient Greek philosophy, and they also studied a wide variety of faiths ranging from Judaism to the Essenians, Gnostics, and Albigensians. The basis of Lukas's faith and view of the world had been laid down by his uncle Franz. His terrible death had shaken that base to its foundations. The official version of his murder was that the bishop had fallen prey to a tragic burglary. This accorded with the facts insofar as the perpetrators had taken only the most valuable objects and most precious antiquarian books from his private library—revealing immense expert knowledge.

What the public didn't know was that the bishop had been the victim of a horrible ritual murder. The perpetrator or perpetrators had chalked a cross on the floor and, in imitation of Christ's Crucifixion, nailed the poor man naked to the floorboards of his study, using long, ancient iron nails for the purpose. This indicated that the burglary and murder had been planned in every detail—what sort of burglar would come equipped with such nails? The murderer or murderers had also cut off and taken the bishop's ears. Their last, inhuman act was to castrate him. Among other remarkable features, the forensic examiner was struck by the fact that while these mutilations should have transformed the scene of the crime into a gory shambles, hardly any bloodstains were found. The terrible deed had been committed cleanly, with surgical precision. The police were confounded by an enigma. Why the brutality? Was the hope to extort still more from the bishop? Or were the murderers perverted, medically qualified anticlericals who had tortured him out of sheer sadism? None of the stolen items had so far turned up with any fences known to the police, making solving the case even harder.

Heinrich von Stetten had offered a big reward for information leading to the arrest of those responsible for his brother's murder, and the police had received numerous phone calls, but every lead came to nothing. There was only one clue, though the detective in charge wasn't even sure it could be construed as such. On the night of his death, the bishop had been surprised at his desk while he was drafting his Sunday sermon. He must have guessed at once that he was doomed to die, because he had left a final message on his notepad: a single large *X*.

Because of the gravity of the crime and the prominence of the victim, the local Bamberg police had requested assistance from the German FBI and had the sermon analyzed by experts. But no one could discern a connection between the sermon and the bishop's death. They agreed on only one thing: that the *X* either stood for the Roman ten or symbolized a secret or unknown factor. They were unanimous in excluding the possibility that it could be the Celtic symbol for man and wife. In short, they were baffled.

What the cryptologists could not have guessed was that the bishop's final message was addressed to one particular person, his nephew Lukas, whom he knew was on the way to Bamberg at his urgent request. During Lukas's childhood, bishop and nephew had employed a kind of secret language in which *X* generally stood for a secret or an unknown, but it also had another, trivial meaning: "Keep quiet!" When young Lukas became overly exuberant in discoursing on Christian or mythical subjects, as he often did, the bishop would signal him to stop by crossing his index fingers over his mouth.

Although Lukas knew what *X* stood for, he did not understand its significance on the sheet of paper. He did not believe that his uncle had drawn it on the sheet of paper by chance. Franz was a man who believed that everyone and everything had a purpose. Lukas knew there was some reason for leaving this final message, but what?

Representatives of the gutter press fell like vultures on the news of the popular bishop's death. And it did not take them long to dig up reports of the earlier death of the bishop's nephew Alexander von Stetten. They could boost their circulation by exploiting the two incidents.

Lukas and Lucie's brother had lost his life in an avalanche disaster nine years earlier. Referencing the earlier death of this heir to an industrial empire, one newspaper boldly headlined an article "The Curse of the von Stettens" and drew parallels with the misfortunes of the Agnelli and Kennedy clans.

Forcibly suppressing his gloomy thoughts, Lukas turned to his sister. "I must go. I've a meeting with the father librarian at ten." He peered at himself in the toaster and muttered, "I think it's stopped," then tossed the ice cube into the sink and quickly washed his hands.

"Wait, Lukas, I think you'll need to change. You can't see in the toaster," Lucie added. "Look at yourself in the mirror."

There was a full-length Venetian mirror outside the kitchen in the hallway. The young priest examined his reflection but could detect nothing untoward.

"What's all this, Father Lukas? Isn't vanity one of the seven deadly sins?" trilled a voice just behind him.

Rabea had recovered her spirits and was back in form. She was leaning against the doorpost dressed only in a towel adorned with the same funny little green frogs from the shower curtain. She had showered and shampooed her hair. Loose and still damp, it fell to her waist in silky, shimmering waves. The reddish-gold mane enclosed her face like an aureole, lending it a hint of magic.

The sudden memory of how her hair had felt, and how intoxicating its scent had been, hit Lukas like a physical blow. Their eyes met in the mirror in a mute dialogue. Visible in his own blue eyes was a hungry look of yearning.

Uh-oh, thought Lucie. She gave her friend a vigorous shove and slammed the door behind her.

Lukas, who was still digesting Rabea's appearance, strove to look as priestly as possible—an impression only spoiled by his ears, which had turned bright red. Hurriedly reexamining his reflection, he finally discovered the problem. The melting ice cube had combined with blood to leave a pink stain on his white collar. "Oh no, I don't believe it!" he exclaimed, and hurried off to his bedroom. His thoughts of Rabea were not exactly affectionate. It was her presence that had set off the chain reaction that had plagued Lukas all morning.

And he had felt so confident earlier that morning. He'd been sure today was an especially good day for him. The thought of Rabea had never crossed his mind. Now she had fallen like a stone into the calm sea of his existence, and the eddies of her impact had stirred up a variety of emotions. What he needed now was some distraction. The peaceful atmosphere of a reading room and, above all, the calming effect of his friend, the imperturbable Simone, would be just the thing. He called goodbye to his sister and Rabea.

"Haven't you forgotten something?" Lucie waved the Vatican envelope at him. Knowing nothing of Bentivoglio's unusual invitation, she assumed that Lukas was going to the Vatican library. He disliked deceiving her, but his superior general's postscript left him no choice. He took the envelope from her with a wry smile and hurried down the hallway to the front door. Flinging it open, he almost collided with a corpulent woman who bared her big teeth at him in a broad smile. He recognized her as the Dutch professor with whom his sister was studying ancient languages.

The woman had often turned up unannounced of late. She always spoke a little too loud and too fast, and concluded every sentence with a booming laugh. She had squeezed her bulky figure into a pink designer costume, and her throat and hands were lavishly adorned with costume jewelry.

Lukas tried to edge past her, but she gripped his arm so hard he spun around and almost bumped into her. "A very good day to you, Father von Stetten. I've brought some cornetti," she trumpeted, brandishing a paper bag in his face. "And I've some great news for Lucie: I've discovered a psammotherapy studio here in Rome." She gave him a comradely slap on the back that nearly brought him to his knees. He must have looked uncomprehending, because she hastened to explain. "Psammo means a bath in hot sand, a practice favored by the ancient Egyptians. Dressed only in a sheet, you lie down in a tub filled with sand heated to a temperature of fifty degrees centigrade. It benefits the circulation and is good for muscle strain. It would do you good too, young man."

Lukas briefly and pleasurably pictured the massive Dutch woman buried beneath an enormous sand dune.

"Ah, what's that I see?" She had spotted the envelope bearing the Vatican coat of arms. "You've also been invited to the reception for the South American delegation the day after tomorrow? Perhaps we'll see each other there. Ah, there's my girl!"

Lucie, who had emerged from the kitchen with a dish towel in her hand, greeted Carlotta van Kampen with a happy smile.

The Dutch professor's incongruous appearance made it easy to forget that she was an eminent authority in her special field, paleography, or the analysis and translation of early Christian manuscripts. She was also a renowned moral theologian and dogmatician who maintained good relations with the Vatican City. It had recently been rumored that the prefect of the Congregation for the Doctrine of the Faith had asked her to write the foreword for his next book. Lucie positively revered her.

Lukas banished all further thought of the professor and endeavored to relish his stroll. He enjoyed walking because he felt it bred a better knowledge of one's surroundings. Besides, he didn't own a car.

Although he had often walked this way before, he discovered something new every time. It might be a fountain, a balcony, a particular piece of ornamentation on a palazzo, or a new ice-cream parlor. Lukas was fond of ice-cream cones.

He turned into the Piazza Navona. Although it was still early, the square was a hive of activity: waiters wiping tables and arranging chairs, artists setting up their easels, and any number of pigeons. They were all waiting for the crowds of tourists who would take the Piazza Navona by storm.

It was just before Ferragosto, also known as the Assumption of Mary, and most of the inhabitants of Rome had fled to the seaside to escape the August heat. Lukas loved the city in August, especially on Sundays, when it grew noticeably quieter. Leaving the piazza, he turned into the Via Vittorio Emanuele II. At the big intersection, where several of Rome's major traffic arteries converged, he was engulfed by the full force of the acoustic kaleidoscope that was Rome in the morning: stationary automobiles standing fender to fender, horns blaring, cabbies yelling at the tops of their voices.

He left the square behind him and entered a small side street leading off the Via Nazionale. The antiquarian bookstore was situated on the ground floor of an old palazzo.

His friend was already waiting for him outside. Father Simone was an endearing sight, not least because of the paunch that attested to his culinary skill. That he enjoyed laughing and told jokes—mainly Jesuit jokes, of which he possessed an inexhaustible repertoire—was immediately apparent from the crow's feet around his eyes. With his tubby figure and naturally developing tonsure, when suitably attired, he resembled the reincarnation of a medieval monk. Right now, however, he was wearing his usual conspicuously colorful clothing: khaki Bermuda shorts overhung by a green-and-orange shirt as capacious as a circus tent, and on his feet, begrimed with the dust of Rome, Birkenstock sandals.

Simone registered Lukas's injuries, the bruise on his forehead and the cut on his chin, with an almost imperceptible lift of the eyebrows.

The two priests exchanged an affectionate hug. "Lukas, punctual to the minute. Is it true you've received permission to poke around in the Vatican's secret library?"

Lukas was momentarily surprised, having learned this himself only around an hour before. Then he remembered that his friend was on excellent terms with the librarian's secretary. He briefly felt tempted to tell Father Simone about his secret appointment, but the superior general had expressly pledged him to silence. Besides, if there were any news from the Borgo Santo Spirito, talkative Simone would be bound to mention it. So he nodded. "You're right. I can't wait to see if I discover something among the documents there that will buttress my theories."

"Yes, I guess it won't be long before I have to address you as *doctor*," Simone said with a grin. "Perhaps you'll soon be called to higher things? As a budding doctor of theology and with a resounding name like yours, who knows?"

Lukas looked askance at him. Simone's little digs about his forthcoming dissertation and the *von* before his name were a running joke between them.

Yet Simone himself had only last year obtained his doctorate with a paper in his own specialty titled, "The Reformation, the Instigator of Witch Hunts, and the Spanish Inquisition." Father Simone had a liking for any subject connected with torture and the Inquisition. He had even gone to Córdoba in Spain to inspect an original seventeenth-century torture chamber and had just published a treatise on the origin of *Cautio Criminalis*, a book published by Friedrich Spee von Langenfeld in 1631. Spee, a Jesuit, had been a humanist and a lifelong and vehement opponent of trials for witchcraft.

Lukas described his friend's passionate interest in methods of torture as "Father Simone's dark side."

Simone hailed from a poor peasant family blessed with more children than bread. The two young men's social backgrounds were as different as their friendship was warm and affectionate.

"Come on, *Father Dr.* von Stetten," Simone said teasingly, "let's go in and work on your future fame. We could also treat ourselves to an espresso first, though. You're not looking your best this morning, and that's not just a reference to those embellishments on your forehead and chin."

Lukas agreed without hesitation, and they made for a café together. Once they had ordered, he took his courage in both hands. "There's something I should have told you a long time ago," he said, and that was how Simone learned the sad story of Lukas and Rabea. All Lukas refrained from telling his friend was why they split up.

"Well, that's a fine dilemma." Simone heaved an audible sigh that sounded, thanks to his deep baritone voice, like a bear growling. "Loyola, the sainted founder of our order, knew why he banned female Jesuits after a one-year experiment. Didn't Hamlet say, 'Temptation, thy name is woman'? Perhaps you ought really to hitch up your habit and make a run for it. I'd be happy to put up a man stranded on the shores of an alluring siren, though if I know you, you'll meet the challenge and resist the eternal temptation of woman."

"Thanks for the offer, but I must cope with Rabea myself. And, for your information," Lukas added amiably, "Hamlet said, 'Frailty, thy name is woman.' A little tip between friends, Simone," he went on, "beware of discussing any profound subjects with Rabea. And since you've just quoted your beloved Shakespeare, please don't mention him in her presence."

"Why?" Simone demanded indignantly. "Doesn't she like him?"

"Not exactly. She's convinced he never existed."

Simone shook his massive head. His suspicious gaze lingered on Lukas's bruise as if he were trying to discover why he seemed to be talking nonsense suddenly.

Lukas enlightened him. "I bet she'd convince you inside ten minutes that no William Shakespeare ever walked this earth, and that all his plays were written under a pseudonym by the owner of the Globe

Theatre in London. The man's name was Edward de Vere, and he really existed. She explained this to me by citing the 150 Shakespeare sonnets, in which his name occurs as Vere or Uvre or de Vere. She also bullied me into reading books—great big tomes by authors such as Looney and Ogburn. They made my head spin so much, I honestly didn't know what to believe. Rabea's a demon with words. She can present her version of events so plausibly, you can't imagine why you ever assumed anything different. She'd give Satan an identity crisis."

As he listened to this exposition, Father Simone's initial frown had given way to a widening grin. "Eureka!" he exclaimed. "An eloquent and intelligent woman arisen from the shores of knowledge. I can hardly wait to meet her. This is exciting."

Lukas looked at him pityingly. He knew Simone would ignore his advice and challenge Rabea at the first opportunity, and he also knew that he would soon be dangling upside down from Rabea's hook, utterly at her mercy.

Simone glanced at his watch and saw that it was almost noon. "Come on, I'm hungry. There's an excellent trattoria around the corner. They make the best linguini in Rome."

Lukas did not feel hungry. He was relieved to have told his best friend about his personal dilemma, but his unease at the superior general's peculiar summons still lingered.

They moved on to the trattoria. Father Simone had not been exaggerating. The linguini was divine and al dente, and the Italian white bread was still warm from the *forno*, but Lukas managed only a few forkfuls—to the delight of Simone, who emptied Lukas's plate as well as his own, mopping both clean with bread.

After their meal, the two men sat in the restaurant for quite a while, philosophizing about a wide variety of things—not including women.

But Lukas's work on his thesis made no progress that day. It was yet another tribute to Rabea's presence in Rome.

***

At the same time, the twenty-ninth superior general of the Jesuits, Ignazio Bentivoglio, was seated at his desk in the curia at No. 4, Borgo Santo Spirito, near the Castel Sant'Angelo. As father general, he was elected for life and bore responsibility for twenty-one thousand members of the largest order in the Catholic Church. He had just dismissed his secretary on some pretext in order to have a few minutes to himself.

The secretary was young and had not been in his service for long. He had been highly recommended to Bentivoglio after his longtime secretary and confidant, Father Bruno Vallone, had lost his life in a hit-and-run accident. According to the police report, he'd been run over while riding his bicycle.

Bentivoglio missed Father Vallone, a serene, even-tempered man who had been his secretary for close to twelve years. Although not inefficient, his youthful replacement was afire with ambition and was frequently overeager, a trait that the septuagenarian father general found exceedingly tiring. Bentivoglio knew from personal experience how insidious the goad of ambition could be. He would have to have a serious talk with the young priest—and soon too. The fact was, he was dying and had little time left. Breathing hard, Bentivoglio propped his bald head on his hands. Cancer had made itself at home in his body and was eating its way outward from within. The terrible pain inflicted by its sharp teeth was visibly exhausting him.

With an effort, he opened a drawer in his desk. There it was, the box of ampoules containing clear liquid: morphine. He wouldn't touch a single one.

Had he heard the journalist Rabea Rosenthal ask Lukas von Stetten whether he was suffering from "old man's curse," he would have answered in the affirmative. He knew that the illness was a curse. He had sinned against God. Everything would have turned out differently had he remained steadfast, but he had failed to resist temptation long ago. Just as the cancer was devouring his body, so had ambition devoured his soul. God had burdened him with the worst of all punishments. He had supported him in his ambitious plans and mocked him by investing him with his order's highest office, but only so that he could fall all the farther. Every day since his assumption of the office of father general had been a personal hell on earth. There hadn't been a day or a night when he was not tormented by knowledge of his deceit and his guilt, but God had hitherto granted him the strength he needed to make good that deceit. The Lord had kept him waiting for thirty years. So the pain was a welcome penance. He sensed that the hour of truth, but also the hour of redemption, was drawing nearer. This was his Golgotha; he would tread the Way of the Cross to the bitter end.

But first he must make amends for an action that lay thirty years in the past. It was a telephone call from his brother Giuseppe that had started it all.

IN THE NAME
OF GOD

Santo Stefano di Sessanio, central Italy—late summer, 1979

The air was shimmering with heat, just as it had done for months. It hadn't rained for three months in Giuseppe Bentivoglio's native district, around fifty miles south of Pescara in the Italian interior. Everything was parched, the countryside brown and water scarce.

Giuseppe, an irascible man in his late thirties, was a bricklayer by trade and foreman of a small local construction firm.

At the moment, Giuseppe was standing at the end of a rectangular pit, supervising the excavation of a swimming pool. He was sweating and swearing, and he furiously plucked at his sodden undershirt. The clients, a wealthy German couple, had bought the half-ruined twelfth-century castle as a prestige object. It had once belonged to one of the most influential aristocratic families in Italy, but a family tragedy was said to have occurred there over two centuries earlier. The ancient building had since been reputed to be haunted.

It was embedded in a natural plateau that looked as if some giant had torn a lump out of the mountainside in prehistoric times. The rear of the castle was protected by an almost vertical wall of rock.

Entering the ruined building had always been strictly prohibited, but to children from the nearby villages of Santo Stefano and Poggio di San Angelo, it had long been a secret stronghold and an incomparable adventure playground. They had ventured inside it for generations.

The digger was slowly working its way toward Giuseppe. This end of the swimming pool was to be seven feet deep. He climbed nimbly down into the pit and ran his eyes along it from one end to the other. Some 150 feet away, between the castle and the swimming pool, stood a small, dilapidated chapel that had once been dedicated to the Virgin. Giuseppe's eye was caught by a flash of light. Reflected by its only intact windowpane, the noonday sun bathed the chapel in fleeting, transfiguring refulgence. Then the sun moved on and the magical moment passed.

Giuseppe signed to Luigi, the elderly digger operator, where to dig next.

All at once, there was a loud, metallic clang. *Dio mio!* Giuseppe immediately sensed what had happened. Now they were in trouble: rock, hard as granite, just because the boss, in order to save time, had dispensed with the usual test drills. Swearing volubly, Giuseppe tore off his cap and flung it to the ground, then fiercely gestured to the digger operator to remain in his cab for the time being. He fished out his industrial gloves, kneeled down beside the place in question, shoveled away the dry soil with both hands—and stopped short: the obstruction felt smooth, not uneven like rock. He fetched himself a trowel and went on digging. Before long, he had unearthed a rectangular slab. It appeared to consist of dark basalt and resembled a tombstone. Had they happened on a hidden burial place? Startled, Giuseppe crossed himself.

He stared incredulously at the engraved inscription and the monogram. *Per la Madonna!* This time Giuseppe even forgot to cross himself. He hastily covered up the slab again with several handfuls of soil, and told Luigi and the other two workmen to break for lunch.

He waited until they had boarded the truck and the vehicle had disappeared around the bend. Then he sprinted over to the castle, where he almost collided with the builder who employed him. "Capo," he said breathlessly, "you must come and look. We've got a problem."

A minute later, Giuseppe and the building contractor, Bruno d'Orazio, a morose-looking man with a badly sunburned forehead, were down in the pit examining Giuseppe's find. The dark slab looked at first like a tombstone, but it lacked the usual particulars like name and dates of birth and death. Instead, it was inscribed with the monogram *IHS*. The letters were curiously entwined, and beneath them was a two-line sentence in Latin.

D'Orazio, who had retained a few scraps of Latin from his school days, gathered that the sentence bore some reference to the honor of God. The monogram looked vaguely familiar to him, but he couldn't recall where he'd seen it before.

Although they had the construction site to themselves, they talked in whispers, having tacitly and swiftly forged a complicity. Before attempting to lever the slab aside with a crowbar, they decided to dig around it in order to preclude the possibility that it was a tomb. They were more inclined to believe that it sealed the entrance to a cave, of which there were many in the area. Many of the old farmhouses, or *rustici*, had grottoes driven deep into the hillside to serve as storerooms for fruit, vegetables, and wine.

Positioning his spade upright at the edge of the exposed slab, Giuseppe drove it into the soil with a vigorous thrust of his work boot. It met resistance less than a foot down. He circled the slab and inserted his spade several times, and each time there was a sound of metal hitting rock. The two men frowned at each other. This meant that it couldn't be a tomb unless the corpse had been buried standing up. The conspirators would have preferred a tomb because it could simply have been moved. Their worst fears seemed to be coming true: the stone slab sealed an entrance leading into the hillside. Giuseppe and d'Orazio found this puzzling. Why should anyone have taken the trouble to seal a cave with an engraved basalt slab a hundred yards from the castle?

D'Orazio thoughtfully scratched his tender, sunburned forehead, and the pain made him wince. *Giuseppe's right,* he thought. *This discovery smells of trouble.* He had already experienced the consequences of an unusual find. At a construction site two years earlier, he had dug up a skeleton ten thousand years old and unwisely informed the mayor of the local town. The latter had reported it to the relevant authorities in L'Aquila because he scented it might pay dividends to himself and his community. D'Orazio's construction site had promptly been invaded by civil servants and nosy archaeologists, and the housing development was quashed by order of the Cultural Heritage Office. His clients had refused to pay him the fees they owed, not that they could be blamed. In turn, d'Orazio had sued them for the value of the work already performed. To this day, he hadn't seen a single lira. The only people to earn themselves fat fees were the *avvocati*, the lawyers.

D'Orazio badly needed the money from this job. His small construction firm was on the verge of bankruptcy. He came to a swift decision: "If we report this find, the authorities will veto the job. I'll get no money, and if I get no money, you won't either, *capisci?* We'll cover the whole thing up again. I'll tell the Germans the swimming pool can't be as deep as they want. We'll slap a layer of concrete over it. *Basta!*"

Giuseppe, thinking of the four—soon to be five—hungry mouths he had to feed at home, agreed. The two men promised each other never to tell anyone of their discovery.

After that, Giuseppe climbed aboard the old digger himself and filled in the excavation site before the other workmen returned.

That night Giuseppe was afflicted by pangs of conscience. Unlike his boss, he had recognized the engraved monogram. He decided at least to inform his elder brother Ignazio in Rome. Ignazio was a priest to whom he could confide his discovery under the seal of confession, so he would not be breaking his promise.

Ignazio came at once. Giuseppe had warned him that his presence must at all costs be concealed from d'Orazio. Everyone in the village knew Ignazio and was proud of their local son, who had risen to become a Jesuit in Rome. It was even whispered that Ignazio might someday become pope: *bene!*

They arranged to meet at the little chapel at midnight. Everyone in the village was asleep including—most importantly—Rosaria, Giuseppe's wife.

Giuseppe had stirred a sleeping draft into her espresso so that he could leave the house undetected. This subterfuge was essential because Rosaria was a human seismograph. The least movement or sound outside of her normal nocturnal routine, and she woke up in a flash. Of course, when Giuseppe had to get out of bed at night—he had a chronically inflamed gut and often suffered from diarrhea—no reaction, peaceful snores. On one occasion, he'd sat groaning on the toilet near to death, but Rosaria had slept the sleep of the righteous. It had taken their whole brood of children, who had anxiously gathered in the hallway outside, to wake her. But he had only to sneak out of bed for a badly needed grappa—just to help him sleep—and Rosaria would be sitting bolt upright in bed.

The brothers greeted one another with a stiff embrace. Ignazio was four years older than Giuseppe and taller and thinner. He already looked ascetic and would look still more so in the years to come. Having early decided to embark on a career in the church, he had studied theology, history, and Orientalism in Rome. At age thirty-eight, he was appointed provincial of the vice-province of the Near East. He had recently returned from there and now headed the Pontifical Oriental Institute in Rome.

The brothers cast an appraising glance at the dark night sky. Late that afternoon the oppressive heat that had prevailed for months had abruptly moderated, and propelled by gusts of wind, heavy clouds pregnant with rain had discharged themselves on the village in a violent thunderstorm.

Although the rain had stopped, everything was permeated with water. Each of the brothers was equipped with a powerful flashlight, and Giuseppe had brought two spades. Slung from Ignazio's shoulder was a large rucksack from which he produced a light nylon climbing rope. This would not be their first expedition into one of the caves beneath the old castle. Even as boys, they and the more courageous of the village lads had ventured deep into the rocky plateau from the cellars of the ruin.

Ignazio and Giuseppe climbed down into the pit. The rain had left muddy puddles everywhere. Giuseppe had used stones to mark the spot where they had to dig. It had started to rain again, just a light shower, and the loamy soil was moist and heavy. They worked doggedly and in silence until, after half an hour, it was done: the dark slab of stone lay exposed in front of them.

Impatiently, Ignazio shone his flashlight on the inscription. Giuseppe had not been mistaken. It really was the "monogram of Jesus"—the first and last letters of the Greek spelling of his name joined together. The letters *IHS* were enclosed by an aureole, and the nails beneath it symbolized the three vows of the Jesuits: poverty, celibacy, and obedience. Engraved below was Ignatius of Loyola's motto: *Ad maiorem Dei gloriam*—To the greater glory of God. That was the first principle of the Jesuit Order, except that someone had clumsily added another two words. Ignazio Bentivoglio stared at the inscription and read it through once more: *Ad maiorem Dei gloriam et Diaboli*—To the greater glory of God and the devil. What blasphemy!

His brother broke the silence. "What does it say?"

"You were right. It's the monogram of the Society of Jesus, together with the motto of Saint Ignatius."

"Well, I'll go and get the crowbar."

The basalt slab was heavy, but the brothers' combined efforts sufficed to lever it up and slide it far enough aside. They were immediately assailed by the smell of decay.

Ignazio's flashlight enabled him to make out a crude iron ladder bolted to the bare rock. Resolutely, he took the rope and tied it around his waist, then kneeled down and shook the ladder to see if it was anchored firmly enough. He secured the other end of the rope to the uppermost rung of the ladder and suspended the flashlight from his neck. He murmured a brief prayer and crossed himself. Whatever awaited him down below, he would cross swords with the devil himself for the greater glory of God. Since reading the blasphemous inscription, he had been filled with a profound sense of vocation. His presence there tonight was not fortuitous. He had been sent to defend God's honor.

"I'll go down alone, Giuseppe," he told his brother. "You stay here and keep watch. Shine your flashlight down the shaft until I use my own to signal that I've made it safely to the bottom."

Giuseppe drew nearer the mouth of the shaft. He'd come to the conclusion that it would have been better to endure his pangs of conscience for a while than telephone his brother. At the same moment, he flinched as a dazzling shaft of lightning zigzagged across the sky followed by a mighty peal of thunder, heralding another storm. The rain fell more heavily now.

To superstitious Giuseppe, this was a bad omen. He'd been uneasy about the affair from the outset, but the feeling that he could rely on his consecrated brother had lulled him into a false sense of security. He quickly crossed himself. "Maybe this wasn't such a good idea," he said. "I've suddenly got the strangest feeling—as if something awful is going to happen. Let's cover it up and forget the whole thing. Please, Ignazio!"

"Nonsense! You aren't scared of a little thunder and lightning, are you?" Little guessing that he was wasting his last chance of averting his fate, Ignazio lowered himself into the opening.

Later, he would spend many a sleepless night remembering Giuseppe's warning. It had, after all, been an occasion that harbored every sign of sinister happenings in store: a clandestine rendezvous between two brothers—one a workman, the other a priest in whom the pernicious seed of ambition was already germinating; a pitch-dark night of lashing wind and rain; and a mysterious shaft that stank of decay. Why hadn't he sensed what his brother had? The only explanation Ignazio could find in later years was that he had been too weak to resist the thirst for glory. He would have failed to recognize the portents of disaster even if the Headless Horseman, hoofs thundering, had galloped straight at him.

The deeper Ignazio went, the stronger the stench became. Before long, he reached level ground. His flashlight revealed that the ladder ended in a small chamber with rough-hewn rock walls. Opposite the ladder was a long, slightly meandering passage, barely the height of a man, that disappeared into the darkness. Looking up the shaft, he signaled to Giuseppe that he had reached the bottom safely. As he turned around, something caught his eye. He shone the flashlight on the wall and discovered a small niche hewn into the rock. In it was a boxlike object. Intrigued, he went closer. It was a small chest secured with a spring lock only. Swallowing his misgivings, he took hold of it in both hands and was surprised to find that it was made of solid lead. He hefted it onto the ground and opened the lock. The chest was empty save for a folded sheet of paper sealed with red wax. Ignazio picked it up. One look at the seal was enough to tell him that it bore the arms of the di Stefanos, the noble family to whom the castle had once belonged. He broke it open.

Stranger,

You who have found this letter and broken the seal, be advised that you should now turn back.

For God in his almighty goodness will in a far-off time to come determine the day on which the light of truth will conquer the darkness of mendacity.

For it is written that only a person of the greatest spiritual purity is destined to reveal the truth of Christendom. Continue on your way and be warned that death and destruction await you, for no one has yet proved equal to this painful ordeal.

For it is true that hatred bedazzled love, greed poisoned hearts, and brother betrayed brother.

Be warned, Stranger: do not court misfortune. Curb your curiosity. Curb your thirst for power and glory. Turn back and leave the secret be.

Be mindful of these words and keep to the path of righteousness. You still have time to turn back and spend the rest of your days in peace.

Piero Alessandro di Stefano
December sixth in the Year of Our Lord 1774

Ignazio lowered the letter. Feeling rather dizzy, he leaned against the wall for a moment. He did not doubt the letter's authenticity. But what truth was to be revealed to Christendom? Why was it hidden?

As a Jesuit he naturally knew that the church harbored many secrets for a wide variety of reasons, and if he had happened here on a hitherto unknown secret, skillfully exploited, it might further his career. He hadn't the slightest doubt that he was the person of the greatest spiritual purity destined to reveal the secret. His heart was pounding, but he got himself under control. The thing was to keep calm and watch for further signs from God. He replaced the letter in the chest. According to the luminous hands of his watch, it was already nearly 1:00 a.m. He cupped his hands around his mouth. "Can you hear me, Giuseppe?" he called. "I've found a passage. I'll be back by two thirty at the latest, you hear?"

"I'm not deaf. Be quick, though. It's creepy out here."

"Good heavens," Ignazio called impatiently, "then wait in my car!"

"All right. Be careful." Giuseppe felt marginally safer only when he was sitting in the car.

Ignazio's suggestion that his brother should wait in the car was not entirely altruistic. Without Giuseppe waiting for him at the mouth of the shaft, he would be able to stow any potential find in his rucksack unobserved.

The beam of his flashlight illuminated some twenty yards of passage before it showed a gentle curve to the left. He felt his way along the wall at a crouch. Iron sconces were mounted on either side every ten yards or so. After fifty yards the passage forked. He had to be almost exactly beneath the Lady Chapel.

He walked a few steps down the left-hand fork, which soon ended in a small, semicircular chamber. Secured to the wall was a ladder like the one by which he had entered. He climbed a few rungs up it until his head almost touched the ceiling, upon which he discerned the outlines of a big slab of stone with a rusty iron ring in the middle. He succeeded in raising the slab far enough to slide it aside. Climbing another rung, he thrust his head and shoulders through the opening. He really had emerged just behind the altar in the Lady Chapel. Something told him he wouldn't find anything there, and he could always find a pretext for exploring the chapel by day.

He preferred to see where the right-hand passage led. Grunting with exertion, he slid the slab back into place and returned to the fork. When he reached the end of his rope, he left it behind. The smell of mold and decay grew stronger the farther into the hillside he went. Suddenly, with a noise like air escaping, Ignazio trod on something soft and was horrified to find that his shoe was embedded in the body of a dead cat. He extricated it in disgust.

How did the cat get in here? he wondered. Gingerly, he made his way farther along the passage, then suddenly missed his footing. He flailed his arms in a panic and let go of the flashlight, which fell into the darkness. Ignazio followed it down.

He was in luck—he did not fall far. He had failed to see a short flight of steps. Unscathed save for a few nasty bruises, he found himself in a tall, circular cavern that looked man-made. One indication of this was a ledge that had been cut out of the rock all around it to form a stone bench that could have accommodated at least fifty people. Ignazio recalled a rumor that after the Jesuit Order had been suppressed, clandestine meetings of its members had taken place in this district. Could he have found their secret rendezvous?

Directly opposite the steps, the ledge was interrupted by an iron-bound door. In front of this, Ignazio made out a cloth bundle. He went over to it.

It proved to be something he had not expected to find on his quest for hidden treasure: a cadaver. Taken aback, he stood looking down at it. The dead man was skeletonized, but his wig and clothes were well preserved. That he had not simply died in his sleep was immediately apparent from the dagger protruding from between his ribs. It had pierced the thick material of his jacket and lodged there. Ignazio estimated the clothing and dagger to date from the late eighteenth century, which meant that the man must have been a contemporary of Piero di Stefano's. Perhaps it was Piero himself. Ignazio said a prayer for the dead and commended the poor soul to God.

After that, he boldly went through the dead man's pockets. He found some Italian gold and silver coins minted in the year 1770, which confirmed his estimate of the period, plus a plain crucifix and a finely chased gold pocket watch. Not having time to examine his finds more closely, he stowed them in the pockets of his jacket. Then he turned to the door, which he unbolted with little difficulty. It swung open to reveal a low-ceilinged chamber in the center of which stood another chest—an exact replica of the one in the niche, but twice the size.

Greedily and devoid of all dignity, Ignazio hurried over to the chest and knelt down in front of it. He remembered his divine mission just in time and uttered a brief prayer, then raised the heavy lid with effort. At first sight, the chest appeared to contain a large number of documents. On top lay another envelope sealed with red wax and bearing the arms of the di Stefanos. Beneath it, he found a packet of letters tied together with ribbon and some loose documents. Impatiently, he picked up the pile and put it on the ground beside him. Lying on the bottom of the chest was a long package tightly wrapped in canvas. He was disappointed to find that it was light. Too light. His hopes subsided. He had subconsciously been hoping for an ecclesiastical treasure—one that had already, in his mind's eye, acquired the dimensions of the Holy Grail. The least his imagination had led him to expect was some precious gold and silver chalices set with precious stones or some saintly relics. He unwrapped the canvas, and his heart beat faster at the sight that met his eyes.

The package contained two well-preserved, sealed cylinders made of goatskin. Ignazio had often seen similar sheaths in collections of ancient texts displayed under glass in the Vatican itself. They were used to protect precious papyri. Did these leather cases contain an unknown gospel? Ignazio restrained himself from examining their contents right away. It was nearly 2:00 a.m. by now. He quickly wrapped them up in their canvas and put the packet under his arm, then gathered up the rest of the documents and hurried back along the passage. He was breathing hard by the time he reached the foot of the ladder.

At the last moment, he remembered Piero di Stefano's letter, which he had left behind in the smaller chest. Having added this to the rest of the documents, Ignazio climbed the ladder and cautiously poked his head out. Nobody there. He climbed out of the hole, reached for his rucksack, and stowed his finds inside.

Just as he finished, his brother came hurrying up. "There you are at last! Did you find anything?"

"No, it was a total disappointment. Just two passages that proved to be dead ends."

"Maybe it's all for the best." Giuseppe hadn't the slightest suspicion his much admired brother was hiding something from him. In his value system, Ignazio occupied a status little lower than that of God. "Come on, let's slide that slab back and cover it all up again."

All traces of their excavation had been obliterated by 4:00 a.m., when the brothers bade each other goodbye.

While Ignazio drove off to meet his fate, Giuseppe slunk home like a whipped cur to face his. Its name was Rosaria . . .

THE POWER
OF POWER

Rome—present day

Punctually at 3:00 p.m., Lukas von Stetten turned up for his interview with Ignazio Bentivoglio, superior general of the Jesuit Order, at the stated private address. It struck him that the headquarters of the Order of Malta was only a few buildings away. In view of its proximity to the General Curia of the Jesuit Order, many conspiracy theorists claimed that the two orders often cooperated in secret.

Lukas had only just rung the bell beside the blank nameplate, as instructed, when the buzzer sounded and a hoarse male voice from the intercom told him to come to the fourth floor.

Bentivoglio, who was wearing a plain gray suit, impatiently beckoned him inside. "Are you sure no one followed you?" he asked, peering down the stairwell. Once Lukas had assured him, Bentivoglio shut the door.

Lukas felt puzzled. The father general was behaving like an apprehensive spy on a hazardous mission.

Bentivoglio led him down a long corridor lined with bookshelves and lit by a crystal chandelier that was strangely askew. It seemed to dispense more gloom than light.

Lukas followed Bentivoglio into a living room at the end of the passage. A large desk sat in front of the window, and on the right-hand wall was a soot-blackened marble fireplace, above which hung an impressive painting of a medieval tournament. The whole room was redolent of scholarship, of ink and ancient vellum, and conveyed the comfort of times gone by. The only incongruous feature was an electric fan humming away in the corner.

Bentivoglio waved Lukas into one of the armchairs in front of the fireplace. "God be with you, my dear brother in spirit von Stetten. May I offer you something? An espresso, some water?"

"Please don't go to any trouble, Father General," Lukas said nervously. "If you're getting something for yourself, some water would be fine."

Bentivoglio brought over two glasses and a bottle of mineral water.

Lukas watched in silence as he poured the water into glasses with a trembling, shockingly wizened hand. Although he had always been an ascetic-looking man, the superior general had lost a great deal of weight since the last time Lukas had seen him in public, over eight months earlier. His sunken eyes were red rimmed, and the skin covering his bald head was as taut as fragile parchment.

Lukas hoped that Bentivoglio had failed to notice how dismayed he was by his appearance, but in vain. He was transfixed by the old Jesuit's gaze, which was still keen and alert.

"Let's cut to the chase, Father von Stetten. Yes, it's true, I'm ill—terminally so. Cancer is ravaging my body. The doctors give me eight to ten weeks at most, but that's unimportant now. I know you were very close to your uncle, Bishop Franz. Were you aware that he visited me here in Rome three days before his death?"

"No, he never mentioned it to me," Lukas replied, feeling hurt.

"Well, he had his reasons. I meant to speak with you long ago, but then I fell ill and had to undergo treatment in the hospital. I sent for you today because I know why your uncle died." Lukas jumped to his feet, and Bentivoglio hurriedly continued. "No, please don't interrupt! I'll answer all your questions, but first I have some questions for you. I must be able to form a definite opinion of your attitude. This conversation will remain between us, of course. We'll equate it to a confession, so anything you and I say today will fall under the seal of the confessional."

Lukas stared at him in consternation. What was the meaning of all this, and how could Bentivoglio know about the circumstances surrounding his uncle's death?

He had been prepared for almost anything—but not the devastating disclosures that followed.

A stunned Lukas von Stetten left the apartment a little over two hours later. He was feeling dizzy with all the thoughts and impressions that were drifting around in his head, and was desperately trying to reach some kind of logical terra firma. Bentivoglio's discussion of his uncle's murder had opened wounds that had yet to heal. Disinclined to go home, Lukas decided to go for a walk and turn the conversation over in his mind. Having begun like an interrogation, it had developed into a passionate sermon and culminated in a shocking admission on Bentivoglio's part.

The superior general's initial questions had related to Lukas's dissertation, in which he endeavored to explain what fateful parallels in historical and political development had led to the Jesuit Order being proscribed by the pope in 1773, just as the no less powerful Order of the Knights Templar had been disbanded more than 450 years earlier.

Bentivoglio had looked him intently in the eye. "You must understand, my young brother in Christ, that I have obediently served the church for over fifty years. Now, at the end of my road, I see many things a great deal more clearly, and I'm profoundly concerned about the alarming demystification of Christendom. More and more people are leaving the church, and many services are being conducted in front of empty pews. Public holidays are what children and adults find most useful about religion. Moreover, recruitment is a matter of concern to us. Within fifteen years, the number of theology students intending to enter the priesthood has more than halved, and the average age of nuns is seventy-five. The last two popes have been mobbed like pop stars on World Youth Day, but very few young people now aspire to the priesthood. But that's just what we need: more young, idealistic priests like you, my son—priests who combat the danger that, in our enlightened age, faith will degenerate into insignificance. But the truly terrible thing is that the church itself is to blame for this misfortune and has brought it about. For in past centuries, it often had to enter into alliances in order to secure its sphere of influence, and it was never too fastidious in its choice of allies.

"God chose me to be his instrument a long time ago. He decreed that I should come into possession of documents that prove that the church deliberately opposed the true bequest of Our Lord Jesus Christ. God sacrificed his son for us in order to open men's souls, but *we* robbed the faithful of the promise of our Lord's message! It was not until I gained access to the hidden secrets of the church in my capacity as father general that I grasped the truth. Behind it all is a secret, millennial plan! Our Lord's true bequest—the thing for which he gave his life's blood—is: *do unto others as you would have them do unto you!* This little sentence harbors the substance of peace, and this change of perspective is the foundation of all morality. It is the essence of neighborliness and tolerance. But we presumptuously reinterpreted his message of pure love into an obligation to act. We used faith as a weapon and set out to impose it on the world. We founded an ecclesiastical state and fought bitterly for power and influence. So many millions died in the Crusades and fell prey to the insanity of the Inquisition.

"How many deaths have we been responsible for in the last two millennia? How many pointless sacrifices besmirch the Christian altar of charity? What is the Vatican today but a ponderous Moloch mired in bureaucracy and composed of mutually hostile vested interests? It is true that the recently deceased pope bravely tried to counter this, but he was worn down by his struggle with the spiritual Sodom and Gomorrah. Of course, there have always been and still are representatives of the clergy who are aware of these terrible failings, but we are all too firmly imprisoned in our own long-standing dogmas. The church can no longer retrace its steps because it would have to own up to two thousand years of errors. Humanity must finally grasp that there's no greater crime than killing in God's name. Religion signifies fear of God. We should serve God, not play God. In the name of Jesus, we must use our power and strength for the sake of peace. The documents I mentioned are the key to all of this." Having exploded his bomb, Bentivoglio looked at Lukas and smiled. "I see I've shocked you. No priest should mount the pulpit and preach to another. Wait!"

He hurried behind his desk, nimbly picking his way over the piles of books strewn across the floor. He opened the top drawer and, with trembling hands, removed a wooden box. Selecting a small key from a bunch, he used it to open the lock on the box. With his free hand he took out a much-used Bible, put it on top of the box, and brought them both over to Lukas.

"I'll tell you the secret of this box in a minute. First, I must describe how these tragic events came about. Over thirty years ago I received a telephone call from my brother Giuseppe. While doing some excavation work in Santo Stefano, he had come across a secret cave. That was where I found these documents. With the assistance of my fellow Jesuit Cataldo, I discovered that they were documents that had disappeared from the personal, secret archive of Lorenzo Ricci, the eighteenth, the last superior general prior to the suppression of our order. Cataldo was murdered soon after their discovery. After his death, I hid the documents in a safe place, where they have remained to this day. That's why I asked you to come here, to bring them to me from their hiding place. But I must warn you, my young friend, it is a dangerous mission. Your uncle died because he recently found a clue to their location. My longtime secretary, Father Vallone, was also killed—allegedly by a hit-and-run driver. I'm under suspicion and beginning to be isolated. The Hydra-headed beast of authority is always watchful. I can sense your spiritual purity, my son. You possess the strength to bear this burden." Bentivoglio paused for a moment, his forehead glistening with sweat. "You'll help me?"

Lukas hesitated briefly, then bowed his head in acquiescence. At the same time, his thoughts were tinged with melancholy. The image of the tormented young woman from his dreams momentarily appeared in his mind's eye.

Bentivoglio nodded solemnly. Taking the Bible, he opened it and watched Lukas as he bent over the little box. It was lined with red velvet and contained a plain, unadorned key. "This little key is the answer. Before confiding the rest of my plans, I should like you to swear on the Bible. No one must know of our conversation here today—it would endanger the lives of yourself and those who share your knowledge. Do you swear this by Jesus Christ Our Lord?"

Once Lukas had sworn on the Bible, Bentivoglio explained that the key belonged to a safe-deposit box and told him the name and address of the relevant bank. "You will rightly be wondering why I didn't send the contents of the safe-deposit box to the Vatican anonymously, or use my status as father general to announce the documents' wondrous reappearance. That, dear brother, is the tragedy of my life. If anything exceeded my burning ambition, it was my cowardly refusal to shoulder the responsibility laid on me by God. I sabotaged his plan and, with blind obedience, subordinated my life to the institution of the church. Power was my dungeon. Yes, von Stetten, I committed a grave sin. I looked into the face of power and realized too late that it was the gargoyle of Satan. Satan is within us, and power sets him free. I forgot the most important thing: that I owed obedience to God alone. In his infinite goodness, he granted me a mystical experience like that bestowed on Saint Ignatius of Loyola, which prompted him to found the Society of Jesus. God revealed himself to me in a vision and enjoined me to fulfill my most sacred obligations."

His recollection of that recent, divine apparition made Bentivoglio's weary eyes shine. "As soon as you have brought me the documents, I shall convene a general congregation of our order. I will invite the international press to it in order to present the documents to the media and, thus, render them accessible to the general public. After that, in full possession of my mental faculties, I shall announce my retirement, the first superior general in our 475-year history to do so. I realize, Father, that my confession has laid a heavy burden on you: responsibility for all the believers in Christendom, perhaps even for the future destiny of humankind. But it is our sacred duty. I don't trust my new secretary, which is why I should also like to ask you to assist me with preparations for the press conference. It must be held at relatively short notice; my plan must not become known too soon because attempts would be made to thwart it. One more thing: a poor soul has been lying in the cave for over two centuries. He should at last be granted a final resting place in consecrated soil. In the safe-deposit box, you will also find a diary in which I recorded the precise course of events. Please hurry, and report back to me by tomorrow evening at the latest. Go now, my son—go with God. *Deus vult*—God wills it so." So saying, the father general blessed him, pressed the key into his hand, and dismissed him.

* * *

Lukas walked briskly to the Parco del Pincio on the hill of the same name above the Spanish Steps. It was still relatively deserted, but at nightfall it would soon be thronged with courting couples.

He found himself an unoccupied bench in the quieter and more secluded part of the park, where the pathway was lined with nearly 230 ancient busts from all periods. The fact that only three of them were of women inevitably made him think of Rabea, who would certainly disapprove.

For the first time since he had begun visiting this place, he had no eyes for the natural beauty around him. Instead, he became engrossed in memories of a day more than twelve years earlier, when Rabea had read an essay to their class in the tenth grade. His lips curled in a faint smile. Who would have thought that Rabea, who had long ago declared herself a fervent atheist, could ever share an opinion with a churchman like Bentivoglio? One particular passage from her essay had lodged in his memory:

> *The church has always claimed to be on the side of the good. What contradicts this are around six million victims of witch hunts plus tens of thousands of Cathars and other so-called heretics and Galileo Galilei. In the early Middle Ages, the pope proclaimed several Crusades with Jerusalem as their objective. The Crusaders left death and destruction in their wake. The church promised that if a Crusader went off to the Holy Land and slaughtered as many infidels as possible, God would personally absolve him from all his sins. The elimination of all forms of heresy was another part of the Crusaders' sphere of responsibility. In 1226 they campaigned against the Cathars on Montségur. Representatives of the church described these heretics to the Crusaders as follows: "A heretic worships the cat, for so the devil appears to him, kisses the same*

*on the rump, brews witch's potions, and whores around
with several women." The so-called heretics, who in turn
described themselves as true Christians, were naturally not
stupid enough to do all these things just when a Crusader
came calling—quite apart from the fact that they didn't
do them anyway. That confronted the Crusader with a
dilemma: How do I distinguish a true Christian from a
true Christian who's a heretic?*

*Since a Crusader was totally unacquainted with set
theory and tended not to be the brightest of men, he solved
the problem in his own way: with the sword, in accordance with the motto, "Better one good Christian too
many than one evil heretic too few." It should be borne in
mind that few noblemen were able to read and write at
this time; they had secretaries and priests for that. All that
was necessary was preached to them from the pulpit—
slowly, because they were Crusaders.*

*Is hell overpopulated with Crusader knights who
wonder where the heretics have gone? Does hell have
a sort of reception or information desk where someone
with a hard-earned absolution from sin in his pocket is
told why he has ended up in hell instead of heaven? The
rule in those days was that the church thought for—and
controlled—everyone. You had only to believe, and if you
didn't, you had to pretend to or you'd roast in hell like a
chicken.*

*So wasn't the Cathars' faith the real, true faith for
which they were bravely prepared to suffer an agonizing
death? They believed in the Christian doctrine of brotherly love and lived by it. They didn't need the church. Jesus
himself had no church.*

I believe that this idea contains the seeds of hope: the modern community of the faithful may be smaller, but those who believe today do so genuinely and with a pure heart. Is goodness confined to those who consider themselves good, or to what enjoys the blessing of a majority like the all-powerful church? In those days, at least, they felt convinced that they were good. In the future, perhaps more enlightened—or should one say less fortunate?— generations will look back on us and define us as evil. At the latest, when Mother Nature hits back because of the irresponsible way we've treated her.

The young Jesuit reluctantly returned from a time of future promise to harsh reality, and the actual reason he was sitting on this bench. He reassured himself that there was no one near, and took the tiny key from his breast pocket. Small and innocuous though it looked, it had seemed to sear his chest like a red-hot seal all the way from the Via Condotti. Although Bentivoglio had given the impression that he was leaving the decision up to Lukas, the superior general's legendary power of personality had not been impaired by his illness, and he had bent the young priest to his will. It was strange, but when Bentivoglio had said he sensed that Lukas was the right man for this mission, Lukas himself had also been overcome by a remarkable degree of certainty.

Lukas did not suspect that someone had followed him from the Via Condotti to the park and was now watching him from behind a hedge. His tail had maintained his uncomfortable position for half an hour. The Jesuit's long reverie had sorely tried his patience. He was becoming convinced that his quarry was simply daydreaming, and so he felt relieved when Lukas produced something from his pocket.

The man withdrew a short distance, though still keeping the young priest in sight, and pulled out a secure cell phone.

The voice at the other end answered at once. "Why keep me waiting so long, Gabriel? What have you to report?"

"Bentivoglio's meeting with von Stetten lasted two hours. Von Stetten is now sitting on a bench in the Parco del Pincio, twiddling his thumbs."

"Good, that gives us time. Anything else?"

"I saw him looking at something. I'm almost certain it was a small key."

"Good, stay with him. I want that key, but first I want to see what he does next. Perhaps he'll do our job for us. Another thing, send a team to his apartment and bug it all over. From now on, I want to know every word that's uttered there and everyone who goes in or out. Understand?"

Lukas returned home just after 9:00 p.m. He had said a prayer in Santa Maria Maggiore and then treated himself to an ice cream. He still had the half-licked cone in one hand when he opened the door.

He had hardly entered the apartment when Lucie came dashing toward him—closely followed by two grim-looking men. Behind them, Rabea was standing in the doorway to the living room with her arms folded and a tense expression on her face.

"Where have you been all this time?" Lucie blurted out. "These gentlemen are from the police—they've been waiting for over an hour for you."

Lucie and Rabea had returned from their extended tour of the city at seven thirty and were just discussing how to spend the rest of the evening when the two men rang the doorbell, identified themselves as police officers, and asked for Father von Stetten. When Lucie told them her brother was out and she couldn't say exactly when he would be back, they politely but firmly requested permission to wait for him in the apartment. She'd tried his phone but, when she heard it ringing from his bedroom, realized he'd left it behind.

As mistress of the house, Lucie had demanded, in no uncertain terms, to know what it was about, but the spokesman of the two had said he couldn't offer any explanation because he needed to speak with Father von Stetten first. He introduced himself as Superintendent Grassa and his colleague as Inspector d'Amico.

Lucie had finally given way and ushered the two men into the living room to wait. The handsome superintendent made himself comfortable on the sofa, with his arms casually spread along the back.

After surveying the elegant living room, the inspector stalked over to the window, which overlooked the Via dei Coronari, and had been watching the street ever since.

Both officers were smartly dressed in three-piece suits despite the August heat. Rabea, who had followed Lucie into the living room and joined her on the other sofa, eyed them with journalistic curiosity.

The superintendent was the younger of the two. Endowed with the dark complexion, hair, and eyes of a southern Italian, he radiated at least as much self-assurance as Silvio Berlusconi. He had angular but regular features and full, sensual lips. His way of smiling, raising the right-hand corner of his mouth only, conveyed a hint of cruelty. All in all, Rabea was quite sure he was a tremendous hit with the ladies.

Whatever he was doing there, Rabea remained on her guard. His obvious attempts to flirt bounced off her ineffectively, whereas Lucie's susceptibility to them earned her a dig in the ribs from her friend.

"Hey, that hurt," Lucie hissed in German, rubbing her side.

"It was meant to," Rabea whispered back. "I know you'd flirt with a stone, but he's a policeman, remember? Government authority. The enemy. So stop making eyes at him until we know what he wants with Lukas!"

Rabea pulled a cheeky face at the superintendent, who had been following their brief war of words with interest. He retaliated by giving her a long look that traveled slowly from her face to her bare feet, and Rabea repaid him in the same coin. Her gaze lingered on his shoes. Not only did he have remarkably small feet for a man, but they were shod in expensive handmade shoes.

The superintendent tried to hold her gaze, but she ostentatiously turned toward his colleague at the window. Had it not been for the watchful look in the inspector's little eyes and the bulge of the shoulder holster beneath the armpit of his jacket, she would never have guessed his profession. Short and tubby, with a rosy complexion and receding hair, he looked like a respectable accountant in his expensive but ill-fitting suit.

In her head, Rabea had immediately invented nicknames for the two policemen: the Panther and Porky Pig. She conveyed her whimsy to Lucie in a whisper, and they both giggled.

This brought them a look of amusement from the Panther.

Rabea tried her luck. "Are you sure you won't tell us why you're here, Superintendent? Perhaps we can be of help."

The superintendent stood by his statement that the matter concerned Father von Stetten alone. He hoped the *belle signorine* would understand.

Lucie sprang to her feet and hurried to meet her brother as soon as she heard the key in the lock.

Grassa pushed firmly past her and proffered the badge identifying him as Superintendent Riccardo Grassa.

"You're Father von Stetten?" he growled.

"Yes," Lukas replied politely, the dripping cone still in his hand, "what can I do for you?"

"You can come with us. I'm arresting you for the murder of Father Ignazio Bentivoglio, superior general of the Jesuit Order."

Lucie uttered a horrified cry and Rabea gasped.

Lukas turned pale as death. "But . . . I saw the father general only this afternoon."

"That's why we're here. It seems you were the last to speak with him—thank you for confirming that. I must advise you that anything you say from here on may be used against you in court. Come." The superintendent took him by the arm.

Lukas stared dazedly at the policeman's restraining hand. He had a sudden, dismaying thought: *the safe-deposit key!* They would search him, find it, and confiscate it at once. He had sworn on the Bible that no one would learn of the contents of the box.

He had to get rid of the key, but how? Feverishly, he racked his brain for a pretext. When another drop of ice cream fell on his hand, an idea occurred to him. He simulated a violent fit of coughing and bent over, gasping and clutching at his chest. At the same time, he felt for the key in his breast pocket. By the grace of God, he managed to get hold of it and thrust it into the ice cream. Lucie had indignantly pushed past Superintendent Grassa and was anxiously slapping her brother on the back, thereby—not that she knew it—obstructing the two policemen's view of him. The inspector stepped forward, handcuffs at the ready.

Lukas straightened up and squared his shoulders. He hadn't a thing to do with the murder. Everything would sort itself out in due time. "Lucie, please get rid of this ice cream so the gentleman here can handcuff me." He gave her a conspiratorial glance that embraced her as well as the cone. He hoped she would get the message. They had often exchanged that very glance in their childhood when sharing a secret. Lucie would discover the key in the ice cream and put two and two together.

But the superintendent upset his plans. He firmly took the cone from him. "No, Father," he said, chuckling, "it would be a shame to waste it."

Lukas stared at Grassa, spellbound. Surely the man didn't propose to finish the ice cream himself? If so, he would have to explain how the key came to be in it.

Grassa misinterpreted his horrified expression. "Oh well, you're welcome to finish it. Who knows when you'll get the chance to have another?" He winked unpleasantly and thrust the cone back into Lukas's hand.

Inspector d'Amico then clasped the handcuffs onto Lukas, took hold of him by one arm, and steered him out the front door.

"*Arrivederci*, signorine, it was a rare pleasure," were Superintendent Grassa's parting words to Lucie and Rabea.

"*Stronzo,*" Rabea said softly, but loudly enough for him to hear. It was Italian for "turd." Then she noticed the neighbor from across the landing, an elderly lady. Her mouth hung open, and her thin lips were smeared with lipstick as were most of her front teeth. The curly-haired lapdog in her arms wore a silly bow on its head and a collar encrusted with artificial diamonds—something Rabea found particularly ridiculous. The eyes of the dog's nosy owner were alight with curiosity.

Rabea pulled a face at the woman, and she indignantly retreated into her apartment.

The few residents of the Via dei Coronari were presented with a bizarre spectacle: a dignified young Jesuit priest being led off in handcuffs by two policemen, a dripping ice-cream cone in his hands.

The two women remained standing in the hallway, transfixed. Rabea, quivering with rage, was the first to erupt. "Arresting Lukas? I just don't get it. That dapper *pappagallo* with his smart suit and his sweet talk—falser than my grandfather's teeth! Lukas needs a lawyer. Do you know of one?"

Lucie didn't respond immediately. She was feeling sick to her stomach. They had accused her twin brother, Lukas, a confirmed pacifist, of murder. Rabea's words seemed to register with her at last. "I'll call my father," she said.

The phone rang in the big mansion in Nuremberg. It was pure chance that Frau Gabler was still there. Instead of enjoying a well-earned rest from her labors, she had once more been searching under the shrubs and hedges on the grounds for the apple of Frau von Stetten's eye, her Persian cat, Isis. This performance, which was repeated at least once a week, had sorely tried Frau Gabler's previously good relationship with cats.

Her knees and back aching, Frau Gabler was looking forward to a hearty supper and a Rosamunde Pilcher adaptation on TV. She was just slipping into her cardigan when the phone in the hallway rang. She was tempted to ignore it, but her sense of duty triumphed.

"Good evening, Frau Gabler, is my father there?"

"Good evening, Lucie. No, I'm afraid not. Your parents are out this evening."

"Then I'll try to reach my father on his cell."

Lucie dialed the number. It wasn't answered until the tenth ring, but it was the indefatigable Frau Gabler once again. She was breathing heavily. Lucie's father had left the cell phone upstairs in his study.

"Do you know where my parents are?"

"They were invited to a private song recital at Herr Fink's. Has something happened?" Frau Gabler asked anxiously.

"Yes, but forgive me, Frau Gabler, I've no time to spare. I must contact my father urgently. Can you call the Finks' number and let him know? Tell him to call me at the Rome apartment."

"Yes, of course, I'll see to it at once."

* * *

While Lucie and Rabea were waiting impatiently for Heinrich von Stetten to call back, they speculated about the reasons for Lukas's arrest.

"Let's approach the whole thing logically," said Rabea. "What are the facts? This afternoon apparently Lukas met with Superior General Bentivoglio. The latter was murdered soon afterward. Our superintendent of police assumes that Lukas was the last person to see him alive, and bingo!"

"He wasn't the last person to see him alive, of course," Lucie amplified. "The murderer was."

"Ergo," Rabea went on, "who killed him? It should be possible to find out, I reckon. After all, not just anyone can waltz into the Vatican. Every visitor has to register with the Swiss Guard, and there must be a couple hundred CCTVs dotted around the walls of the Vatican State. Even if the murderer entered legitimately, he'd have had to get past Bentivoglio's secretary," she reasoned, not knowing that neither Lukas's meeting nor the murder had taken place there at all.

"If it's true what you said this morning about him being seriously ill with cancer, he didn't have long to live in any case. The murderer could have just waited for him to die." Lucie shook her head. "What if it was suicide? Maybe the police have simply misinterpreted the crime scene?"

"I don't think so," said Rabea. "Grassa seemed too sure of himself, or he wouldn't have arrested Lukas so quickly. I'm less interested in *who* murdered the superior general of the Jesuits than *why* he was murdered at this particular moment."

"Aha, and that brings us to the question of motive. Okay, Columbo, I can tell you've already formed a theory. Shoot!"

"I'm sure you remember I mentioned I wanted to interview Bentivoglio? Well, in preparation for my planned interview I recently did some thorough research into the Society of Jesus. How much do you know about the Jesuit Order, Lucie?"

"Oh dear, to my shame I have to admit my knowledge of it is based largely on historical novels. Until Lukas joined the club, I regarded all Jesuits as fanatical demagogues, but I do know that the order was founded over 450 years ago by a Spaniard named Loyola, and that Jesuit priests are regarded as a Catholic elite because they allow only the best and brightest to join their ranks. That's the lot."

"Not bad at all," Rabea said approvingly. "However, I'm now going to give you a crash course. The order was founded in 1534 by a Basque nobleman named Ignacio de Loyola just when the established church was undergoing the greatest crisis in its history. It was the time of the Reformation. Half of Europe was in the process of abandoning Catholicism: England and Scotland, the whole of Scandinavia, France, Poland. There are a great many Catholic male orders: Benedictines, Franciscans, Dominicans, et cetera, but traditionally the superior general of the Jesuits occupies the top spot, which makes him the second most powerful man in the ecclesiastical hierarchy after the cardinal secretary of state. He's also known as 'the black pope.'

"But none of the orders was ever as controversial, gained or lost as much power, or was so persecuted, its members often being deported, imprisoned, or murdered. With one exception: the legendary Knights Templars.

"In 1773, at the zenith of its power, the Jesuit Order was personally banned by the pope, even though it was the only one out of all the fraternities to be bound to him by a special vow of obedience. The precise circumstances that led to the suppression of the Society of Jesus have never been fully elucidated to this day. It was not reinstated until forty-one years later. The Jesuits' list of enemies at this time reads like a *Who's Who* of Europe's leaders: the pope and all the heads of the royal houses led by those of arch-Catholic Spain, France, and Portugal. Even our old Reich Chancellor Bismarck feared them like death and the devil, which was why he branded them enemies of the state in 1872. Why were those in power so mortally afraid of the Jesuits? Because the order had a partial monopoly of male higher education and owned a college or university in almost every major city. The best known is Georgetown University, founded in Washington, DC, in 1789. The order wielded an immense influence over the education of the future elite, especially in Europe, because the Jesuits built religious instruction into their entire education. Sounds like indoctrination, doesn't it? Today the order maintains one hundred eighty universities in seventy-five countries, plus fifteen hundred schools. A list of their alumni would surprise you, Lucie. It includes Voltaire and Descartes, Heinrich Heine, and James Joyce, not to mention the film directors Buñuel and Hitchcock. Quite a few former Jesuits are employed as management consultants in German industry alone. But what I find most objectionable is the so-called Jesuit doctrine. This propagates a relativism of values that doesn't preclude the right of resistance, up to and including the assassination of tyrants. There is also the principle of secret reservation, in other words, cleverly disguising the truth in the interests of damage control or in order to preserve a secret.

"A great principle, that! All it really signifies is that the end justifies the means. But to get to the heart of my theory: I'm sure that in 1773 the Jesuits suffered the same fate as the Templars. They had become too powerful and influential and knew too many secrets. One of them must have been so dangerous that the church felt existentially threatened. The heads of the order currently wield as much power and influence as they did in its heyday in the mid-eighteenth century, except that they've learned from past mistakes: now they operate in secret. But I've discovered indications that the order is active in establishing a new world order. They make deals and conspire with the powerful, especially the usual suspects, the freemasons and the knights of the Order of Malta, many of whom hold key positions in politics and industry. The order has created numerous enemies over the centuries. Grassa will soon come up against them in the course of his inquiries. He'll be swamped with suspects and motives, believe you me. And that," Rabea concluded, quite mistakenly, "is what'll get Lukas off the hook, because he's utterly remote from the machinations of the order's top brass."

Lucie was looking rather puzzled after Rabea's extended monologue. "Wow! I always knew the Jesuits weren't an innocuous, hymn-singing outfit, but you make them sound as if Lukas had joined the Mafia."

"The order really does have various links with the more orthodox Catholic Mafia families. For the moment, though, let's forget my theory that someone has discovered a dark Jesuit secret. Let's think as naively as our superintendent would. The commonest reasons for murder are jealousy and rapacity, followed by revenge. We can rule out jealousy, I guess, which leaves us with rapacity and revenge. Bentivoglio must have known the murderer because the latter had access to him. You're right: if he hated Bentivoglio so much, why didn't he simply wait for him to die in pain?"

"What if it was euthanasia?" Lucie suggested. "A man of the cloth can't kill himself because it'd be a mortal sin, so he asks someone else to do it for him. That someone else bungles the job so badly, it looks like murder."

"Hmm, we should give Grassa some food for thought. Maybe Bentivoglio learned a secret in the confessional and was eliminated by someone who couldn't afford any accessories after the fact."

"But isn't confession sacred? A priest isn't even obliged to turn in someone guilty of a capital offense. I can't see that principle being violated by the Jesuit in chief."

"Maybe he just appealed to the murderer's conscience," said Rabea. "The murderer got cold feet and killed him in the heat of the moment."

"Have you considered the possibility that the murderer may think Bentivoglio confided his secret to Lukas? Then Lukas would also be in danger."

Lucie did not know she had hit the nail on the head. She'd been racking her brain over the conspiratorial glance her brother had given her. She felt sure he'd meant her to do something with the ice-cream cone.

Lucie had also picked up other signals from Lukas, one of them being that he knew he was in a jam. There had to be more behind his arrest than the precipitate action of an ambitious police superintendent.

Rabea broke in on her thoughts. "Don't worry, Lucie. Bentivoglio was probably murdered by someone who knew him, the motive being some secret known to him in his capacity as superior general. What do you say we—"

Her musings were interrupted by the telephone.

Heinrich von Stetten, the patriarch of the family, and his wife, Evelyn, were sitting beside their hosts at a house in Grünwald, listening enthralled to an aria from *La Traviata* performed by a new star in the operatic firmament, a beautiful Russian soprano. Heinrich gave a start when someone tapped him on the shoulder.

Indignantly, he turned his head to see the Finks' butler, a brawny individual who could have landed a job with any private bodyguard agency. He assumed his old friend Fink had mobilized him for the evening because of the not inconsiderable array of jewels displayed by the ladies on the invitation list.

The butler-cum-bodyguard bent over him. "An urgent message for you, sir. Please would you call your home at once."

Evelyn looked at him inquiringly.

He gave her shoulder a reassuring squeeze and told her in a whisper that it was an urgent call from overseas.

She eyed him with a look of mute suffering and flashed her hostess an apologetic smile. Both women were inured to their husbands being called away at all hours of the day or night.

Heinrich von Stetten loosened the collar of his shirt. He was feeling faintly uneasy. As he followed the butler, his thoughts went back to a day in the Frankfurt Airport VIP lounge nine years earlier, when someone had tapped him on the shoulder in the same way and asked him to come to the phone.

That was when he had received the news that his son Alexander had lost his life while skiing off piste at Chamonix. He and a friend had ignored an avalanche warning. Alexander . . . his eldest son and heir, only twenty-seven years old. His pride and joy. He should have taken over the firm.

The baron called his home from the Finks' hallway. Then, in response to Frau Gabler's request, he anxiously dialed the number of the Rome apartment.

Lucie answered at once. "Daddy?"

Thank God. Relief flooded through him. His daughter's voice sounded calm enough. Things couldn't be too bad.

"What's so important, Lucie?"

"They've arrested Lukas, Daddy. You must do something at once."

"What? What nonsense is this?"

"No, it's true! Lukas saw the superior general this afternoon. When he came home, the police were waiting for him. They arrested him."

Heinrich shook his head bemusedly. "They arrested Lukas just because he saw the superior general?"

Lucie didn't reply. Instead, he heard another woman say something in the background. Then the receiver changed hands.

"Hello, Uncle Heinrich, Rabea here."

Ah, Rabea, thought von Stetten. She was never far away when things happened, but he was relieved to hear her voice. Rabea would keep a cool head in any situation. He knew her almost as well as his own children; after all, she had grown up with them. He was fond of Rabea. Although her disrespectful manner had thrown him occasionally, he always preferred strong personalities to obsequious yes-men.

Rabea gave him a succinct overview of the situation.

Heinrich retained his composure. He took it for granted that Lukas had absolutely nothing to do with Bentivoglio's murder, so he felt sure the matter would soon be disposed of. His son seemed to have been in the wrong place at the wrong time. All Heinrich had to do was see to it that the affair was settled swiftly and discreetly, so the press didn't get wind of it. His firm had numerous government contracts, and a son suspected of murder would stir up a lot of dust in official circles.

"Right, Rabea. Tell Lucie not to worry. I'll deal with everything. And tell her Lukas will be home by tomorrow. If the two of you hear anything new, call me at once. And not a word to Evelyn, please. Good night."

"Shit," said Lucie. "We'll probably have to sit around for hours without knowing what's happening to Lukas."

"We don't have to," Rabea told her. "The superintendent didn't invite us to come to headquarters with him, so we'll invite ourselves. Let's see how he enjoys our company. I'll camp outside his door until he lets Lukas go."

Lukas von Stetten rubbed his eyes in a daze. It was just after 1:00 a.m., and he was alone for the first time in over three hours. Superintendent Grassa had been questioning him until only a moment ago. Everything had happened so quickly: his arrest, his drive to headquarters, the interrogation. Lukas was not only feeling exhausted but suffering from a sore throat. Inspector d'Amico's driving was to blame for that.

Lukas had awkwardly finished off his ice cream in the back of the police car and lodged the little key under his tongue. Keeping it there was not a long-term solution, of course, and he realized he would have to think of something more practical. Unfortunately, the boorish style of driving favored by Grassa's colleague d'Amico put an end to that. Disaster struck during his very first reckless maneuver: he slammed on the brakes, causing Lukas to swallow the key. This time the ensuing paroxysm of coughing was genuine. The tiny key stuck fast in his throat, causing him to retch and gasp for breath.

Superintendent Grassa, who was sitting beside him in the back and had watched his coughing fit with interest, finally intervened. He slapped Lukas brutally on the back with the flat of his hand, thereby dislodging the key, which slid painfully down his prisoner's gullet.

They had reached headquarters without further incident. There, Lukas patiently underwent the usual procedures, which included photographing, fingerprinting, and a body search. His clerical garb caused a considerable stir, arousing the interest of the policemen present and one or two delinquents. A prostitute who was being led away to the cells made him an unmistakably suggestive offer involving a special discount for gentlemen of the cloth. Rabea would have been tickled by her delicate phraseology.

Suddenly, the door of the interview room opened again. The superintendent returned, followed by an elderly man with a snow-white mane of hair. The newcomer, who barely came up to Grassa's shoulder, was wearing a pale-gray suit, a bilious-green shirt, and a canary-yellow necktie. Father Simone would at once have asked the name of his tailor.

Grassa was visibly disgruntled by the presence of the stranger, who gave Lukas a friendly nod. His German was clumsy but quite comprehensible. "Good evening, Father von Stetten," he chirped in a strange falsetto. "I'm your attorney, Dottore Carlo Pierangeli. Your father sent me."

Lukas sprang to his feet at these words.

"We can leave at once. I have already settled all the formalities with the superintendent. There's no reason to hold you here any longer." That explained the look on the superintendent's face, which was reminiscent of a hungry predator robbed of its prey.

Another joyful surprise awaited Lukas outside. Lucie and Rabea hugged him in delight.

"You haven't seen the last of me, *Reverend*," Grassa growled softly. Pierangeli had rained on his parade more than once in the past, and he hated lawyers almost more than priests. What particularly irked him was that the most expensive star attorney in Rome had been employed to defend von Stetten. That the German priest had access to such contacts and money had given him food for thought.

He beckoned d'Amico into his office with an imperious gesture. "I want you to stick to that Jesuit like glue. He stinks to high heaven. Find us some evidence. Bug his apartment and his phone. I want to see a report on my desk every evening. What he says, who he meets, when he shits, when he fucks—everything. *Avanti*, get cracking!"

Grassa took off his Brioni jacket and loosened his necktie. His good looks and lack of scruples, coupled with his keen intelligence and analytical turn of mind, had paved the way for a lightning-fast upward career trajectory to the youngest departmental chief in the capital's homicide division. Grassa inspected his carefully manicured nails. Nothing in his current appearance was reminiscent of the unkempt, ragged orphan who had haunted the docks and markets of Naples in hopes of stealing enough to eat. Nothing apart from the fine white lines on his palms: vestiges of the scars inflicted by the matron of the orphanage to which he had eventually been consigned. He had stoically endured the humiliation and pain, inspired even then by his burning self-pride.

Grassa opened the window and looked up at the starry sky, which overlay the roofs of the Eternal City like velvet, enfolding it like a mother cradling her newborn child. "*Par tibi*, Roma, *nihil*," he murmured. Rome, you're beyond compare.

He loved the atmosphere that came over Rome at this hour. He smiled in a way that emphasized the cruel streak Rabea had noticed. This was the hour of lawlessness. This was when Rome witnessed most of the crimes of violence that provided him with a living. At night, the superintendent liked to prowl the quiet streets by himself, taking possession of the city like a lover. At night, the city and its secrets belonged to him. The time would come when they belonged to him by day as well.

Grassa was not feeling tired in the least. On the contrary, this latest case had invigorated him. Anticipatory energy was coursing through his veins. The murder of the superior general of the Jesuits was a career-boosting stroke of luck, and its solution, which was imminent, would mark the next stage on his road to success. His practiced instinct told him that the priest was hiding something.

After gazing out once more across the roofs of "his" city, Superintendent Grassa shut the window. He spent the rest of the night immersed in his files while the Eternal City slept.

With a sigh of relief, Lukas subsided against the leather upholstery of Pierangeli's Mercedes. His throat hurt like hell. At the same time, his stomach signaled that he was famished. He called his father to briefly thank him, then conversation lapsed. Father and son never had much to say to one another. Lukas anxiously inquired after his mother, but was assured that she knew nothing about the whole affair. They said a subdued goodbye, after which Attorney Pierangeli exchanged a few words with von Stetten senior on the subject of their course of action. Lukas was still suspected of murder and had been released on certain conditions only, the surrender of his passport included. For the moment, he was permitted to leave the Via dei Coronari apartment only in order to meet with his attorney.

Back home, Rabea said, "We all need some shut-eye. I hope you'll be able to sleep after all this excitement, Lukas. Or do you have other plans?" she added as he made for the kitchen and flung open the door of the refrigerator.

"Yes," he said, "food." He took out some garlic and Parmesan cheese.

Half an hour later Lucie and Rabea marveled at the quantities of *spaghetti all'aglio e olio* Lukas managed to devour. In view of the amount of garlic he'd used, they had declined his invitation to eat with him.

Apart from satisfying his hunger, Lukas had another reason for his extravagant use of garlic: it was the only laxative he knew of aside from sauerkraut and vinegar. There wasn't any sauerkraut in the house, and he had no wish to dose his sore throat with vinegar. That left the herbal all-purpose weapon. He shoveled two platefuls into himself and drank vast amounts of plain water.

After that, he sat back in his chair, shut his eyes, and reviewed the day's events in his mind. Bentivoglio's death had changed everything. Quite unexpectedly, he was sitting on a dead man's secret. Did he, Lukas, have to make a decision, the magnitude of which had deterred Bentivoglio himself? It was a decision concerning the disclosure of a momentous secret, one whose significance—and potential detriment— to the church might, according to the late father general, be immeasurable.

The young Jesuit once more remembered his uncle's final message. What if the *X* on the half-finished sermon really had been a message relating to Bentivoglio's secret? Where lay the connection between Bentivoglio's revelations and what his uncle Franz was said to have discovered a short time ago? Bentivoglio had assured him that he would understand the connection as soon as he opened the safe-deposit box. Whichever way Lukas looked at things, he always came to the same conclusion: he couldn't shirk his mission.

A loud rumble from his stomach reminded him of the requirements of the moment. Until now he had successfully suppressed the thought that there was a substantial risk the key might perforate his gut during the digestive process, leading to a fatal infection.

Lucie and Rabea, who kept him company in the kitchen, refrained from asking him any questions while he was eating. Lucie told him about the afternoon they'd spent together. First, they had accompanied the Dutch woman to the psammo studio and sampled the method of relaxing in a heated sand bath. Rabea privately thought it would have been far more relaxing if the professor hadn't talked incessantly. It had been a hard job to get rid of the talkative woman for the rest of the day.

After that the two had gone for a walk across the Piazza Navona, then strolled on toward the Piazza della Rotonda and the Pantheon. Lucie had explained that for centuries architects had been mystified by the dome of the latter, the secret of whose perfection they'd been unable to fathom.

After landing at the famous Caffè Greco on Via Condotti, Lucie and Rabea had returned home at around 7:30 p.m.

When Lukas pushed his plate away at last and wearily closed his eyes, Rabea briefly allowed him to luxuriate in the delusion that he was to be left in peace.

"All right, Lukas," she began. "We've known ever since you were arrested that you met with the superior general. What did the boss want?"

Superintendent Grassa had asked him the same question, and added, "Why did you murder the superior general of the Jesuits, von Stetten?" Lukas shut his eyes again.

"Come on," said Rabea, "it's obvious there's some connection between your visit to the old boy and his murder."

Although Lukas had no intention of initiating Rabea or Lucie into Bentivoglio's lethal secret, he realized he would be unable to avoid revealing a few superficial details. He began by telling the girls that the conversation had, at Bentivoglio's request, taken place in a private apartment on Via Condotti, not at the Vatican. They had talked about Uncle Franz, who had recommended him to Bentivoglio, and about the progress of his dissertation.

Rabea declared herself dissatisfied with this. "You mean to tell us it was just an innocuous chat between the superior general and one of his junior priests? Sorry, I just don't buy it."

Lucie, who sensed her brother's growing uneasiness, touched Rabea on the arm. "Give him a break. He's had a hard day. Tomorrow"—she glanced at her wristwatch, which showed it was just after 2:00 a.m.— "I mean *today*, is another day." She yawned uninhibitedly and pulled Lukas to his feet. "Come on, little brother, beddy-bye."

Rabea shrugged her shoulders. "You're right. Let's call it a day."

Lukas lay down in his room and waited for his meal to take effect, which it soon did. He made it to the bathroom just in time. Worried, Lucie knocked on the door, but he sent her away, telling her it was just a minor stomach upset. Almost one hour of discomfort later, the key lay disinfected on the ledge beside the sink. He sluiced his face with cold water. What he badly needed now was a shower. When he finally left the bathroom, however, Lucie and Rabea were barring his path.

"Okay, little brother, out with it!" growled Lucie, stamping her foot, which was encased in a slipper resembling a sheep's head. "Your behavior's pretty weird, don't you think? You don't even like garlic, yet you polish off a whole bulb and then barricade yourself in the john for an hour. I want to know what's up."

Lukas stared at her foot, simply to avoid looking into two pairs of beady eyes, one steel blue, the other emerald green.

"I'm waiting," Lucie snapped.

All at once, while Lukas was searching for a credible answer, they heard a strange howl followed by a scratching sound.

"What was that?" asked Rabea, turning in the direction from which the sound was coming. She paused beside the front door.

"I'm sure it's just the little dog of that wacky contessa across the way. Who knows," said Lucie with a malicious sidelong glance at Lukas, "perhaps it's suffering from the same trouble as my beloved brother."

At that moment, the howls resumed even louder.

"Can it be running around out there on the landing?" Rabea opened the front door. Sure enough, the contessa's brown-and-white lapdog was scrabbling desperately at the door of its mistress's apartment. Every now and then, it stopped scrabbling long enough to raise its head and utter another heartrending howl.

Rabea kneeled down beside the little animal. "Poor little thing," she cooed. "Did the old hag shut you out, then?" She extended a fist so that the little shih tzu could sniff it. The dog regarded her briefly with its big brown eyes, then went on scratching desperately at the door.

Lucie and Lukas had followed Rabea out onto the landing. She looked up at them. "The old woman must have let it out to do its business. Think I should ring the bell, or should we keep him for a little while—give her a bit of a scare for forgetting about her dog?" Cautiously, she took hold of the animal's collar.

It gave a pitiful yelp. Startled, Rabea took her hand away. It was smeared with blood. "The poor little creature. It's hurt!" Picking up the dog with care, she carried it inside.

"Come on, let's look after you." She deposited the trembling animal on the kitchen table. "Lukas, I need a pair of scissors and some iodine for disinfection."

While he was hurrying off, she turned to Lucie. "I'd like to put a dressing on the wound after cleaning it, so he or she can't scratch itself. Which are you, I wonder?" Bending over the animal for a moment, she discovered two rows of teats that told her she was dealing with a little girl dog.

Lukas returned with a dressing and handed her a pair of scissors—plus, with a rueful smile, a bottle of grappa. "Sorry, there's no iodine in the house, but maybe alcohol will do."

Rabea grinned. "I'll take what I can get. Would you mind holding her, please?" She spoke soothingly to the trembling animal, then gingerly took hold of its collar and, avoiding the wound, cut through it. A little disk dangling from the collar was engraved *Stellina*. The dog looked up at her. "So that's your name, is it, Stellina?" When she trickled some of the spirits on a cotton ball, the dog lifted her black button of a nose and sniffed, then winced a little as Rabea cleaned the wound. Stellina kept still until the procedure was over and Rabea applied the dressing.

"There, my little heroine. It'll soon stop hurting. Now we'll go and wake your mistress." Rabea picked the dog up. Before Lucie and Lukas could react, she had pushed past them and planted herself in front of the door across the landing. The shiny brass plate below the doorbell bore the ornate inscription:

FRANCESCA BUONAVENTURA-ANGELI
CONTESSA DI MONTEBELLO E VALLEVERDE

Rabea rang the bell. The dog was resting its forepaws on her arm, and she felt every muscle in its body tense.

Lucie and Lukas had followed her out. Lukas craned past her and tried to detect some movement through the peephole.

"Oh my God!" Lucie covered her mouth suddenly. "What if the old lady took her dog for a walk and got mugged!"

Rabea and Lukas exchanged an eloquent look. "Come off it," said Rabea, "you've been watching too many Hollywood B movies. I'm sure there's a simple explanation. She probably had too much Montebello e Valleverde vino to drink and is sleeping it off. Poor little doggy, your mistress is a bad mother." She tickled the putative victim's head, and Stellina trustingly nestled against her.

"All right," said Lucie, "come on, let's get to bed."

She and Rabea were back inside their apartment and had already reached their bedroom when they noticed that Lukas hadn't followed them.

He was still standing irresolutely outside the contessa's door.

"What is it, Lukas?" Rabea called. "Did you hear something?"

"I don't know." He shook his head. "I have such a funny feeling. Maybe something's happened after all."

He'd had the same sort of odd sensation that morning and paid it no attention—a fatal error. His inner voice had just made itself heard once more. Should he call the police? If it turned out that the old lady had had a drop too many and was sleeping the sleep of the just, as Rabea had surmised, he would look ridiculous and could poison neighborly relations forever. The contessa was the most prickly tenant in the building as it was.

He was still debating with himself when he heard a faint jingling sound. He turned his head to see Lucie waving a bunch of keys at him. He recognized it as his own. As the son of the building owner, he occasionally stood in for the building manager and possessed a set of passkeys.

"I can't just break into my neighbor's apartment. What if she's in there and screams the house down? What if someone calls the police? I already had that pleasure once today."

"I'd hardly call it a pleasure, Father Lukas," Rabea interposed, "but if you think we should see if the old girl's all right, I'll take over."

Lukas look alarmed, and she reassured him. "Don't worry, I'll be diplomatic."

Now it was Lucie's turn to exchange an eloquent glance with her brother. Neither of them had any great faith in Rabea's tact or diplomacy.

Without waiting for an answer, Rabea set the dog on the ground and took the keys from Lucie. The third key fit, and the heavy door swung inward. The little dog scampered past her.

The contessa's apartment was considerably larger than Lukas and Lucie's, but its most conspicuous feature was the ostentatious display of wealth. Stretching away in front of the three intruders was a hallway lavishly furnished with small inlaid tables and gilded Louis XVI chairs. Leading off it were several double doors, and at the far end was a baroque mirror that filled the entire back wall.

"Talk about overkill," said Lucie as she sauntered past the gilt-framed pictures. "Madame de Pompadour would have felt at home here."

"Typical case of status symbolism." Looking around for the dog, Rabea spotted it scratching at the farthest door.

"I seem to remember that's the door to the master bedroom," Lukas thought aloud. Rabea looked at him inquiringly, and he added, "I saw the plans when this building was converted."

"Let's go and see, then. Come on."

Lucie followed Rabea with alacrity, but Lukas stayed put.

Rabea was concentrating on the little dog, which had started to howl, so she was halfway along the hallway before she noticed his absence.

"What's the matter, Lukas, growing roots in that doorway? It was your idea to check on the old lady. *We* could have been in bed already."

After a last despairing glance over his shoulder at their own apartment, Lukas capitulated. As he walked toward Rabea, he became suddenly aware of her titillating appearance. He gazed at her hair, which was loose and looked like a reddish-gold shower of sparks. He also registered her dainty femininity emphasized by her short nightie. It didn't help that he was also presented with an all-around view courtesy of the mirror at the end of the hallway, which brazenly revealed Rabea's delectable backside in its flimsy briefs. Priest or not, he had been born a man. That part of his body, forbidden to function by his vow of celibacy, reacted against his will and demanded its unpriestly due. He was appalled when he remembered he was wearing only thin cotton pajamas, the trousers of which would inevitably reveal the nature of his reaction.

Feigning another coughing fit, he bent over and waited until he could straighten up without betraying himself. The deliberate coughing made his throat hurt even more, but the pain was more than welcome at that moment. He found a harmless focal point—his sister Lucie— and assumed an expression appropriate to a Sunday sermon. He hoped Rabea hadn't registered her dire effect on him.

But when he raised his head, one look into Rabea's eyes sufficed to tell him that his mishap had not escaped her. He was faintly surprised to see, however, that her bright eyes were entirely devoid of mockery. Instead, they seemed to convey muted regret. A sudden, delicate, and alluring *what if* hovered between them and nestled into their consciousness like a fragile strand of gossamer.

The dog, whose howls were impressively amplified by the lofty walls of the hallway, reminded them abruptly of their reason for being there. This wasn't the time or place. A few steps brought them to the door of the contessa's bedroom.

Rabea hesitated for only a moment, then pushed the door open. The little dog promptly shot past her into the room, which was dominated by a grandiose four-poster. The damask bedspread, which looked rather rumpled but had not been turned down, was sprinkled with pink dots like confetti. The curtains flanking the ceiling-high windows were pale pink, and the entire room was papered in pink as well. Old rose prevailed in the case of the Chippendale sofa, the two upholstered chairs, and the ankle-deep carpet. There was no wardrobe, but there were two cloth-covered doors in the left-hand wall. One of them was ajar and led to a dressing room; the other was closed. The little dog was up on its hind legs outside the closed door, scrabbling to be let in.

"Oh my God," Rabea groaned. "Old rose hell. Who is her goddamned interior decorator, Elton John?"

"Do you know Mr. Bubble?" Lukas asked her.

She stared at him, puzzled by this seemingly irrelevant question. "No, why do you ask?"

"It's a brand of pink bubble gum—you can buy it at any supermarket checkout or espresso bar in Rome. The contessa was married to its inventor or the heir—something like that. Maybe that's why she's so fond of pink."

"I see. Incredible anyone could become so damned rich on chewing gum." Rabea shook her head, and Lukas was once more fascinated by the iridescence of her auburn hair. His overactive subconscious had nothing better to do than defy him once again and conjure up the image of a little frog princess lying on the four-poster bed. It took all his willpower to banish this inappropriate idea.

"Where's Lucie gone?" asked Rabea, looking around for her.

"Wow, she's got more shoes than I have," said Lucie's voice, which was heavily tinged with disbelief at the fact that anyone could surpass her at that discipline. She emerged from the contessa's dressing room wearing an enormous hat that looked as if it had been made for the races at Ascot.

"Lucie, are you crazy? Put that thing back at once!" Lukas looked around anxiously as if he expected Superintendent Grassa to walk in at any moment and catch them burgling the place red-handed.

"Ouch," he said. Something sharp scratched his bare ankle. He looked down and saw the contessa's little shih tzu. It had evidently grown impatient and was now resorting to violence in hopes of persuading one of the bipeds to open the door at last. "All right, we'll look for your mistress."

The dog turned and trotted back to the closed door. Lukas, with his hand on the handle, hesitated. He gave Rabea and Lucie a sidelong glance, but there was no help from that quarter. He knocked on the door.

"Contessa, are you in there? Can you hear me? It's me, your neighbor, Father von Stetten. I was worried because I found your dog out on the stairs. Contessa? Can you hear me?" He knocked again, louder this time. No answer. "Contessa, I'm coming in now; please don't be alarmed. Contessa?"

He slowly depressed the gilded handle. The door swung silently inward and the bathroom light came on at the same time. It was obviously linked to a movement sensor. A smothered cry rang out beside him. Rabea had grabbed his arm. Lucie gave a horrified exclamation. The little dog bounced up and down in front of the huge bathtub, feverishly wagging its tail. The contessa was lying full-length in the brimming tub, but she wasn't enjoying a relaxing bubble bath: she couldn't have been more dead.

"Oh my God, I don't get it. That's all we need," Rabea said angrily.

Lukas stared at the contessa in consternation. He'd been prepared for anything but this.

"I'd call this a really juicy run of bad luck, Father Lukas," Rabea went on. "I suppose you haven't put your foot in it with the Almighty recently, have you? If you'd only been arrested on suspicion of murder, we wouldn't need to worry, but now we're up to our necks in it."

Lucie was staring at the contessa's corpse as though hypnotized. "You think she drowned in there?" she asked in a whisper.

"In a Chanel dress, Lucie?" said Rabea. "Honestly!"

The contessa was not a sight for sensitive eyes. The look in her lifeless, dilated eyes revealed the horror she must have felt in her last few moments. Her features were grotesquely contorted by her death struggle, and her blue-black tongue, which protruded from between her lips like a ripe plum, left no doubt as to the cause of death. She had been strangled.

Rabea at once suspected that she had not died in the bath. Her searching gaze fell on the contessa's hands and their artificial fingernails, several of which had broken off. Suddenly remembering the pink dots on the bed, she went back into the bedroom. Sure enough, several of the nails were lying on the rumpled damask counterpane. The contessa had been strangled on her bed and had desperately clawed at her assailant or assailants.

Why the latter had put her in the bath and filled it for no apparent reason was something that at first defied Rabea's comprehension. She continued to scrutinize the bath and its contents. In the bottom of the tub, she made out some strange white crystals. "I wonder . . ." she murmured, frowning. Though both Lukas and Lucie were used to the sight of dead bodies—Lukas as a priest and his sister as an archaeology student inured to mummies—they watched Rabea's actions with incredulity.

Rabea went over to a stainless steel garbage can beneath the marble sink and opened it. Inside she found several crumpled 500-gram packs that had contained *sale grosso*, or coarse salt. "Damn it, I can just see Superintendent Grassa waltzing in here. I've no wish to help him have a triumphal orgasm. Maybe we should simply take the dog and lock up again. We were never here, right?" she said unexpectedly.

Lukas gave her a wry smile. "It's our duty to call the police. We don't have the slightest connection with her death, so we've nothing to fear."

"You didn't have anything to do with Bentivoglio's death, but they arrested you," Rabea reminded him, but then gave in. "All right, truth is always the best weapon. Anyway, this place must be plastered with our fingerprints. I can't imagine how many things your inquisitive sister has touched." With a reproachful sidelong glance at the person in question, Rabea removed an expensive crystal bottle of perfume from Lucie's hand and put it back on the shelf.

"I'm nervous, that's all," Lucie said weakly.

"I've one condition, Lukas," Rabea went on in a voice that brooked no opposition. "Before we call the police you owe us some answers. Two murders in one day, and you're in the vicinity of both crime scenes. That's no coincidence, and that's just what our ambitious superintendent will think. I've a theory, Lukas. The contessa was a particularly inquisitive type, and that was her undoing. She must have seen something she shouldn't, and the killer or killers wanted to prevent her body being found too soon. In this heat, the smell of decay would soon have become noticeable, so they put her in the bath and shook in several kilograms of salt. That would have preserved the body for a while, and that's what worries me. The killers weren't expecting any friends or relations to find her in the near future, or they wouldn't have bothered with the salt. They obviously had a very clear idea of her habits, so they must have kept watch on her for days, and they also had the salt ready. That shows it was an absolutely professional job. Her murder served only one purpose: to cover something up. It's all connected with Bentivoglio's murder. So out with it, Lukas: What are you hiding from us?"

Lukas made one last attempt to prevaricate. "How do you know it wasn't a simple burglary that went wrong?"

"Don't insult my intelligence, Lukas! We both know this wasn't a burglary. You saw the open jewel casket in the bedroom. It can hardly have escaped you that the contessa owned half of Tiffany's. Even the dumbest thief would have stumbled over tidbits like those."

"Okay, Rabea," he sighed. "I share your opinion that the contessa's murder wasn't just chance, but Bentivoglio made me swear on the Bible that I wouldn't divulge the subject of our conversation. Besides, knowing about it could put you in danger too."

"Lukas, the man who made you swear that oath has been murdered, and so has an innocent woman. Under those circumstances, I hardly think your oath is still valid. Or do you think Bentivoglio was counting on departing this life so soon after your visit? This has given the affair an entirely new dynamic. You want to wait until someone else is murdered?"

"Lukas," said Lucie, "I can sense how perturbed you are by this whole affair, but what makes you think the killers haven't long ago concluded that we're already in the know? Superintendent Grassa certainly thought so." She took his hand, turned it over, and laid her cheek against his palm in a touching gesture of affection.

Lukas was suddenly struck by a new idea. *Had it really been pure chance that Rabea turned up just when all these difficulties arose? Why had she wanted to interview Bentivoglio, of all people?* He immediately regretted his suspicion—of course Rabea could have had no knowledge of Bentivoglio's secret. It had always been like that, though. As soon as she was in his vicinity, reprehensible characteristics deep inside him seemed to awaken. But why whenever something went wrong with his life did he always try to burden her with the responsibility? The young priest was honest enough with himself to see his thoughts for what they were, the product of his male-dominant subconscious. He knew his subconscious blamed Rabea for only one reason: because he responded to her *against his will*—both physically and emotionally.

Two pairs of eyes, one blue and one green, regarded him calmly. He conducted a mute dialogue with Rabea's green emeralds. It was still there, their ability to communicate with the eyes alone, as if a single synapse were all that separated their thoughts. *Let me help,* said her eyes.

It's too dangerous, his own replied.

I'm not afraid.

I know. It's me who's afraid.

Rabea sensed the decision tilting in her favor. "You've got to tell us."

He heaved another sigh. "Very well. Bentivoglio told me that as a young Jesuit he came into the possession of some sensational documents that had been stolen from our order in 1773, during the turmoil following its suppression. Instead of taking them to his superior at once, he hung on to them and studied them with a fellow Jesuit. The latter was murdered soon afterward, and Bentivoglio became frightened. After that, he kept them hidden in a safe-deposit box outside Rome. He was too ill to fetch the documents himself, so he asked me to do it for him. That's all. I was merely to act as his errand boy." He refrained from mentioning the plan to convene a general congregation of the order and hold a press conference thereafter, which was a purely internal matter. He saw Rabea's dubious expression.

"As a young Jesuit?" she said. "He must have kept them stashed for decades."

"Almost thirty years exactly."

"Why did he want to get them back now? What sort of documents are they? Did he tell you anything about their contents?"

"Almost nothing."

Rabea interpreted his unhappy expression correctly. He had told them as much as he could reconcile with his oath on the Bible.

Lukas felt in the breast pocket of his pajamas and took out the symbol of his dilemma, the tiny gold-colored key.

The three of them stood side by side like conspirators, staring at it, spellbound. Even Lukas did, as if he needed the key to convince himself once more that everything that had happened that day had not sprung from his own imagination.

A strange mood had taken possession of the trio, rendering all their senses more acute.

It was the hour when night expired, giving birth to a new day.

From the outside, the white Fiat Ducato van that had been parked on the Via dei Coronari since the previous afternoon was no different from the thousands that could be seen in Rome every day. With dented front and rear bumpers and mottled patches of rust, the van had seen better days. Its unsightly appearance was intentional and conducive to its special function. It helped it to recede into a gray zone where no one noticed it.

If anyone had nonetheless deigned to look twice at the vehicle, they would have seen the words *Lavanderia Luigi Rossi* emblazoned on its sides in big black letters, and they would have promptly dismissed this unimportant information from their mind. If anyone had been lucky enough to inspect its interior, however, they would have whistled through their teeth. Instead of laundry baskets, it contained the most modern high-tech equipment imaginable: state-of-the-art computers, highly sensitive bugging devices, and a phalanx of expensive monitors. Neither the CIA nor Mossad was better equipped.

But what use was the most sophisticated bugging operation if the sound receptors—bugs, in the vernacular—were located in the wrong apartment? Or rather, if the persons you wanted to eavesdrop on were in the wrong apartment? The two men whose clearly defined task it was to discover what Lukas von Stetten and Superior General Bentivoglio had spoken about were just missing a firsthand account of it.

The younger of the two appeared to be dozing in the passenger seat in spotless overalls. The driver's seat was empty. Passersby might have taken him for an apprentice waiting patiently for his boss, but this peaceful impression was deceptive. The man was wide awake. From beneath his long lashes, he was keenly observing his surroundings, poised to react to the least sign of danger. Fresh-faced and fair-haired, he exuded a kind of perfidious innocence that made him look much younger than his thirty years. Having grown up on a pig farm in the Po Valley, he endeavored to shake off the stench of his childhood by dressing with the kind of stylish elegance that cost a lot of money. Many a woman of mature years eyed him wistfully on the street, never guessing that his angelic appearance concealed a venomous soul. The innocent-looking young man was nothing other than a professional killer.

His evil career had begun early. Even as a child he had stolen cats and subjected them to lethal torture—his first taste of the power of life and death. His hard-pressed parents had had him committed to a home for problem children in response to vehement complaints from his teachers and the parents of his classmates. He committed his first murder at thirteen, his victim being one of the teachers at the home. After that, his movements became untraceable.

His employers appreciated the fact that he planned and executed his contracts meticulously and down to the last detail. His operations spanned the whole of Europe. There wasn't an authority, from the

German CID to Scotland Yard and Europol, that hadn't put him at the top of their most-wanted list, but he made fools of them all. He had never been arrested, nor did the authorities know what he looked like—because none of his victims ever survived. That was how he came to the attention of the Protector, who wanted him all to itself. The killer named a sum, and the Protector not only paid it but also gave him an important position in the organization. The killer called himself Gabriel, which suited him. He really was as handsome as an archangel.

The other man in the van was seated at one of the monitors. He was wearing headphones and fiddling with various controls. The work area in front of him resembled a trash can. It was littered with empty paper cups, unappetizing leftovers, and a brimming ashtray. Unshaven and wearing a grubby set of overalls stretched tight over his paunch, compared to the refined good looks of his colleague, he looked like an uncouth peasant. Massimo Trapano was, in fact, a genius who had occupied a special place of trust within the Protector's organization for over twenty years. He was uninterested in the money he earned from his activities on behalf of the outfit. He made more than enough from the patents he owned. Trapano and the Protector were bound by more than secular, material interests: they were fighting on behalf of a noble cause.

Trapano swore softly. There was no sound from the priest's apartment, but he thought he detected some faint vibrations emanating from his bugs, an almost imperceptible electronic signature. He fiddled some more with his various keyboards and controls, turned on another amplifier here and an additional monitor there. Clamping the headset to his ears with both hands, he listened intently. He cursed the inquisitive mutt for alerting its mistress, but the whole mess was attributable to his colleague's arrogant behavior. His only task had been to watch the building, wait until the coast was clear, and then tell Trapano when he could sneak into the apartment unobserved. At 9:30 p.m., when she left the building to walk her dog, he had given Trapano the green light. But for some reason, she had stopped short outside the front door and turned back. Gabriel claimed to have had no time to warn him, but Trapano suspected the delay was deliberate. For what had his youthful colleague done to remedy this alleged mischance? Simply lived up to his nickname, the Executioner. Trapano had tried to prevent the execution, but had been quelled in his opposition with a single sentence: "She's seen us."

Trapano normally kept his distance from the base criminal members of the Protector's retinue, but too much depended on this job—they might be on the verge of a breakthrough. Being so close to success, the Protector wanted nothing left to chance and had teamed him up with the Executioner.

Like his colleague the Executioner, Trapano was arrogant and infatuated with his own abilities—an explosive combination that had long ago led to a potentially disastrous loss of touch with reality. Because his activities for the Protector had always been confined to installing and dismantling bugging devices and monitoring and analyzing what they gleaned, he believed that he himself was no common criminal. But he realized that he had crossed a line yesterday. A human being had died. He'd heard the old woman desperately pleading for her life and seen her wet herself in terror, seen her face turn blue and her limbs go limp.

And as if that were not enough, there had been another foul-up. While Trapano was installing his devices in the von Stetten apartment, Gabriel had said he would "see to the dog," but the confounded animal had given him the slip and roused the neighborhood with its yapping. They'd been compelled to quit the apartment prematurely. Trapano had been able to install only half his bugs and none of his personally developed minicameras. Only von Stetten's phone, living room, and bedroom were equipped with monitoring devices. For the first time in his many years of work for the Protector, Trapano had failed to finish the job and was having to make do without any visual transmissions.

The irony was that it was only the contessa's murder that prompted Lukas to break his oath and take the two women into his confidence—but their conversation was in the contessa's apartment itself, not in von Stetten's apartment, where the bugs had been activated.

Dismayed silence reigned in the murdered contessa's bathroom.

Rabea was the first to regain her composure. She carefully took the safe-deposit key from Lukas's palm and eyed the object, turning it over in her hand as if hopeful that its secret would be revealed before her very eyes. "So Bentivoglio has decamped to the Elysian Fields and left you sitting on a whole heap of problems. I call that bad luck and a half."

Before Lukas could say anything, they were startled by a loud bark. Spinning around, they saw the dog make for the door like a furry cannonball. Standing there was an elderly matron in a floral apron, screaming at the top of her voice—the contessa's cleaning woman.

Superintendent Grassa's face looked inscrutable, but he was inwardly jubilant. The case was developing just to his taste. First the murder of the superior general of the Jesuits, for which he had at once been able to produce a suspect, and now another murder, the victim being the suspect's next-door neighbor. There had to be a link between the two killings. It promised to be a quick job, and the press would once more splash his name in the papers in connection with a sensational case.

Inspector Corrado d'Amico had been questioning the cleaner, who sat sobbing in an armchair. He hurried over to Grassa.

"Well, Corrado, what have we got so far?" the superintendent asked in a businesslike tone. His eyes roamed the contessa's bedroom and came to rest on Lucie, who was standing beside the bed with another policeman and the little dog, which was sitting at her feet. Grassa registered her baby-doll getup with raised eyebrows. Lucie returned his gaze with a certain defiance, conscious of her provocative effect. Meanwhile, the inspector had launched into his dispassionate report.

"We have the body of a woman, age around sixty, and identified as Contessa Francesca di Montebello e Valleverde, the tenant of this apartment. Preliminary findings suggest that she was strangled, and dumped in the bathtub postmortem. Time of death: last night, probably before midnight. The autopsy will narrow it down, of course. The deceased was found by that lady in the armchair, the cleaner, Anna-Maria Petrullo. That's to say, the whole situation is a bit confusing. She says someone was there before her. She's in shock—I still haven't gotten much in the way of definite information out of her. We were alerted not by her but by Lucie von Stetten, the sister of the priest we questioned yesterday. He seems to have flown the coop with that redheaded journalist. I thought you'd probably like to interview the sister yourself." D'Amico concluded his report with a suggestive glance at Lucie's baby-doll.

Grassa scowled at the innuendo before switching on an instant smile and turning in Lucie's direction. Spreading his arms wide, he hurried over, took hold of her right hand, and planted a kiss on her knuckles.

Lucie suppressed an impulse to snatch her hand away and gave him her most dazzling smile instead. Rabea's instructions had been to gain time.

"Signorina von Stetten, delighted to see you again so soon. As I'm sure you'll understand, I'm anxious to discover what you're doing here in the victim's apartment." Grassa took her gently but firmly by the elbow. "Come, let's find a quieter spot. We're only getting in the way of my colleagues' work. Let's go to your place."

He led her purposefully out of the apartment and across the landing. The little dog had trotted after her. "Would you be kind enough to open the door?"

"Oh, my goodness, I forgot my key in all the excitement. How am I going to get in?" Lucie's expression was lamblike in its innocence.

Grassa eyed her skeptically. "Stay right where you are, signorina. I'll be back." Three minutes later, he returned with a sour-faced police locksmith. He pointed imperiously at the door.

The man kneeled down in front of it. Outwardly antiquated, the lock's innards were consistent with the most modern technology.

"Please be careful," cooed Lucie, "that door is on the national heritage register." Her charm bounced off the locksmith. "Is the key on the inside?" he growled.

Lucie told him no, but of course it was. Rabea, who knew all the tricks, had seen to that.

Grumbling to himself, the locksmith got busy with his tools. Grassa was growing increasingly impatient. At last, there was a faint click, and the door swung open. The man noted the key on the inside and glowered at Lucie.

"Whoops," she said, innocently shrugging her shoulders.

"After you, Signorina von Stetten," Grassa said politely.

Lucie touched him briefly on the arm. "Make yourself comfortable in the living room, Superintendent. I'm just going to put on something more appropriate." The superintendent's expression left her in no doubt that he had no objection to her getup, but he nodded.

Lucie took as much time to change as seemed even remotely acceptable before rejoining him. She was now wearing white linen shorts and a sleeveless blouse knotted below her breasts in such a way as to reveal her tanned tummy. She had little more on than before, possibly less.

The superintendent was yelling into his cell phone when she returned to the living room. "Hell and damnation! I'll call you back right away, and then I'll expect to hear how this could have happened!" He hung up and turned to Lucie. "Signorina von Stetten, you're a feast for the eyes, and I enjoy every minute I spend in your company, but I'm fast running out of patience. I need to know your brother's whereabouts."

"My brother? He went out early this morning, but he didn't tell me where." This was true. Rabea and Lukas really hadn't told her where they were going.

Grassa planted himself in front of Lucie and looked her in the eye. "Signorina von Stetten—" he began, but she interrupted him with a winning smile.

"Do call me Lucie, Superintendent."

"Lucie, I feel flattered, and I'm most appreciative of your attempt to flirt with me, but your brother's in an extremely awkward position. So I'll ask you one more time: Where is he?"

"I honestly don't know."

"All right, Lucie, where's your redheaded friend. Rabea, isn't that her name? Did she go off with your brother?"

This time Lucie didn't hesitate. It was information she could afford to give. "Yes, the two of them left together."

Her reply seemed to satisfy Grassa. He turned away and looked down for a moment at the crowd of people on the Via dei Coronari. The whole neighborhood was out. The Forensic Institute's ambulance was just driving up to collect the contessa's body.

Grassa turned back to her. "Lucie, I already know that your brother went off with Rabea. Since he was under house arrest, I had him watched by one of my men. His last report this morning was that he was following the pair. Unfortunately, I've just been informed that my officer has been found dead. His throat had been cut."

Yet another murder! Lucie was profoundly shocked by this news.

Grassa's instinct told him that her consternation was genuine. "You see, Lucie? The situation is serious. Three murders in less than twenty-four hours. The dead policeman leaves behind two young children. What am I going to say to his widow?" He lowered his voice. "Your brother and your girlfriend are in extreme danger. I can protect them, but only if you tell me what you know."

"Very well. Last night, after we found the contessa's dog out on the landing, Lukas became worried about her. He knew she sometimes had a drop too much to drink. Being the son of the owner of the building, he had a passkey. We found her dead in the bath. Then Rabea told my brother to come clean."

"Well?" Grassa said impatiently. "What did he say?"

"He said the superior general had hidden something a lot of people are after, and he told Lukas to go and get it for him. That's all I know, Superintendent. Then the cleaning woman found us."

"And your brother never told you what Bentivoglio had hidden?"

"No, but he intended to go and get it with Rabea."

"And you really don't know where they went?" Grassa persisted.

"No, but they planned to be back by this evening."

"I know you and your brother don't have a car here in Rome. How about the journalist?"

"Rabea came here from the airport yesterday in a taxi."

"Is either of them carrying a cell phone? Can you call them?"

Lucie shook her head. Rabea owned two cell phones: one registered in her name, which she had deliberately left in the bedroom, and a prepaid one whose number she'd declined to reveal.

While the superintendent was issuing further instructions by phone, Lucie felt a sense of dire foreboding. The unknown murderer or murderers were hot on the heels of Lukas and Rabea.

"Where are we going?" Lukas asked Rabea breathlessly as he pounded along behind her toward the Pantheon.

"The multistory parking garage on Via XX Settembre. The editorial office has a car for me there. It isn't in my name, so nobody knows about it. I received the key by messenger. We'll drive to the bank, open the safe-deposit box, see what's in it, and then decide if we hand it over to your Jesuit bosses or simply burn it."

Lukas had halted abruptly. "Wait. I know you, Rabea—you can smell a big story. Whatever we find in that safe-deposit box is *my* problem, and *I'll* decide what to do with it."

"All right, Father Lukas, calm down. First we'd better see what it is. Don't look around, by the way, but I think we're being followed."

"What gives you that idea?"

"It wouldn't be the first time. I've often stirred up dirt when researching a story, and not everyone likes that. You develop a sixth sense. Grassa must have put him on our tail, I guess. We'd better separate. If there's only one of them, he'll have to decide who to follow. You're the chief suspect, so he'll go with you. Let's meet at the multistory garage exit in half an hour. I'll pick you up there."

Rabea disappeared around the next corner. As she had predicted, the man continued to follow Lukas.

The Protector's two men in the van had also spotted the couple's departure. Trapano had sent Gabriel after them, then called the Protector to report the latest developments and continued to monitor the priest's apartment.

The conversation in the drawing room between the superintendent and the Jesuit's twin sister had mitigated their missed opportunity the night before. Lucie's statement confirmed that they were on the right track at last. Bentivoglio must have been in possession of the missing documents for a long time. And he must have been aware of their potentially explosive nature, which was why he had locked them away. Shortly before his death, he had passed the secret on to Lukas von Stetten, and he and the red-haired girl appeared to be going to collect them. Trapano informed the Protector of this gratifying news on his encrypted cell phone.

Although Gabriel had never let the organization down on a job and was already hot on the priest's heels, the Protector had a secret backup plan. They were so close to the objective to which the Protector had dedicated most of its life.

Having promptly issued the relevant orders, the Protector strolled out onto the balcony of its suite at the Hotel Hassler, overlooking the Spanish Steps. From there, the head of the organization had a magnificent view of the sun-drenched roofs of Rome and Vatican City. The Protector smiled as its gaze lingered briefly on Saint Peter's. If the safe-deposit box contained what it surmised, the day of vengeance was not far off.

Gabriel was crouching beneath the steps leading up to a house on the Via Barberini. He felt the blood rushing through his veins—the murder had aroused him. It was a pity he couldn't amuse himself with the little redhead right away. He thought about the dead policeman, whom he'd left lying in a rapidly expanding pool of blood. What an amateur!

He wrapped the bloody knife in a handkerchief. He would have to hurry if he didn't want to lose sight of the redhead.

Rabea scanned the Piazza di Spagna mistrustfully. She'd been sure the man who had followed her was after Lukas. *There must have been two of them,* it occurred to her. The man who was following her now seemed smarter than the one she'd spotted at the Pantheon. Although she'd employed various tricks, like stopping suddenly and looking around or examining the reflections in a shop window, she hadn't identified her tail.

Gabriel was enjoying himself enormously. This cat-and-mouse game appealed to him. The redhead seemed to have smelled a rat, but she didn't stand a chance against a pro like him. He looked forward to her next move but was disappointed when she made no further attempt to spot him. Annoyed, he decided to spice things up a bit.

On the Largo di Santa Susanna, he broke cover and strolled openly along in a gaggle of tourists, and when they turned right in the direction of the Piazza della Repubblica, he walked on alone by himself and followed Rabea up the Via XX Settembre. They were now separated by only five yards or so. At close range, Gabriel treated himself to a long look at Rabea's swaying buttocks in their denim shorts. It titillated him to picture what he would do to her later.

He didn't waste a single glance on the half-dozen nuns coming toward him, but his quarry suddenly did something quite unexpected: she darted into the middle of them. The effect of this was explosive. The nuns scattered like a flock of pigeons startled by a gunshot—in fact, Rabea almost thought she saw a few feathers fluttering into the air.

Grabbing a particularly stalwart nun by the arm, she cried, "Please help me! That man is stalking me. He's been harassing me!"

Gabriel's lecherous expression was still imprinted on his face, so the nuns didn't doubt her.

Appalled, he saw every one of the pious ladies assume a look of grim determination. As though in response to a secret word of command, they hemmed him in, vituperating and brandishing their purses. One of them even beat him with her umbrella, though God alone knew why she was carrying one on such a fine day.

By the time the nuns had finished with him and swept off on a wave of righteous indignation, the redhead had vanished.

Gabriel experienced a surge of murderous hatred. The little witch would regret this. Feverishly, he debated his next move. Where could she have gone? There was a bus stop across the street, but he ruled that out at once. Stazione Termini, Rome's central station, was too far to the right. A taxi? She'd had plenty of time to take one. What else was there in the neighborhood? He turned on the spot. Suddenly, he sighted a notice board. A multistory parking garage. Of course, she must have a car. He set off hastily.

* * *

Lukas gave a start as a car blew its horn right beside him. Rabea, who was behind the wheel, snapped, "There you are at last. Quick, get in. We must get out of here. I had a pretty persistent tail."

He opened the passenger door of the dark-blue Fiat and got in. "Sorry," he said breathlessly, "I bumped into someone from the seminary."

"Okay." Rabea gave him a brief, sidelong glance as she threaded her way into the traffic. She was making for the Tangenziale, Rome's ring road, and from there to the A24, direction Pescara. "You must be tired. Try to sleep a little. It's at least a two-hour drive."

"I don't think I can sleep. I could eat something, though."

"You mean you're hungry again already? Incredible! I'll stop on the expressway."

"Wouldn't that be too dangerous? What if someone sees us?"

"Nonsense. You stay in the car, and I'll go in and get you something. It's vacation time. I won't be noticed; the cafés are usually teeming with people. Grassa doesn't have a clue where we are. I think we'll be safe from him until tonight. Besides, there's Lucie. She'll keep him busy."

Gabriel was in luck this time. He had picked up the trail of the redhead and the priest at the multistory, and hot-wired a Lancia Ypsilon. He was following the Fiat at a distance of three cars. However, the redhead now knew what he looked like. For the first time in his life, he had underestimated an opponent.

Lukas woke up just as Rabea pulled up outside an expressway café with a sign that read "Autogrill." He glanced at his watch. It was a little after 10:00 a.m.

"Hello, sleepyhead," Rabea said brightly. "You were obviously more tired than hungry. How about a spot of breakfast?"

Not for the first time, Lukas wondered where she got her energy. He felt shattered. "Where are we?"

"Still around thirty miles from Ancona. Then comes another twenty on the expressway and a bit of ordinary road. Another good hour, I'd say. What shall I get you? A cappuccino and cornetti?"

"Yes, please, plus two ham and cheese on toast."

"Okay, I won't be long. Meantime, get out and stretch your legs a bit, but stay near the car."

When Rabea returned to the car ten minutes later, carrying two paper bags, Lukas was nowhere in sight. Just as her blood pressure was about to go through the roof, she saw him hurrying back from the direction of the toilets.

"Sorry," he called, "it was urgent."

"Come on, get in."

"Mmm, that smells good," he said, rummaging in the paper bags. Unerringly, he fished out a ham and cheese on toast and sank his teeth into it.

Rabea covertly studied him in profile. It had always surprised her, the animal greed with which he assuaged his hunger. He had displayed the same avidity during their tempestuous affair.

Her memory of their erstwhile relationship conjured up a host of emotions. She'd had plenty of time to think back over her life during those months in prison in Iraq. Out of false pride, she had destroyed not only her love but also her friendship with Lukas. And since then, she had been driven by anger. She knew, however, that her anger was far more deep-seated than just that—caused, as it had been, by the two men she'd loved most in this world.

First, her grandfather had denied her the wish she'd cherished with all her childish heart, and then Lukas had cheated her of her love by choosing the priesthood. The men and their religions had robbed her of everything, and since then she could find no peace. Sometimes she wondered whether she hadn't subconsciously courted death in order to punish her grandfather and Lukas. It was an appalling idea, and one she was ashamed of, but the subconscious was a powerful weapon and often directed against oneself.

Rabea shook off the memories and started the car. "All right," she said, "let's get it over with."

Back on the expressway, she said, "We haven't had a chance to discuss the subject, but these documents Bentivoglio hid in the safe-deposit box—what exactly are they, do you think?"

"I don't know, Rabea. I told you: he simply asked me to play errand boy."

"I asked you what you think, not what you know," she retorted sharply. "As father general, Bentivoglio would have had access to a lot of ecclesiastical secrets. What could have been so important that he personally shut it away? He was on the right side, wasn't he? Why was he murdered? What interest me most are the questions he asked you. Questions are often more informative than answers. I think he asked you about your thesis because it deals with Loyola, the founder of your order, and the political parallels between the suppression of the Templars and the Jesuits. I think there must be some connection."

"Oh, that's too speculative for me."

Instead of replying, Rabea passed him a bottle of water.

After opening the bottle and handing it to her, Lukas took a drink from it himself. The moment his lips closed around the neck, it flashed through his mind that Rabea's lips had only just touched it. To banish the thought, he went on rather too hurriedly, "I was the nephew of his friend Bishop Franz—that was Bentivoglio's only reason for sending for me."

"I was afraid of that answer. You're fobbing me off because you're loath to discuss the subject. I think they may be confidential church documents that provide evidence for why the Templars were banned in 1307 and the Jesuits in 1773. The charges against both orders, which were surprisingly similar, related to sodomy, devil worship, and regicide. Murder, Lukas! To this day, wild rumors persist about a secret treasure in the Templars' possession, which Pope Clement V was anxious to acquire with the help of Philip IV of France. That hypothetical treasure never came to light. What if the Jesuits found it later and hung on to it? Perhaps the Vatican caught on and the same wretched process began all over again: suppression, persecution, torture. Death to the Jesuits!"

"Please, Rabea." Lukas was looking pained. "Must you always dissect everything and come to the worst possible conclusion? The church committed a great many mistakes in the past, I admit, but that's very far from saying that the Vatican must be behind these murders." Privately, he admired her perspicacity. He had been thinking along similar lines, thanks to the allusions Bentivoglio had made, but he wasn't prepared to share his suspicions with Rabea—at least not until he'd been able to look at the documents himself.

"Don't be so sensitive," she—of all people—told him. "I've another suggestion. Let's talk about the real, extant Gospel of Mary, fragments of which reputable theologians have been able to reconstruct. What if Bentivoglio's bequest is a fully preserved gospel by a female disciple of Jesus—Mary Magdalene was far from the only one—which categorically states that Jesus rejected any idea of a male hierarchy and placed men and women on an equal footing in life *and* in the church. After all, the first three early Christian centuries were matriarchal in nature— the catacombs beneath the Vatican contain dozens of graves belonging to Christian priestesses. Besides, I've no need to tell you how close Jesus the Jew was to the ideas of the peace-loving Gnostics and, later, the Cathars, who regarded woman as the life-giving element. To the churchmen of the time, though, equal treatment for women was out of the question. The emergence of authentic writings by a male or even a female contemporary of Jesus proving that the church has exploited and censored its own God would be meat and drink to all its critics."

"Yes, and to you in particular," Lukas retorted lamely. He knew this argument and its target of old. "Don't start all *that* again, Rabea. I know how upset you are by the church's patriarchal system, and I don't deny that the Vatican made mistakes in the past—mistakes affecting the sciences as well as women." He found the subject distasteful.

Sure enough, a storm broke over his head. "You can't be serious! You call millions of witch-hunt victims and the torturing of eminent scientists like Galileo or the murder of Giordano Bruno *mistakes*? The Inquisition burned Bruno at the stake. How often have you walked past his statue in the Campo de' Fiori? And what about the mass burnings of major scientific works? How much precious knowledge was lost due to ecclesiastical ignorance, delaying human development by a thousand years? Here's a choice example for you. Modern technology was able to render the original text of a palimpsest legible. It was unknown treatises by the Greek mathematician Archimedes, who lived around twenty-three hundred years ago. A monk overwrote them with some so-called important verses from the Bible in the twelfth century. Archimedes had described integral and differential calculus, which wasn't rediscovered for another eighteen hundred years. It's the basis of all modern sciences and technologies, mechanical engineering, electronic data processing, and space travel. That book could have changed the world, Lukas, if a monk hadn't run out of paper. People might have shed their small-mindedness far sooner, and Christianity and Islam would have failed to gain such a hold. Who knows, maybe the world would be better off today without the three major religions?"

"Haven't we already discussed this a thousand times? Cults and religions are as old as humanity itself. It's in the spiritual nature of human beings to seek the truth."

"Bah, they won't find it in religion. Religion doesn't proclaim the truth. It asserts and dogmatizes it. The word *Islam* simply means 'submission.' Religions preach love of one's neighbor but practice nothing but intolerance. And then when it comes to the rights of women or homosexuals, all religious leaders are suddenly at one. When will they ever understand? Where does it come from, all this hatred for dissenters, for other skin colors, other traditions? And where has it all led to so far? Only to miserable wars, Lukas, yet the highest form of human evolution is peace. But the church has never been interested in peace. It loves and needs war. Bad times are what guarantee it a bumper harvest of souls."

Rabea's freckles were glowing, but she suddenly and surprisingly changed tack. "Sorry, I've strayed too far from the subject. I do have a third theory. It supplements my first, actually, but you won't like it any better." She gave him no time to respond. "The fact is, nobody yet knows why your order was banned in 1773, but we do know who reinstated it. I'm talking about Napoleon, not the reigning pope. That the ban on your order was revoked in 1814 was down to him alone. Napoleon himself was a product of the Jesuits—he'd absorbed their geopolitical hunger for power. Outcast Jesuits in Corsica seized on the young general at an early stage in his career. Wolves always scent their own kind, and they recognized his potential. At their instigation, Napoleon tried to persuade the pope to come to France, but the old gentleman failed to survive the journey over the Alps. Napoleon also plundered the Vatican archives and had everything he could lay hands on carried off to Paris. What did he or the Jesuits hope to find? Clues to the whereabouts of the Templars' treasure, which may have been taken from them in 1773? The next pope didn't reinstate your order until Napoleon had locked him up for five years. That's a historical fact."

"Really, Rabea." Lukas shook his head in disbelief. "I never cease to be amazed by the way you mingle fact with speculation. You attach too much weight to the theories of people like Manhattan and Phelps."

"Fancy you boning up on the opposition," she said derisively. "So you've read Avro Manhattan's *The Vatican in World Politics*, have you? Then you may also have heard of the remarkable interview given by Jon Phelps about his theory of a secret world conspiracy involving the Jesuits, the freemasons, and the Order of Malta. You know as well as I do that they all hate us Jews as much as they hate the Protestants, and in no country more than in America. Phelps considers the Jesuit superiors masters of agitprop and thinks they have a perfidious plan to unleash jihad on the United States, which they hate, and consequently on Israel. When he was asked how they proposed to do this, he said that in their place he'd launch a frightful terrorist attack inside the US that would prompt the Americans to march into Iraq."

"Well," Lukas said indulgently, "it isn't difficult to cite something that's already happened."

"Wrong. He gave that interview in May 2000, a year before the attack on the Twin Towers. Maybe Phelps and all the other people who take a critical view of your order are right? Maybe they're unjustly pilloried as crazies. Who knows how many conspiracy theories are propagated by the perpetrators themselves? Discrediting your opponent with information and disinformation is a time-honored tactic. But I don't rely solely on Phelps & Company. I've done some thorough research on the Jesuit Order myself because I'm working on a book about the best president the US ever had. That's why I wanted to interview Bentivoglio." Rabea inserted a pause for effect, a faint smile lurking at the corners of her mouth. She obviously found it enjoyable to zigzag Lukas through the labyrinth of her argumentation.

"Oh, come on," he said, "Abraham Lincoln's assassin definitely wasn't Catholic, and there's no proof of Chiniquy's 1886 allegation that he was murdered on the instructions of the Jesuits."

"But Charles Chiniquy was a Catholic and a fundamentalist priest who was excommunicated because he had dared to draw attention to abuses within the church. He was also an intimate friend of Lincoln's. Abe had defended him against his severest critics, the Jesuits, and won the case—hence his dictum: 'The Jesuits never forgive and never forget,' which showed that he was well aware of the danger threatening him. But actually, I wasn't talking about Lincoln at all, though I'm glad you added to the list of Jesuit conspiracies by yourself. I was talking about John F. Kennedy."

Lukas was taken aback. He had never heard of a conspiracy theory that linked his order to the murder of JFK.

"In 1979 a committee of inquiry conceded that his murder wasn't the work of a lone operator. Our present state of knowledge indicates that his assassins were hired on instructions from Castro, and Castro was educated by Jesuits. Lee Harvey Oswald, his alleged assassin, was only a fall guy who had met with his cousin, a Jesuit, two weeks before JFK's murder. It's a fact that the Jesuits backed the Vietnam War. Spellman, the senior cardinal of the time, paid so many visits to US troops in Vietnam—he called them 'Soldiers of Christ,' incidentally—that the media talked about 'Spelly's war.' It's no secret that the Jesuit Order held shares in armaments firms like Lockheed and McDonnell Douglas. They made money from the Vietnam War, whereas Kennedy wanted to prevent it at all costs. Sadly, history proved him right—he could have saved his country and its mothers a lot of grief. Kennedy also wanted to clip the CIA's wings because he had learned that his own secret service had betrayed him over the Bay of Pigs—with the help of the Mafia. There was a reason for this: the Mafia and the CIA were both very interested in abandoning Cuba to Fidel Castro. Goodbye to Cuba's casinos and nightspots, hello to big money in Las Vegas!"

"Fine," Lukas said teasingly, "so the Jesuits murdered Lincoln, meddled in the Vietnam War, and conspired with the CIA and the Mafia to murder JFK. Napoleon can think himself lucky he died a more or less natural death."

"Save your sarcasm, Lukas. Napoleon did just what they wanted by ravaging half of Europe. May I remind you of the word *regicide* in the 1773 indictment, and of the fact that Jesuit doctrine approves the murder of tyrants? King or president—when it comes to murder, there isn't much difference."

"Well and good, but what does this have to do with Bentivoglio's murder and his safe-deposit box?"

"When researching the Kennedy-Jesuit connection, I discovered indications that your order has a secret protocol in which your superiors have drawn up a plan for Catholicism to attain world supremacy. It's a fact that the Jesuits have always had a hand in international politics. Would no less than thirty-nine Catholic rulers have expelled them from their countries otherwise? Never have those in authority been so united, either before or since, and that's a historical fact. One of the doctrines in the secret protocol is said to be: give pleasure. Well, after Kennedy's murder, a whole entertainment empire was created in Las Vegas with the Mafia's assistance. When people pursue their pleasures, they're blind and deaf to what's going on around them. *Panem et circenses*—bread and circuses, know what I mean? We've become a digitally controlled fun-and-games society, Lukas. Underlying it all is a system, a perfidious agenda. Could Bentivoglio have discovered this very protocol and hidden it in the safe-deposit box? I've tried to research the protocol in the Jesuit archives in Rome. Unfortunately, *all* documents later than 1921 are under lock and key and may only be released by the father general himself in conjunction with the senior librarian. Interesting that the Jesuits should lock up all the most recent documents. That applies to Kennedy's case as well, where the release date of the inquiry file has been put forward to 2029. *They* actually murdered the only Roman Catholic president the US has ever had. I admire JFK. He wanted to prevent a terrible war, and now they usually portray him on television as merely a womanizer, as if they want that to be his only legacy—an image perfectly agreeable to the Jesuits, who don't like women."

"Our order has many enemies, I know, and we feature in nearly every global conspiracy theory. There are plenty of nuts convinced that our founder, Loyola, was sent by Lucifer. But you surely can't believe all this unfounded nonsense."

"Don't be so patronizing, Father Lukas. I don't have to believe it. You're the churchman—you're responsible for belief. I'm a journalist. I put facts together until I form a clear picture of something. Besides, what are conspiracy theories other than disguised political statements? For me, the Jesuit Order stinks to high heaven, and it can be linked to nearly every drumbeat in history. All the good guys like Lincoln, Martin Luther King Jr., the two Kennedy brothers, Sadat, Rabin, were murdered. Just like your Jesus. The Talmud says, 'He who saves just one person, saves the whole world.' Jesus was a Jew, and I believe he genuinely wanted to save the world. All we haggle over today are arms and oil. Our society is characterized by the lust for profit and power. Incidentally, Loyola was a member of the Alumbrados in Spain, the Illuminati, as we call them today, another obscure, secretive organization associated with the Jesuits." Once again, Rabea abruptly changed tack. "What do you know about the Council of Trent?"

Lukas looked baffled. "It opened in 1543 and went on for eighteen years. It took place more than two decades after Luther's Reformation and was intended to devise measures that would reinvigorate the church."

"That's a polite way of putting it. The Council of Trent had only one fundamental purpose: to condemn every product of Luther's Reformation. Yet the Reformation was the best thing humanity had produced in fifteen hundred years. It's the origin of civil rights, international law, and political freedom as we know them today. But the established church was interested in only one thing: the Reformation's threat to its authority and supremacy. What I'm getting at is this: at the fourth session of the council, the right of free speech and freedom of conscience was anathematized. *Anathematized*, Lukas! No one was to have the right to choose their religious denomination or express their opinion freely. That's ecclesiastical dictatorship for you. Hitler followed suit. One of his first acts in 1933 was to order the summary arrest of every journalist who had ever been critical of him. Truth always dies first. What can be worse than a religious intolerance that seeks to rob people of their spiritual freedom?"

Lukas heaved a sigh. "I know all this. Many thanks for regarding me as a member of a gang of villains, but we're living in the here and now. Times have changed, and so has the modern church. You can't blame it for all the transgressions of past centuries. We've learned from our mistakes, but one can't reverse the course of a historical tradition nearly two thousand years old, not overnight."

"But don't you see? You aren't trying to reverse—you're plowing straight on. Women still don't have equal rights in the church, which opposes contraception and abortion. It would rather children came into the world to die a miserable death of AIDS or starvation. Why do you think I'm telling you all this? Because it saddens me to see you being exploited by *them*. Ordinary priests like you are an advertisement for your order, grassroots men of profound faith who bring good into the world. You lull your pure souls in the gentle breeze of faith and fail to notice that the world is in the teeth of a hurricane. Wake up, Lukas. You're just a prisoner, the fettered, exploited captive of a snowballing system of power created by greedy men who purport to be acting in the name of God. It's people like you for whom they cast their nets. It's fishers of souls like you who have preserved the church's true source of power from time immemorial: the massed ranks of the faithful. They have been its sole foundation for nearly two thousand years. It wasn't God that created man, but man that created God. You serve a false master." Wearily, Rabea brushed a moist strand of hair off her forehead.

Lukas glanced sideways at her, a look of deep sadness in his eyes.

For a while neither of them spoke. Lukas didn't know what to say. Rabea had often argued fiercely with him in the past, of course, but he'd always felt it was because she didn't want to give him up—because she wanted to persuade him not to dedicate his life to God and the church. Her outburst today was different, however. He could sense her desperation, and it pained him to see her in such a state. He almost got the feeling that his decision in favor of the order still rankled with her. Yet it was she who had left him and gone to bed with another man on the very day he'd planned to ask her to be his wife.

"I'm sorry," she said, capitulating once again. "I'm tired of the everlasting struggle. I've seen too many deaths in the past few years. Too many people I knew have met a violent end. I've learned how precious life is and, above all, how precious the time at our disposal. Yet we squander it as if we will live forever. It isn't a question of whether there's a God, but what we make of our lives. We don't have to love our neighbors the way it says in the Ten Commandments, but surely we can at least accept them as they are. And if they're of a different faith, who cares? Why do some people always pass judgment on others? Why do we regard ourselves as smarter and better than others?" Rabea glanced at Lukas, as if to gauge his reaction.

"I realized I had to change my life, and I came to Rome to discuss what happened with you. I know it's too late for us to be together, but it's never too late for friendship. What happened in Munich stemmed from a misunderstanding I never resolved, purely out of pride. I was immature and silly, and I'm ashamed of it. I went to Munich that time because of your phone call—" She broke off abruptly. Something in the rearview mirror seemed to have caught her eye. "Damn it, I think that dirty devil is following us again." She floored the gas pedal, overtook a milk tanker, and pulled back into her lane again.

"The police? Are you sure? I thought you gave him the slip?"

"I did," she said, "but somehow he's managed to pick up our trail again. He's definitely not from the police—I've a nose for these things. Sorry to tell you this, but the bad guys are after us. He probably belongs to the outfit that bumped off Bentivoglio and the old lady."

"If he's following us, we can't risk going to the bank."

"We'll have to shake him off again."

"Right. And how do you propose to do that? In case you hadn't noticed, this Fiat has a maximum of sixty horsepower under the hood."

"Never fear, you Christian automobile expert. Watch this." Rabea reduced speed a little and downshifted into third.

The driver of the milk tanker behind them immediately closed up. When he noticed that the Fiat didn't intend to put on speed, he signaled left and pulled out.

As soon as Rabea saw this in the rearview mirror, she suddenly accelerated and the tanker had to pull in again. Their tail had to be behind the tanker, because he wasn't visible in the mirror. This process was repeated twice more until the tanker driver angrily blew his horn.

After around three miles, an exit sign loomed up ahead. Rabea drove parallel to the exit lane with the tanker close behind her, which obscured the pursuing vehicle's view of her Fiat. The driver honked at her again. Looking in the rearview mirror, she saw him signaling his incomprehension at her constant changes of speed. He had already indicated left again in order to overtake her little Fiat, when she suddenly downshifted again into third, floored the gas pedal until the engine screamed in protest, and shifted back into fourth. At the last moment, with a squeal of rubber, she swerved down the exit road, just missing her pursuer. A look to her left showed her that he'd been unable to follow in time and had now shot past her along the expressway. She grinned happily and glanced at her pale-faced passenger in quest of applause.

"I'm impressed," Lukas said with a wry smile, still bracing himself against the glove compartment. "Is that what they teach you in journo school?"

"Well, if you've picked up some red-hot copy and need to smuggle it over a frontier, you do learn a few tricks over the years. It worked, didn't it? We're rid of the guy. Now make yourself useful. There ought to be a map in the glove compartment."

"What, no GPS?"

"I hate the things. Check exactly where we are and what the next exit on the expressway is called. Our tail will turn off there, double back, and pass us coming the other way. We must get off this road as soon as possible. Driving through the little hill villages would be best."

Lukas opened the glove compartment and caught his breath.

"What's that?"

"What's what?"

"There's a gun in your glove compartment."

"Really?" Rabea shook her head. "Damned careless of the editorial staff. Many of my foreign assignments are on the risky side, so my profile says I must always have access to a gun. Someone in the Rome office must have been a bit overzealous—they forgot it only applied to crisis zones."

Lukas refrained from commenting. While he was tracing possible routes on the map with his forefinger, Rabea drove on contentedly. It really would be a stroke of bad luck if their pursuer picked up their trail again.

It wasn't, in fact, bad luck, just technology. Gabriel, the Executioner, had seized his opportunity while Rabea was in the café, Lukas in the toilet, and the car momentarily unsupervised. He had stowed the bloodstained knife in the trunk together with a GPS transmitter, one of Trapano's many useful toys. Consequently, he knew where to find the couple at any time—provided they didn't change cars, which he considered unlikely. He had driven too close behind deliberately. It enhanced the fun of the game.

"Well, have you found us a route?" asked Rabea.

"Yes, we should soon be coming to a village named Borgo di Elia. Just after that, there's a fork to the left. Then we make for Montecarotto, up in the hills." Lukas paused. "Say, weren't you going to tell me something earlier—something about your reason for going to Munich? You mentioned a phone call, didn't you?" He was glad they could talk about it at last. Like her, he had long been mentally burdened by what had happened and the unforgivable way he had acted.

"That's right. I overheard your phone call with the bishop, and so I went to Munich because I needed someone to talk with and Lucie was out of reach in Egypt at the time. I was so desperate, Lukas, and—" Once again she got no further because her cell phone rang.

"Hell, who is it now? My phone's in the side pocket of my bag." Lukas took it out and handed it to her.

"Rosenthal," she said.

"Oh, hello Bea, at last. Where are you? I was worried. Are you all right?"

"I'm sorry you couldn't get through to us. It was probably all those tunnels between Rome and Pescara. Wait, I'll put you on loudspeaker so Lukas can listen in."

"Hello, little brother," said Lucie.

"Hi, Sis, you sound worried. What's the matter?"

"I don't know how long I can talk for. Grassa's hanging around. I've got some bad news. There's another warrant out for your arrest, once again for murder."

"What nonsense!" Rabea exclaimed. "He couldn't have killed Bentivoglio more than once."

"Not Bentivoglio. Worse. Grassa had Lukas shadowed by one of his detectives. Unfortunately, the man was found with his throat cut. Grassa thinks it was Lukas. I've already called the attorney."

"Hell!" Rabea drew a deep breath. "We mustn't lose our nerve. Tell the attorney we'll be back this afternoon. Lukas will turn himself in, and the whole business will be settled. We'll talk again soon, Lucie."

Rabea hung up. "I think I know who killed the policeman," she mused aloud. "I'll bet it was the guy that followed me, the one I shook off. You've no need to worry about that arrest warrant, Lukas. I'm your alibi. Now I can hardly wait to see what Bentivoglio and his goddamned safe-deposit box has in store for us."

They passed the road sign for Angeli di Mergo soon afterward. Rabea slowed down, and they scanned both sides of the street. "There it is," she exclaimed, "next door to the pharmacy: Banche delle Marche. Nice and inconspicuous." She sounded disappointed. Since several people had already been murdered because of this safe-deposit box, the affair had taken on huge dimensions. She'd subconsciously been expecting a Swiss fortress of a bank complete with armed policemen guarding an armor-plated door. Instead, they found themselves outside a little provincial bank housed in a shabby four-story building with peeling walls. The building also accommodated several apartments and a pharmacy, which was twice as big as the bank. Freshly washed laundry fluttered from the balconies overhead.

"And this building contains what may be the most dangerous documents in Christendom?" Rabea murmured incredulously.

"I think it was very smart of Bentivoglio. Who would suspect it of anything so extraordinary?" said Lukas. "How do we go about this? Got a plan?"

"We don't need a plan," Rabea said firmly. "Just give me the key. I'll go in and get the stuff while you wait in the car. Let's just hope some overly efficient cop hasn't circulated your arrest warrant and we end up in a provincial jail." She grabbed her big crocodile handbag, said, "Back in a tick," and disappeared into the bank.

Lukas kept watch on the entrance.

He failed to notice the white Lancia Ypsilon that pulled up outside the little bar across the street a minute later. The driver got out and went inside the bar, then stood looking out the window with a glass in his hand.

* * *

Rabea entered the bank via a revolving door. Halfway around it clicked to a stop, so she couldn't walk straight in. All Italian banks were protected in this way. It enabled the staff to check who was coming in and, at the same time, prevent too many people from entering the bank at once. Only one customer was standing at the counter with his back to her, while a red-faced clerk attended to him. The door buzzed twice, a little green light came on, and she was at liberty to enter.

The clerk craned his neck.

The customer, a corpulent farmer in bulging overalls, also turned to look.

Rabea said a polite *buon giorno*. She showed the clerk her key, asked him in Italian where the safe-deposit boxes were, and wondered if there were any formalities to be completed. She had gotten her German passport out just in case.

"No, no, signorina, there's no need for any formalities, really not," she was assured. The bank teller, whose name tag identified him as "Sig. Frollino," surreptitiously eyed her legs as he spoke. Signore Frollino had not even glanced at the key or her passport. "We're in the Marche here, the safest region in Italy. Honest folk, one and all. If you have the key, signorina, that legitimizes you. I'll show you where the strong room is." He left his workstation by way of a folding counter and beckoned to Rabea to follow.

"You'll excuse me for a moment, Pepe," he called over his shoulder with the look of a man who had just been entrusted with a task of greater importance.

Pepe leaned against the counter with the patience characteristic of an Italian mountain peasant. His eyes caressed Rabea's backside.

Signore Frollino led her into an adjoining room full of discarded office furniture and a multitude of dusty files. Crossing this, he opened a heavy armored door. The claustrophobic room beyond was barely ten feet square, windowless, and smelled musty. The walls were lined with numbered lockers. Rabea scanned the rows for No. 34.

She hurried over to it, kneeled down, and inserted the key in the lock. She was about to open the locker when she became aware that the bank teller was still hovering in the doorway. She turned to him and raised her eyebrows. From the look in his eyes, the locker had not been their focal point.

Caught in the act, Signore Frollino cleared his throat. "I'll leave you to it, then, signorina," he said, and disappeared.

Rabea breathed a sigh of relief, but for safety's sake, she pushed the door closed after him. Then she kneeled down in front of No. 34 and opened it. Withdrawing the steel container, she set it on the dusty floor in front of her. Until now, she had only acted as the situation demanded, but the moment she had the drawer of documents in front of her, something strange happened. Her chest felt so constricted, she could hardly breathe. *Not scared, are you, Rosenthal? Don't be ridiculous.* It took all her willpower to suppress her mounting panic. There being no rational explanation, she blamed her sudden anxiety on the window-less room, although she'd never been prone to claustrophobia before. She forced her trembling hands to open the steel container.

The first things she unearthed were a battered deed box and a long-ish object wrapped in some form of oilcloth. Curiously enough, the latter seemed warm to the touch. The deed box was unlocked. On top, she found a packet of letters tied up with ribbon. She took them out. Beneath them lay an exercise book. Flicking through it, Rabea saw that every page was handwritten in Latin. She laid it aside. Finally, she took out a drawstring bag made of blue velvet. Rabea took only a brief look at the contents, a few gold and silver coins and a gold watch bearing an engraved coat of arms. At last, she turned to the oilcloth bundle, which turned out to contain two leather cylinders. Bingo! Similar document cases could be found in paleography museums. She resisted the tempta-tion to open them at once and wrapped them up in the oilcloth again. Last of all she checked the locker to make sure she hadn't overlooked anything, then slid the steel drawer back into place and locked it. The key she slipped into the pocket of her denim shorts. Having put every-thing back in the deed box, she stowed it in her capacious handbag and then clamped the leather cylinders under her arm and returned to the bank lobby. The clerk was chatting with the same customer as before. Rabea's return silenced their conversation as abruptly as if she'd pressed a "Mute" button.

She said a friendly *grazie* to the clerk and was about to give the revolving door a push, relieved that everything had gone so smoothly, when the clerk called her back. "Signorina, just a minor matter."

Rabea drew a deep breath, molded her features into a radiant smile, and turned. "Yes, Signore Frollino, what is it?"

The clerk's rubicund face turned even redder, this time with plea-sure at the fact that she had registered his name, even though it was printed in bold on his tag. "If you wouldn't mind signing a receipt for the contents of your safe-deposit box?"

Rabea came back to the counter and bent over the slip of paper. Frollino handed her a ballpoint pen and indicated the relevant spot with a dirty fingernail. She skimmed the short declaration. It confirmed that she had found the contents of the safe-deposit box intact. Rabea scrawled an illegible signature and left the bank.

Lukas hurried eagerly toward her. "Well? Everything all right?"

"Let's go." Rabea deposited the elongated bundle on the backseat. Lukas nearly dropped her handbag when she thrust it into his hands.

"What have you got in there, bricks?" he asked in surprise.

"Later. I'll tell you in the car. Let's get out of here."

Gabriel had seen the bundle under Rabea's arm from inside the bar. He left his observation post at the window, got into his car, and followed the signal from the Fiat. He felt sure the redhead and the priest would not be able to restrain their curiosity for the three hours it would take them to drive back to Rome. They would look out for some hotel where they could inspect the contents of the safe-deposit box in peace and quiet. He would do just the same if he had made a sensational find. His plan was simple. He couldn't achieve much while they were on the move in their car, but as soon as his targets came to rest in a hotel room, he would pounce. He would eliminate the priest first and then devote himself to the redhead. He ran his tongue over his lips at the thought. Sadistically aroused by anticipation of an orgy of violence, he gripped his crotch.

He was right in his supposition. Rabea called her friend Isa, an author who had some years earlier bought and restored an old farmhouse near San Quirico, less than twenty miles from Angeli di Mergo. Rabea hadn't thought of her until she saw the place name on a signpost. Isa had often invited her to stay, but she'd never found the time. She got through to Isa in Germany and was told where the house key was hidden for the benefit of spontaneous visitors. At Isa's place, they could examine the contents of the safe-deposit box undisturbed, whereas in Rome they would be greeted by a reception committee headed by Grassa.

Isa's house was rather secluded and not easy to find. "There's the little chapel she mentioned," said Rabea. "We have to turn left here, then along the farm track and past the olive grove. There it is, the yellow house with the green shutters. Looks cozy, doesn't it, Lukas? It's like that house we always dreamed of. Remember how we—" She broke off abruptly. Lukas, who had turned to her in surprise, saw that she was fiercely biting her lower lip.

Rabea sensed his gaze and assumed the look of a person who had long since given up dreaming about anything. She turned into the entrance too fast, and the little car went bouncing over the unsurfaced driveway. She had to brake hard to prevent it from crashing into the door of the big barn next to the house.

Lukas had shut his eyes in apprehension.

Rabea flung open the driver's door and got out.

Lukas opened his eyes again. He estimated that there was no more than a hair's clearance between the bumper and the barn door.

Rabea had already gone around the car and opened his door. Eying Lukas defiantly, she hefted her handbag off his lap, shouldered it, and strode off.

Lukas knew no one else who could be as eloquent without saying a word.

Of course he remembered the little yellow house. As children they had often roamed the woods in their neighborhood, especially after reading *The Lord of the Rings*. Captivated by the charm of the story, they had imagined they were hobbits wandering through the forbidden forest and braving the many dangers lurking in the shadows. On one of these excursions, they had come upon a deserted forester's cottage. The spring sun, whose golden fingers were touching the trees, had bathed the house in a surreal glow. It was a place full of magic and secrets, and they genuinely felt transported to a magical land of elves. The garden had run wild but was already displaying its springtime splendor. The daisies, pansies, tulips, and narcissi were a riot of color. Rabea had immediately fallen in love with the enchanted cottage, which became *their* house. The pair of them visited it as often as they could. They tidied up the garden and dreamed of living there someday. On one occasion, the forester caught them there, but he good-humoredly left them in peace. The dilapidated cottage became their refuge. It patiently witnessed many quarrels and temperamental outbursts (Rabea), followed by tearful, tempestuous reconciliations (also Rabea), and the first, shy kisses of their young love. The house was privy to all their dreams. It was there that they had come of age and forged plans for the future.

All this flashed through Lukas's mind in a fraction of a second. He picked up the oilcloth bundle and hurried after her.

The wrought-iron garden gate was secured only by some green wire. Rabea unwound it and walked quickly across the natural stone terrace to the barbecue, followed by Lukas. She felt around in the cold ash, then fished out the key and hurried up the steps to the front door, which she opened. They found themselves in a high-ceilinged hallway. A door on the left led to the big farmhouse kitchen.

"Make us an espresso, Lukas, would you? I'm going to find the bathroom. My hands are filthy."

Rabea returned soon afterward, smelling of rosewater soap. She took her cup from Lukas with a grateful smile but avoided his eye. "There's a huge table in the living room across the hallway," she said. "We can spread everything out on it."

The living room, with its natural stone fireplace and comfortable red sofas looked so snug that Lukas couldn't suppress the wistful feeling he was there on a romantic vacation with Rabea.

Rabea, who had no idea what he was thinking, made straight for the table in front of the picture window, which afforded a magnificent view of the Marche's undulating landscape. The table could have seated a party of twelve. She took the bundle from Lukas, deposited it on the table, and opened her handbag.

"I'll quickly show you what's in the deed box, then we'll see what that oilcloth contains." Without waiting for an answer, she opened the deed box and removed the contents. She opened the drawstring bag and took out the pocket watch. The coat of arms on the back displayed a knightly shield, and above it a cross surmounted by a sun and three stars arranged in a semicircle. Then she shook out a dozen gold and silver coins, all of them minted around the middle of the eighteenth century. Next, she turned her attention to the packet of documents. She carefully undid the blue ribbon with which they had been tied together and picked up a thick sheet of paper covered with writing. "What a nuisance," she said, pulling up a chair. "A secret code. Just numbers and letters, some of them in mirror writing, probably done with a stencil.

Still, first things first. You'd better sit down, Lukas. Who knows, you might be bowled over otherwise."

Rabea was already reaching for the oilcloth bundle. As she did so, her braid brushed Lukas's arm. He caught her faint scent of flowers and stole a glance at her as she opened the bundle with a flourish. His throat contracted with sudden yearning. As long as he'd been apart from Rabea—unable to see her, feel her presence, and breathe in her very special scent—he'd managed to lead a life remote from her. But her proximity brought back all his carefully suppressed memories of the times they had spent together.

Rabea's cell phone broke the spell. She turned to reach for her handbag, which was the only reason she spotted the shadowy figure behind her and reacted instinctively. With a strength Lukas would never have thought she possessed, Rabea pushed him off his chair just as a shot rang out. On her feet already, she kicked the startled gunman in the crotch with all her might, the way Jules had taught her. He staggered backward and fell to the floor, doubled up in agony, and she quickly disarmed him.

"Dirty swine!" she yelled, kicking him in the ribs. The phone emitted two more rings, then fell silent.

"Lukas, you're bleeding!"

"What?" He felt his head and stared in bewilderment at the smear of blood on his hand.

"It's only a graze," she told him reassuringly. "I'll see to it in a minute, but first we must tie up this swine. Here, take the gun. If he moves, shoot him! I'll find something to tie him up with."

She soon returned with a length of washing line. Despite the gravity of the situation, she couldn't help grinning at the sight of Lukas. The gun might have been a stinking fish, the way he was holding it: two-handed and as far away from his body as possible.

She kneeled down behind the killer, wrenched his hands behind his back, and secured them tightly, then did the same with his ankles.

Gabriel had debated whether to launch himself at Lukas regardless of the pistol, but it might have gone off by itself. Besides, he was crippled with pain. He decided to wait for a better moment and gave Rabea a look of pure hatred. "It isn't over yet, you bitch!"

"Now I'm really scared," she sneered. "Look at you: you're tied up, your balls are pulped, and you're all on your own. I know your type. You're a lone operator, so stop boring me!"

Rabea might have looked tough on the outside, but her heart was pounding. That had been a damned close shave. If her phone hadn't rung, she and Lukas would probably both be dead. She got up and went over to the sideboard against the opposite wall. Knowing that her friend Isa was almost pathologically well organized, she found what she was looking for in the second drawer down: a stack of snow-white napkins, ironed and starched—they couldn't have been more sterile. Taking out two of them, she gave one to Lukas to help him stanch the blood from his head wound. The other, with a malicious smile, she stuffed into Gabriel's mouth.

She inspected her handiwork with a contented air. "He'll make a nice gift for our superintendent." She turned to Lukas. "You're bleeding like a stuck pig, but don't worry, the bullet only grazed you."

"I do feel a bit dizzy, but I've often felt worse in the boxing ring. Are *you* all right?" he asked, looking at her elbow, which displayed a nasty bruise.

"I didn't notice a thing at the time, but it is hurting a bit now." She winced a little and rubbed her arm. "That wound of yours should be disinfected. I'll go and see where Isa keeps her first-aid box. Be back right away."

Lukas eyed the bound figure in front of him. Gabriel suddenly reared up and mumbled something behind his gag. Startled, Lukas retreated a step, but his prisoner promptly subsided again. He was clearly in severe pain. Rabea seemed to have wrecked his family planning for good, which explained why he was looking so stunned.

Lukas went back to the table. He was clamping the napkin to his head with one hand, so he put the gun on the table in front of him to fish Rabea's cell phone out of the side pocket of her handbag. The display read "Caller Unknown." He was just dialing Lucie's number when someone pounced on him from behind. Lukas crashed facedown onto the table.

Gabriel had managed to free himself and seized the opportunity to pin Lukas down beneath his full weight. He tried to reach the pistol at the same time, but it was buried beneath Lukas's body. Lukas tried desperately to shake him off. The napkin adhering to his head wound now served as a target. Gabriel drew back his fist and landed a merciless punch full on it.

The blow sufficed to put Lukas briefly out of action. Feeling his resistance lessen, Gabriel slid off him, caught hold of his leather belt from behind, and tried to haul him up from the table. Lukas instinctively clung to it with both hands, but with a violent effort, his assailant managed to heave him aside. Before he could react, Gabriel had snatched the gun off the table and put it to Lukas's temple.

Feeling the cold metal against his head, Lukas regained his senses in a flash. He had the presence of mind to yell, "Run, Bea!" while waiting for the fatal shot to ring out. Gabriel's finger was already tightening on the trigger . . .

Lukas flinched when he heard a violent blow, but he felt no deadly bullet.

Was this the swift, painless death that snuffs out life in the blink of an eye? He was surprised to note that his brain must somehow be functioning in spite of everything. He would have been unable to ask himself that question otherwise. The thought made him open his eyes. The first thing he saw was what he had seen last: the killer standing beside him with the gun to his head. But his all too handsome face was frozen in a look of surprise. As though in slow motion, the man's arm sagged, his fingers relaxed their grip, and the gun crashed to the flagstones. He subsided onto his knees and toppled over sideways, allowing Lukas to see Rabea.

She had been standing just behind the killer and was positively quivering with rage. She was holding a fireplace poker in her hand, poised to deliver another blow. Her green eyes were flashing, her braid had come undone, and her pale face was framed by hair that now cascaded to her hips. To Lukas she looked like one of the ancient Furies come down to earth from Olympus.

"That goddamned B-movie Rambo," she said. "I don't understand how the guy could have freed himself so fast. I know I tied him up properly. Are you all right?" she added solicitously.

"I'm feeling a bit weak at the knees. That's the second time you've saved my life today."

"Pure self-interest. We've still got things to do, remember?" Rabea camouflaged her feelings with a faint smile. *My God, if I'd been even a split second slower . . .*

"Is he really dead?" Lukas whispered.

"I think so, I caught him full on the back of the head," she replied dispassionately after feeling in vain for a pulse. The lengths of washing line were lying loose on the floor. She picked them up and examined them more closely. "Look at that, Lukas." She held up one end.

"Looks like a clean cut."

"Exactly. I wonder . . ." Rabea patted the man's waistband. Sure enough, beneath his loose shirt he'd been wearing another leather belt with a pouch attached. Concealed in this were an assortment of useful tools, which had enabled him to break into Isa's house unobserved. And on one of the leather sheaths in the middle was the small knife he had managed to extract, despite his bound hands, and use to sever the rope.

"Smart, eh? Pretends to be completely out of action and cuts himself loose in readiness to strike at the right moment. Did you see this? One of the leather sheaths on his belt is empty, and it's the shape and length of a sizable knife. Could have held the weapon our pretty boy used to kill Grassa's man in Rome." Rabea tried again to feel Gabriel's pulse. "I don't get anything. I think he's really had it, but safety first. In my unfortunate experience, the meaner the bad guys are, the tougher they are too. To be on the safe side, I'm going to tie him up again."

"Shouldn't we call a doctor?" Lukas ventured to suggest. "He is a human being, after all."

"He isn't a human being, Lukas. He's an anomaly, a devil on two legs. I know his type. I've met them often enough in Gaza, Iraq, and Afghanistan. They're the devil's mercenaries. They hugely overestimate their own importance. They kill for money, and what's far worse is that they find it fun. They get off on their power over life and death."

"He's a human being and God's creature all the same," Lukas insisted. "No matter what he's done, it's not for us to judge him. I'm going to say a short prayer for his soul. You go and get a blanket."

Although Rabea cast her eyes up to heaven, she let him have his way and returned with a wool blanket, which in her view was wasted on the man. Lukas carefully covered him up. When he continued to kneel there indecisively, Rabea hauled him gently to his feet. "Believe me, Lukas, the world is a good deal better off without him. Come on, Isa's bedroom is upstairs. I want you to lie down for a bit while I see to your wound and put a bandage on it. You're looking quite green about the gills, my dear." Mechanically, she picked up her cell phone and slipped it into the pocket of her denim shorts. Then she took him firmly by the arm and led him upstairs to the bedroom, which looked like something out of a Jane Austen novel.

Rabea made at once for the huge bed and folded back the bedspread to reveal white sheets with crocheted lace edges. They gave off a faint scent of lavender. Lukas thought he had never seen a more inviting place to sleep.

"Wow," said Rabea, "if I'd known what a cozy little nest Isa had made for herself, I'd have looked in on her sooner."

"Hmm, after the mess we've made of her living room, I doubt she'll ever invite you again." Lukas's tone was unusually curt.

She left him alone in the bedroom for a moment while she moistened a hand towel in the bathroom and found the first-aid box she'd dropped in favor of the fireplace poker.

She sat down on the bed beside him and snipped away the hair around the wound with a pair of scissors. Then, taking him gently by the back of the head, she drew him toward her, heedless of the fact that his blood was staining her T-shirt.

Quite unexpectedly, he found his face buried in Rabea's shoulder while she gently cleaned his wound. It had been six years since he'd been as close to her. Conscious of the warmth emanating from her body, he inhaled the delicate scent of her skin, which conjured up memories of happy times gone by. He was so abruptly and intensely overcome by long-suppressed emotions, he found it hard not to sigh.

"Does it hurt much?" she asked anxiously, sensing his tension and misinterpreting it.

Rabea had so often deliberately flaunted her charms and shamelessly provoked him, and Lukas had always resisted her and proved the stronger. But it was at this of all moments, when she was lovingly ministering to him quite oblivious of her effect on him, that he found himself jolted out of the self-control he had so arduously maintained for years. He realized how simple it could all be. The adrenaline rush of the life-threatening situation they'd just survived was undoubtedly playing its part in generating the almost sensual certainty he felt, but did he have the courage to turn back? Yes! He was free to live as he wished—he could leave the Jesuit Order.

Intoxicated by Rabea's proximity and his unfulfilled yearnings, Lukas forgot everything else around him. He forgot the dead man downstairs and the dangers that stemmed from Bentivoglio's secret. He no longer knew where and what he was. He knew only that he wanted Rabea, now and forever.

He slowly raised his head and sought her eyes, then plunged deep into those emerald seas. There was so much love and desire in his gaze that Rabea immediately understood. She shivered. They were very close now, their faces only an inch or two apart.

Lukas read the acquiescence in her eyes and gently put his lips to hers, enjoying every second of this longed-for but unexpected moment. Their lips explored each other, recognized each other. For a while, they merely held one another close, made sure of one another. Then their kisses became more passionate, and they hurriedly divested themselves of their clothes. Their naked bodies clung to each other, their arms and legs entwined. Lukas groaned, unable to wait any longer, he desired her so much. Her slender thighs parted all too readily, and he entered her in a single, sinuous movement. He took her in an act of concentrated ardor, savoring every inch of his movements inside her. Only gradually did his rhythm accelerate and his thrusts become harder. Rabea relished his strength, clamped her own slim hips to his. She understood Lukas. Like him, she wanted to assure herself of his physical presence, of the fact that they were really there together, one body—one.

He cried aloud in ecstasy as if he wanted the whole world to share in his happiness, and then he clasped her to him, trembling. They had both arrived in another world, their own cosmos of love. For a while, time stood still just for them.

Afterward, sated and content, they lay there closely entwined. She enjoyed the throbbing of his rapid heartbeat against her ear.

"Tell me," he asked randomly, "who or what is Rambo?"

"Oh no!" She covered his face and chest with countless featherlight kisses. "What made you think of that now?"

"There are so many thoughts whirling around in my head, I probably picked out the most trivial," he replied, one hand resting proprietorially on her soft, cinnamon-colored hair. His fingers toyed with the ringlets, in which a shaft of sunlight was bringing out a multitude of colors. Fascinated, he saw them repeated throughout her cascade of hair. Framed by that incandescent aureole, she looked like a seductive siren.

"Oh, Rambo's just a Hollywood invention, a traumatized Vietnam vet whom nobody wants and who wipes out half the US army and police. Nobody important, but everyone knows him. Except you, of course. I bet you've never heard of Britney Spears either," she said teasingly, drawing a circle around his navel with her wet tongue.

"Sure I have," he murmured, stretching luxuriously under her caresses. To prove it, he hummed a few bars of "Baby One More Time." Wrapping both hands around her slender waist, which they almost encircled, he lifted her in one powerful movement onto his hips. She was now sitting astride him.

He hesitated for one tiny moment because he thought he heard an inner voice. Could his twin sister be calling him telepathically? But the moment of unease passed when Rabea, with a sigh, shut her eyes and lowered herself onto him, absorbing him completely. Triumphantly, she flung her head back. Her long mane of hair tumbled down her back, and a few strands tickled his thighs.

Now it was Rabea who determined their rhythm. She savored every single moment that Lukas was at her mercy and deep inside her. She toyed with him, curbing his excitement and repressing her own, until she could restrain herself no longer, and fiery lust erupted from the core of her, engulfing her and carrying her away.

Later, sweaty and exhausted and drunk with happiness, she lay flat on top of him. He tenderly caressed her face with his fingers and planted a gossamer kiss on her forehead. "I love your forehead," he said. "It's soft and white, like ice cream."

"You mean that's all I am to you, a fairground treat?" she said with mock indignation, rubbing her hard little nipples against his chest.

Lukas heaved a blissful sigh. If she went on doing that . . .

"No, I'm besotted with you," he protested. "I'd like to nibble you for all eternity. And that enchanting little snub nose . . ." He brushed it gently with his lips. "It's as sweet as cherry ice cream with Amaretto. And your lips . . ."

"What about my lips?"

"Your lips"—he kissed them—"are as fruity as an ice cream made of ripe grapes and more intoxicating than any wine. And your skin is as irresistible as a fresh peach ripened under the summer sun. I'd like to lick every square inch of you, kiss every freckle." He seemed to be about to do so, because he rolled over so that Rabea was lying beneath him. "Your nipples are like delicious ripe gooseberries, just made for me to taste their sweetness." His hot mouth sent pleasurable frissons through her body. All at once, he was back inside her, and they made love again, but this time without any wildness. Gently and affectionately, they assuaged the longing that had grown inside them over the years. Afterward they lay facing each other side by side. In the midst of this absolute bliss, Rabea had a sudden thought. She stiffened. "My God, Lukas, I've taken no precautions. It's been a long time, you know."

Lukas gently lifted her chin, and ardently gazed deep into her eyes. "Well? Isn't a child begotten in pure love the acme of happiness and the fulfillment of God's creation?"

The truth of that statement, so lovingly and honestly uttered, so overwhelmed Rabea that it abruptly punctured her mood of enchantment. It reminded her of what she'd done. She had to tell him at once about the letter from Switzerland. She sat up. "There's something you should know. I did something I'm not proud of, truly. I—"

That was as far as she got. Lukas put a finger to her lips. "Shh, nothing matters now but us," he broke in firmly. "Forget about the past, Rabea. I've loved you all my life, and I don't know how I managed to live without you these past six years. Nothing you did in the past can alter my love for you. God truly loves anyone on whom he bestows the gift of true love. You don't believe in him, but it doesn't matter, because he believes in you. Remember your sixth birthday, when you told everyone you were going to marry me? You were right, Rabea. We belong together. My decision to enter the order was a mistake. I'll always love God, but I know that I love you as much and need you even more. From now on, only the future counts. Bentivoglio landed us in this mess, but let's get it over with, and then my mother can finally have the grand wedding she's been planning for me since I was born."

"Lukas, please, it's important. I have to tell you, because—"

The ringtone of Rabea's cell phone played the role of destiny for the second time that day. She almost swore at it, but when she saw through the window that the sun had passed its zenith, she realized they should have been on their way back to Rome a long time ago. Lucie was bound to be worrying about them—that must be her on the phone. She stood up and reached for her shorts, giving Lukas an incomparable view of her bare backside while she was on the phone.

"Hello, hello, there you are at last. Where on earth are you?" said a tearful female voice. It wasn't Lucie's, but it sounded vaguely familiar. "Who is this?" Rabea demanded.

"Please, you must come back at once. Something terrible has happened." The voice drifted off into hysterics without answering her question. Rabea suddenly recognized the voice: Lucie's garrulous professor with whom they'd recently had breakfast.

She put her hand over the phone and turned to Lukas. "It's Lucie's friend, that crazy Dutch professor. I wonder how she got my number. She's blathering about something—I can hardly understand a word she says."

The caller made it no easier for her; she continued to sob.

"Hello, Professor Van Kampen? Is that you? Please calm down!" she exclaimed. At that moment, the phone changed hands. Rabea was so startled, she almost dropped her own phone. She instinctively picked up her T-shirt when she recognized the man's voice at the other end of the line. It was Superintendent Grassa.

"*Buon giorno*, Signorina Rosenthal. The lady here wouldn't give me your number—she insisted on calling you herself. I'm sure Signore von Stetten is with you. Please put it on speakerphone, so he can listen in."

Rabea did as she was told and gave Lukas a reassuring glance.

"It's about your sister, Signore von Stetten. She has disappeared."

Lukas sat up with a start, all the blood draining from his cheeks. "What do you mean, disappeared? She isn't under arrest. She can leave the apartment any time she likes. I'm sure she's just gone shopping."

"I'm sorry, but the matter is serious—there's no possibility of a mistake. We're sure she has been abducted. There are signs of a struggle in the kitchen—your sister must have resisted—and we've found a rag soaked in anesthetic. I suggest you return at once and tell me, at long last, what's going on here. You should cooperate. This isn't just about you anymore—your sister's life is at stake."

"But . . . who would abduct Lucie?" Lukas said haltingly as the news bit into his consciousness like acid.

Rabea, who saw that the same thought had occurred to them both, muted the phone. "You're thinking what I'm thinking, aren't you? There's only one reason for her abduction, Lukas. It was the guys that murdered Bentivoglio and your neighbor. They obviously know about the key to Bentivoglio's safe-deposit box. Bet you anything it won't be long before we get a call from them: Lucie in return for Bentivoglio's documents. Damn it, Lukas, I'd like to know exactly what it is, this can of worms he landed us with. We'll take the stuff to Rome, and whatever it is these guys want so bad, they can have it. There's too much blood clinging to it."

She pushed the "Mute" button again. "If I understood you correctly, Superintendent, Lucie was kidnapped from the apartment right under your nose. The whole building is swarming with your men, and they didn't notice a thing? If anything happens to her, I'll hold you personally responsible. I'll set the police commissioner and the whole of the Italian press on you and make sure your career is over, understand?"

she snarled. It was fortunate the superintendent couldn't see her pacing up and down the bedroom naked.

"Please calm yourself, signorina!" Grassa said soothingly. His voice had lost much of its customary arrogance. "Attributions of blame won't help Signorina Lucie now. Kidnapping someone from a building full of policemen takes some doing. We're dealing with absolute pros here. That's important, because it means that Signorina Lucie is all right. If they'd only meant to warn her brother, they'd have killed her on the spot and left her corpse behind. The fact that they took her with them proves they want something. It's what underlies every abduction: a trade. Signore von Stetten, am I right in thinking you're in possession of something the kidnappers are anxious to lay their hands on? If so, bring it here!"

Lukas, who had groaned aloud at the word *corpse*, took the phone from Rabea's hand. "Superintendent, we're on our way. We'll meet at the apartment in about two and a half hours."

"Wait," Rabea said, taking the phone back.

"Superintendent, before we head back, I'll give you an address. There your men will find the dead body of a man who tried to shoot Lukas. I was compelled to hit him on the head with a poker. Lucie informed us that one of your detectives was killed. Our assailant was definitely involved—I spotted him following me in Rome. I even have some witnesses: a party of nuns. It shouldn't be hard to trace them. More when we get back. And listen: if there are any developments, call us at once. You have the number now . . ."

THE GENETICS
OF SUFFERING

Lukas and Rabea avoided each other's eye as they gathered up their scattered clothes and got dressed in silence. Their consciences were pricking them. While they were abandoning themselves to pleasure, Lucie had been kidnapped.

What's happening to her? Rabea wondered. She started to pull on her T-shirt, but it was smeared with Lukas's blood. Heedlessly, she let it fall to the floor and opened Isa's clothes closet. Isa was taller and far less petite, but she found a low-cut white peasant blouse whose cleavage could be gathered with ribbons. Her eye fell on a denim shirt that obviously belonged to Isa's husband. She picked it up.

"Here, better put this on, Lukas, your shirt is covered with bloodstains." When, instead of responding, he slipped into his stained shirt, she touched him gently on the arm. "You can't be seen in public like that."

Somewhat more abruptly than he intended, he snatched his arm away. "Do you think I'm the least bit worried about a bloodstained shirt? Damn it, don't you understand? They've got Lucie. I sensed it earlier, while we were in bed. She called me! She was scared, and I took no notice because I was blinded by lust. Even that dead man downstairs didn't put us off!" Lukas was quite beside himself and shouting now. He had gripped Rabea's slender shoulders, and she was half-suspended in his arms like a lifeless puppet. Ablaze with fury, his eyes met her calm green gaze. Suddenly ashamed because he had taken out his anger on her, he let her go, but the tumult within him had yet to subside. He punched the wall several times, leaving behind a trace of blood from his grazed knuckles.

"Please, Lukas, it's not your fault. We're a hundred fifty miles from Rome. We couldn't have prevented her abduction anyway."

Rabea didn't doubt for a moment that Lucie had called her brother. It was the power of blood and love that linked the twins so closely.

But Lukas was temporarily unable to accept reason. He had defied God and given in to his desire. He had taken what he had long thought of as his due, and God had punished him by taking Lucie.

In her turn, his attitude made Rabea boil with rage. How could Lukas so quickly forget their hour of bliss and disavow the perfect moment they'd just shared? She clenched her small hands as if preparing to drive God from the bedroom with her fists. Just now, she had been ready to give Lukas up of her own accord. She had meant to confess the truth at last, well aware that it might have ended their love and could even have deprived her of his friendship. But now that the battle wasn't hers to decide, God having once more stretched out his greedy hand for Lukas, she was ready to fight for her love to the last breath.

"Lucie's abduction has nothing to do with divine retribution. If anyone's to blame, it's Bentivoglio. The church invented celibacy a thousand years ago for one reason only: in order to dominate you priests. Do you know what Foucault wrote? That the first act of human freedom consists in gaining control over one's own body. That's just what *they* want to prevent. They enslave our bodies, our souls, our spirit. They exercise power over us only when we feel unworthy. Love of power coupled with religious fanaticism is a dangerous mixture. It's the mortal enemy of love and tolerance, precisely the values your Jesus espoused. That was his message, which is why they nailed him to the cross. Believe me, the religious and political leaders of this world don't want humanity to be contented. A contented person is free from fear, but the prerequisite of power *is* fear. That's why they've tried to make humanity afraid since the beginning of time: afraid of the Last Judgment, of eternal damnation, of woman, the corrupt sinner, and in recent times even of a war involving nuclear and biological weapons—weapons invented by humans themselves. They've made a pact with fear. I've nothing against faith, Lukas, as long as it gives people spiritual support, comforts them, inspires them to do better. Jesus was undoubtedly a man of goodwill, but his self-appointed representatives on earth have been betraying him for centuries. They pervert his legacy by claiming the right to kill in his name! Their hypocrisy makes me sick. I'm a Jew, Lukas. I carry the genetics of suffering within me. No race has suffered more than we have from the powers that be and from religious persecution. None has been so often expelled, murdered, even gassed. And what has our endurance earned us? A country of our own that was taken away from another people and has to be defended with tanks? I'm afraid, Lukas—afraid we may become like those who have persecuted us. Your God may have created the earth, but humans have created what shouldn't exist: war. Please don't make our love responsible for Lucie's predicament. Don't let that steal our love. Love is the only thing that can heal this world."

Rabea hadn't planned that speech. She had simply flown off the handle, frustrated at the unfair turn of events. The words had come bubbling up of their own accord. She now felt as if they had drained all her energy. She knew that her passionate outburst hadn't helped Lukas understand her feelings any better.

He was staring at her, his eyes unnaturally bright. "My goodness, Rabea. Why do you hate God so much?"

There was a brief pause before she answered, "Perhaps because you love him so much." She hadn't been able to resist that. She realized it only widened the gulf between them, but she suddenly didn't care, she was so tired of arguing. No one could run up the same hill again and again without becoming exhausted.

"Let's go and get Lucie back," she said. She stood up and left him on his own in the bedroom.

Wearing the denim shirt after all, Lukas joined Rabea in the living room a little while later. She had stowed the papers again. Now she shouldered her bag and silently handed him the heavy deed box. They both avoided looking at the killer's body.

Two minutes later, they were driving along the village street in the direction of the expressway.

Lukas was sitting in the passenger seat like a stone statue, out of his mind with fear at the thought that Lucie was in the control of the same killers who had tortured his uncle to death.

Rabea, who was conscious of his mounting desperation, glanced at him briefly. "We'll get Lucie back. I forgot to tell you, Grassa mentioned that your old man's already on his way to Rome."

Lukas and his father had last seen each other at Franz's funeral three months earlier. The same night, in his grief, Heinrich von Stetten had picked another quarrel with his surviving son. He couldn't forgive Lukas for choosing God over him—something he had in common with Rabea.

"Pass me my cell phone, Lukas?" she asked. "I have an idea. I know someone who can help us to find Lucie." As she drove onto the expressway, she searched her phone's contacts list, keeping one eye on the road. When all was clear, she dialed the number.

A familiar voice answered. "Rabea? Good to hear from you. It's been a while. Lucie calls me far more often."

"I'm sorry. I'm a naughty girl, but we'll talk about that later. Listen, I need your help. Lucie has been kidnapped in Rome. Can you come? I'll give you the address." She reeled it off without waiting for an answer. She knew that Jules could be relied on and would come at once. She was right.

Jules asked no questions. He simply said, "I'm on my way."

After she ended the call, Lukas looked at her questioningly. "Who was that?"

"If anyone can help us, it's him—" Rabea began. She suddenly uttered an expletive.

Lukas's head had been turned toward her, so he hadn't noticed the policeman on the shoulder signaling her to pull over.

"Damn, damn, damn! If they check our papers, they'll know there's an APB out for us. That means they'll take us with them and confiscate the car and its contents. We're in the Marche and Rome's in the Lazio region. If the police have an argument over whose meat we are, it could take time. Maybe we should risk it and just keep driving."

Rabea, who had already taken her foot off the gas pedal, was about to floor it when Lukas restrained her. "No, Rabea. It could be just a simple traffic check. If we run for it, he'll just radio a colleague, and they'll stop us at the next intersection at the latest."

She finally pulled over around sixty yards from the police car. While watching the approaching cop in the rearview mirror, she hissed to Lukas, "Look, we can't risk them taking the scrolls and the deed box and us being stuck here for hours. Lucie's life is in the balance. If I have to get out, I'll go around the back of the car and open the trunk, whether he asks me to or not. That'll obstruct his view of you so you can slide behind the wheel. If there's a problem and he won't let us drive on, I'll slam the lid. That's your signal. Drive off at once. Don't worry—I'll hold them up. If necessary, I'll stage an epileptic fit in the middle of the road. Leave the car someplace and get to Rome by public transport. Then go to your friend Father Simone, the guy Lucie told me about.

I'll call you on my cell phone—here, take it. They can't do anything to me. I'll inform Grassa." While explaining her plan she'd been feeling under her blouse. Some remarkable contortions enabled her to extract her white bra.

"Are you crazy? You can't get undressed now!"

"I'm only enlisting the help of Gina and Sofia."

"What?" Lukas's expression made it clear he thought she'd flipped.

"Gina Lollobrigida on the left and Sophia Loren on the right. I told you I'd distract them. We're in Italy—it's never failed before." With an impish grin, she undid the ribbon on her neckline and pulled the blouse far enough off her shoulders to reveal her cleavage. The blouse itself was slightly transparent, so without the bra, her nipples were clearly visible. She handed her bra to Lukas, who stuffed it into the glove compartment just before the policeman tapped on the driver's window.

"*Buon giorno*, signorina. I'm afraid you were going a little too fast. Do you have your license and your papers, please? This is a rental, isn't it?"

The young cop had given Lukas only a fleeting glance, being far more interested in Rabea's cleavage and her bare brown legs in their denim shorts. He flicked through her papers. "Ah, *tedesca*, German. And what brings you to our beautiful country, signorina?" he asked with a winning smile, bending down with his eyes glued to her neckline.

"We've been visiting a friend in Mergo." Rabea threw back her auburn mane in order to stimulate the cop's imagination still more and distract his attention from Lukas. The young man's Adam's apple bobbed. He could clearly see that the signorina wasn't wearing a bra.

"Hmm, everything seems to be in order. No ticket this time, but drive a bit slower from now on, signorina, *bene*?" He returned the papers.

Rabea was about to breathe a sigh of relief when the cop added, "Please could you open your trunk?" He had thought of a better way to admire her bare legs.

Lukas, who was meantime watching everything in the rearview mirror, noticed that the cop in the patrol car had picked up his phone and was speaking into it. He fervently hoped the man wasn't phoning in their license number and description. Completely ignored by the cop who was fixated on Rabea, Lukas was relieved he hadn't been obliged to put her plan B into effect. The potentially explosive situation seemed to be defusing itself. The trunk was surely empty.

In fact, their situation was far more tenuous than they assumed. If Rabea opened the trunk, they would have real problems when the cop found the knife wrapped in a bloodstained handkerchief—courtesy of Gabriel.

Rabea's hand was already feeling for the button. She pressed it and the lid of the trunk sprang open with a click. She had inserted her fingers under the edge of the lid and was about to lift it when the other cop called, "Davide! There's a serious accident on the expressway near Jesi North. We're wanted right away to help regulate the traffic."

The young cop cast a last, regretful glance at Rabea. Then, clutching his holster with one hand and his cap with the other, he sprinted back to the patrol car, which sped off with blue lights flashing and siren wailing.

Rabea gave them a friendly wave. "Phew, that was a close call."

Lukas was also relieved, though he felt she'd rather overdone the display of her charms. "You didn't even get a speeding ticket," he commented incredulously.

The drive proceeded without further incident. About halfway to Rome, Lukas took over the driving. Both of them were wholly engrossed in thoughts of Lucie.

Rabea took a preliminary look at the exercise book whose contents were written in Latin. It looked to be a sort of diary kept by Bentivoglio. Although her Latin was rusty, she managed to decipher some of it.

They had almost gotten to Rome before they broke the oppressive silence and discussed what to do next.

* * *

Lucie recovered consciousness. Her head and neck were aching like mad, and she had a revolting taste in her mouth. She was lying on her stomach in a dark, cramped space and hurting all over. She couldn't tell which was making her feel more nauseated, the anesthetic or the disgusting gag in her mouth. *Hell,* she thought, *I've been kidnapped again!* She couldn't help remembering what Jules had told her in Beirut. After her rescue, he'd said that the possibility of being kidnapped was about as remote as the chances of winning the lottery. *Great,* she thought wryly, *I've hit the jackpot twice.* She was so angry at the predicament, her rage outweighed her fear. Although Jules had considered it unlikely that it could ever happen again, he'd spent several days giving her and Rabea a crash course on what to do. Lesson number one: act dumber than you are.

Hell, she thought, *Lesson number one ought to be: How do I avoid being sick with a revolting gag in my mouth?* She forced herself to breathe deeply through her nose, and the feeling of nausea gradually retreated into her stomach. Good, act dumb. In her case, that probably meant concealing the fact that she'd recovered consciousness.

Lesson number two: assess the situation. Her wrists were handcuffed in front of her, and she was half-lying on her outstretched arms. She alleviated her discomfort a little by rolling over, then raised her hands, and yanked the dirty rag out of her mouth. Relieved, she drew several deep breaths. She had already grasped that she was in the trunk of a car. Next, she tried to open her smarting eyes. Her nose was smarting too, presumably an aftereffect of whatever they'd knocked her out with. Her eyes slowly accustomed themselves to the semidarkness. Okay, lesson number three. What was lesson number three? Oh, yes: Do your kidnappers or the place where they're holding you prisoner display any weaknesses? Any opportunities to escape? None, unless she wanted to jump out of a speeding car with her wrists manacled.

That led to lesson number four: What can be done to improve the situation? Lucie was an expert on handcuffs thanks to Jules's training.

First, she tried to get hold of one of the two hairpins she'd always worn since Beirut. One of them must have been lost during the struggle in the kitchen, together with an earring, but the other was still there. She mislaid it in the darkness for a few alarming moments, but managed to find it again. Putting it in her mouth, she raised her hands and tried to recall what Jules had taught her. It seemed to take her half an eternity, and she'd almost abandoned hope when the handcuffs finally clicked open.

The car was now jouncing over a potholed road at high speed. She braced her feet against the side and tried to spot something in the gloom that might indicate the make of the car. Jules had told her that for safety reasons, the trunks of American automobiles had to be openable from the inside, but even if this didn't apply, she still had her hairpin. Jules had practiced this with her too. Although it had been tough, she thought back with gratitude to the hours she'd spent sweating in a trunk in the sweltering heat of Beirut. Feverishly, she felt for a little lever on the underside of the lid—and found one. It was an American car! She could hardly believe her luck.

Next was lesson number five: collect as much information as possible about your surroundings and your kidnappers. Lucie recited Jules's instructions to herself: *Listen to their voices. How many men or women? Who's the leader? Do the voices sound old or young? Languages or dialects? Do they call one another by name, mention times or places? Any special smells or sounds? Any roadblocks? Any church bells or animal noises? Any sound of rushing water that would indicate the proximity of a river? Type of road? Asphalt, unpaved, serpentine, straight?* Although car noises were all she could hear, she felt convinced that they were driving along a bumpy, deserted country road. Well, every journey ended sometime, and that was when she meant to seize her opportunity.

The moment came sooner than she expected. Shortly afterward, the car made a sharp left turn and slowed down. Feverishly, she felt for the handcuffs and put them on again without engaging the locks. She had the presence of mind to stuff the filthy gag back in her mouth, then rolled back onto her stomach.

Not a moment too soon, because the car pulled up and a door opened. Steps approached and someone opened the trunk. Lucie sensed a faint movement as someone bent over her—someone who stank of stale sweat and nicotine. All at once, the person gripped her shoulder and shook her so violently that her head hit the weather-strip seal. She managed to stifle a cry of pain, but her heart was racing. The man let go of her. She was thanking her lucky stars, when he slowly slid a calloused hand up her bare leg. He was breathing heavily now, and his hand was inexorably approaching the point at which she would no longer be able to restrain the impulse to bat it aside.

"What are you playing at?" snapped a commanding voice. The searching hand was withdrawn. "You were supposed to see if she's awake. The Protector expressly forbade us from touching her. Shut the trunk and get the gas. I need a piss."

The lid came crashing down. She heard the nozzle being inserted in the tank and a loud gurgle as the gas pump started up. Nauseated, she tugged the gag out of her mouth. It took her only a second to make up her mind. This was probably her last chance to escape before the kidnappers reached their destination. Who knew where they were taking her and how closely guarded she would be there? Cautiously, she cracked the lid. If the Groper, as she'd christened him, had a clear view of the back of the car, her escape bid would end before it had begun. She was in luck. He was standing with his back to her around twenty-five yards from the car, battling with a recalcitrant cigarette machine. There was no sign of the other man.

Noiselessly, she climbed out of the trunk, crouched down, and surveyed her surroundings. She was at a small gas station in the middle of nowhere. Behind the counter in the little glass booth she made out a middle-aged woman in a smock.

It took Lucie less than a second to determine that she couldn't turn to the woman for help without endangering her too. Immediately beyond the gas station was a steep, grassy slope, and above it a densely wooded hill. Her one chance was to take advantage of the element of surprise and make for the woods. Rounding the car at a crouch, she sprinted across the forecourt and clawed her way up the slope on all fours. She was halfway up it before her escape was discovered.

She heard the men yelling behind her and redoubled her efforts, then plunged into the woods and zigzagged through the trees. She realized that her white linen shorts would show up like a flag and offer a good target, and she could already hear the men crashing through the undergrowth behind her. Although she estimated that her lead was less than two hundred yards, the sound of breaking twigs indicated that they were not gaining on her fast, if at all. After a minute or two, the trees thinned. Before her lay a huge field sprinkled with sunflowers in bloom. She paused for a moment to get her bearings. A distant mechanical hum attracted her attention: a tractor was slowly putt-putting across a field, but it was too far away.

On the left-hand edge of the woods, Lucie spotted a paddock in which two horses were peacefully grazing. She sprinted over to it, but slowed to a walk before she reached the fence and slowly climbed over it. An experienced horsewoman, Lucie checked out the younger and stronger-looking horse with a practiced eye, then quickly plucked a handful of grass and held it out. The mare submitted her to a brief, melancholy gaze before accepting this gift. Lucie gave the animal a soothing pat, and it snorted and butted her with its head. Just then, she spotted movement at the edge of the woods.

The two kidnappers had emerged from the trees, but the mare's bulky body was still concealing her from their view. Cautiously, she seized the animal's mane and vaulted onto its back. Seeming less startled than puzzled, it pranced to and fro as she bent low over its neck with her fingers buried in its mane. The kidnappers sighted her just as she dug her heels into the mare's side, and a shot whistled past only a few feet way. Whether because of that or Lucie's heels, the mare reared, bounded forward, and made straight for the fence at the far end of the paddock. Horse and rider cleared it in one mighty leap and galloped off across the open field. Risking a look over her shoulder, Lucie saw the two men turn and run back into the woods, presumably to fetch their car.

She had to get to a telephone as quickly as possible. Between two large fields, she made out a farm track. The horse headed straight for this as if it knew it. The track was wide enough for a car, and it wouldn't be long before the kidnappers found it. It rose gently, and after rounding a bend, Lucie found herself confronted by a range of hills with a *rustico*, a small farmhouse, in front of it. To her great relief, she saw an elderly woman forking manure into a wheelbarrow in the yard. When she heard them coming, she lowered her pitchfork and stared at them with her mouth open.

The mare came to a stop beside her and whinnied.

Before Lucie could get a word out, the old woman let fly. "What do you think you're doing riding our Mona Lisa? Get off her at once!"

Her dialect was so broad Lucie could scarcely understand what she was saying. All at once, however, the indignant expression on the woman's face was replaced by a look of horror. She was concentrating so hard on the horse that its rider's disheveled state had escaped her notice. Lucie's blouse and shorts were torn in several places, and she was bleeding from a gash on her cheek.

Dismayed, the old woman let go of her pitchfork and clapped her work-worn hands together. "*Dio mio!* What happened to you?"

Lucie slid slowly off the horse. It was only now that shock really set in. Her legs felt like rubber. Swaying, she clung to the mare's neck.

The old woman saw this and gripped her arm with surprising strength.

"My name is Lucia von Stetten. I was kidnapped from my apartment in Rome this morning, but thanks to Mona Lisa, I managed to escape." She patted the mare. "Signora, I need your help. The men are still after me. Could I please use your phone?"

"Of course. Come into the house, signorina. You can leave Mona Lisa outside here. She'll find her own way to the stable." Once she realized she was dealing with a foreigner, the old woman tried to moderate her dialect. Briskly, almost gaily, she hurried on ahead of her guest and into the house. Lucie couldn't resist the impression that she welcomed this break in her daily routine.

She followed the woman through the low doorway into a dark, pleasantly cool entrance hall pervaded by the delicious scent of freshly baked bread. She suddenly felt not only thirsty but also ravenous.

"Here's the telephone. Please help yourself." The farmer's wife pointed to an old-fashioned push-button phone on a chest of drawers in the hallway, which also bore some family photos and a vase filled with artificial flowers. Above it hung a faded portrait of Pope John XXIII. "I'll get you a glass of water, signorina," the woman said, and disappeared into the kitchen.

Lucie picked up the receiver and dialed the number of the Rome apartment in hopes that Grassa might still be there and could send help at once. She tried twice in succession, but the answering machine cut in immediately each time. It had to be defective, because she was unable to leave a message. Disappointed, she hung up. It occurred to her that she'd forgotten to ask the old woman exactly where she was. Then she tried Rabea's cell phone, but a monotone computerized voice informed her that Rabea was *al momento* unavailable. No one answered the phone in the Nuremberg mansion either. Frau Gabler was using the vacuum cleaner, and her mother, Evelyn, had gone out, blissfully unaware that her daughter was in danger. Her husband hadn't wanted to worry her yet. Her father's cell phone was switched off because he was on a plane bound for Rome.

* * *

It was Lucie's bad luck that she had tried to call the Rome apartment just as a police technician was doctoring the phone and connecting it to police headquarters in case the kidnappers called. In the process, he had also discovered the high-performance bug installed by Trapano. This had alerted Grassa to search the apartment; additional monitoring devices had been found in the living room and bedroom. The superintendent was seething with rage. He couldn't help wondering who would be interested in eavesdropping on the young Jesuit—aside from himself, of course. What riled him most of all, however, was that someone had gotten there before him.

Where the hell are they all? Lucie wondered.

Her Good Samaritan returned from the kitchen with a tray. "Well?" She gestured to Lucie to follow her into the living room. On the tray were a bottle of water, bread, butter, some juicy prosciutto, and a bottle of iodine and some bandages.

"Where are we, actually? Is there a police station somewhere near? Maybe someone could come and pick me up?"

"*Sì, sì,* of course. We can call the police in Monte Alto. The phone book's in the top drawer of the chest."

Lucie went back into the hall. She discovered a 1989–90 edition of the phone book under some old newspapers. She dialed the number for the police station. Engaged. Then the Italian emergency number. Engaged.

She was beginning to feel as if everything was conspiring against her. Two armed gangsters were after her, and here she was, helpless, stuck in a farmhouse with an old woman. Despondently, she returned to the living room. "I can't get through to anyone. The police number was also engaged. I'd like to thank you for your kindness, but I don't even know your name."

The old woman took her hand and patted it. "My name is Anna Sassi. Just call me Anna. Go on, try again, then have something to eat. That always helps," she said encouragingly. Her tone conveyed an implicit belief that a good meal could instantly banish all concerns. She had already loaded a slice of bread with spicy prosciutto and pushed the plate toward her. Overcome with hunger at the sight of this simple delicacy, Lucie needed no second bidding.

Anna delightedly watched her guest sink her teeth into the crusty bread. Suddenly, Lucie dropped the slice of bread on the plate and jumped up. Footsteps could be heard outside in the hallway. She was desperately looking around for some means of escape when a tall, heavily built man walked into the living room.

Anna's wrinkled face broke into a happy smile. "Don't be afraid, Lucie, this is my son Alfredo. Alfredo, this is Lucie. We must help her. She's been kidnapped—she's frightened."

Alfredo extended a callused hand. The aroma of manure he gave off was clearly attributable to his bespattered overalls. He displayed no surprise, as if he found it quite normal for his mother to be entertaining a kidnapped stranger in the living room.

His calm demeanor became comprehensible when he said, "I thought it must be something of the kind when I saw you galloping off on Mona Lisa. I was the man on the tractor—I saw the two men who were after you. Have you informed the police, Mamma?" A calm and collected individual, it seemed, Alfredo had his mother's kindly eyes.

"It's permanently engaged," said Lucie. She went out into the hallway and pressed the redial button, only to get the busy tone once more.

Alfredo had followed her. "Still engaged?"

"Yes, but I must go. It'll be only a matter of time before the men turn up here."

Alfredo thought for a moment. "Even if we got through, the police would take fifteen minutes to get here. I suggest I take you there in my van."

She almost hugged him in relief.

"Mamma," he said, turning to his mother. "Just in case, go and get our pump-action and my hunting rifle. I don't like surprises."

"Good idea, Alfredo." Anna bustled off.

"May I use your toilet?" Lucie asked.

"Of course. It's along the hallway and around the corner to your right."

Lucie was about to pull the chain when she heard a car drive up. Thinking it was Alfredo, she peered out the little toilet window, which overlooked the yard—and recoiled in alarm. It was the kidnapper's car. Cautiously, she raised her head again. The two men were just getting out.

Alfredo went to meet them with a friendly smile.

Without warning, the older of the two gunned him down with a single shot. Utterly horrified, Lucie saw the big, strong man topple over like a felled tree. At the same moment, the thought of Anna flashed through her mind. *They'll kill her too!* She had to face them. Feverishly, she wrenched at the bolt on the wooden door, but it stuck, now of all times. At last it gave. Panic-stricken, she was hurrying along the hallway when two shots rang out in quick succession.

Oh God, she was too late. They'd already killed the old woman.

She dashed around the corner and stopped abruptly, brought up short by an unexpected sight. Anna was standing to the left of the open doorway with a huge pump-action shotgun propped on her skinny hip, loading it with shells from her apron pocket. "Stay under cover, girl!" she hissed at Lucie over her shoulder. "I got the cowardly swine who shot my Alfredo. The other bastard is hiding behind the car."

Suddenly some more shots rang out, one of which hit the door frame. Anna hastily withdrew her head. Without breaking cover, the old woman raised the shotgun, thrust it around the door frame, and responded by discharging a broadside in the direction of the kidnappers' car. She couldn't aim properly without endangering herself, but a metallic clatter signified that she'd hit the vehicle. That was enough to keep the man's head down for the moment.

"I've an idea, Lucie. Come here to me, slowly, keeping close to the right-hand wall—the man won't be able to see you from that angle." A moment later, when Lucie was hugging the wall just behind her, Anna whispered, "Can you handle my shotgun, girl?"

Lucie could only nod, staggered by Anna's transformation from a motherly old woman into a formidable Amazon.

Anna was busy reloading the shotgun with nimble fingers. She thrust it into Lucie's hand. "If the bastard moves, pull the trigger!"

"Where are you going?" Lucie asked in a sudden alarm, because Anna was preparing to leave her on her own in the doorway.

"Alfredo's rifle is in the living room. I may be able to get the fascist swine from the window. As soon as I call *now*, just blaze away!" She flitted off with the verve of a young girl.

Lucie concentrated hard. Unlike Anna's, her hands were trembling. Drawing a deep breath, she plucked up her courage and thrust the heavy shotgun around the doorjamb, inch by inch. The man promptly fired several shots in quick succession. She darted back under cover but kept the shotgun at the ready, expecting to hear Anna's voice at any second.

"Now!" came the cry from the living room a moment later. Aiming blindly, Lucie blazed away with the pump-action until it was empty, then stood there exhausted, her ears aching from the din.

Startled to feel a sudden hand on her shoulder, she spun around. Anna, holding a hunting rifle with a telescopic sight cradled in the crook of her arm like a baby, regarded it fondly. "Alfredo's," she said. "He always forbade me to touch it." A single tear rolled down her cheek.

She looked up at Lucie, who was over a head taller. "It's over. I saw the bastard run off down the hill. A pity, I thought I'd hit him." She stomped out into the yard.

Lucie followed her, feeling lousy. After all, she was the one who had lured Alfredo's murderer to this house. What could one say to console a mother who had just seen her son gunned down before her eyes?

The first thing she noticed was a hen lying dead in the midst of a cloud of feathers, a few of which were still drifting to the ground. *Great,* she thought. Old Anna had dealt with the kidnappers almost single-handedly, whereas she herself had dispatched a broiler.

Her comrade-in-arms, still holding the hunting rifle, was standing over her son's murderer, who was lying on his back only a few yards from the front door. The man had taken a load of shot full in the stomach and was lying in a rapidly expanding pool of blood. He was whimpering and clutching his shattered body in a pitiful way, as if trying to stanch the blood welling between his fingers. Lucie's nostrils were assailed by a revolting smell. Its source puzzled her until she saw to her horror that something in addition to blood was spilling between the man's fingers: his guts—hence the appalling stench of excrement. She promptly threw up.

Alfredo was lying between his murderer and the dark-colored Ford. Anna kneeled down behind him and tenderly pillowed his head on her lap. Death must have been instantaneous, because his face still wore the friendly smile with which he'd greeted the killer.

The fatal shot had hit him in the heart at close range. There was very little blood. To be more precise, there was no blood at all, just a small black hole in his shirt that marked the place where the bullet had pierced it. Suddenly, Alfredo uttered a groan. His mother gave a start and feverishly felt his chest. There was a pocket at the precise spot where the bullet had hit him. Reaching inside it, Anna pulled out a badly battered snuffbox with a bullet embedded in it. Formerly her husband's, it had now saved her son's life.

Alfredo groaned again and opened his eyes. The first thing he saw was his mother's tear-stained face bending over him upside down. He looked incredulously from her to the battered metal box in her hand.

Then he felt his chest and grimaced with pain. "That's the last time you complain about me taking snuff, Mamma."

Laughing and crying simultaneously, Anna clasped him to her bosom. Lucie also hugged him, feeling highly relieved, and Alfredo welcomed her embrace in spite of the pain it caused him.

A cheeky hen strutted up to the kidnapper, whose tortured breathing had now fallen silent forever, and gave his limp hand a couple of pecks.

Lucie noticed that the dead man was still gripping his automatic. On impulse, or perhaps because she remembered that Jules had taught her to, she kicked the gun away. It went slithering under the car.

Now that she was safe, Lucie's thoughts returned to her brother. Feeling strangely restless at noon that day, she had obeyed a powerful urge to call him at once, but had failed to reach him. She'd been kidnapped from the apartment only a short time later.

Frozen with fear when the man clamped the anesthetic-soaked rag over her nose and mouth, she had called Lukas with her mind. She briefly thought she'd gotten through to him, only to be suddenly confronted by a yawning black void. She had even felt that he'd deliberately shut himself off from her. That alarming sensation of emptiness still lingered inside her. Her mental connection to Lukas had always given her a feeling of strength. Now her mind was suddenly invaded by a new and frightening thought. It hit her like a thunderbolt: *My God, Lukas had been in great danger.* Something had happened to him. Hadn't they shared everything since their earliest childhood, cuts and bruises included? She recalled how, on the same day and over twenty miles apart, they had each broken their left arm.

A muffled ringtone broke in on her thoughts. It came from the direction of the dead man. Should she answer? Why not? Lucie traced the sound to the man's right-hand trouser pocket. Bravely ignoring the stench, she fished out the phone with two fingers and glanced at the display. The call was anonymous. She pressed the key. *"Pronto?"*

"Who's this?" snapped a brusque female voice.

"Cleopatra," Lucie trilled quick-wittedly. "Who are you?"

A click. The woman had hung up.

"What is it? Who was that?" Anna and Alfredo had come over to her.

"Strange." Lucie frowned. "It was a woman, and she sounded pretty sore."

"The kidnapper's wife, maybe?" Anna wondered aloud. "Tell me, girl, why were you kidnapped? Are you rich or famous, or something?"

"Well, my family might be described as wealthy, but I don't think my abduction had anything to do with money. It's more likely to be connected with some business of my brother's. But it's a long story, Anna. Please could we go back inside? I'm feeling rather queasy."

"Of course, girl," Alfredo answered in his mother's place. "I reckon a grappa would do us all good." From the look Anna gave her son, it seemed he never passed up any opportunity for a grappa.

Alfredo left them alone in the kitchen long enough to make another attempt to get through to the nearest police station, but the number was still engaged.

Anna had already produced a bottle of the Italian cure-all. The first grappa found its way into Lucie's stomach almost by itself, suffusing it with comforting warmth and loosening the knot of fear a little.

Alfredo drained his glass in a practiced manner, heaved a blissful sigh, and sent another chasing after it. "Go on trying for the police, Mamma," he told Anna. "I want that scum out of our yard as soon as possible. I'll drive Lucie to Monte Alto myself. I'll get changed quickly, then we'll go." He heaved himself to his feet and plodded out of the room. Lucie knew he was trying not to show it, but his chest had to be extremely painful. Anna followed him out to the phone.

Despite the soothing effect of the alcohol, Lucie was feeling lousy. She had now been on her feet for nearly thirty hours, and in the last few of those hours had been drugged, kidnapped, shot at, and compelled to witness a brutal would-be killing. She was in a self-destructive mood that led her to blaming herself for everything that had happened. It was only because she had borrowed the horse and asked Anna for help that the kidnappers had come here. She had put the old woman in mortal danger, and the men had almost killed Alfredo, whose survival was little short of a miracle. Hot tears sprang to her eyes.

The old woman came back and sat down beside her. Noticing Lucie's tears, she took her hand. Lucie smiled at her. She had never met anyone like Anna before. What was the source of her strength, her courage? She had to be well over seventy and had just seen—or thought she'd seen—a man kill her son, but she had kept her head and taken her gun and avenged his supposed murder.

"I'm blubbering like a baby," Lucie sniffed.

Anna produced a handkerchief from her apron and handed it to her. "I got through to the police at last, and they're sending someone at once. But Lucie, girl, why so sad?"

Lucie turned her tearful face to Anna's. "Oh, Anna, I'm so terribly sorry," she burst out. "This is all my fault."

"Yes, you're right, of course," said Anna. "If you hadn't been kidnapped, and if the mare hadn't been in the paddock, and if Alfredo hadn't been out in the field, and if we didn't live here . . ." She gently lifted Lucie's chin and compelled her to look straight into her own kindly eyes. "Lucie, my dear, we could carry on this way and go back to Adam and Eve. Look, Alfredo and I are God-fearing Christians like my late husband, Enrico, God rest his soul. Our faith and our love of God and Our Lord Jesus Christ are simple and good. Even if God had taken my Alfredo from me today, I'd have been consoled by the knowledge that he was with my husband, Enrico, and his two little sisters. I'd have wept for Alfredo until my heart drowned in tears, of course, but sooner or later we're all reunited in heaven. I believe that, and so does my Alfredo. Today, the Almighty chose not to summon either me or Alfredo, so all is well."

Lucie listened to the old woman with amazement. Anna's fervor and her ability to express herself in lucid, simple words reminded her of someone. She wondered again where Anna got her incredible spiritual strength, although she already knew the answer. Anna had just given it to her. Her faith was the source. All at once, Lucie knew who Anna reminded her of: Lukas. He too possessed a special gift for consoling people with a few simple words, imparting some of his strength and giving them hope. She was overcome by an ardent yearning for her brother. The bond between them had been abruptly renewed, her special link with him restored. Gratitude flooded through her.

"Feeling better, my dear?" Anna inquired with a little smile. "Hungry? Shall I make you a ham sandwich?"

"Very kind of you, Anna, but no thanks. I mentioned my brother earlier. I think the two of you would like each other. Lukas is more than just my brother: he's my twin. I'm sure he already knows I was kidnapped. I can sense he's very worried about me. I'd like to try to call him."

But she seemed to be jinxed. Rabea's cell phone was again out of reach. Discouraged, Lucie put the receiver down. Anna, who had been watching her fruitless efforts, was standing in the doorway, drying a glass on a dish towel. "Don't worry, my girl. Alfredo will drive you to Rome right away. I'll cope with the police on my own. I've known the *capitano* since he was a baby."

"No, Anna. The kidnapper who got away may be hiding somewhere out there, and he's armed. They didn't plan this on their own. I heard them talking about their boss. What if the man comes back with reinforcements?"

"One more reason for you to get out of here at once. I'm not scared, and I've got a decent gun," Anna said grimly. "Let them come, the fascist swine. This time I'll be ready for them."

Lucie couldn't help smiling at her fierce determination. Anna's description of her son's would-be murderer as a "fascist swine" had given her food for thought. "Tell me, Anna," she said, "how come you're so good with guns?"

"Oh, that's easy." Anna shrugged her scrawny shoulders. "It's all the fault of the last damn war. In 1943 the fascists wiped out my family. I was only twelve at the time, all on my own, close to starving and in despair. That was when Enrico, my future husband, found me. He belonged to the resistance and he took me with him. The partisans became my new family. Enrico taught me to shoot and fight. More importantly, he taught me never to give up on life. Life is far too precious—it's a gift from the Almighty himself. Enrico taught me faith and love, and he taught me that neither can exist without the other. The two are one. My husband helped a lot of people and revived their hopes, but that's a long time ago." Anna sighed faintly, immersed in the distant past. The memory of it lit up her wrinkled face like a shaft of sunlight, mysteriously rejuvenating it. For one magical moment, Anna resembled the young bride in the wedding picture on the chest of drawers.

"So you were a partisan who fought against Mussolini and the fascists?" Lucie said, impressed.

"Yes, and against the Germans too. But, as I say, that was a long time ago. Let's worry about the here and now. I want you to get into Alfredo's van and leave here right away. I know our capitano, little Benini. He's no fool, but he's put on a bit of weight. I could feed my two pigs by the time he gets into his stride, so please go with Alfredo. Do it for me. Above all, do it for your twin brother, *sì*?"

Although not unmoved by Anna's urgent appeal, Lucie struggled with her urge to leave the farm. She was loath to leave the old woman on her own. She was still wondering what to do when events sped up. Just as Alfredo came downstairs, they heard the sound of a motor vehicle coming quickly up the road on the other side of the farmhouse. The engine roared intermittently as it rounded the S-bends at speed.

Remarkably agile for her age, Anna jumped up and hurried out of the kitchen into the room Alfredo used as an office. It had a small window that overlooked stretches of the serpentine road.

Alfredo and Lucie followed her. Together, they peered out the window. Sure enough, the vehicle came into view, clearly visible on a straightaway between two bends. But it wasn't the police. An unknown German SUV, it briefly disappeared, then came speeding around the barn built into the hillside only thirty yards or so below the house.

Alfredo and the two women were running out of time. Resolutely, Anna turned to Lucie, who was frozen with horror. "Now we're in trouble. They're here already. You can't leave by the front door, and Alfredo couldn't squeeze through this little window. You must go on your own. No buts, just do as I say—at once! Climb out and run to the barn. Our van's in there and the key's in the ignition. Alfredo and I will hold them off." She opened the window and pushed Lucie toward it.

"Lots of luck, my girl. God be with you. No arguments. *Avanti!*" Before Lucie could object, Anna clasped her around the waist, lifted her off her feet, and, with Alfredo's help, maneuvered her out the window.

Lucie realized she had no choice. The farmhouse obstructed the view of the barn, which was lower lying, so she managed to get to it unobserved. She opened the barn door and climbed into the vehicle. It was as Anna had said: the key was in the ignition. The vehicle was an old white delivery van, but it started at once. Lucie floored the gas pedal, the engine screamed, and the van almost leaped out the barn. Accelerating, she turned sharply to the right onto the road just as the first shots rang out behind her.

She hoped God had nothing better to do at that moment than come to the assistance of Anna and Alfredo. Then she had to concentrate on the road, a seemingly endless series of tight S-turns winding down into the valley. Feverishly, she checked the rearview mirror again and again to see if the silver SUV would appear. Her fears for Anna and Alfredo rapidly mutated into blind panic, until she eventually succumbed to irrational delusions and was overcome by a single thought: she must turn around and go to their aid. But the narrow roadway fell away steeply on the valley side, and there was no room to do so. She wouldn't be able to turn around until she reached the foot of the hill, when it might well be too late. At last, after what seemed ages, the road leveled out.

Lucie cast another nervous glance at the rearview mirror and swung her wheel over at the same time, which proved to be a mistake: she almost collided with a police car speeding around the next bend. Both vehicles skidded to a halt, tires screaming. Lucie, who hadn't fastened her seat belt, was pitched forward and hit her head on the windshield. Momentarily dazed, she remained slumped in her seat. The doors of the police car burst open, and two uniformed cops hurried over to her. The older of the two opened the driver's door, and Lucie fell straight into his arms.

"Good heavens, signorina, what were you thinking?" With his help, Lucie tottered over to the side of the road and lay down.

"Benito, *avanti*. The signorina has a head injury. Go and get the first-aid box from our car and call an ambulance. Then close off the road. One accident is enough."

Lucie was heartened by the policeman's considerate manner.

"Please," she said, "you've got to hurry. I've just come from old Anna Sassi's place up the hill. She and her son are being attacked by armed men. Listen, they're shooting up there." She gripped the man's arm. He stared at her incredulously, and for a moment, she could see he was wondering whether the bang on the windshield had scattered her wits. Then more shots punctured the silence of the valley. She found them reassuring because they meant that the brave pair were continuing to hold their attackers at bay.

The older policeman, who introduced himself as Sergente Federico Olivo, was Capitano Benini's deputy and had been dispatched by him to see if all was well with "crazy old Anna." Olivo had been in the area on another assignment, hence his prompt arrival. He now had to concede that the signorina was right: shots were definitely being fired up the hill. A fine hunter himself, Olivo noted that it wasn't one of the usual battues for hare or wild boar, which sounded different; there was no hysterical barking from any accompanying pack of hounds. Besides, he recognized Alfredo Sassi's delivery van. The experienced officer was a good judge of people and felt sure the young woman wasn't the type to steal other people's vehicles, so Alfredo must have lent it to her himself.

Suddenly another car, a sky-blue Fiat 500, came around the bend. At the sight of the other policeman, who had just marked the spot with a warning triangle, the driver braked so violently that he took the bend almost on two wheels. An elderly man in a black cassock, he hitched up his skirts and hurried over to them. "What happened? Can I be of help?" he exclaimed in concern. Regardless of his age and his cassock, he kneeled down beside Lucie.

"Father Serrano, this is perfect timing!" Sergente Olivo sounded relieved. "The young lady was involved in a minor accident. She doesn't appear to be badly hurt, but Benito has called an ambulance to be on the safe side. Please stay with her until it gets here. We have to check on old Anna up the hill." He turned to his colleague. "Benito, come on, up to the Sassis' farm! Call for backup and keep your gun handy!"

Lucie suddenly felt a little better. The sergente seemed to know exactly what to do.

Minutes of apprehensive waiting ensued. Meantime, the priest busied himself with the first-aid box, disinfected Lucie's wound, and applied a Band-Aid. She meekly submitted to his ministrations. "I expect you're very worried about Signora Anna, aren't you? But fear not, signorina, our Anna is indestructible. The Almighty keeps a special eye on her."

The priest was a very good-looking man for his age, Lucie noticed. He had kindly eyes, like Anna, and his face seemed to emit a gentle glow. Strangely enough, it was his very gentleness that triggered a sudden fit of anger in her, a kind of safety valve that released her pent-up concern for the Sassis and her brother. "The Almighty may keep a special eye on her," she said, "but he hasn't exactly been doing overtime lately."

"I can see you're angry," he replied, frankly and without malice. "Why don't you tell me what happened?"

Lucie suddenly felt it was right to unburden herself to an unknown priest beside a dusty country road. He listened patiently to her hurried outpouring of words, but he listened even more intently to what she didn't say.

"Dear child, may I ask your name?"

"Oh, of course. Lucie von Stetten."

"I am Father Stefano Serrano. It's my job to look into people's souls. I feel sure that, if old Anna were here, she would tell you what I'm telling you now: whatever happens, this day is a part of her destiny." Serrano saw Lucie struggling with herself. Suddenly and almost simultaneously, they both became aware that silence had fallen. No more shots could be heard.

Serrano smote his brow and jumped up. "By our Savior, why didn't I think of it sooner?" he cried. "What if the criminals have put Olivo and Pitti out of action too? Then you would still be in danger, Signorina Lucie. We mustn't stay here. Can you stand?" Although freckled with age, the hand he held out felt remarkably strong as he hauled Lucie to her feet without more ado. "We'll take my car and leave Alfredo's van here. I know of a little clearing farther along the road. We'll wait there." He took Lucie's arm and led her over to his car. The Fiat was several decades old but looked in excellent condition. Lucie squeezed into the passenger seat.

The little car puttered a couple hundred yards, turned off down a track flanked by conifers, and pulled up in a small clearing. They got out of the car. "I know a spot where we can get a good view of the road," said Serrano, and he set off through the trees, crouching low.

Lucie, who couldn't fail to notice the adventurous glint in his eyes, realized to her surprise that he was no stranger to this unusual form of activity, namely, creeping up on people unobserved. It wasn't in keeping with the average routine of a country priest, but she got the impression that he relished the situation.

Halfway there, they heard a faint ringtone. "That's a cell phone," said Lucie.

Father Serrano halted abruptly and slapped his brow again. "By Saint Paul," he said, "I'll forget my head next. I acquired the thing very recently, and I simply can't get used to it." He hurried back to the Fiat and fished the phone off the backseat. After a moment he called to Lucie, "Thank God, it's Olivo, and all is well! Anna and Alfredo are safe." He handed her the phone with a little smile.

"Lucie, my girl," said Anna's voice.

"Thank God. Are you really all right, the two of you?"

"We're fine. Olivo said you had an accident."

"It's nothing. Alfredo's van isn't even scratched."

"Oh, I'm not worried about the van, girl. Take care of yourself and God bless you."

"You too, Anna. And thank you again for everything."

Serrano took the phone back. He listened for a moment. When he hung up, he told Lucie that Anna had asked him to drive up to the farm and pray with her. He wanted to wait until the ambulance arrived, but Lucie persuaded him to go at once. The ambulance would be there any moment, she said.

With a sigh, the old priest gave way. Lucie waited until he'd disappeared around the next bend, then hurried back to Alfredo's van and drove off in it. Her one thought now was to get home to her brother.

* * *

Ten minutes later, the radio started squawking in Olivo's patrol car, which was parked close behind the Mercedes SUV that had held the kidnappers' B team.

Unprecedented pandemonium reigned in the normally quiet and secluded farmyard. Still hysterical after all the gunfire, hens and geese were fluttering around the vehicles and the plastic sheet covering the body of the dead kidnapper. Sergente Olivo had kept an admirably cool head in all this chaos. Unlike his young colleague Pitti, who had sustained a flesh wound in the shoulder, he was unhurt. Driving the agitated birds in front of him, he went over to his car and grabbed the chattering radio.

The puzzled caller was the ambulance driver, who had arrived at the stated location and looked around in vain for an injured young woman. What was he to do now?

Olivo immediately jumped to the right conclusion and inquired after Alfredo Sassi's delivery van, but that too had disappeared.

He accepted the inevitable, not having the time or personnel to follow the young woman, whose statement he needed for his report. He would worry about that later. At least he had statements from Anna and her son. He instructed the ambulance to come to the farmhouse so that the paramedics could attend to his colleague Pitti and the two crooks in custody. One of them was in a really bad way, and the other—thanks to Anna's marksmanship—had a bullet lodged in his thigh. Anna and Alfredo themselves had gotten away without a scratch.

In the living room of Lukas and Lucie's Via dei Coronari apartment there was more noise and turmoil than at any child's birthday party, though the atmosphere was not as festive.

Heinrich von Stetten had arrived in Rome shortly after Rabea and Lukas got back. The patriarch, who had a poor opinion of the Italian authorities and had no intention of continuing to entrust his daughter's safety to them, had brought his own security chief, an Englishman and former SAS officer named James Fonton, plus several of Fonton's team. When he saw how crowded the apartment was, Fonton sent two of his men downstairs to wait in their car.

What with Superintendent Grassa, Father Simone, the little attorney Carlo Pierangeli, and the inescapable Professor Carlotta van Kampen, who sat enthroned on the sofa like a large pink elephant, a total of ten people were herded together at very close quarters. The room was oppressively hot. Diverse though the members of this motley company were, concern for Lucie was the thing that united them all. They were trying to compensate for their collective impotence by speculating wildly in German, Italian, and English. They talked and talked without really saying much. All were so engrossed in their respective conversations that none of them noticed a figure standing in the doorway with Stellina in its arms, listening in amazement to the babble of voices that filled the air. Odd words could sometimes be distinguished.

"If anything happens to Lucie," Heinrich von Stetten announced in German, controlling himself with an effort, "I'll pursue the cowardly swine to the ends of the earth . . ."

"Now might be the right time for a prayer. Hope is balm for the soul," Father Simone's bass voice purred in Italian. He directed his comment to Lukas and Rabea, who were standing at the window deep in conversation, as he draped his arms around their shoulders. This interruption earned him a thunderous look from Rabea, who seemed to think that prayer would be the last thing on her agenda at this moment.

"Gentlemen, gentlemen, not so loud," Professor Van Kampen called in stentorian tones, "or we may not hear the phone."

Meanwhile, Superintendent Grassa was barking into his cell phone and taking out his frustration on some wretched subordinate.

The person in the doorway called out, "Seems like quite a party. Am I invited?"

The surprise was absolute. Its effect was comparable to that of a hand grenade lobbed into the middle of a crowd. Like a multicellular organism whose links had been severed, everyone milled around.

Something clicked inside Lucie. She just had time to put the dog down before she was overcome by a paroxysm of laughter.

For a moment, some of those present clearly wondered if they were hallucinating. Then Lukas, Rabea, and Heinrich von Stetten converged on Lucie, nearly hugging her to death in their relief. In order to get some air, she eventually had to extricate herself from their loving embrace.

Rabea was sniffing and sobbing with abandon. Lukas and his father, who had feared the worst, were also weeping unashamedly.

"Thank God you're safe, my girl," said Heinrich von Stetten, struggling to regain his composure. He clasped her to him once more. Lucie, who had never seen her father in such a state, was profoundly touched.

Grassa pushed rudely past him and came straight to the point. "Signorina von Stetten, we're all extremely relieved to see you safe and sound. I—that's to say, all of us—would like to hear your story. What exactly happened?" Something seemed to have thoroughly blighted Grassa's luxuriant flower garden of pleasantries.

What Lucie didn't know was that her father had already pulled some strings, and that less than an hour ago, Grassa had a rather one-sided phone conversation with Italy's Minister of the Interior, who was furious. The latter had brusquely demanded that Grassa produce some quick results, or else . . . Grassa could well imagine what the "or else" would mean for his career.

At this point, Carlotta van Kampen intervened. Her bulky figure parted the group around Lucie like Moses parting the Red Sea. Thrusting everyone else aside, she draped a muscular arm around Lucie's shoulders and applied pressure, almost asphyxiating her, then towed her vigorously over to the living room door. "Really, Signore Grassa, what a boorish fellow you are," she snapped. "Can't you see the girl's quite hysterical and needs rest? What do you think you're doing, pestering the poor dear like this?" And she swept out with defenseless Lucie in a kind of armlock.

Rabea followed them into the bedroom, grimly determined to get rid of the Dutch woman as soon as possible. Lucie might be in a bit of a state, but she certainly wasn't hysterical. Professor Van Kampen's obtrusive presence was driving them all up the wall. Lukas and Rabea had only just returned to the apartment when she bore down on them in the hall like a frigate under full sail. Since then they'd been at great pains to avoid her and her incessant questions. Getting rid of her seemed to be just what Lucie wanted, judging by the look of entreaty she'd given Rabea when suddenly captured by her.

Thwarted, Grassa glared after the three women. He had to conduct some inquiries, after all, and Lucie was his principal witness. In search of help, he turned to Heinrich von Stetten, whom he acknowledged as the supreme authority in the room next to himself.

Von Stetten laid a hand on his shoulder. "Professor Van Kampen is right, Superintendent," he said. "Be patient. My daughter has been through a great deal today. I realize that your prime concern is to catch the perpetrators. Believe me, there's nothing I want more than to bring them to justice, but give my daughter time to recover. I should also be obliged if you would see to it that a doctor takes a look at her."

Elegantly outmaneuvered and temporarily entrusted with another task, Grassa sent for a doctor, then went to the apartment next door to check on the progress of inquiries into the contessa's murder.

With Grassa gone, Heinrich von Stetten beckoned to his head of security. "Fonton, don't let my daughter out of your sight from now on. I want her guarded by two of your men at all times."

Fonton nodded imperturbably. He'd been accustomed to receiving orders for over twenty-five years, first from his superior officers in the army and since then from his employer of eight years' standing. He transmitted the order to his men, who left the room at once. One of them took up his post at the front door, the other in the hallway immediately outside Lucie's bedroom.

Father Simone, ever practical, offered to get some refreshments and disappeared into the kitchen. Lukas, who was anxious for a private word with him, followed. While his friend was checking the contents of the refrigerator and cabinets and ruefully shaking his head at their vacancy, Lukas got busy with the espresso machine.

"What's on your mind?" Simone asked with his head in the fridge.

"I forgot myself today and did something unpardonable."

In Lucie's bedroom, Rabea was trying to bid the Dutch woman a tactful goodbye. "We're very grateful for your help, Professor Van Kampen, but we can manage on our own now. Lucy needs rest, as you say. She'll call you tomorrow, when she's feeling better."

"I wouldn't dream of leaving the poor girl alone with that ghastly man Grassa, not when she's so upset." Ignoring Rabea's broad hint, Van Kampen took hold of a button on Lucie's blouse. She evidently planned to undress her like a little girl. Lucie gave Rabea a please-do-something look.

Rabea, who decided that diplomacy wasn't her forte after all, linked arms with the big woman, thanked her again for her help, and hauled her to the front door like a small tug towing an ocean liner.

Obviously unused to such unceremonious treatment, Van Kampen was so taken aback she submitted to it without protest. Before she could utter a word, she was out on the landing and the front door had already shut behind her.

"Phew!" Rabea blew a strand of hair out of her eyes. "That's that." To her surprise, she heard a faint growl and looked down to see Stellina at her feet. The little dog clearly shared her aversion to the Dutch woman. Rabea headed back to the bedroom.

"She may be an eminent authority," Rabea said to Lucie, "but don't you find her a bit too pushy?"

"Oh, Carlotta's not so bad. She means well, believe me. She worries about me. And she's a first-class teacher. I'm learning a lot from her."

"Maybe, but Stellina can't stand her. She growled at her."

"Really?" Lucie cast a thoughtful glance at the dog, which was just making itself comfortable on her bed. "It's true she can be a little tiring sometimes," she conceded at length, clearly more open to trusting the dog's instinct than her friend's. Then she had another thought. "But now I'd like to know why you look like a cat that's just won a lifelong supply of tuna."

Rabea gave a little start. "What do you mean?"

"Come on, you can't fool me. Spit it out."

"You really are one of a kind, Lucie." Rabea shook her head incredulously. "You're kidnapped and come home covered in scratches and with a face like a patchwork quilt, and all that interests you is why I'm looking happy. I'm happy to have you back safe and sound. How else should I look?"

"Sure, but because I've been having such a lousy time, I badly need some good news. I won't take a shower—I'll stink the place out—until you tell me what's going on between you and Lukas."

Congratulations, thought Rabea, impressed. If that wasn't further proof of the mutual empathy between twins!

"You've no need to flutter your eyelashes in that innocent way," Lucie persisted mercilessly. "I'm listening . . ."

At the same time in the kitchen . . .

"I'm listening," Simone repeated, regarding Lukas keenly from beneath his bushy eyebrows. When Lukas still said nothing, he growled, "Well, well, something unpardonable, was it? Then let me guess. I'll just say a five-letter word: *Rabea.*" He added, "Frailty, thy name is man."

Lukas visibly quailed. "You're right, Simone, I completely lost my head today. I think we were attacked by the man who murdered my uncle and Bentivoglio. He tried to shoot me, and Rabea was forced to kill him with a fireplace poker. She saved my life—the bullet only grazed my skull." Mortified, he pointed to the Band-Aid on the back of his head. "We were pumped full of adrenaline and had just survived a murderous attack. It simply happened." His voice had grown steadily quieter toward the end.

Simone screwed up his eyes and glowered at him. "Ah, I understand. You don't dare say it out loud. By all the saints!" he roared suddenly. "Nobody knows what God looks like, but believe me, I know he has *very* big ears. Don't be bashful. You can say it out loud. It's written all over your face, my friend. The two of you fell on each other like hungry wolves."

Lukas drew in his head like a tortoise.

In the bedroom . . .

"My God, Lucie, we were out of our minds. We simply tore the clothes off our bodies."

In the kitchen . . .

"It was terrible, Simone. I seemed to lose control of my senses, my actions. I felt intoxicated."

In the bedroom . . .

"It was wonderful, Lucie, just like the old days. The old intimacy was suddenly there again. It was as if we'd never been parted."

In the kitchen . . .

"I behaved like a wild animal, Simone. I find it hard to look her in the face."

In the bedroom . . .

"Lukas was so passionate. We couldn't get enough of each other."

In the kitchen . . .

"Don't glare at me like that, Simone! I realize things can't go on this way, and I have to think seriously about my future. Today has changed a lot of things. First, though, I must settle the Bentivoglio business, and for that I'll need your help. Please don't abandon me now."

In the bedroom . . .

"You've no cause to look so pleased, Lucie. Today hasn't changed a thing. Lukas and I had a spat immediately afterward. We're barely talking now."

"Bah, that means nothing," Lucie retorted gaily. "You always were that way. Some people need a postcoital cigarette; you two argue. So what? You love each other even when you're sore at each other. I know that, otherwise you wouldn't mind so much. My goodness," she went on, rolling her eyes, "what a fuss about nothing. You're grown-ups now, not teenagers. You ought to know what you want and, what's more important, how to get it."

"It isn't as simple as that, take it from me. Anyways, first we must get rid of this ridiculous murder charge and decipher Bentivoglio's riddle, then we'll see." Rabea stood up. "Well, now you know everything. Into the shower now, no arguments. I hesitate to tell you this"—she pretended to sniff her friend—"but you really do stink like a farmyard complete with a dung heap."

"No wonder." Lucie hopped off the bed and gave her a cheeky grin. "That's just where I've come from."

Lukas and Simone started when the kitchen door abruptly opened to reveal Superintendent Grassa with a cell phone in his hand. They felt instantly apprehensive.

"Signore von Stetten, I've just received an extremely interesting phone call. My men went to the address in Mergo given to us by Signorina Rosenthal and examined the house in question. Unfortunately, there was no sign of any body. How do you account for that?"

Lukas jumped to his feet. "But that's impossible. Both Signorina Rosenthal and I saw the man lying dead in the living room. He couldn't possibly have been alive. There was blood and . . ."

"Hmm, that's another curious thing, Signore Jesuit. My colleagues found no traces of blood in the living room, either on the floor or on the poker. Both had been wiped as clean as a baby's bottom. They did find two bloodstained shirts, some bloodstained cotton balls, and a tuft of fair hair in the bedroom. Oh, and by the way, I'm given to understand that a certain bed was found in a rather rumpled state." The superintendent grinned suggestively and looked at Lukas like someone whose poor opinion of Catholic priests and their extramural amusements had just been confirmed. He strode briskly across the kitchen and sat down immediately opposite him.

At a loss how to respond, Lukas sank back into his cane chair while Simone greeted Grassa's remark with a glare and a snort of indignation.

"Well, *Father*, I'm not in the least interested in where and how often you and Signorina Rosenthal get it on, being only an earthly authority. I think you'd better sort that out with your boss up above. I have three murders to solve. However, and this will really surprise you, I'm temporarily inclined to believe you and Signorina Rosenthal."

After this revelation, the superintendent sat back with a complacent air. Lukas looked confused.

"Ah, you're wondering why? The answer is simple: no one in your position, not even you, would be stupid enough to send the police to your love nest and confess to another murder. Corpses have been littering your route for thirty-six hours and your twin sister was kidnapped. You stubbornly deny any involvement, and then supply me with a fourth corpse for which you and Signorina Rosenthal claim to have been responsible, even though it can't be found at the stated location. Why in God's name would you do anything so stupid? There's something fishy going on here, and I'm going to get to the bottom of it. But I warn you, if this is just a diversionary tactic on your part, I'll find out. Then neither God nor your expensive lawyer will help you. I've already sent a forensic team to assist our provincial colleagues, but it'll be hours before their preliminary results are available. If there ever was any blood at the location you gave us, we'll find traces of it," the super-intendent said. "I went easy on you while your sister was missing"—he omitted to mention that this was on the orders of the Minister of the Interior—"but now I must ask you some questions. You know there's another warrant out for your arrest, and I could have you taken away at once, so think carefully before you answer. Although you were under house arrest, you and Signorina Rosenthal left the city this morning. By so doing, you risked forfeiture of your bail and immediate arrest. I know from your sister that Bentivoglio requested a meeting with you yesterday. What did he tell you just before his death, and why did you visit that house in Mergo?"

Before reaching the apartment in Rome, Lukas and Rabea had agreed to aim for maximum credibility by more or less sticking to the truth if questioned. They would, however, keep quiet about the most important thing of all: the contents of the safe-deposit box. The docu-ments had now been safely stowed away in another safe-deposit box in Rome, which Father Simone had rented on their instructions. Lukas had realized that they couldn't possibly turn up in Via dei Coronari with the scrolls or Grassa would promptly confiscate them as evidence. They still didn't know who their adversary was, and they couldn't run the risk that his arm might extend to the police.

So Lukas had called his friend Simone and given him the bare bones of the story and asked him to meet them outside a bank in the Centro Storico. The whole handover had taken less than two minutes. Rabea had had the idea of removing the scrolls from their leather cyl-inders and taking the latter with them in case the bank teller in Mergo testified that he'd seen her with them, but they wanted to try to with-hold them from Grassa for as long as possible.

Lukas had been very doubtful that they would manage to smuggle the distinctive leather sheaths into the apartment unobserved, but the hullabaloo when they arrived came to their aid. Although there were a lot of people outside the building and inside the apartment itself, the stairwell was deserted, so Lukas had stowed the sheaths behind a big vacuum cleaner in one of the wall closets on the stairs.

At Lukas's request, Simone had asked no unnecessary questions but dealt with the matter swiftly and efficiently. Just before Lucie's return, he had turned up at the Via dei Coronari apartment and surreptitiously slipped Lukas the key to the new safe-deposit box.

Lukas cleared his throat before answering Grassa. "As you know, Superintendent, Father General Bentivoglio was terminally ill. That was why he asked me to hear his confession in place of my uncle, Bishop Franz. After that, he gave me the key to a safe-deposit box with instructions not to open it until after his death. Its contents were not earthly treasures, he assured me, but documents pertaining to the church alone. We went to the bank today in hopes of finding clues to his murder."

"Oh, and it never occurred to you to share your knowledge and ask me to accompany you to the bank?"

"I couldn't do otherwise than I did—you've got to understand. It was Bentivoglio's express wish that I alone should access the contents. I had to swear to that on the Bible, and as a priest I'm bound by that oath."

Grassa looked as if he'd bitten into a lemon. "I guess you must have made an exception for Signorina Rosenthal, eh?"

Lukas, who couldn't think of a good answer, preserved an embarrassed silence.

Grassa planted his elbows on the table and propped his chin on his folded hands. "Who is this Bishop Franz, and why did you hear Bentivoglio's confession in his place?"

A shadow crossed Lukas's face. "My uncle, Franz von Stetten, was the bishop of Bamberg. He was also a close friend and fellow student of the father general's. He was murdered three months ago."

"Hmm." The superintendent appeared to turn this over in his mind. "Was his murderer caught?" he asked. When Lukas shook his head, Grassa continued, "It could be a coincidence, of course, but it could also mean that this whole business started three months ago. In any event, I shall investigate this and request your uncle's records from my German colleagues. Now, Father von Stetten, I think I've been patient long enough. What did you find in that safe-deposit box?"

The hour of untruth had come. Lukas recalled Rabea's admonitions. *Answer promptly, and look him straight in the eye. If you have to look somewhere, look to the left, never down and to the right. Look right and you're lying, look left and you're trying to remember—an experienced detective knows that. Keep your answers short and succinct and don't stray into elaborate explanations.*

"Nothing. The safe-deposit box was empty." The lie was out. He did his best to look straight into the superintendent's eyes.

Father Simone, who had no knowledge of secret service interrogation techniques, looked down and to the right in embarrassment.

"What do you mean *empty*?" Grassa snapped.

"There was nothing there. It was empty. Someone must have gotten there first. After all, Bentivoglio hadn't checked on it for thirty years."

"Good God, von Stetten, you really expect me to believe that story? It stinks to high heaven!" Grassa jumped to his feet and paced up and down the kitchen. At this point, Rabea's prepared text ran: *Believe what you like, Grassa, but it's the truth.* However, Lukas's outburst of criminal energy was exhausted, and he couldn't get it out. It remained stuck somewhere between his conscience and his vocal cords.

Grassa went to the kitchen door, opened it, and called to a policeman in the hallway, "Bring Signorina Rosenthal to me at once." He turned to Father Simone. "I spy a coffee machine. I wouldn't mind taking you up on your offer."

While Simone was busying himself with the machine, Rabea walked into the kitchen.

Grassa and Lukas both jumped up, and the superintendent gallantly pulled a chair out for her.

"How's Lucie doing?" Lukas asked anxiously.

"Remarkably well, physically as well as mentally. Her cuts and bruises aren't bad, and the doctor has just arrived. He'll examine her right away. Ah, Father Simone, just what I need." Rabea took the cup of coffee intended for Grassa and thanked Simone with a smile charming enough to make a polar bear sweat but completely wasted on the priest, who muttered something unintelligible and hid his crimson face in the refrigerator.

Rabea got the message at once: his best friend had already confessed to his terrible transgression. She was amused to think that Simone was probably crossing his fingers behind his back and longing for a return to the days when witches were burned at the stake. She turned to Grassa. "What can I do for you, Superintendent?" she asked, smoothing her hair back with both hands so that he could see she wasn't wearing a bra. This time, however, it failed to have the desired effect. Grassa refused to be distracted.

"Signorina Rosenthal," he said sternly, "this morning you and Father von Stetten went off to examine a safe-deposit box in a bank. According to him, he was given the key by the late superior general. He now alleges that the safe-deposit box was empty. What do you say to that?"

"What Signore von Stetten told you is correct. The safe-deposit box was indeed empty. We got there too late." Lithely, Rabea crossed her bare legs. Still unaware of the bloodstained knife in the trunk, she added, "If you don't believe us, search us and the car."

"We will, never fear. Will you also tell me which bank you visited? We shall check the truth of your statements on-site."

This was their Achilles' heel. She had signed a receipt confirming that she'd had access to the safe-deposit box. However, on the drive to Rome, she'd checked the crumpled counterfoil in her handbag and found it made no reference to the contents. She had merely confirmed in writing that the box was there—it might just as well have been empty. Given that the bank lobby had been quite gloomy and the clerk busy leering at her bare legs, she hoped he hadn't noticed the two leather tubes under her arm.

"You will see, Superintendent, that it's quite possible someone emptied the box before we got there. The bank is a very small provincial branch with no security precautions apart from the usual electronic door. Anyone with a key to a safe-deposit box can walk in there. I didn't even have to show a power of attorney. The lockers are in a small room off the main lobby with no CCTV. The locks are extremely simple and contain few tumblers—an amateur locksmith could pick them with the appropriate tools."

"You seem to know a great deal about security precautions and locks, Signorina Rosenthal," Grassa said sourly. "I don't believe a word of your story, but I can't disprove it for the moment. Kindly give me the key to your rental car. We'll have it forensically examined."

Rabea stood up and was fishing the key out of her hip pocket when the doctor summoned by Grassa put his head around the door.

Grassa jumped up at once. "Well, Dottore, how is Signorina von Stetten? May I proceed to question her?"

"Er, I didn't realize it was so urgent. Her father was most insistent, so I gave the signorina a sedative injection. She's fast asleep." The doctor sounded uneasy. It had just dawned on him that he'd inadvertently contravened the superintendent's wishes.

Grassa eyed him indignantly. "Well, since there's nothing I can do about it for the present . . ." He turned his attention to another target: Lukas.

"Thanks to your attorney and Signorina Rosenthal's confirmation of your story, I'll refrain from taking you into custody right away," said Grassa. "However, my men will remain here to ensure you don't run off on any more unauthorized excursions. I shall expect you at headquarters at nine o'clock tomorrow morning, together with your sister and Signorina Rosenthal, to take down your statements. Nine on the dot, understand?"

"Yes, of course," Lukas said hurriedly, relieved to be rid of him for the time being.

"Good. Dottore, a word with you!" With an imperious gesture, Grassa beckoned to the doctor to follow him out.

Father Simone, leaning against a kitchen cupboard, had been listening to the question-and-answer session, at first in amazement but then with growing disapproval. Once the superintendent and the doctor had left the kitchen, he drew himself up to his full, imposing height, marched to the door and, after checking the hallway, firmly closed it. That done, he slowly turned to face Lukas and Rabea, folded his arms, and glared at them ominously.

Lukas shifted uneasily on his chair while Rabea submitted her fingernails to an impromptu inspection.

"Well," said Simone, "that was an extremely interesting performance you gave, the two of you. What was the name of the play, *How to Lie Successfully to the Police*? Congratulations, it was star quality. I've asked you no questions, not what I had to deposit in a bank in double-quick time, nor why. I did it because I'm your friend, Lukas, and because you said I must trust you. I did so blindly, but now that I've unexpectedly embarked on a criminal career thanks to you two, I'm sure you'll agree that it's high time you gave me an explanation."

"Of course, Simone," Lukas said. "There simply hasn't been time until now."

Having concluded a full account ten minutes later, Lukas awaited his friend's reaction. Simone had sat down in the meantime and was thoughtfully twisting his bushy eyebrows. Without warning, he burst out, "By Saint Ignatius, now I need a drink! Any grappa in this place?"

"Right away." Lukas jumped up and returned with an almost full bottle. He poured Simone two fingers and watched him drain the glass at a gulp, then push it toward him for a refill. Lukas hurriedly complied, looking like a penitent schoolboy who hoped his teacher's expected reprimand would not be forthcoming after all.

"Well now," said Simone, when the second glass of grappa had gone the way of the first. He folded his big hands over his paunch. "What a mess! You're quite sure, Lukas, that the gang that kidnapped your sister was also responsible for the deaths of your uncle Franz, our father general, and your neighbor across the way?"

"Yes, and don't forget Grassa's detective. So far, this mysterious business has cost the lives of four innocent people—well, six counting Bentivoglio's secretary, Vallone, and his friend Cataldo."

"And all because of some old documents. What on earth have you dug up, you two? Satan's diary?"

"Not us, Simone, the father general," Rabea interjected. "Unfortunately, we still haven't had time to look at them."

"What? You mean you haven't read the documents at all?" Simone said excitedly. "Why not? If I understood Grassa correctly, that was your whole reason for going there this morning."

Lukas blushed to the roots of his hair, and Rabea discovered another fingernail that needed attention.

"I see. Well, then . . ." Simone mumbled, turning red himself. "What do you think is going to happen now?" he went on angrily. "You've just told the superintendent a pack of blatant lies. This isn't just a question of solving several murders—his career is at stake. The man is intensely ambitious. He won't rest until he's unearthed the whole truth, Lukas, and he'd love to put you behind bars. The safe-deposit box is the key to everything. And who, pray, is in possession of its allegedly nonexistent contents? You, Lukas. You're both out of your mind and in urgent need of an exorcism against stupidity. As soon as Grassa discovers the safe-deposit box wasn't empty—and for that he only needs the testimony of the bank teller in Mergo—you'll be in custody quicker than I can say a Hail Mary."

Rabea, who had completed her obligatory manicure, saw Lukas looking more and more browbeaten by his friend's tirade and felt it was time to intervene.

"It isn't as simple as that, Simone. Lukas only did what the father general asked, which was to take sole charge of the safe-deposit box and its contents. He had to swear that on the Bible. What would you have done in his place, Simone, ignore Bentivoglio's wishes and break a sacred oath? Which is more important, God or earthly jurisdiction? An oath sworn on the holy Bible or an unavoidable lie to a police superintendent?"

Rabea glared at Simone defiantly. He managed to withstand her green fire for exactly two seconds before lowering his eyes. He then reached for the slender bottle and, Adam's apple bobbing, treated himself to a third slug of grappa. Rabea found this an answer in itself.

"You see, Simone, all we did was bow to the force of circumstance. Besides, if the documents are what we think they are, they're worth a fortune. American software moguls are prepared to pay astronomical sums for ancient manuscripts. Bill Gates spent thirty million dollars on some original da Vinci texts. If Grassa had learned of the documents now, he would have fitted Lukas up with the classic motive for murder: greed. That's why we can't risk handing them over to an ambitious policeman. We must find out who's behind the murders first."

Although Simone said nothing, he signified his acceptance of her line of argument by pouring another glass of grappa and pushing it toward her instead of drinking it himself.

Rabea nodded and accepted his peace offering. She raised the glass to him and knocked it back—a mistake for someone who seldom drank spirits and who also hadn't eaten. Within seconds, her stomach felt vaguely queasy.

"Simone, what was that you said earlier about refreshments? Lukas says you can conjure something good out of nothing. Would you mind?"

"Of course, of course." He jumped up with alacrity.

Lukas noted with surprise that even his best friend wasn't immune to Rabea's charms.

"While I'm making a couple toasted sandwiches," said Simone, "perhaps the two of you would let me in on your plans?"

"Oh, sorry, no ham for me, thanks," Rabea told him. "Well, this is what I was thinking: Lukas is under house arrest and can't leave the apartment till tomorrow morning and then just for questioning, but we can move about freely. I'd like to go straight to the bank with you and fetch those documents from the safe-deposit box. Next, I plan to scan them and study them tonight. By tomorrow morning we should have some preliminary results that will clear Lukas and pacify Grassa."

"How do you propose to smuggle them past Grassa's guard dogs and into the apartment?" Simone asked.

"Oh, I won't scan the scrolls here. We'll go to your place, or rather, your brother's. Lukas told me he's away on vacation and you have a key to his apartment. Being a software technician, I'm sure he'll have all the necessary equipment there, including a scanner."

The look Simone gave Lukas could no longer be described as friendly. The two of them had cornered him—he couldn't back out. Fortunately, the grill's high-pitched beep announced that the first toasted sandwiches were ready. The kitchen was pervaded by the delicious scent of freshly toasted bread.

"Do you have any idea who could be interested enough in the documents to murder for them?" Simone asked as he passed them their sandwiches.

"We can only speculate. There are simply too many potential candidates, but I naturally have a few theories," Rabea said with her mouth full.

To Lukas, the word *theories* instantly sounded an alarm bell. It called to mind the drive to Mergo and Rabea's lecture on the Jesuits' alleged skulduggery. Simone wouldn't like that at all. He made a surreptitious attempt to warn her off, but she deliberately ignored it. "One thing's for sure," she went on. "The criminals' behavior indicates that they're aware of the documents' nature and value. Of course, we can't exclude the possibility that a gang of well-organized treasure hunters is behind the whole thing."

That sounded unwontedly innocuous by Rabea's standards, and was miles away from her usual conspiracy theories. Lukas was just breathing easier when she continued.

"However, I do have a theory that certainly won't appeal to you two." She sounded uncharacteristically hesitant. Lukas, accustomed to hearing Rabea provide her personal opinions on all and sundry without the slightest sign of diffidence, was filled with foreboding.

"I doubt if it could be worse than what I've already heard today," said Simone, who was inexperienced in the ways of Rabea.

"All right, let's approach this forensically. First the facts. One: the surveillance of this apartment with expensive electronic gizmos that aren't available on the open market. Two: ruthless murders that bear the unmistakable signature of professional killers. Question: Why has everyone who has so far come into contact with Bentivoglio's bequest been murdered? Who can afford to employ one or more professional hit men? But the most important question of all is: What prompted one of the leading members of the church's inner circle to hide the documents for over thirty years? There can be only one answer: they contain a dangerous secret—dangerous either to the Jesuits themselves or to the Vatican. Since Bentivoglio was the Jesuit in chief, it wouldn't be absurd to at least speculate that the Vatican has a prime interest in the documents."

Having linked the Vatican to a dangerous conspiracy and the murder of several people, Rabea calmly stood up and took a third toasted sandwich from Father Simone's hand before he dropped it, which he had shown every sign of being about to do.

Simone stared at her as if she were an apparition, his fat lower lip trembling with suppressed rage. Just when the silence threatened to snap like an elastic band, he erupted with the violence of a volcano.

"That's the most monstrous insinuation I've ever heard in my life. You dare to accuse the holy Catholic Church of these abominable crimes? Find some other dimwit to help you, not me!" He plucked the dish towel from his arm and hurled it onto the countertop. He was about to storm out of the kitchen when Lukas sprang to his feet and caught him by the arm before he could reach the door. He had never seen his friend in such a state, but then, Rabea had a regrettable knack for arousing violent emotions in people.

"Simone, please stay!" Lukas entreated. "You mustn't take that at face value. Rabea said it was only a theory. She's a journalist, don't forget. It's her job to suspect there's something sinister underlying everyone and everything. We need you, Simone. All we're interested in is the truth. Please help us to unearth it!"

His words had a noticeably calming effect on Simone. "Anger is a bad adviser, it's true," he said. "Of course I'll stay, if only to give this daughter of Eve a piece of my mind!" He glared at Rabea.

Anyone else would have been intimidated, but this particular daughter of Eve seemed wholly unimpressed. Still chewing, she regarded Simone from beneath her eyelashes. She loved provoking other people—making their blood boil and then placating them with a few well-chosen words. She wiped her mouth on a paper napkin, stood up, and stretched like a cat in the first sunbeam of spring.

Only then did she go over to Simone, rest her little hand on his shoulder, and say, "Mmm, that was good, Simone. Lukas was right when he told me you were the finest cook in Italy. You can turn even a simple toasted sandwich into a poem. He also said you've created a lot of your own recipes. Maybe you could put them together for me sometime, and I'll try to place them with some magazines. I know an editor who'd jump at a Jesuit cook. Well, now it's your turn. You ought to eat something too. Then you can tell us *your* theory."

Defeated, Simone gave in and let himself be led back to his chair like a little boy. "Very well," he harrumphed.

Welcome to the club! Lukas thought to himself. The little witch knew exactly which buttons to press to manipulate her victims at will.

Now it was Rabea's turn to take over the kitchen. "You too, Lukas?" she asked, brandishing a knife.

"Sure," he replied promptly.

"All right, friend Simone, what's your interpretation of recent events?"

Simone needed no second bidding. "In the first place, Rabea, there's a sizable snag to your theory. Why on earth should our father general have personally and at risk to himself preserved documents hostile to the church, when he himself was one of its most senior representatives? If they really are as dangerous to the church as you claim, it would have been logical for him either to destroy them or bury them in the innermost recesses of the Vatican's secret archives. Why all the palaver?"

"You're right, Simone." Rabea wiped some marinade off the counter. "Except that they may be hostile to the church or the Jesuits but not to the *faith*."

"Aha, Lukas, did you hear that? Now we're getting closer to the truth. Your sharp-witted friend draws a distinction between holy mother church and our order *and* the faithful. I can't wait for her to explain the difference."

Simone leaned back in his chair with a complacent smile. Rabea was poaching on his personal territory. He savored this theological tidbit even more than the delicious aroma of the toasted sandwich Rabea had just handed him. He could hardly wait to shoot her down in flames.

Lukas noted his friend's smug expression with an uneasy feeling in the pit of his stomach. He knew there was no holding Rabea back now.

If Simone thought he was going to spring a trap on her, he had failed to see that its jaws had long been poised to close on another victim.

"As you know," said Rabea, "nothing remains of the original four gospels of the New Testament. The very earliest copies date from the fourth century. However, there's now sufficient evidence that those copies were adapted to conform to the prevailing Roman ideology—in other words, censored. They were commissioned by the Roman emperor, Constantine, and jointly produced by bishops subservient to Rome at their first great council in Nicaea, Turkey, in 325. What would happen if authentic versions from the first century turned up two thousand years later? What if they confirmed that Jesus had a wife? I should add that it's wholly unimportant whether or not he was married because marriage doesn't necessarily make a man a good husband or an advocate of equal rights. It would be far more dangerous to the established church if it turned out that Jesus's only true bequest had been withheld from the faithful in favor of the sole supremacy of the Roman Catholic Church. I'd call that antichurch but not antifaith."

Father Simone greeted Rabea's exposition with a weary smile. She didn't seem too familiar with the material. *She probably couldn't even name the four Evangelists!* Besides, she'd given herself away. All that concerned her was the age-old question of priestly celibacy. That was the crux of it; she wanted Lukas for herself.

"My dear child, you really shouldn't concern yourself with things you know nothing about. I hardly believe the documents are writings relevant to the holy mother church or Christianity. If they're as old as you claim, they're more likely to resemble those from the caves of Qumran, which are attributed to the Essenes, a Gnostic sect. The Qumran scrolls are known to date from the first century but have nothing to do with our Savior. Among other things, they contain a complete copy of the book of Isaiah from the Old Testament—a copy, moreover, that's almost identical to the present book of Isaiah, which proves how accurately copyists have always worked. That accuracy would certainly have been observed when copying the gospels. No, I'm sure the criminals are just a well-organized gang of treasure hunters."

Lukas had been concerned by Simone's condescending "dear child," but he really felt a sinking feeling when Simone smugly told Rabea not to trouble herself with things she knew nothing about—Rabea, a walking encyclopedia who meticulously researched every subject she took an interest in.

With a saccharin smile, Rabea served them another toasted sandwich apiece and wiped her hands on a kitchen towel. "Shall I put another on?"

Lukas seized the chance to wave a white flag. He felt sure she would grasp the ambiguity of his reply. "No thanks, Rabea, that's quite enough." To make doubly sure, he gave her a look that begged her to spare his friend further punishment.

"Thanks, I'll have another. They're very tasty," Simone said approvingly. He sat back in his chair with an air of pleasurable conceit.

Rabea's mouth twitched in an almost imperceptible smile. Lukas knew what that meant: her main course may have been a toasted sandwich, but her dessert would be a Jesuit priest.

"It isn't quite as simple as that, friend Simone. Think for a moment. If they were merely harmless Gnostic texts, why would Bentivoglio have hidden them away for thirty years? Why set up such a conspiratorial meeting with Lukas? No, his behavior would be totally illogical. The documents must contain something dangerous—something that could compromise the Jesuit Order as well as the church. Would you grant me that much, Simone?"

The plump priest nodded reluctantly.

"Good. So back to my 'not antifaith' theory. As you know, the four gospels of Matthew, Mark, Luke, and John came into being between the two major insurrections in Judea in AD 66 to 70 and AD 132 to 135, but during the persecution of the Christians early in the fourth century, all the early Christian documents we know of were lost or destroyed.

Nearly five thousand copies originated at that time, but all of them, unfortunately, were produced by guardians of orthodoxy. That is to say, they were prepared in conformity with Rome in order to pave the way for a merging of the Romans' polytheism with the new, Christian monotheism."

At that point, Simone interrupted Rabea with a challenging question whose answer he already knew. "What does 'prepared in conformity with Rome' mean?"

Rabea took up the challenge. "In 325, Emperor Constantine ruled a Roman Empire already crumbling at the edges. In order to consolidate his authority, he was compelled to allow his subjects to practice the religion that had recently gained the upper hand: Christianity. He skillfully managed to cannibalize the original state religion, the Sol Invictus, or Invincible Sun, cult with the Christian religion, which was itself mingled with elements of Judaism: Jesus was a Jew and deeply rooted in Jewish tradition. For example, Christians would still be celebrating the Jewish Sabbath as a sacred day of rest if Constantine hadn't decreed that it be transferred to Sunday, the holy day of his own cult. Constantine never was a Christian—he remained faithful to Sol Invictus until he died. Early Christian leaders had to obey Roman orders to reinforce their authority. That's why the *Roman* governor of Jerusalem, Pontius Pilate, who ordered the Crucifixion of Jesus, gets off relatively lightly in the gospels. According to historically attested sources, he was in fact a venal drunk whose own superiors were later compelled to depose him for brutality. Amazingly, the Evangelists acquit him of responsibility for the death of Christ and put the blame on Jewish law. The story still peddled to this day is that the Jews crucified their own Messiah—a deliberate, deceitful lie! Our Jewish high council, the Sanhedrin, could only have condemned Jesus to death by stoning if found guilty. The cross was a uniquely Roman method of execution. It proves that Jesus was subject to *Roman* jurisdiction and a *Roman* sentence. On the grounds of Pilate's proven venality, I share the belief of many biblical scholars that Joseph of Arimathea, a wealthy Jewish citizen of Jerusalem, bribed Pilate so that he could place his own tomb at Jesus's disposal. In those days, no victim of crucifixion would have been entitled to a ritual burial. Some scholars even claim that Joseph and Jesus had concocted a dangerous plan to fake the latter's death on the cross. As many as five hundred crucifixions a day were taking place at the time, so it would have been hard to keep track. Joseph of Arimathea doesn't only appear in the gospels, by the way. He features in many legends including the Arthurian, where he's described as keeper of the Holy Grail. But to go back to the Council of Nicaea: that was where Jesus, who had hitherto been revered as a man, acquired divine status. Suddenly, 325 years after his violent death, Jesus ceased to be a normal, mortal Messiah and became a god! It was another piece of manipulation to accord with the wishes of Constantine, who wanted to amalgamate the Christian and Sol Invictus cults. The bishops invoked Saint John's Gospel, which is known to have originated 160 years *after* the death of Jesus. It speaks of him as the Son of God, admittedly, but putting the words in context, we learn that his message to posterity was this: *We are all children of God. Know yourself and you will discover the divine within you.* Jesus was a Gnostic and his message was Gnostic. *Gnosis* is Greek for "knowledge." Goodness comes from humankind, not from God! But the new Roman Christians now did to others precisely what had been done to them for 300 years: they persecuted all the Gnostics who adhered to the true message of Jesus, killing them and destroying their writings. No one is crueler than a victim of cruelty—sad, isn't it? But I'd better get to the point before I send friend Simone's blood pressure off the scale." Rabea had noticed his face growing redder. The only reason he'd restrained himself when she mentioned the possibility that the Crucifixion had been faked was that Lukas had laid a soothing hand on his shoulder.

"The fact is," she went on, "I got a little start on you because I was able to root around in Bentivoglio's notes during the drive back here. It's clear that one of the scrolls really is an original gospel from the first century. Bentivoglio even indicates that it almost triggered a grand conspiracy against the established church in the last third of the eighteenth century. And it seems that there may be a connection with the suppression of the order in 1773. If Jesuits were involved in such a conspiracy, it means that Bentivoglio had discovered the true reason for the order's suppression, and this would explain why he hid the documents. He also mentions a treasure—'the greatest treasure in Christendom,' are his exact words." Rabea looked at her watch. "Hey! It's getting late—past three thirty already. On your feet, Simone. Let's go, or the bank will be shut."

She jumped up and looked at him challengingly. Simone was so taken aback, he continued to sit there as if he'd taken root. Having mentally prepared what he considered a brilliant response to Rabea's blasphemies—for instance, that Jesus most certainly *had* described himself as the Son of God during his lifetime—he felt like a starving man whose meal had been whipped away at the last minute.

Lukas had to admire Rabea's tactics. In a very short space of time, she had not only rubbed his friend's nose in her interpretation of ecclesiastical history but also served them both up with a thoroughly audacious theory and then left it hanging in the air.

Simone cleared his throat, looking scandalized. "You know, Lukas, I must correct myself. I was wrong. Rabea is no daughter of Eve; she's the serpent itself. If Adam fell for her in paradise, how are you to resist? May God help you, because I certainly can't. I can't cope with her myself, as you can see. *Arrivederci*, Lukas, I'll call you later."

Rabea was already waiting for Simone in the hallway, her laptop stowed away in her crocodile handbag.

Lukas followed them as far as the front door, where a police sergeant marked the limit of his territory, and then watched them disappear into the no-man's-land of the stairwell. He felt uneasy letting them go off on their own.

Not wanting to join his father and the attorney in the living room, Lukas decided to see if all was well with Lucie. He exchanged a few words with the bodyguard outside, then cautiously opened her bedroom door.

The shutters were closed, and the room was in total darkness, but the light from the hallway showed him that his sister was curled up motionless in bed. She was breathing evenly. Stellina was keeping watch at the foot of the bed. Lukas sat down in an armchair beside the window and followed the dog's example.

The Protector's secure satellite phone rang.

"Yes?"

"The journalist and the fat priest have left the apartment. Shall we follow them?"

"Are they carrying anything? A big bag or a rucksack?"

"Not really. The woman has her handbag with her, that's all."

"Stay where you are. Von Stetten has the documents. The whole palazzo belongs to his family. There are dozens of places he could hide them from the police. Anything else?"

"Yes, in addition to the policemen on guard, there are five private goons in our way. Two upstairs in the apartment, three downstairs in a car. The old man brought them with him. We'll definitely need reinforcements for tonight."

"I'll see to it. Meanwhile, keep your eyes open."

Rabea and Simone got down to work as soon as they reached the apartment near the Trevi Fountain that belonged to Simone's brother Filiberto. Scanning the documents was a laborious task. Bentivoglio's notes amounted to more than fifty pages, each of which had to be placed on the scanner separately. While one of them was doing this, the other worked on translating the Latin notes.

Rabea had taken advanced Latin, but she was so rusty that Simone soon took over the translation himself. By tacit agreement, the Jewish atheist and the conservative Jesuit instituted a temporary truce.

Rabea treated herself to a break from the monotony of scanning and let Simone take over while she skimmed the documents from the deed box once more. Not all the envelopes contained endless columns of letters and numerals. There were also brief notes and receipts, some in Italian and many dated. She suddenly noticed that the scanner had fallen silent. Evidently unable to resist his curiosity any longer, Simone was examining the scrolls, which they'd removed from their leather sheaths.

Simone felt magically attracted to them. One of them seemed to give off an inexplicable warmth. He had unrolled it on his brother's desk with the greatest care, holding down the ends with his fingers. He didn't dare weigh it down with books for fear of damaging the ancient papyrus. The contents of the second cylinder, several rolls of younger parchment, were lying alongside it. The papyrus of the older scroll was far more brittle, and the writing faded but still legible.

"This is an Aramaic script," Simone said to Rabea, who had come over to him. "What's interesting is that the scroll appears to be original, whereas the second cylinder contained a dozen neatly written copies."

"It's a pity they copied it several times instead of producing a translation," Rabea said disappointedly.

"Yes, nothing's ever simple, is it?" sighed Simone. He eyed her covertly. Could she sense it? He had known as soon as he had touched the ancient document that the words on it were sacred.

"You mean you can't read Aramaic?" she asked.

He shook his head.

"Too bad. Then I'll go on looking. Maybe I'll find a translation."

Since almost all the documents were in code, the pile of encoded and presumably more interesting documents steadily grew. At last, Rabea came upon a detail that was not enciphered. It was a list of European universities with a note appended:

My dear brother in Christ, here is the list you requested of me.

She got out her laptop and looked up something on the Internet. That was interesting. The find reinforced one of her theories. She glanced at her watch: time for another call to Lukas. She had promised to call him every hour. Phoning was safe. They knew the Via dei Coronari apartment was bug-free, thanks not only to Superintendent Grassa but also to Lukas's father, who had insisted on having it scrubbed again by Fonton's team.

She dialed the number.

"Rabea!" Lukas sounded relieved. "Any news?"

"Not so far. We started with scanning Bentivoglio's Latin notes— most are already on the laptop. Simone is taking a preliminary look at the contents of the two cylinders. The scrolls are in Aramaic, and one of them appears to be very old indeed. Simone can't tear himself away from it, even though he can't read Aramaic. He's absolutely transfigured—you'd think he'd inhaled too much incense." She glanced at Simone with an amused smile, but he was so engrossed, he didn't even hear her remark.

"That's great," Lukas replied, but he was puzzled. Simone could indeed read Aramaic. If he felt the need to lie, he must have his reasons. What could they be? "Have you discovered anything else?" he asked.

"Yes, but only fragments. The documents are all jumbled together: letters, lists, receipts. It looks to me like someone cleared their desk in a hurry and stuffed everything into a bag quite indiscriminately. Much of it is in code. I have a program on my laptop that can crack the most common codes of the past four hundred years, so perhaps we'll be in luck. But I'll worry about that later, when we get back to the apartment.

One thing I can say, though: there's something odd about the stuff that isn't in code."

"How do you mean?"

"It's just a feeling. It reads too innocuously, like the boring drivel people put on postcards. It's as if they were reassuring each other that all was quiet on the western front. On the other hand, I did discover an interesting list of the European universities in existence around 1750. It could support my theory of a potential conspiracy against the Catholic Church toward the end of the eighteenth century. Let's say I'm a conspirator and want to spread an important message as quickly as possible. How do I go about it? I'd take a leaf out of Luther's book! He did it successfully over two centuries earlier, even though he didn't originally plan it that way. It was his students at Wittenberg University who duplicated his Ninety-Five Theses and circulated them. In those days, students were the surest and fastest system for disseminating information, almost like a nonelectronic precursor of the Internet. Without them and Gutenberg's printing process, which was invented a short while before, the Reformation could not have happened as it did. But let's wait until Simone has translated Bentivoglio's Latin notes. Then we'll know more. Is Lucie awake yet?"

"No, she's still fast asleep."

"That's good. Are you all right?"

"Yes, aside from the fact that I'm suspected of several murders. I'd give anything to be with you at this moment."

"Be patient. I estimate we'll need another hour. The scroll is hard to scan because of its size, and we have to handle it very carefully."

"Call me when you're through? Oh, just a moment, Lucie's bodyguard wants me for something. Don't hang up."

Rabea heard him talking with someone in the background, then he came back on the line. "There's someone at the door, apparently, but Grassa's man won't let him in. Call you later."

Rabea cautiously tackled the next document. The envelope was blank, like all of them, but she was astonished to find the seal still intact. She broke it open and withdrew a closely written sheet of paper. Suddenly, she turned pale. "Goddamn it!" she exclaimed.

Simone was jolted out of his preoccupation. "What is it? Found something?"

"Far worse. I forgot something important. In all the hullabaloo over Lucie's return, I forgot to warn Lukas a friend of mine was coming."

"What's so bad about that? Do they know each other?"

"Well, yes," she sighed. "Lukas broke his nose."

"In that case, he's got nothing to fear. Lukas, I mean."

"I must call him at once." She pressed the redial button. This time it was a while before anyone answered.

"Von Stetten residence." It wasn't Lukas.

"Rabea Rosenthal here. Who's this? Where's Father von Stetten?"

"Oh, please excuse me. Walter König here. I work for Herr von Stetten senior. We saw each other earlier. Father von Stetten is being patched up in the bathroom. There's been a bit of a scrap."

"What happened?" Rabea demanded breathlessly.

"A stranger came to the door and asked for you, Fräulein Rosenthal. The Italian policeman was reluctant to let the man in, but he insisted—said it was about Fräulein Lucie's kidnapping and that you'd asked him to come to Rome. We went and got Father von Stetten, and then it happened. The two of them seemed to know each other. Father von Stetten just said 'You?' when the man drew back his fist and punched him on the nose. It all happened very quickly. Now they're in the bathroom, as I said."

"What, both of them?"

"Yes. I heard the stranger say something like 'Now we're even.' Then he handed Father von Stetten a handkerchief because his nose was bleeding and helped him to his feet. They disappeared into the bathroom after that, but don't worry, everything's quite peaceful. The stranger told me to bring some ice cubes from the fridge—they're melting. If that's all, I should take them in there."

"Please ask Father von Stetten to call me back, all right? Thanks." Rabea closed her cell phone, looking thoughtful. The stranger was Jules, of course. Typical of him to sock someone and then minister to him.

Lukas called ten minutes later. "Rabea? You wanted me to call you back?" His voice sounded rather nasal.

"Oh, dear, Lukas," she said meekly, "it's all my fault. I didn't have the chance to tell you Jules was coming. Does it hurt a lot?"

"I'm becoming used to looking like Rudolph the reindeer."

"How are you getting on with Jules?"

"We've had a nice talk. I now know you never had an affair, and I apologized to him for behaving like an absolute idiot. When this Bentivoglio business is over, we'll talk about everything." Lukas sounded subdued.

"It was my fault, Lukas—my stupidity and pride. I should have told you the truth about Jules long ago, but I was so terribly angry with you, and I wanted you to be jealous. I wanted you to feel as lousy as I did after listening in on your phone call to Uncle Franz."

"But . . . I don't quite understand," Lukas stammered uncomprehendingly. "What do you mean? What phone call?"

"It was soon after our vacation together—those four days beside Lake Garda, remember?"

How could Lukas ever have forgotten the happiest days of his life? Donna Rosa's romantic little boardinghouse right beside the lake? Rabea and he had seen little of the unspoiled little town and its old castle—they'd seldom left their room, or their bed.

On the day of their departure, they'd quarreled over something trivial at the breakfast table, with the result that they barely exchanged a word on the drive home to Nuremberg. Lukas had dropped Rabea at her grandparents', and she'd swept off without saying goodbye. Two days after that was the last time he had seen her—until yesterday.

"The next day," Rabea went on, "I noticed that I'd left my camera in your glove compartment and went over to your parents' house. Frau Gabler let me in. I didn't want to bump into you, so I was sneaking along the hallway to pinch your car keys when I heard you on the phone to Uncle Franz in your father's study. You told him our vacation had helped you make up your mind, and you'd come to a decision. Peering through the doorway, I saw you wave a bunch of papers in the air and then put them on the desk. I crept in after you'd gone and found the entrance forms for the Jesuit seminary. You had decided against me and in favor of the church. If it had even been another woman, but the church . . . It broke my heart. I was determined that you should never learn how much you'd hurt me, so I went to Munich to weep on Jules's shoulder. Jules and his boyfriend, René—he was the one who let you into the apartment—had moved to the living room couch, giving me their bed. The next thing I knew, poor Jules went sailing across the room, and you were standing over the bed looking down at me with that terribly wounded expression. You thought Jules was my lover, and that I'd consoled myself with him. I knew then that you were suffering as much as I was, and that's why I never cleared up the misunderstanding. Why should I have? After all," she concluded resignedly, "you'd abandoned me to become a priest."

An alarming silence prevailed at the other end of the line. Then Lukas heaved a sigh. "Oh, Rabea, we're the dumbest sheep in God's flock. We tore each other to shreds for no good reason and then out of false pride took refuge in the wrong way of life. I'd called Uncle Franz to tell him that I *wasn't* going to enter the seminary because I wanted to marry you. *That* was my decision, and he accepted it. Damn it all, Rabea. I'd already bought a ring and was planning to bear you off for a romantic picnic that evening, but when I got to your house, your grandmother told me you'd gone away. The next morning I called Lucie in Egypt, and she thought she knew where I might find you. I just can't take it in, Rabea. So much sorrow and suffering for nothing. Why didn't you come and see me before you ran off?" he cried. Then, because she didn't speak, "Rabea?"

"I'm still here, Lukas." Rabea's voice seemed to come from very far away. "Oh my God, what have I done to us, what have I done to *you*? All these lost years! I cheated fate. Why do I always have to wreck everything? I don't deserve you. If you want nothing more to do with me after this Bentivoglio business, I'll understand. I'll disappear from your life for good, I promise. Perhaps you'll be able to forgive me sometime." She sounded drained.

"You think we'd be better off if you did? After what happened at your friend's house today? No. Besides, didn't we discuss this subject long ago? 'Love means never having to say you're sorry,' remember?" he said, quoting from *Love Story*, her favorite movie.

"No, Lukas, I don't deserve your absolution. I've wrecked our lives," she replied miserably. She fended off his forgiveness. No one could be guiltier than her.

"Don't start all over again and make the same mistake twice," Lukas told her gently but firmly. "Leave the past alone, Rabea. We weren't just lovers, remember, we were good friends as well. That bond will be between us forever. Let's concentrate on the present—it's exciting enough. All right?"

"All right, but it isn't quite as simple as that." Rabea reflected that she was carrying an additional, unpardonable burden of guilt, but she temporarily lacked the courage for another confession. Besides, some throat clearing on Simone's part reminded her that she wasn't alone.

"Trust me, Rabea. We'll talk about everything in due time. First things first. Have you discovered anything?"

"Yes, a sealed envelope. It obviously never reached its destination or was never sent. The coat of arms is the same as the one on the pocket watch. I've compared the handwriting, and it strikes me that the writer must also have compiled some of the coded columns of figures. He was certainly the author of the mysterious list of universities. Listen, this is what he wrote:

Dear brother in Christ Francesco, greetings,

Do not be surprised at the bringer of this missive, a Dutch merchant. He is not in the know and must be duly recompensed. I write to you in great haste. I believe the enemy is on our track. If you hear no more from me, I beseech you to continue our work on your own. Remember what we swore to each other on the day of Saint Ignatius.
The church is nothing without faith and the faithful.
Farewell, my brother. I entrust our sister, Emilia, to your care. We shall see each other again in another life.

Your brother, Emanuele"

Rabea waited in vain for some reaction. "Well, what do you think?" she demanded impatiently. "It was clearly written by one priest to another, and they seem to be in deep water. At last, we've got some names we can work with. Looks like an interesting lead."

"It is interesting, but let's talk about it when you get back."

"Sure. Can you pass the phone to Jules?"

A moment later, her ear was filled with Jules's powerful, French-accented baritone. "Hello, Rabea. I was glad to hear that Lucie is safe. Lukas says you're both up to your eyes in new adventures. Now that I'm here, is there anything I can do to help?"

"Hi, Jules. Sorry you bumped into Lukas right away, but I gather you settled the matter in accordance with your own sense of justice," she said teasingly.

"Oh, unpaid bills are a bad thing. They pile up and bar your path to paradise. But everything's fine now—the father and I are the best of friends. When are you coming? Or should I come to you?"

"No, better stay there. We'll come as soon as we're through. I must get back to work; Simone's already looking quite reproachful. Wow, that Jesuitical stare—it's like a death ray! Shalom, see you later." Rabea had taken refuge in flippancy as usual. She did not want anyone to know what was going on deep inside her, and how ashamed she felt about what resentment had made her do.

"No jokes about death, even in fun," Jules told her reprovingly, but she'd already hung up.

THE GOSPEL
OF LOVE

The Protector sat at a paper-strewn desk in a palazzo in the diplomatic quarter of Rome. Although the Protector showed no outward sign of fury, inwardly, it was in a state of extreme agitation. After more than twenty years of devoted effort and research, all of which had cost a fortune, the Protector had succeeded in finding out who was in possession of the documents. It had been so close to its objective—revenge had been within its grasp—and then everything had gone wrong.

The electronic surveillance had been amateurish and far too quickly detected, and the kidnapping thwarted by the victim herself. Two good men arrested, another dead. Even the ever-reliable Gabriel had failed for the first time. Seated across the desk with a bandage around his head, Gabriel looked contrite.

The Protector knew the sadist's remorse was a charade. Gabriel was acquainted with only two emotions: hatred and pleasure, which he derived only from inflicting physical pain on others.

The Protector did not know that another mistake had been its own: giving the orders not to follow Rabea and Father Simone when they left the apartment and instead depending on keeping Lukas von Stetten under surveillance. It had relied on its informant at police headquarters, who had said the supposed documents had been found neither on the young priest nor confiscated, so he must somehow have managed to smuggle the scrolls straight past Grassa and hidden them somewhere in the apartment. The Jesuits were too damned smart. Bentivoglio had kept the secret under wraps for decades. Why should young von Stetten be any less cunning?

The Protector had run out of patience and could wait no longer. It had flown its best men in from all over Europe. The final plan was as risky as it was simple and diabolical: once the men guarding the von Stettens had been eliminated, the twins would be captured. Then Gabriel would torture Lucie before her brother's eyes until he voluntarily surrendered the documents. The threat alone would probably be enough to sway the young Jesuit.

"Get out of my sight, Gabriel! And don't disappoint me a second time!" the Protector said ominously.

"Ma, che cavolo!" Father Simone burst out suddenly, glaring at the scanner.

Rabea looked up with a smile. Simone had just invoked a cabbage.

"Something's gone wrong with the scanner; all it's producing now is black images. As a layman, I'd say a fuse has blown, or something. Sorry, I'm afraid I can't go on. The thing needs repairing."

"There's bound to be a computer store somewhere nearby. I'll try googling." It didn't take Rabea long. "Here, I've found one near the Colosseum." She dialed the number on her cell phone, described the problem, and pretended she needed the scanner urgently for her doctoral thesis. Could a technician be sent over right away? Not possible, said the manager; he was alone in the store. But he suggested she bring the machine in for a diagnosis within the next hour.

"I'll go," said Simone.

Rabea called Lukas briefly to tell him about their technical glitch, which would delay them considerably. They wouldn't be back before 9:00 p.m., she told him.

Impelled by curiosity, she sat down at the desk in Simone's place. His excitement over the scroll hadn't escaped her. Gingerly running a finger over the ancient characters, she was abruptly aware of a strange but pleasant sensation of warmth. She had been feeling bad since her phone conversation with Lukas and their mutual confessions, but all at once, she was filled with renewed confidence. As she brushed the hair out of her eyes, the pencil she'd stuck behind her ear fell to the floor. Bending down to retrieve it, she spotted a sheet of paper protruding from a drawer. She quickly compared the handwriting with another page of Simone's notes. It looked as if he had already embarked on a translation of the scroll, but why had he hidden it from her in the drawer? And why had he pretended not to know Aramaic? Her hands started trembling almost as soon as she began to read. She now understood Simone's shining eyes! What she read was so unique and sensational that she could hardly wait to show it to Lukas. It was so wonderful that her wounded soul absorbed the healing words like a sponge.

Having already transferred the scanned documents to her laptop, she synchronized all the data on her smartphone as well. Then she redevoted herself with fresh courage to the documents on the floor. Picking up a crumpled sheet of paper, she smoothed it out. It was an old receipt dated from the end of 1774. Suddenly she stopped short, her freckled face on fire. A name had caught her eye: Leysieffer, and she knew she'd heard it in some other context. She remembered the source of the name even before she'd fed it into her laptop. "Shit!" she exclaimed. She'd been wrong—it wasn't the Vatican that was after these documents. She owed Simone an apology.

Some rapid research on the Internet confirmed her suspicions, and she called a colleague at her old editorial offices in Berlin who owed her a favor, and asked him for some additional information that was unobtainable on the Internet. Fifteen minutes later, he called her back. Rabea now had an address. She typed it into her laptop at once. The first thing that came up was a property advertisement. The building had recently been put on the market. The bird was preparing to fly the coop!

So that Simone wouldn't worry about her disappearance, she left a message saying she would call him on the way. Then she pocketed the slip of paper bearing the address and set off. It was shortly after 8:00 p.m.

Whistling to himself, Father Simone came pedaling around the corner on his old bike. He was just about to open the front door of the apartment house when something caught his eye. In the midst of a group of tourists, he thought he glimpsed a slender, rapidly receding figure in denim shorts and a white blouse. Then, in the glow of a streetlight, he saw an auburn braid swinging to and fro. So it *was* Rabea, but where was she off to? Not to Lukas, anyway, because she was heading fast in the opposite direction. What was he to do? He had to decide.

He heard one of his brother's neighbors coming down the steps. Thrusting the repaired scanner into the hands of the bewildered young man, he said he would pick it up later and hurried off down the narrow street in pursuit of Rabea. He swiftly caught up—they were separated only by a few tipsy English tourists—and was about to make his presence known when he suddenly decided it was rather fun to shadow her. It couldn't hurt to see where she was headed.

They got to the Via XX Settembre by way of several side streets. Passing the Porta Pia and the British embassy, Rabea turned into the Viale del Policlinico.

Father Simone, mopping his moist brow with a handkerchief, started to regret his hasty decision to tail Rabea. Not only had darkness fallen, causing him to almost lose sight of her several times in the dim street lighting, but he was handicapped by his corpulence and lack of cardiovascular fitness. At last, after a twenty-minute trek, Rabea seemed to be nearing her objective. Having crossed the Piazza della Croce Rossa, she made for the Via di Villa Patrizi, where Rome's diplomatic quarter began: quiet streets in which lonely mansions and grand palazzi led a secluded existence behind high walls.

Rabea neared an imposing, three-story eighteenth-century house on the edge of a wide expanse of greenery. It was in total darkness apart from one lighted window on the second floor. Nearly all the shutters were closed, and the façade was only dimly illuminated by streetlights.

Rabea strolled past the house, carefully keeping to the shadows. Then she retraced her steps and came to a stop immediately opposite it in a spot half-hidden by flowering oleanders. She eyed the ochre-yellow building intently. Each of the tall, round-arched windows was surmounted by a fierce-looking gargoyle, and below the roof ridge was a whole row of particularly ugly demons whose contorted faces were presumably intended to deter evil spirits. The house was enclosed by an eight-foot stone wall broken only by a pair of solid iron gates with CCTV cameras mounted on either side.

Rabea was so intent on the house that she failed to notice Simone until he tapped her on the shoulder. Startled, she spun around.

"Well, Mata Hari, are we spying on someone or just out for a romantic stroll?" Simone gave a self-satisfied grin. He looked immensely pleased with the success of his surprise.

"Damn it, Simone. Do you have to sneak up on people like that?"

"Yes, if you sneak off like this. Where are we, and why are we lurking in the bushes? What's so interesting about the person who lives here?"

"He's probably responsible for all our troubles. I came across a name in Bentivoglio's papers and did some research, *ecco qua*. Anyway, it isn't true that I disappeared without leaving a message. I left you a note saying I'd call you on the way." She instinctively felt in the pocket of her shorts and found it was empty. She hurriedly patted the other pocket. "Shit, I must have forgotten my cell or lost it. Damn!"

"Perhaps it slipped out of your pocket when you were spreading those papers out on the floor." Simone helped her look around for the phone in the grass at her feet, but without success. He straightened up. "That's enough botany. We'd better call Superintendent Grassa and get him to do the dirty work. After all, that's what the police are there for."

"Shh, not so loud," Rabea whispered. "I'm still not a hundred percent sure. I'd like to look around a bit first." She produced a pocketknife and operated a mechanism with her thumb and forefinger. Out sprang a miniature picklock. Jules had given her the tool some years earlier.

Simone stared at it aghast. "What do you mean, look around a bit? Surely you don't intend to break in?" he asked with a hint of panic in his voice.

"Take it easy. Let's just wait and see for the moment, okay?" Rabea could literally smell the fat priest's agitation—he was sweating profusely. He was beginning to get on her nerves, and she cursed herself for failing—for once—to note whether she was being followed. If she had, she would soon have spotted Simone and persuaded him to go back and carry on with the important task of translating the documents.

Only two vehicles had driven past the house since their arrival. Now a white delivery van appeared to be slowing down. "I think something's happening," she whispered.

Sure enough, several lights had come on inside the house, and the semicircular forecourt, which could barely be seen over the wall, was now lit by two lamps. The delivery van pulled up, engine idling, immediately outside the gates. Almost silently, they swung inward. The van drove in, and they closed again at once.

In the few seconds during which Rabea and Simone had an unobstructed view of the house through the open gates, they made out several men standing in front of the house. All were dressed in black and at least two of them had balaclavas pulled down over their faces in spite of the warm night.

Simone hunkered down on the grass. "Well, I think you've proved your case, Mata Hari. Unless those gentlemen are going to a costume ball in the middle of August, I'd say they were up to no good. *Now* can we please call Grassa?"

Rabea felt almost sorry for him, but before she could reply, she was dazzled by the beam of a halogen flashlight. A male voice said, almost jocularly, "Well, well, what have we here?"

Rabea, who assumed it was a park attendant or policeman, quick-wittedly hurled herself at Father Simone, who was crouching down beside her, and bowled him over. Lying on top of the startled priest, she kissed him passionately in simulation of a courting couple—which would account for their presence behind a bush. She secretly gave thanks to whomever for the fact that Jesuits didn't wear monastic garb, but her bright idea was a failure.

"I must say, Fräulein Rosenthal, you lead an interesting love life. Earlier today with the handsome young Jesuit and now with another gentleman here in the park. That's enough, though. Come with me. Someone wants a word with you."

Rabea let go of Simone, who audibly gasped for breath and remained lying on his back like an overturned beetle. She found herself looking into the muzzle of an automatic pistol, which was rendered all the more ominous looking by the silencer attached to it. She was utterly astonished to recognize the man who was pointing it at her and smiling broadly.

"You?" she exclaimed incredulously. "The worms should have been at you by now. Your skull must be harder than granite."

"Not as hard as my dick, lady," purred Gabriel. "It takes more than a tap on the head with a poker to finish me."

"You know each other?" Simone demanded a trifle suspiciously.

"We met earlier today," said Gabriel. "Sorry to have deprived you of the pleasure of my untimely death, but that's enough talk." With a jerk of his gun, he shooed them across the street and keyed a four-digit code into the pad on the gatepost. The gates swung open.

Some wooden packing cases were stacked on the steps leading up to the front door of the house, and several men emerged from the house, carrying more packing cases. Just then, the gates opened again, and a black truck pulled up immediately behind the white van.

The present owner of the house really was in the process of moving. *But why?* Rabea wondered. It seemed illogical. They still hadn't attained their objective, which was to gain possession of the documents from Bentivoglio's safe-deposit box.

No one paid much attention to Gabriel and his two prisoners. Rabea, who had witnessed many preparations for military operations, was strongly reminded of the intense activity preceding a special-forces raid. Then another alarming feature caught her eye: one of the men was trying on a gas mask. Gabriel hurried them up the steps and into the house.

Rabea tried to catch a glimpse of the boxes' contents, but the lids were all nailed down and bore no inscription. The one thing common to them all was that they were adorned with neat black crosses. And from the strained look on the men's faces, they were heavy.

Gabriel herded them to the back of the entrance hall, which was two stories high. Half-hidden behind a fan palm was an elevator onto which he herded them. When the door closed on them with a faint hum and the elevator silently descended, the digital display indicated that they had stopped two floors down. The door slid open to reveal a long passageway with walls of rough-hewn rock punctuated at irregular intervals by steel doors. Neon tubes provided harsh artificial lighting.

Rabea heard Simone breathing heavily beside her. He was sweating like a suckling pig at a hog roast. She took his big, moist hand in hers and squeezed it. When he turned to her in surprise, she gave him an encouraging nod. She knew that nothing numbed the senses like fear, and they would need all their courage and intelligence for the coming encounter—Rabea thought she knew who awaited them at the end of the passage.

Gabriel gestured to them with his gun to walk on for a few yards, and then called, "Halt! Very touching, this hand-holding, but that's enough. Turn to face the wall and spread your legs, hands above your heads!"

Rabea, who was familiar with this procedure, did as she was bid. Gabriel searched them both very thoroughly. She trembled to see him take possession of Simone's bunch of keys. Then he opened the nearest steel door and pushed Simone roughly into an empty cell.

When she started to follow him, Gabriel grabbed her arm and hissed, "Not you." He locked the door of Simone's cell and led her to the cell next door. The heavy steel door clanged shut behind her, but even so, she was glad to be relieved of his presence for a while. The man had a way of looking at her that made her skin crawl to the roots of her hair. She was engulfed by total silence and a feeling of complete isolation.

Meanwhile, Lukas had been trying Rabea's cell phone and the apartment's landline almost every minute. Jules was sitting in the kitchen with him. Each had a mound of cold spaghetti in front of him.

"How far away is Simone's brother's apartment?" Jules asked.

"On foot, around twenty minutes."

"Right, then we'll wait another five. They could be on their way back. If they don't turn up, I'll go over there and make sure all's well." Lukas had briefed Jules on everything that had happened, from Bentivoglio's murder to Rabea and Simone's scanning operation.

"I'll come with you," he said spontaneously.

Jules raised his eyebrows.

"Yes, yes, Jules, I know I'm under house arrest, but I'll go mad if I have to sit around here idly any longer." Lukas jumped to his feet so violently that the chair fell over backward.

"Easy, Lukas! You'll only compound your problems if you leave here. If you're caught outside, you'll go straight to the pokey. I'll leave at once. We'll know what's what in twenty minutes at most."

Lukas grimaced in disgust, but he conceded that Jules was right. He described the route and watched Jules produce some useful items of equipment from his traveling bag. Apart from a pair of black leather gloves, they included a powerful halogen flashlight, a thin but extremely strong nylon rope, and an exact duplicate of Rabea's pocketknife with the built-in picklock. Last of all, he took an automatic pistol from the side pocket of his bag and stuck it in his waistband.

"How did you manage to smuggle that onto the plane?"

"No need. I called an old friend in Rome and met with him shortly before I came here. He lent it to me. I never go on an operation unarmed." Jules slipped off his brown moccasins and exchanged them for a pair of black sneakers.

"Incredible," Lukas said disapprovingly. "Everyone here seems to know someone with access to weapons. First Rabea and now you."

"Look who's talking," Jules retorted. "May I remind you of a certain German company that manufactures munitions?"

That hit home. Lukas promptly conceded. "After all that's happened so far, I guess it's only sensible to fight the enemy on equal terms." He accompanied Jules to the front door.

Grassa's man planted himself in front of it and eyed them suspiciously, but stood aside when Lukas said goodbye to Jules and stepped back into the apartment.

Lukas was faced once more with long, apprehensive minutes of waiting.

The Protector was seated in a subterranean chamber in which the walls were dominated by countless monitors. Most displayed deserted spaces and some the activities in progress in the forecourt, but the Protector was interested only in the two that transmitted pictures from the prisoners' cells. The male prisoner had sat down on the floor with his back to the rough stone wall and closed his eyes. His lips were moving in prayer. The Protector sneered contemptuously. The female prisoner was fiddling with her hair as she paced up and down her cell. Suddenly she came to a stop and stared straight at the tiny lens of the minicamera embedded in the wall between two blocks of rough-hewn stone. So she knew she was being watched.

Someone entered the room. Without turning around, the Protector asked, "Where did you pick them up?"

"In the park across the way."

The Protector glanced at a platinum wristwatch. "Hmm, we must find out how they discovered this address and what else they know. Tonight's operation must not be compromised, not for anything. Did they have a cell phone with them?"

"No, neither of them. I searched them thoroughly."

"Search the place where you found them again. I don't want any surprises. They may have informed someone first, or their phones could have been tracked. After that, bring them both here, but gag and blindfold them."

Ten minutes later, Gabriel reappeared with the two prisoners. He had gagged and blindfolded them, and handcuffed their wrists behind their backs. Taking them roughly by the shoulder, he thrust them down onto two chairs.

Absolute silence prevailed for a while. Being deprived of sight, the prisoners registered every little sound. They could detect that someone apart from their captor was also in the room. That someone stood up and walked slowly around them.

The Protector deliberately intensified their feelings of helplessness by leaving them in a state of uncertainty. Using a voice modifier, the Protector finally spoke.

"Well, well, if it isn't Rapunzel and Friar Tuck. You've already made the acquaintance of my friend Gabriel, so let's not beat about the bush. Gabriel is an expert personal information gatherer. There's no pain barrier he hasn't crossed. Tell me what I want to know, and I'll let you go—though my friend Gabriel would be deeply disappointed if you talked without his assistance. Where are Bentivoglio's papers?"

With a jerk of the head, the Protector instructed Gabriel to remove Rabea's gag.

"Let my companion go," Rabea said immediately. "He doesn't have anything to do with this business. He's a nobody."

Father Simone drew himself up and grunted indignantly.

The Protector ignored him. "Answer my questions and don't waste my time! Where this priest is concerned, I don't believe a word you say. The man's a Jesuit, and they're the worst of the bunch. They're God's jackals!"

"I'm no fonder of papists than you are, but this one really is harmless. Let him go, and I'll tell you what you want to know. What do you say? Do we have a deal?"

Simone, who had grown more and more restive, stamped his foot angrily.

Rabea couldn't see him, but she registered the vibrations of his anger. Didn't the idiot realize she was trying to save him?

But the Protector was undeceived in any case. "I think our brother here would like to tell us something. What does Rapunzel say to that? Shall I remove his gag, or do you want to continue your fairy tale?"

The Protector nodded to Gabriel to remove Simone's gag.

The Jesuit gasped and seemed about to hyperventilate.

"Simone, hold your tongue, we . . ." Rabea said loudly, but she got no further. Gabriel slapped her face so hard that she would have fallen over complete with chair if he hadn't caught hold of her. Her mouth filled with the metallic taste of blood.

Simone had indignantly risen from his chair at the sound of the slap, but his attempt to intervene was promptly checked by Gabriel, who hit him on the head with his pistol butt.

"That's enough," decreed the Protector. "Our guests are not in agreement, I gather. Gabriel, take feisty Friar Tuck to the TC as arranged. Have fun, you two," it added in an amiable, conversational tone of voice, as if Gabriel and Simone were off to a party.

Gabriel's face broke into a diabolical grin. The Protector's order was exactly what he was hoping for. Simone, a rivulet of blood trickling down his forehead, was grabbed by the arm and yanked off his chair. Stumbling along in Gabriel's grip, he turned in Rabea's direction once more as if to say something, but his gag had been replaced.

"Chin up, Simone," Rabea called after him. "Everything'll be okay."

She heard a drawer being opened, then shut again.

"What is Gabriel going to do with Father Simone? What does TC mean?"

Before the Protector could answer, someone else entered the room and whispered something Rabea couldn't hear. Then the sound of receding footsteps told her that, for the time being, she was all alone with her profound concern for Simone.

* * *

Dragging the handcuffed priest behind him, Gabriel kicked open another steel door and paused briefly to remove the prisoner's blindfold and gag. In the light streaming into the chamber from the brightly illuminated passage, all Simone saw at first was that the floor, walls, and ceiling were bare rock. It was like being in a dark, menacing cave.

Gabriel pushed Simone roughly up against the wall. "Don't budge," he commanded. Lighting a torch, he used it to ignite others until the chamber was bathed in a flickering glow.

Each torch seemed to cast another dark shadow of fear across Simone's soul. Since he was fourteen and Crucio's gang had beaten him up and burned him with cigarettes until he told them where his brother Sebastiano was hiding, he had known that God would someday call him to account. Three days after his betrayal of his brother, Sebastiano's dead body had been dumped on the doorstep of his parents' home. They had mutilated him and cut his tongue out. The sign around his neck read "Traitor."

Sebastiano, who had tried to quit the gang when its methods became steadily more brutal, regretted his youthful sins and planned to become a priest. Haunted by the word *traitor* ever since his brother's death, Simone was living Sebastiano's dream. He, Sebastiano's kid brother, had become a priest in his place.

Simone felt afraid, but he thought of God and said a short prayer. At once, he felt courage and confidence flow back into him. "Myrrh and incense!" he exclaimed cheerfully. "This isn't what I'd call a cozy boudoir. Did your interior designer have a particularly bad day?"

Gabriel, who had been waiting for Simone's reaction to the décor, was indignant. He was proud of the place, every detail of which had been designed to replicate a torture chamber from the dreaded Spanish Inquisition.

"Do you know what humans have in common with ants?" Gabriel asked, gesturing with his gun toward a long, heavy wooden table.

Leather straps were attached to each of the four corners, and these, in turn, were attached to a number of wooden cogwheels of different sizes.

Simone peered in amazement at this original example of a medieval rack. Generations of woodworms had gnawed through the wood.

"I think," he said in answer to Gabriel's question as he studied the rack with a fascinated eye, "that they're the only other living creatures on earth to wage war on their own kind."

Gabriel, who noted that his victim's knees were not yet knocking with fear, gave an evil grin and nodded. "Yes, and there's more to learn from them. Ants in the Amazon basin construct traps the thickness of a finger with lots of little holes in them. Then they wait inside for some tasty tidbit in the shape of a locust to land on it. When it does, they grab its feet from beneath so another member of the colony can happily bite it to death. After that, it's dismembered into bite-sized morsels, and the ants have a banquet. There's nothing more cruel than nature, don't you agree?"

Simone didn't find it funny to be compared to a tasty tidbit. Above all, though, he felt there was nothing more cruel than man himself. He answered, "Well, I never. What diabolical little creatures! I found your biological discourse most interesting, believe me, but don't you have a job to do?" He was becoming more and more calmly resigned to his fate.

"No need to remind me. Get undressed. Take everything off, underwear included." Gabriel was satisfied to see a first hint of panic cross Simone's face.

"Everything?" Simone was prepared to endure all the pain in the world, but the thought of having to strip naked shocked him profoundly.

It wasn't the first time Gabriel had observed this phenomenon in priests. They seemed more attached to their clothes than to life itself. "Everything. Chop, chop! I'll be glad to help," he said menacingly. "Your Lord Jesus didn't have a stitch on either, when he was crucified. It was prudish Christian artists who put the diaper on him later."

Simone had not noticed any movement on Gabriel's part, but a switchblade suddenly clicked open in the man's right hand. Simone slowly started unbuttoning his shirt.

"You're the first Jesuit I've 'interrogated.' They say you're a damned tough breed. I heard the Native Americans liked to roast Jesuits over a slow fire. What makes you so different from the other brethren, and why can't people stand you?"

Simone, who was just taking off his sandals, had regained his composure. "I don't think Jesuits are anything special, but if the subject interests you, I'll tell you a little joke. A Benedictine, a Dominican, a Franciscan, and a Jesuit are sitting in a room together, praying, when the light suddenly goes out. The Benedictine steadfastly goes on praying, the Dominican launches into a long-winded lecture on the nature of light and darkness, the Franciscan praises God for the gift of mercifully unrevealing gloom. And what does the Jesuit do? He goes out and changes the fuse."

"Very funny. Now I'll tell you one. Do you know the real reason why people prostrate themselves during a papal audience?"

Simone dutifully shook his head.

"They're all trying to look beneath the throne of Peter. It was stolen from the infidels on one of the Crusades. Imagine the pope's posterior reposes on a throne engraved in Arabic with the words: 'There is no greater god than Allah, and Mohammed is his prophet.'" Gabriel laughed.

"Well, the next time I call on His Holiness, I'll try to peek beneath his throne." Simone stood up straight and faced Gabriel naked. Dressed only in his dignity, Simone looked him resolutely in the eye.

Gabriel returned his gaze with eyes of stone in which the torches were reflected like little flames of cruelty. Simone understood their message: he would never have another opportunity for an audience with the Holy Father.

Gabriel regarded Simone's neat pile of clothes with contempt. He gave them a kick. "One thing's for sure: you Jesuits have no fashion sense."

"We don't need one. We don't itch, that's the main thing. Have you ever tried on a monk's habit? The brethren weren't to be envied."

Stung by his victim's refusal to be intimidated, Gabriel shoved him toward the rack. "That's enough talking. Get up there, fatso!"

Hampered by his ample physique, Simone complied with difficulty. When he was lying full-length on the table, Gabriel attached the straps to his wrists and ankles and tightened them. Without warning, he turned the crank and ratcheted up the tension by one notch, eliciting a startled groan. His unfortunate victim now lay at full stretch, muscles and sinews taut to the breaking point, big pale stomach reminiscent of a beached whale. His brow was beaded with sweat, and he yearned for the moment when Gabriel would finally ask him a question. Only then would he be able to show God how steadfast he was.

Gabriel turned the crank until the pawl engaged in the next notch of the ratchet. Simone emitted a bloodcurdling scream as the first sinew snapped.

The Protector returned to the control room fifteen minutes later. Rabea's limbs had gone to sleep from being tied up like a parcel, but her mind was all the more alert.

"Where were we? Oh yes, you wanted to know what TC means. It's short for torture chamber. Gabriel has fitted up a little playroom down here. He's extremely creative in a perverted way."

Rabea decided to lay her cards on the table, poor though her hand was. Now that Simone was no longer there, she thought it unnecessary to go on playing games.

"Isn't it a bore, using a voice modifier? I know who you are, Professor."

"Clever girl."

Rabea felt her blindfold being removed. "In that case, we won't be needing that anymore."

Carlotta van Kampen looked down lovingly at her prisoner. In contrast to her usual gaudy clothes, she now looked as if she'd stepped out of a Paris fashion magazine. She was immaculately made up and coiffured, and her face had lost all its harmless naïveté. Rabea's eyes were drawn to the professor's perfectly manicured hands. She was wearing a single ring on her left hand, a magnificent black diamond. But it wasn't the ring that had attracted Rabea's attention so much as the scissors the Dutch woman was toying with. She casually snipped the air a few times, then went behind Rabea's chair. Rabea could guess what she had in mind. Sure enough, a strong hand yanked her head back roughly by the braid, then cut it off close to her scalp. The sound of the scissors sawing through the thick skein of hair pierced her to the marrow.

"I've wanted to do that since the first time we met." Van Kampen tossed the braid on the floor. "Well, what was in Bentivoglio's safe-deposit box? Secret transcripts? Long-lost gospels? An anti-Bible?"

"How should I know?" Rabea was surprised at how light her head suddenly felt without the braid. It was a strange sensation.

"You were observed with the priest today, fetching the documents from a safe-deposit box in a bank in the Marche. You then hid them in the Via dei Coronari apartment. I don't care to wait any longer. We're going to get them tonight."

This news made Rabea's heart skip a beat. *The men in balaclavas in the forecourt!* They were planning a raid on the von Stetten apartment. While she was swiftly calculating the odds of survival of the occupants, who had been reinforced by Uncle Heinrich's men, it suddenly occurred to her that it wouldn't be a fight of man against man: to her horror, she remembered the gas mask she'd seen. If the raiders used gas, the defenders wouldn't stand a chance. Wondering desperately how to prevent the raid, she bluffed.

"Sorry to disappoint you, but the safe-deposit box was empty."

"Nice try. You entered the building with the leather cylinders. I do know from my police informant that you didn't take them into the apartment with you, or our formidable superintendent would have confiscated them. And if they were empty, why go to so much trouble? This is your last chance to answer my question before I turn you over to Gabriel."

"Carry on—feel free. I can't tell you what I don't know." Rabea realized she had nothing to lose. Judging from the readiness with which she'd been informed about the planned raid, the Dutch woman took it for granted that Rabea would never get a chance to warn anyone.

"You're becoming tedious. Never mind, your boyfriend, the priest, will be more cooperative. We'll nab his beloved sister. You wouldn't believe how quickly a pretty face can be disfigured with a knife. It's one of Gabriel's specialties."

"You filthy bitch! Haven't you even a spark of decency? Lucie is a friend of yours."

But the Dutch woman ignored her outburst and went over to the console in front of the monitors. Her manicured forefinger pressed a button and a screen lit up. Then, with a contented smile that imbued every little wrinkle around her mouth and eyes with malice, she turned to Rabea.

Rabea stared in horror at the screen, on which Simone's naked form could be seen stretched out on a kind of rack, his pale face contorted with pain. Just then, Gabriel bent over him with a knife in his hand, briefly obstructing Rabea's view. A moment later, he straightened up. Simone's head was now bleeding profusely—from the place where his right ear had once been.

Gabriel held up the severed ear, grinned at the camera, and tossed it carelessly into a wooden bucket beneath the rack.

"Oh my God, what are you doing to him, you piece of shit! No more, stop it at once!" Rabea cried, tears of desperation and impotence springing to her eyes. Beside herself with fury, she strained at her hand-cuffs. For the last half hour, she had been surreptitiously trying to open them with a hairpin, which Gabriel had missed when he searched her.

"Oh, pipe down! To Gabriel, that fat priest is just an appetizer—he'd much sooner amuse himself with you. Anyway, the Jesuit doesn't deserve your pity. Jesuits have plotted and murdered their way down the centuries, fomenting wars and revolutions. Who saw to it that Louis XIV revoked the Edict of Nantes, which had granted religious free-dom to the French? The Jesuits. Where was ETA, the Basque terrorist organization, founded? At the Jesuit University of Bilbao. Jesuits are agitators. You're a Jew, Rabea. Why has your race survived every mas-sacre, every attempt to exterminate it? Because it endured every form of adversity, and that was its strength. Now, however, Israel is supported by America and demonstrates its strength through force of arms. Israel is surrounded by enemies, and America is preparing to become number one on the list of most-hated nations. Underlying all this is an ingenious plan. The Jesuits have always been enemies of the Jews. They want Jerusalem back—that arch-devil Ignatius of Loyola wanted it ever since going on pilgrimage there. How long will Israel survive? So don't con-demn me for allowing Gabriel his little bit of fun with the Jesuit. He's only doing what the church has done for nearly two thousand years. Come, I've made inquiries, and I know you hate the church as much as I do. You pine for that handsome priest who chose the Vatican SS over you. For two thousand years, the Catholic Church has been nothing more than an international conspiracy against Jews and women. It's our common enemy. I don't want to harm either you or Lucie. On the contrary, I want you to join me."

"It's worth discussing, but first you must call off your torturer," Rabea said firmly.

"Very well, but I warn you: if I harbor the slightest suspicion that you're lying to me, I'll tell him to carry on." Van Kampen stood up and pressed a button on the console. "Gabriel," she said, "take a short break and offer the father some hospitality. I'll call you later." She turned off the sound.

Rabea shut her eyes. She had secured Simone some breathing space. Now she had to kill some more time. It must be nearly 10:00 p.m. by now, and she felt sure that after waiting in vain for her promised phone call, Jules would go to Simone's brother's apartment to see if all was well. What with the calls on her laptop account and her cell phone, which she hoped she'd left behind and not lost, she had given him enough clues to put him on the right track.

"There's a lot of mental activity going on behind those freckles, I can tell. I'm listening."

Rabea opened her eyes. "Good. I applaud your summary of the conspiracy theories about the Jesuits' machinations. You're right. The documents do exist—I was actually able to take a look at them. But before I tell you what I know, would you permit me to ask you a personal question?" By flattering the professor and feigning interest in her personally, she was hoping to get her to talk and gain more time. One did not have to be an expert psychologist to tell that the woman was a born egomaniac and liked talking about herself most of all.

The Dutch woman registered Rabea's journalistic tone of voice at once. Being a scientist of repute and a bestselling author, she had given countless interviews in her life. "If it would help to convince you of my worthy intentions, yes. What interests you so much?"

"How is it that a refined and cultured woman like you will stop at nothing to gain possession of Bentivoglio's documents, resorting to kidnapping, the crudest kind of torture, and even murder? Why soil your whole life's work?"

From the way her captor's perfectly made-up eyes narrowed with hatred, Rabea knew she'd touched a nerve. The professor caught the ball and ran with it.

"Because it was a refined and cultured priest who ruined my mother's life, and mine as well. She became his housekeeper as a young orphan of sixteen. She was slightly disabled and limped, which had made her the lowest of the low at the orphanage. She thought she was in heaven when she found employment with a priest. But her heaven proved to be a hell. I found her diary. My mother was a simple woman who expressed her suffering in simple words, but they burned their way into my soul. The priest, who was almost thirty years her senior, violated her the very first night. My mother was a girl of not quite sixteen and knew nothing of men. He came to her nearly every night thereafter, and his practices became more and more perverted. My mother wanted to run away, but she knew that no one would believe her. The word of a respected priest against that of a young, disabled orphan? After years of martyrdom, she became pregnant and managed to hide her pregnancy from the priest until it was too late for the abortion she knew he would have forced her to undergo. After I was born, my mother looked after me in a touchingly maternal way. But my life changed when I grew bigger and the priest started to take an interest in me. My mother's response to this was absolutely hysterical—she never let me out of her sight, but she couldn't prevent it. One day, when I'd just turned eleven, 'Uncle Father' collected me from school and drove me to a hut in the woods. He hurt me, then put the fear of God into me and threatened me with dire consequences if I betrayed our secret. From then on, my mother often dozed off at the supper table and slept like the dead. I realized only later that he was drugging her with a powerful sedative. Those were the nights he always got into my bed. At fifteen, I became pregnant. My mother took the priest to task, and the next morning she was dead. The doctor, a good friend of the priest, did not doubt his allegation that my mother had felt unwell the night before and complained of pains in the chest. The day of the funeral, I went to the police. Instead of believing me, they sent me back to him. That night I slept with a knife under my pillow. When he came to my bed, I tried to stab him—unsuccessfully. He locked me up in the cellar, and the next morning he had me taken away and confined in a Catholic home for problem children. I refused to submit and wrote the bishop a letter telling him the whole story. A few days later, I was transferred to the secure wing, where I was sedated for months. They took my child away at birth and then sterilized me. I finally realized things couldn't go on that way or I'd die, so I learned to be obedient and became a model pupil. I knew my time would come. Revenge is a patient beast."

Rabea suppressed a shudder and strove to maintain her objective, journalistic demeanor as the Dutch woman continued her tale.

"I have devoted my whole life to planning my revenge on the Catholic Church. In order to defeat my enemies, I plunged into their world and studied theology, dogmatics, and early Christian languages. I earned my success with hard work. I have now assembled sufficient evidence to prove the criminal machinations of the Vatican. It has cost me a fortune. The documents from Bentivoglio's safe-deposit box are only the icing on the cake of destruction. Can you imagine how the public will react when a theologian of international repute suddenly changes sides and produces an irrefutably destructive dossier on the established church and the way it has betrayed its adherents for two thousand years? Goethe said doubt grows with knowledge, and I'll make them doubt, believe me! I've studied the historical figure of Jesus for decades. He was just an itinerant preacher like many who roamed the country at that time, but he had charisma. His message of neighborly love and peace won him many followers in subjugated Israel. It was his good fortune that Emperor Constantine found Christianity of use in trying to save his doomed Roman Empire. It was *never* about Jesus or his message and always about male dominance. Three hundred years after his death came the birth of that collection of fairy tales, the Bible. The bishops compiled it to suit themselves and for their own exclusive benefit. They cheated their master, Jesus Christ, out of his message, but betrayal always reposes on weak foundations and the established church is displaying deep cracks. The faithful are staying away because they aren't so easily deceived these days. The Catholic Church is tottering, and I plan to give it the coup de grâce."

The Dutch woman's face was only inches from Rabea's. Spittle had accumulated in the corners of her mouth, and her eyes were blazing with fanaticism.

In truth, Rabea's views about the church were not that different, and she could sense that what Van Kampen had told her about her childhood was true—even if her story did sound like a poor script for an even poorer soap opera. But Rabea could not abide that the woman believed it gave her the right to torture and murder; it made her incredibly angry.

As the professor spoke, Rabea was tormented by the images of poor, mutilated Simone, but she knew it wouldn't do him any good to lose her temper. At pains to sound distressed, she said, "I'm very sorry for you and your mother. I can understand your hatred, but you can't blame the church and the entire priesthood. It was the act of one misguided man. He alone was responsible."

Van Kampen took a few seconds to regain her composure, but when she eventually broke the silence, her eyes were clear and she spoke as if addressing her students in the lecture hall. "You're wrong," she said. "It still goes on. In the United States in 2002, dozens of priests were charged with abusing underage children. The church had covered up their crimes for decades. Austria was rocked by a similar scandal a few years ago. The church has since been compelled, especially in the United States, to close down dozens of parishes. It's selling off its assets because it needs the money to compensate families whose children have been abused by pedophile, usually homosexual, priests. Approximately two billion euros! Instead of protecting children, the church abuses them. The homosexual priesthood is gaining ground; they've set up a universally accessible website of their own—via a Turkish server, of all things! They have a peculiar sense of humor, too. The Catholic Church claims the story of creation for itself, right? God created Adam the man, but he also created his physical desires. He created paradise, the tree of knowledge, the serpent, and the apple. Eve took the apple and was kind enough to share it with Adam, and for that, God drove her out of paradise. Ever since then, according to the church, woman has been to blame for everything. Did you know that 96 percent of all crimes of violence are committed by men, and that 85 percent of all prison inmates are also men? And they say that woman is evil! God's self-appointed representatives on earth, *they're* the source of all evil. I'm going to root them out and—"

She was cut short by a phone call. Incensed by the interruption, she snatched up the receiver. "Yes, what is it? Wait till I get there!" She was about to leave the room when she turned. "I shall expect some answers when I return." Without giving Rabea another glance, she strode out.

Rabea stared spellbound at the silent monitor, which was still showing pictures from Gabriel's torture chamber. Simone was clearly in considerable pain, but Gabriel had bandaged his head with strips of gauze that ran around his head and under his chin, lending him a mummylike appearance. Leaning nonchalantly against the rack, Gabriel seemed from his gestures to be conducting a one-sided conversation with his victim.

Rabea tried to ignore the screen, but she continued to stare at it almost compulsively, like someone suffering from toothache who keeps probing with her tongue. She was still staring when Van Kampen briefly entered the screen for a word with Gabriel. Before she went out again, she gave the camera a knowing smile.

Rabea had a sudden thought. Did the room she was in contain a camera that was watching her? She carefully scanned every corner of it. Nothing. Either the camera was so tiny and well hidden as to be invisible to the naked eye, or the control room itself was not monitored. She took the risk and stepped up her attempts to free herself from the handcuffs. With her wrists manacled behind her back, it was extremely difficult to introduce the hairpin into the locks, but she managed it after what seemed like an eternity. They opened with a faint click.

Murmuring "Thanks, Jules," she removed the handcuffs, kissed the maltreated hairpin, and replaced it behind her ear—which abruptly reminded her that she hadn't much hair left to stick it in.

On the spur of the moment, she quickly turned on all the other monitors. Sure enough, on one of them, she could see Van Kampen. The professor was in the entrance hall in conversation with a man dressed from head to foot in black. Rabea scanned the console. Perhaps she could turn on the sound and discover what they were talking about. The screen was numbered, so she took a chance and turned a knob bearing the same numeral. It was too much of a good thing: the professor's voice reverberated around the control room. Startled, Rabea killed the sound at once and listened. To her immense relief she could hear nothing but her own heartbeat, which seemed to ring in her ears.

She carefully turned the knob until the professor's voice was little more than a whisper. ". . . another few hours to the operation, but I want you to leave right away and take up your positions. I'll expect a situation report every half hour."

The man gave her a military salute and disappeared from view, to reappear soon afterward on the monitor displaying the activities in the forecourt. Rabea heaved a sigh of relief: Van Kampen did not make for the elevator but turned toward a door on her left. Rabea closely studied the other screens, but she did not reappear on any of them.

On the other hand, she blanched to see the van containing the raiders drive out the gate followed by the heavily loaded black truck. A second delivery van drove up and was promptly boarded by several more men. The only other vehicle remaining out front was a black limousine, presumably Van Kampen's.

Rabea's eyes strayed back to the screen on which poor Simone could be seen. His eyes were closed. Was he asleep or had he lost consciousness? Then she noticed something that made her blood run cold:

Gabriel had disappeared. She spun around in panic, half expecting to find him right behind her, grinning derisively, but there was no one there.

Feverishly, she looked around for a weapon. She could see nothing but the big and unwieldy pair of scissors, so she took the hairpin and concealed it in her palm. According to Jules, nothing was more effective than an invisible weapon.

On impulse, she returned to the table in front of the monitor wall. Crawling beneath it, she discovered the main distribution box and pulled out all the cables.

Then she went over to the door and peered around the corner. The passage was deserted. The torture chamber had to be behind one of the numerous steel doors that led off it on either side. She set off in search of Simone.

Jules was standing outside the front door of the old apartment house. Having checked the address Lukas had given him, he pressed several bell buttons at random. The door buzzed open. He counted to twenty-five, then stole up to the fourth floor. He cracked the lock on the apartment door in a matter of seconds. The interior was brightly illuminated.

"Hello? Anyone here? Rabea? Father Simone? It's me, Jules."

No answer. Jules surveyed the small apartment. Four doors led off the bare little hallway. Three gave access to a neat kitchen, a spartan bedroom, and a tiny bathroom. All seemed to be in order.

The fourth door led to a room in utter chaos. The massive desk in front of the only window was strewn with faded documents, some of them half–rolled up and frayed at the edges. Jutting incongruously from among the ancient papyri was a laptop, open and humming to itself. A large flat screen was standing on the tiled floor with some cords lifelessly trailing from it. It had clearly yielded pride of place to the laptop. More documents were strewn over the floor. Jules began by trying the automatic redial of the telephone on the desk. A Trattoria da Gino answered—a dead end unless you were hungry. He was just turning his attention to the laptop when a digital ringtone sounded. Following the sound to its source, he found a cell phone under a stack of papers on the floor. The display showed a Rome number. He knew it, having memorized it only half an hour earlier.

"Hello, Lukas, Jules here."

"Damn it, Jules, what are you doing with Rabea's cell phone?"

"I've solved the riddle of why she didn't answer your calls: her phone is here in the apartment, but she's not. I've found a note from her to Father Simone, telling him she'll call him on the way. Unfortunately, it doesn't say where she was going."

"Where on earth can they be?"

"Give me a few minutes, Lukas. I'll check Rabea's e-mails and the last few calls she made on her cell phone. Don't do anything stupid." Jules doubted his inquiries would be facilitated if Lukas broke out of the apartment with Grassa's army hot on his heels.

Frustrated, Lukas put the receiver down. He vented his anger by thumping the table with his fist, but his outburst was short-lived. He bowed his head and ran his fingers through his mop of fair hair, making it stand up in all directions. Nothing was more irksome than being condemned to inactivity when you were worried about someone. Worse still, he was a prisoner cooped up inside his own four walls.

His spirits lifted at the sight of his sister, who had just emerged from her bedroom looking refreshed. "Lucie!" he exclaimed, hugging her so hard she gasped for breath.

"Ouch, you're squashing me. What's wrong? Has something else happened?" Her Lukas-sensitive antennae had picked up a signal.

He brought her up to date with the latest bad news.

"Disappeared, you say? Both of them? Hmm." Lucie remained surprisingly calm. Stellina, having followed her out of the bedroom, was watching her intently. "Jules knows what he's doing. I'm sure he'll find them."

Deep inside him, Lukas felt a tiny twinge of jealousy. Both Lucie and Rabea seemed to have absolute faith in Jules's abilities, whereas he had to sit around uselessly.

When the cell phone rang, he grabbed it like a drowning man. It was Jules. Lukas put the phone on "Speaker."

"I think I've found a lead. I noticed that the scanner was missing, and one of the last numbers dialed on Rabea's cell belonged to a computer store in the neighborhood. I got through to the owner, who confirmed that a Father Simone had been with him until shortly after seven thirty getting a scanner repaired. So he must have disappeared sometime after that. If he'd returned to the apartment, the scanner would be here. Oh, just a moment, someone rang the doorbell." Jules returned. "That was a neighbor. He bumped into Simone around eight, just outside. He thrust the scanner into his hands and asked him to hang on to it, then walked off. Another thing: Rabea looked up some very informative pages on the Internet and put a call through to Berlin. I called the number myself. The man, a colleague of hers, was cagey at first. He didn't seem particularly impressed when I said she might be in danger, but I managed to convince him in the end. I got an address out of him. Know what I think? Rabea took off on her own, and Simone followed her. What do you reckon?"

"Typical of Rabea to go swanning off on her own."

"And that crazy Simone had nothing better to do than go scurrying after her. It's just before ten thirty now. I'm going to the address. If I haven't reported back in an hour, send the police there, okay?"

"Yes, but be careful, Jules." Lucie wrote down the address.

"That's why I'm still alive." He hung up.

Lucie chewed her thumbnail for a moment, thinking hard. "I have an idea," she said.

She left the kitchen and walked down the hallway in her nightie, which covered very little of her slender form; the little dog, Stellina, devotedly trotted in her wake. She yawned a "Good night" to the bodyguard outside her bedroom door and nodded to Grassa's man, who had peered around the living room door.

Minutes later the apartment rang with the horrified screams of a woman in extreme distress. They came from Lucie's bedroom. Gun at the ready, the bodyguard dashed into the room. The second bodyguard went thundering in after him, followed by Grassa's man.

Lucie was lying there with the covers pulled up to her chin, screaming. Stellina was barking frantically and bouncing around on the bed.

All three men stared wildly around the room, which was only dimly illuminated by the light from the hall. The older bodyguard turned on the light, signaled to the younger, and dove into the bathroom, from where he called "Secure!" a moment later. Grassa's man wrenched open the door of Lucie's walk-in wardrobe, while the younger bodyguard stationed himself at the foot of the bed, ready to shoot anyone who dared approach his charge.

It very soon became clear that no intruder was present, but Lucie continued to scream. The older bodyguard gripped her arm and said in German, "Please calm down, Fräulein von Stetten, everything's under control. There's nobody here." Stellina abruptly stopped barking and eyed the man suspiciously, then growled and went for him. Lucie just managed to grab her in time and clasped the animal to her breast. "Brave little girl," she whispered.

"What happened?" asked the man beside her.

"There was someone outside the window. I distinctly heard him rattle it," Lucie said in an apprehensive voice. The other bodyguard hurried over to the window, opened it, and inspected the front of the building.

"Look, there's no one there. Perhaps you just imagined it or had a bad dream. I'll stay in the room if you want."

Lucie was about to reply when the man turned his head as if something had struck him. "Hey, where's your brother?"

Because they were speaking German, Grassa's man didn't understand his question, and Lucie tried to signal him to say no more, but in the meantime, Grassa's man seemed to have had the same idea. It was highly unlikely Lukas would not have reacted to his sister's screams.

Startled, he spun around and dashed out.

Lucie's idea had worked. Lukas had taken advantage of the temporary confusion and decamped.

Both German bodyguards eyed Lucie with amusement. She merely shrugged and gave them a mischievous grin.

Grassa's man returned, his cell phone already to his ear. All the color had left his face. Lucie didn't envy him.

Lukas was walking as fast as he could. If he maintained this speed, he would be there in less than twenty minutes. Jules wouldn't be able to get there much faster by car because he had to keep to the main streets, whereas Lukas could take shortcuts via side streets and pedestrian precincts. On the other hand, Jules had fifteen minutes' start. Lukas, who had taken Lucie's cell phone with him, dialed his number while walking.

"Hello, Jules. I'm on my way to you."

"By the beard of the Prophet!" Jules exclaimed. "Didn't I tell you not to do anything stupid?"

"Don't worry, nobody followed me. I got out through the old cellar connected to the building next door. We discovered it during the conversion a few years ago. Where shall we meet? I think there's a small park near the road. Wait for me at the entrance."

When he got there barely twenty minutes later, there was no one to be seen. Then Jules materialized beside him.

"There you are at last. I've already done a bit of recon." The two men stole closer, shielded by the oleander bush Rabea and Simone had crouched behind earlier. "Something seems to be going on. Half a dozen men are busy loading a truck. I haven't spotted any guards on patrol. They probably feel secure because of their CCTVs, and the alarm system is probably switched off because of their constant comings and goings. We're going in."

"Just like that? How?" Lukas eyed the wall dubiously. It was at least eight feet high.

"On my own I'd use a grappling hook and rope, but since you're here we'll use the oldest method in the world: a leg up."

"Oh." Lukas swallowed hard.

"Come on." Jules darted across the street at a crouch, and they worked their way around to the rear of the house.

Jules had already identified a stretch of wall that lay in the semi-darkness between two streetlights. The night was starlit, the air fragrant with summer. A wonderful night for a stroll, but not as good for people who wanted to melt into the darkness.

Jules scaled the wall first with Lukas's help, then sat astride it and hauled him up. They landed on the lawn of the well-kept grounds. "It's a huge place," Lukas whispered. "Any idea how and where we can get in?"

Jules produced his smartphone. "I got a friend to send me the plans of the house. It was sold to a Lebanese businessman in the late eighties. He developed the cellars into a sort of fortress. They run beneath the house, all the way across the park, and come out somewhere in the Cloaca Maxima." Jules tapped the display, which showed a part of the ground plan in miniature. "According to my information, the place was resold eight years ago to a shady organization based in the Cayman Islands. We'll start by searching the cellar and work our way systematically upward. There are two possible ways of getting in." He called up another ground plan. "Elevator or external staircase. We'll take the stairs." Suddenly he swung around, grabbed Lukas, and with a single, vigorous movement, thrust Lukas behind him.

"What's up?" Lukas whispered.

"Shh, don't move," Jules hissed. "Not unless you've got a rump steak with you."

Before Lukas could make sense of this, a dark shape flew at them from out of nowhere.

Jules lunged at the shadow, grabbed it left-handed by the throat, and hammered it between the eyes with his right elbow. It emitted a strangled yelp and fell dead. All this happened in a fraction of a second.

Lukas could now see that the thing lying at Jules's feet was a powerful Doberman with a long pink tongue protruding from its jaws.

The former secret policeman stood there foursquare, listening intently. "Careful, they usually guard in pairs. Keep your head down!"

Too late: Lukas had only just spotted a movement out of the corner of his eye when a second animal sprang at him and knocked him over. His reflexes sharpened by fury at the series of obstacles that kept him from rescuing Rabea and Simone, Lukas drew back his fist as he fell and punched the dog hard on the head. It gave a little yelp and subsided onto the grass, out cold.

"Not bad, Lukas," Jules whispered. "Come on, the stairs are over there."

Lukas followed him over to a flight of stone steps on the right-hand side of the house. Once Jules had checked that they were not under CCTV surveillance, they started down them.

The worn steps ended in a small landing with a rusty iron door. Jules picked the lock with a weary smile, but the door opened with a creak that would have awakened the dead. Startled, the two cat burglars, master and apprentice, stopped short and listened. All remained quiet. The voices of the men in the forecourt continued to carry faintly to their ears.

"That's typical," Jules whispered. "The more guards, the easier it is to break in somewhere. They all rely on each other."

The door opened onto another half landing from which more steps led down to the upper of two basement levels. Jules stole down the steps and peered around the corner. Ahead lay a long, neon-lit passage hewn out of rock. They descended some more steps to another landing. According to the plan, it led to the lowest level.

"Heavens," said Lukas, "this is an absolute labyrinth. How on earth are we to find them?"

"One thing at a time. We'll proceed systematically," said Jules, who was studying his display again. "According to the plan there are only two basement levels. We'll work our way all along this one to the end, where there's supposed to be a control room equipped with monitors. They could be useful to us. An elevator giving access to the ground floor is also located there."

Jules took the lead. The air smelled only faintly of mold, so the basement obviously had a first-class ventilation system. The musty smell did not intensify until they went farther along the various passages. As they checked each one, Jules marked it on his smartphone. The layout was simple: a main, central path from which additional passages branched off in both directions, some of them as much as twenty yards long but all ending in a U-turn that led back to the central thoroughfare.

They reached the control room without incident. Jules hurried over to the screens and tried in vain to turn them on. In search of the problem, he crawled under the console table and found that the cables had been disconnected. He was crawling out again, at a loss, when he saw Lukas staring at something with utter horror in his eyes. Hurrying over to him, he spotted the cause of his consternation: Rabea's severed braid was lying at his feet.

Jules noticed the open handcuffs under the chair. "Know what I think happened, Lukas? Rabea gave them the slip—she managed to free herself. Smart girl. Come on, let's go look for her."

Lukas remained rooted to the spot. "But her hair . . ." he blurted out.

"Is just hair—it'll grow again. Leave it, man!" Jules snapped when Lukas bent down to retrieve it. "Either you come with me or I'll go look for Rabea on my own. Then you'll have plenty of time to weep over her hair. Which is it to be?"

"All right, let's go."

Halfway along the passage they heard two men coming toward them, arguing loudly.

They just had time to squeeze into one of the cramped cells and close the door. The men disappeared in the opposite direction. They were tiptoeing on when cries rang out behind them. Someone light-footed came hurrying in their direction, closely pursued by the heavier footsteps of two men. All at once, Rabea darted around the corner.

Jules grabbed her and thrust her and Lukas into the next cell. He followed close behind. The two men who had been squabbling earlier rounded the corner just as Jules shut the door.

He signed to Lukas to stand on the other side of the door; it wouldn't be long before the men checked the cell for Rabea. Then he signaled for her to stand against the wall opposite the door so that she would be the first thing they saw.

One of her pursuers kicked the door open with his booted foot. His eyes shone with triumph at the sight of her. Unfortunately, the other man made no move to follow him in. He remained outside with his gun leveled at Rabea.

She grasped the tricky situation at once. Lukas and Jules would have to take advantage of the element of surprise in order to overpower both men simultaneously. The second guard must not be allowed to fire a shot and raise the alarm. It was the lecherous look in the eyes of the intruder that triggered a flash of inspiration: the two men's place in the pecking order seemed obvious. While the first, a beefy thug, was leering at his helpless prey, the other man, clearly accustomed to letting his pal go first under all circumstances, waited his turn.

Although robbed of her loveliest attribute, her wealth of auburn hair, Rabea threw back her head and raised her arms in a provocative movement that emphasized the firmness of her breasts. At the same time, she almost imperceptibly rolled her hips.

In an instant, the cornered quarry had transformed herself into a seductive siren. "Hey," she called to the man in the doorway, "you want your pal to have all the fun?"

The man promptly took the bait.

Sinuously, Rabea sank to the stone floor in order to compel the first man, from whom her invitation to his partner had elicited an indignant grunt, to bend over her.

Her plan worked. The second guard barged into the cell while Rabea's brutish admirer tugged feverishly at his zipper. She could already smell his foul breath when Jules and Lukas struck.

Jules grabbed her bewildered assailant and hurled him at the wall headfirst. The man slumped to the floor unconscious with his trousers at half-mast. Meanwhile, Lukas put his own victim out of action with two well-aimed punches to the head and jaw.

Rabea jumped to her feet. "About time too!" she said angrily. "What the hell took you so long? I couldn't have laid a clearer trail."

"Yes, and we're glad to see you too. Nice hairdo," Jules retorted, looking at her shorn head. Lukas was about to say something when she silenced them both with an impatient gesture and gave them a brief account of Father Simone's martyrdom.

Before they left the cell, Jules swiftly searched the unconscious guards and manacled them with their own handcuffs. He also took their weapons and smartphones and gagged them with strips of cloth torn from the would-be rapist's shirt. Then he followed Rabea and Lukas out and bolted the door of the cell.

Jules took the lead with his gun at the ready, and they reached the torture chamber soon afterward. Gabriel had still not returned.

Simone was a terrible sight. He was still lashed to the rack, and the bandage around his head was sodden with blood. Rabea heard a hissing intake of breath behind her as Lukas took in the details of the scene. Jules cut the leather straps and, with Lukas's assistance, carefully helped the injured man down off the rack. Simone couldn't stand properly, thanks to the torn tendons in his leg, and he swayed precariously. The two men tried to lift him back onto the rack, but he shook his head in dismay.

Rabea hurriedly looked around for a chair, but all she could find was a wooden bucket under the rack. To her horror, it contained Simone's severed ear. Deciding that this was no time for sensitivities, she quickly inverted it, and Simone, naked as the day he was born, subsided onto the improvised stool. *Probably the first man who ever sat on his own ear,* she thought hysterically.

Lukas, who had found Simone's heap of clothes, draped his shirt over his knees. Jules kneeled down in front of him. Having conjured some bandages and a splint out of his rucksack, he temporarily immobilized the priest's injured leg.

While Jules was attending to Simone, they discussed in whispers what to do next. Neither Jules's smartphone nor those of the two guards had any reception inside the rocky vault. They would have to go upstairs in order to notify the police. Rabea and Lukas urged Simone to come with them right away, but he vehemently insisted on staying behind. He could hardly walk, he pointed out, and carrying him—at this he gestured at his vast bulk—was out of the question.

Jules took no part in the whispered argument but silently agreed with Simone. Time was short. Rabea and Lukas eventually prevailed. The sadist could return at any moment. Jules put one of the guards' guns in Rabea's hand. Then the two men took the injured priest under his arms.

This time Rabea took the lead. Her escape did not appear to have been discovered yet, but the alarm might sound any second. All of their nerves were taut to the breaking point.

Their plan was simple: they would barricade themselves on the landing behind the steel door to the basement, where they would have reception and could summon help. There they would also be able to hold off potential attackers for a while. They went as fast as they could with the injured Simone, who felt guilty for burdening Lukas and Jules with his considerable weight. They had almost reached the last bend before the steps when suddenly things started to happen very quickly.

Someone darted around the corner, lithe as a feline predator, and knocked the gun out of Rabea's hand, simultaneously firing several shots at the three men. Even before Father Simone felt the impact of the first bullet, he pushed Lukas and Jules violently backward, then crashed to the ground like a felled tree. The other two rolled away and instinctively sought protection behind the open steel door of a cell. Jules drew his gun, ready to fire, but the man had already grabbed Rabea and was holding her in front of him as a human shield, his pistol to her temple.

It was Gabriel. He grinned. "Father von Stetten, the knight in shining armor, eh? Do you know your uncle's last words were of you, not of his God? Now throw me your guns and come out with your hands up, or I shoot her."

"No!" Rabea said sharply when she saw Lukas preparing to comply. She gave Jules an imploring look to which he responded with a flicker of the eyelids. Instantly, despite the arm around her throat, she struggled with all her might, compelling Gabriel to tighten his grip. Then she pushed off with both feet so that for a fraction of a second, and at the risk of throttling herself, her full weight hung from his arm. By the time he grasped her intention it was too late.

Jules fired at once in response to her signal and shattered Gabriel's kneecap. The sadist doubled up with a cry of rage, releasing Rabea, who promptly took possession of his gun. The sadist who so much enjoyed inflicting pain on others was getting another dose of his own medicine. "You'll pay for this, you bitch," he snarled at Rabea. Contorted with hatred, his angelic face resembled one of the gargoyles on the front of the house.

The whole thing was over so quickly that Lukas was left thinking Jules had cold-bloodedly risked Rabea's life. What if he had hit her? Oblivious of the danger they were in, he vented his anger.

"Are you completely out of your mind?"

Jules was unmoved by his outburst. "Calm down. We'd practiced that."

"You taught Rabea that move?"

Just as he had in Munich when Lukas broke his nose, Jules marveled at the way the levelheaded Jesuit priest's feelings for Rabea could transform him into a raging fury. "Okay, *pax!* Those shots will have carried. We'll be getting some visitors any moment."

A loud groan made Lukas turn around. *Simone!*

Rabea was already crouching beside his supine form. To her horror, Simone had been hit in the chest and stomach. Gravely wounded, he was breathing with the utmost difficulty, each breath accompanied by a gurgling sound. The bloody bubbles forming at the corners of his mouth made it obvious that his lungs were filling with blood. Rabea pillowed his head gently on her lap. With tears in her eyes, she looked up at Lukas, who had kneeled down beside her and taken Simone's hand.

They all knew he was past saving. A tremor ran through his massive body. His face looked as if the lifeblood were draining from it.

Simone gathered his strength for the last time. His pale lips moved in an attempt to shape some words. Lukas put his ear close to the dying man's lips to catch his final message. "The documents . . . important . . . mustn't fall . . . wrong hands . . ." Father Simone, who had loved life and sampled all its culinary delights, had died a senseless death.

For a moment, the other three were imprisoned in a sort of temporal vacuum. Rabea the Jew, Lukas the Christian, and Jules the Muslim joined in an unspoken prayer that knew no religion.

Then the unthinkable happened. The click of a safety catch echoed from the rocky walls of the passage. Jules spun around. Gabriel had sat up and was pointing a small-bore pistol at them. It had presumably been hidden in his boot. Jules cursed his negligence in failing to search the man. Such a thing would never have happened to him in the old days.

"I told you I'd make you pay, you red-haired witch," Gabriel snarled. "See you in hell!" And he pulled the trigger.

Almost simultaneously, Jules raised his gun and fired several shots at him, while Lukas, in an attempt to shield her, threw himself on top of Rabea, who was still cradling Simone's lifeless head in her lap. He was momentarily obstructed by Simone's hand, which gripped his in death.

Jules hurried over to Gabriel and satisfied himself that the killer could do no further harm. He took the little automatic from his lifeless hand and applied the safety catch.

"The bastard's dead," he said, "but I reckon even hell will spew him up." Then, seeing that Lukas was still sprawled across Rabea, he added, "You can get off her now, Father Lukas."

Lukas froze in midmovement.

Jules instantly grasped that something was wrong and kneeled down beside him. "Oh no . . . Rabea, no!"

A red stain in the center of Rabea's white blouse was quickly expanding. Her breathing was rapid and shallow.

"Quick, Lukas, fetch the dressings from my rucksack! We must stop the bleeding." While Lukas hastened to comply, Rabea tried to sit up.

"No, lie nice and still." Jules stripped off his T-shirt, rolled it up, and gently bedded her head on it. Taking her blouse by the hem, he ripped it down the middle and carefully examined the wound, which was alarmingly close to her heart. When Lukas returned with the first-aid kit, he told him to lift her under the arms so that he could apply a firm dressing.

Rabea groaned during this procedure but remained conscious. "How bad is it?" she asked. Her voice was little more than a whisper.

"It doesn't look good," Jules replied honestly, "but you were lucky. The bullet missed your heart. You need to get to a hospital right away. I'll fetch help and lock the two of you up in a cell meanwhile. Six inches of steel ought to keep you safe. Here, Lukas, take the guards' guns."

They carried Rabea carefully into the nearest cell, followed by Father Simone. Jules locked them in and locked all the neighboring cells as well. He took Gabriel by one leg and was dragging him to the staircase when he heard footsteps approaching. They hadn't discovered him yet, but Gabriel's body would show them the way. No matter. He let go of him and took the stairs two at a time, making plenty of noise so as to lure them away from the others. His plan worked. He had reached the first landing and opened the low door leading to the upper level when the first shots hit the wall close beside him. He dove through the door and raced on up the stairs. Moments later he was up the second flight and facing the last steel door. He hesitated, hoping that no unpleasant surprises awaited him behind it, but he had no choice—he couldn't go back. Whipping the door open, he charged out with his head down and instantly collided with a man.

They rolled around on the ground, panting and exchanging punches, until Jules gained the upper hand. Seated astride his adversary, he was about to put him to sleep with a final punch when someone caught his arm from behind. "Don't, Jules. It's Grassa."

Jules stopped short. "What are you doing here?" he asked, staring up at Lucie as if she were an apparition.

"I'll tell you later. Where are Lukas and Rabea? And Father Simone?"

Before he could answer, the grounds were flooded with light and a megaphone voice loudly announced that the property was surrounded by police. Anyone on the premises was ordered to come out with their hands up. Jules could now see that the place was swarming with policemen.

Grassa, already back on his feet, was wiping the grass off the trousers of his linen summer suit.

Jules hurried back to the steel door, but his pursuers had retreated in the face of such overwhelming odds. Still a trifle mistrustful, Grassa had followed him over to the entrance. Jules gave him a brief account of the situation, and the superintendent beckoned to some of his men, who drew their guns and cautiously descended the stairs.

Lucie remained behind to wait for an ambulance, which had been summoned.

Grassa's men reached the locked cell door unopposed. Behind it, they found Lukas in despair. Rabea had lost consciousness, and her freckles stood out dark against the alarming pallor of her face. To see her lying there so inert, with a blood-soaked dressing on her chest, one might have thought she was dead.

Lucie, who appeared with the emergency doctor soon afterward, must have thought so because she uttered a cry and would have hurled herself on her friend if Jules hadn't restrained her. "Don't worry, Lucie, she's alive and she's tough. Let the doctor do his work."

The doctor, who with his team had entered the cell at her heels, unceremoniously thrust her aside and ordered everyone out except the members of his medical team. After a cursory glance at Simone's dead body, he devoted himself at once to the living. While he was issuing his instructions, Lukas and Jules took a sobbing Lucie between them and followed Grassa out into the passage.

The superintendent checked on the progress of the police search by radio, then turned to the two men and glared at them with his arms folded on his chest. "Well," he said in an ominously calm voice, "I'm listening."

Lukas, with one arm around his sister, left the talking to Jules, who gave Grassa a brief outline of what had happened in the last few hours. The superintendent was enough of a pro to restrain himself, at least temporarily, from losing his temper.

After that, Lucie told Lukas and Jules how the two German bodyguards had grilled her after her performance in the bedroom. They had convinced her that her brother and her friend were in danger and might need help, so she had told them the address of Father Simone's brother.

Like Jules, the two men were able to follow Rabea's trail. They drove to the house with Lucie, and spent a few minutes watching the place. They were still uncertain what to do when chance came to their aid: the gates opened to let another truck out, and Lucie, who was watching the forecourt through the bodyguards' binoculars, recognized the kidnapper who had escaped from the Sassis' farm. Grassa was informed at once, and he and his men turned up within fifteen minutes.

Unnoticed by Lucie, who was having a word with Grassa, Lukas whispered something to Jules and sneaked off down the passage.

A few minutes later, things started to move again. The medical team left the cell with Rabea. Her frail form looked as small as a child's beneath its blanket. The doctor walked alongside the gurney holding the drip attached to her left arm. When he saw that Lucie and Jules were preparing to approach the gurney, he restrained them with a peremptory gesture, "She's stable," he said, "but she must be operated on without delay."

"Wait!" whispered Rabea, turning her head to look at Lucie.

The doctor gave a brief order, and the medics came to a halt.

"Where's Lukas?" she asked softly.

Jules bent over her. "He refused to leave your braid behind. He's gone to get it."

"What an idiot!" She smiled faintly. "What about the woman? Have you got her?"

"What woman?" everyone said at the same time.

"Professor Van Kampen, your so-called friend. She's the head of this goddamned gang. Hasn't she been arrested?"

"We've arrested six men so far. There wasn't anyone else in the building." Grassa was already yelling fresh orders into his radio.

"Then she's escaped. She . . ." Rabea's head sank back, and she passed out again.

Lucie stared at her in disbelief, momentarily reluctant to believe what she'd just heard. Her motherly friend was in charge of this vile gang of murderers? Had Rabea been imagining things? No, it was true! She recalled the imperious female voice on the kidnapper's cell phone. It was *her*. An unpleasant thought occurred to her. She turned to Jules in sudden alarm. "Damn it! What if she's still here?"

Jules seemed to have had the same idea. "Lukas," he called, and disappeared down the main passage.

Rabea's severed braid was still lying exactly where he had last seen it. For a moment, Lukas stood looking down at the rope of auburn hair. The sight of it evoked a multitude of emotions. At last, he pulled himself together and bent to pick it up. Just then he felt a stab of pain in his right shoulder. Instinctively, he fell sideways, grabbing his assailant's ankle and yanking her off her feet. She yelped in surprise, and the scissors clattered to the floor.

Rabea's hair had probably saved his life. If he hadn't bent down, the scissors would have gone far deeper. As it was, the surprise attack had inflicted only a superficial cut. Lukas scrambled to his feet and prepared to repel another onslaught. To his bewilderment, his assailant was Lucie's friend, the Dutch professor who had lately developed an irritating habit of turning up at the most unsuitable moments. How had she gotten here, and why had she attacked him?

The woman had obviously hurt herself in falling. Seated on the floor, she felt the back of her head and groaned. One of her shoes was lying several feet away. For one brief second, Lukas felt there was something odd about the look of appraisal she gave him from beneath her false eyelashes, but the impression was so fleeting, he thought he must be wrong.

Her blue eyes were guileless as she looked up at him. "Good heavens, it's Father von Stetten," she gushed. "Can it really be you? God, I thought you were one of them. What are you doing here?"

Having initially regarded her with suspicion—after all, she had just tried to stab him with a pair of scissors—Lukas came a step closer. "I was about to ask you the same thing, Professor." He kneeled down beside her to check on the severity of her injury.

The cut on the back of her head was bleeding, but she waved him away. "No, no, I can hardly feel it. What about you, though? My God, to think I almost killed you!"

While helping her to her feet, he couldn't refrain from asking her how she came to be there.

"I was abducted like your sister, probably because they needed my professional expertise. I overheard them talking about some ancient manuscripts that needed translating. Then there was an alert of some kind and my guards rushed off. Luckily, I managed to free myself, but when I heard shots and footsteps approaching, I flew into a panic. I snatched up the scissors and stabbed you on the spot. I'm so sorry."

"Come on, let's go. There's nothing more to fear. Superintendent Grassa and his men have everything under control." Lukas took her arm, but she checked him with a gesture of entreaty. "Would you be kind enough to bring me my shoe?" She pointed to her bare foot and coquettishly wiggled her well-pedicured toes.

As Lukas turned to fetch the shoe, his eye was caught by the reflection of a neon tube in one of the inactivated screens. Also visible in it was an incredible sight: with an agility that belied her physical bulk, the professor had retrieved the scissors from the floor and was about to attack him once more. Lukas reacted instinctively yet again: he dodged aside and the blow landed on thin air. A victim of her own momentum, the professor went sprawling. Robbed of her prey once again, she uttered a scream of rage. Lukas hurled himself at her, and they went rolling across the floor.

Then a piercing cry of agony reverberated around the walls. Lukas stared at the blood on his hand and the limp body of the woman beneath him. The scissors were protruding from her chest. Dazedly, he scrambled to his feet, picked up Rabea's braid, and fled from the room.

At the end of the passage he encountered Jules, who hurried toward him exclaiming, "Allah be praised, there you are! Rabea recovered consciousness just before she left. Don't worry, Lukas, she'll make it. She told us that the Dutch professor, Lucie's friend, is the head of this murderous outfit. She must still be somewhere in the building."

"I know. She's in the control room. Dead."

Lukas stared past Jules with a blank expression, clasping Rabea's auburn braid to his chest like a sacred relic.

"At last!" Lukas sprang to his feet. He had already spent hours in the waiting room of the Santa Maria Hospital, which boasted neither windows nor air-conditioning, and the atmosphere was oppressively warm.

It was shortly after 5:00 a.m. by now, and another fine summer day was preparing to enfold Rome in its scorching embrace. Lukas looked terrible. He was still wearing the clothes stained with Rabea's and Simone's blood.

Shocked by the sight of him on arrival, a young nurse had mistakenly thought he was badly hurt. He'd found it hard to convince her that all he needed was a shower, a change of clothes, and some good news.

A surgical team had been fighting for Rabea's life for over four hours, and at last the door had opened and the visibly exhausted surgeon appeared, still in his bloodstained gown and removing his mask as he came in. *Rabea's blood,* Lukas thought with a shudder as he hurried toward him.

The surgeon checked Lukas with an experienced hand. "Steady, all went well. We managed to remove the bullet. It punctured a blood vessel near the heart, but the heart itself is undamaged. The patient is doing as well as can be expected. She's asleep now. Come back early this afternoon, and you can pay her a brief visit."

Lucie came over to Lukas and hugged him. "You heard that, Lukas? She's doing well. Our Rabea is a tough nut. Go on. Go home with Jules. You really could use a shower. I'll stay here and let you know as soon as she wakes up, okay?"

"No," he said. "I abandoned her for too long. You go with Jules." He hugged Lucie back and gave her a perfunctory kiss on the forehead.

She understood what he meant and didn't insist. "All right, we'll come back in two hours at the latest, bringing you some breakfast and some clean clothes. Lukas . . ." She hesitated for a moment, then went on, "We ought to inform her grandfather. After all, he's her only living relative. Please do that, will you?"

The realization that he'd entirely forgotten about Rabea's grandfather made him squirm with embarrassment. Lucie squeezed his arm and gave him her cell phone.

Lukas braced himself to call the rabbi. The old gentleman could be very blunt. Lukas's memory was indelibly imprinted with the phone number of the little house on the edge of Nuremberg where Rabea had spent her childhood and where he had so often been a guest.

Rabbi Rosenthal answered after the second ring. He was already up and about in spite of the early hour. He was appreciative that Lukas had called him, and he evinced no displeasure at the belated way in which he'd been informed of his only grandchild's condition. He had only one request, and that was that Lukas should give Rabea a message from him when she woke up. Lukas promised to let him know at once if there was any change.

The call left him feeling exhausted and lonelier than ever. He became painfully aware how good for him his sister's soothing presence had been.

Jules and Lucie, accompanied by Lucie's father, returned at around seven o'clock, when the hospital came to life and resumed its daily routine. Lucie infused the waiting room with her characteristic vigor and self-assurance. Once Lukas had reported no new developments, she took charge. Forceful as ever, she persuaded the nurse to allow her brother to shower in one of the washrooms reserved for patients.

It was amazing what water, soap, and clean clothes could achieve. When Lukas emerged fifteen minutes later, he was looking almost himself again. His somber expression was all that said otherwise.

He was met in the waiting room by the delicious aroma of fresh coffee. Out of the picnic basket Lucie had brought with her, she conjured up cornetti and hot cappuccinos in cardboard cups, plus orange juice and her obligatory colorful napkins. Lukas's attempt to refuse the food foundered on her sisterly authority. She got a cornetto down his gullet by warning him that she'd feed it to him piece by piece if necessary.

Von Stetten senior, who had already been briefed on the situation with Rabea by Lucie and Jules, brought good and bad news with him. The bad news was that Professor Van Kampen's body had not been found, either in the control room or elsewhere in the building. Contrary to Lukas's assumption, it appeared she was not dead, and either made off by herself or with someone's assistance.

Grassa had immediately instituted a nationwide manhunt, notified all airports, and set up roadblocks around Rome. A special team was currently combing Van Kampen's residence for secret passages. The house itself had already been cleared of all furniture and was devoid of any clues to her machinations. As for the men in custody, they had so far remained silent.

Where Bentivoglio's murder was concerned, however, some progress had been made. One of the men detained at the house was the late father general's new secretary, which at least indicated a connection between Van Kampen and his murder. Now that Lukas was no longer the only suspect, Grassa was following up this new lead. He had also enlisted the help of major international police authorities like Interpol and Europol.

When Lukas heard that the Dutch woman probably wasn't dead, he realized that he hadn't given any further thought to her until now. "How did Rabea pick up her trail?" he asked.

"I think I can answer that," said Jules. "In order to trace Rabea and Simone, I went back through Rabea's research, which led me to Van Kampen's house. I surmise that Rabea found something in Bentivoglio's documents that linked Van Kampen to these mysterious happenings. She then got in touch with a journalist friend and asked him for further information. Van Kampen married very young to Jaap Leysieffer, a Dutch diamond merchant forty years her senior. Leysieffer controlled almost the whole of the South African diamond market. He was one of the wealthiest and most powerful men in the world. He had survived a mine disaster as a young man, and was confined to a wheelchair thereafter. He lived in seclusion—few people even knew he was married. Van Kampen became his widow and sole heir after only three years. Leysieffer died in circumstances that have never been entirely clarified: he and his bodyguards died in a car crash, and the dead driver was held responsible because he had a high concentration of cut cocaine in his blood. Carlotta van Kampen reassumed her maiden name after his death and ran the business with an iron hand. A world-famous patron and art collector, Leysieffer left his young widow a collection of important early Christian writings, which she steadily augmented. All this must have aroused Rabea's suspicions."

In other good news, Heinrich von Stetten's Italian attorney had that morning obtained a deferment of Lukas's summons to police headquarters. "That leaves only your violation of house arrest. Our attorney is preparing to represent this as a case of force majeure." Von Stetten senior was about to add something when his cell phone rang and he left the room.

"Here, have another." Lucie handed Lukas a cornetto oozing vanilla cream. He took it mechanically but didn't eat it. Jules, by contrast, silently devoured one cornetto after another. Lucie gave her friend a covert, sidelong glance. Something was obviously bugging Jules.

Von Stetten senior reappeared. "Lukas, a word with you."

"Can't we talk later, Father?"

"No, this is important. We'll go and sit in my car. Lucie can always come and get you if there are any developments."

Lukas followed his father outside.

Von Stetten silently opened the passenger door, walked around the car, and got in behind the wheel. He came straight to the point as usual.

"I know why my brother Franz was murdered. It's time I let you in on a family secret. All these untoward happenings—the appalling murders of Franz and the father general and Lucie's abduction—are all directly connected. I myself learned the secret from Franz, who happened on it by chance. I won't ask you to never divulge what I'm going to tell you, but you should carefully consider what effect your actions would have on our family and our business."

Lukas was dumbfounded by his father's words.

"Three months ago, I returned from a business trip to Asia and found your mother in a state of excitement. She told me to call Franz at once and put a crumpled slip of paper in my hand. Franz's manner on the phone was like something out of a cheap thriller. He asked me to meet him at the stated address and to take the utmost care to ensure I wasn't followed. The old fisherman's hut to which the slip of paper directed me turned out to have long been a secret retreat of your uncle's." Von Stetten hesitated as though he found it hard to go on. "I've never told the police, Lukas, but I was the last person to see your uncle alive. He was murdered the same night. Immediately after our conversation, Franz called you and asked you to come to Bamberg. The rest you know. He had already been found by the time you got there, and you had to identify him. Franz was doomed to die because some workmen found a secret cache of books in my library. The legend turned out to be true: there really was a family treasure. Even the books on their own—first editions of works by famous scientists and theologians—were worth a fortune. And concealed in two dummy volumes were caskets containing eighteenth-century Venetian gold coins and a pound of exceptionally pure diamonds and other precious stones. Most informative of all, though, were the documents and the journal that constitutes our family chronicle. It was begun by Alexander von Stetten starting when he settled in Nuremberg in 1778, and then painstakingly kept until 1814, the year of his death. After that, it was carried on by the eldest son. The entries end on May 28, 1916, shortly before my great-grandfather Heinrich died. Both his sons, Alexander and my grandfather Ferdinand, were army officers killed in the First World War. Heinrich must have feared the worst, because he saw to it that the entire treasure was walled up in the library before he died. My father, Heinrich junior, was only four at the time, too young to be initiated into the family secret, which the diary states was passed on to the eldest son by word of mouth only. That was why it lapsed into oblivion over the course of time. But the real family secret, Lukas, is the incredible story recounted in the journal. I must go back a bit: I'm sure you've heard of Paititi?"

Lukas nodded.

"Then you'll know that the media often confuse Paititi with El Dorado, the legendary Land of Gold. But Paititi is a legend of its own. Translated, it means 'Lost City of the Incas.' It was the mysterious refuge of the last Incas in the east of Peru. Although Francisco Pizarro overthrew the Inca empire in 1533, it was another forty years before the conquistadors managed to capture Vilcabamba, where the last Inca ruler, Túpac Amaru, had taken refuge. Túpac was killed, but a group of Incas got away and took their legendary treasure to a place of safety. This story was first confirmed in 2001 by the Italian archaeologist Mario Polia, who had rediscovered the journal of the missionary Andrea Lopez. Writing around 1600, Lopez described a city rich in gold, silver, and precious stones, and called Paititi by the natives. Lopez informed the pope of his discovery, and there are conspiracy theorists who assert that Paititi's exact location has been kept secret by the Vatican ever since. It is supposed to be in the largely unexplored Madre de Dios region east of Cuzco, or east of Lake Titicaca in Bolivia. But everyone has been looking in the wrong place, because *this*, Lukas, is our family secret: *we* are in possession of the secret treasure map. It was in the journal found by Franz. The true name of our ancestor, Alexander von Stetten, was Piero Alessandro di Stefano, and he stole the map from his younger brother Emanuele. Emanuele was a Jesuit, like you. Not just any old priest, he served as personal secretary to Ricci, the last superior general before the suppression of the Jesuits in 1773. Ricci, who knew that his order was doomed and that he himself would soon be arrested, was anxious to prevent some special documents in his secret archive from falling into the hands of the Vatican, so he instructed his secretary to preserve them. Emanuele fled in the confusion that prevailed during the order's final days and hid at the di Stefano family's castle in the middle of Abruzzo. From there he got in touch with other Jesuits, and they met several times in a cave beneath the castle. Among other things they discussed was the treasure map. Some of the Jesuits demanded that it be handed over. Convinced that the pope could be bribed, they

planned an expedition to Paititi to acquire the means of buying back
their power. Emanuele envisaged something else, however. His brother,
Piero, described him as a pure soul, an idealist who had placed himself
at the service of God out of profound faith and a steadfast belief in
his vocation. As Ricci's secretary, he had access to the inner circle of
power. Although the order forbade its members to take an active part
in secular politics, Emanuele knew that in practice it did little else. It
constantly meddled in the affairs of the Catholic countries of Europe
and their colonies, and the Jesuit father confessors to the royal houses
were diligent spies. What shocked him most of all, however, was his
realization of the extent to which the church had cheated the faithful
out of Christ's true bequest from the very first. While in exile, Emanuele
failed to convince his brethren that it was their duty to reform the
established Catholic Church. Instead, they quarreled with him over
the treasure map. Disappointed by their greed, he produced the map,
held it to a flaming torch, and burned it before their eyes. That was the
end of their secret meetings. But Emanuele had burned a copy, not the
original, because he planned to travel to South America himself and
return the map to its rightful owners, the Indios. At that point, his
elder brother, Piero, stepped in. Having eavesdropped on the meeting
and seen through Emanuele's plan, he demanded the map for himself.
His journal does not describe what happened then or what became of
Emanuele. He merely reports that he shouldered a heavy burden of
guilt and brought misfortune upon his brother and his sister, Emilia.
Years later Piero turned up in Nuremberg. Fabulously wealthy by then,
he bought himself a patent of nobility and settled there under the
name Alexander von Stetten. He regretted having betrayed his younger
brother to the end of his days.

"Now you know about the stain on our family name, Lukas. There's
a curse on us, hence our family's many misfortunes. Franz was convinced of that, anyway. They tortured him because they were after the
treasure map, but the fool told them nothing. Whoever *they* are, they

believe that it's in our possession. In fact, it's securely locked up in my office safe. After the First World War my father parlayed the little that was left of our fortune into a business of worldwide repute, but it's all worth nothing. Your brother, Alexander, is dead, and we almost lost Lucie as well. And for what? Are we to atone for our ancestors' mistakes for all eternity?"

Distraught, he hit the steering wheel with his fist. Lukas was shocked. He thought of the dead man in the cave of whom Bentivoglio had spoken. Could that have been his ancestor Emanuele? Was his family's wealth and reputation founded on theft, betrayal, and fratricide? A lot of puzzling events were finally fitting together to form a convincing picture. He had encountered the name di Stefano once before: in the father general's confession. It was on land formerly owned by the di Stefanos that his brother, Giuseppe Bentivoglio, had discovered the Jesuits' secret cave in 1979. Later, when Bishop Franz von Stetten turned up in Rome shortly after the discovery in the library, his old friend Ignazio must have been dismayed to perceive the connection between the two finds.

What was he to do now? The documents and scrolls were in Simone's brother's apartment. His father was right. To make the discovery of the treasure map public, thereby publicizing his family's disgrace as well, was a grave decision.

Van Kampen was still at large. Who else apart from her knew of the family secret? Lukas's heart suddenly froze. The X on his uncle's sermon! Of course, Franz knew the secret and had read Alexander von Stetten's journal. Did his final message refer to the demand not to make the treasure map public because he feared that its rightful owners, the people of Peru, would brand the church thieves? Or did it mean that his conservative uncle Franz was against Bentivoglio publishing the documents because he feared for the reputation and heritage of the church?

"It's your decision, Lukas," said his father.

Lukas hesitated for a moment. Then, awkwardly, he put his arm around the old man's shoulders. The two of them spent a while in silent communion.

The only person taking any notice of the two men in the car was an inquisitive girl who turned to admire the luxury rental before lighting a cigarette and hurrying on. As Lukas mechanically watched her receding figure, his eye was caught by a car on the other side of the street. He could have sworn the man at the wheel had just lowered a pair of binoculars. He dismissed the thought when the car drove off.

"I'm sorry, Lukas." Von Stetten senior had recovered his poise. "It'd be best if you came to Nuremberg as soon as possible to look at the journal and the map yourself. I'll leave Fonton and his team here for your safety. Kiss Lucie for me and give Rabea my best wishes. She's a tough girl—I'm sure she'll soon be back on her feet. Come home soon, the two of you—your mother misses you both."

His father had put on his dispassionate industrialist face again. He waited as Lukas got out of the car, then nodded to Lukas and drove off.

More interminable hours of apprehensive waiting went by before the doctor reappeared. "You'll be glad to hear," he said, "that the patient is awake and would like to see you."

A few minutes later, dressed in sterile clothing, the three of them entered the small intensive care room.

The room was bare apart from the bed, a mass of medical equipment, and a simple crucifix on the wall. The usual faint smell of disinfectant hung in the air. Having enjoined them to make it short and sweet, the doctor left them alone.

Rabea's slender form was almost engulfed by the apparatuses to which she was hooked up. Her cropped auburn hair provided the only touch of color and lent her an impish appearance. She tried a faint smile when they came in, but it got stuck around halfway.

Lukas, overcome with emotion, kneeled down beside the bed and rested his head on the palm of her little hand.

Lucie and Jules came around to the other side of the bed. Lucie brushed the damp strands of hair off her friend's forehead, while Jules, shoulders drooping, stood beside her. He looked like a man in the dock awaiting sentence.

Sensitive as ever, Rabea at once realized what was troubling him. Although her voice sounded fainter than usual, it was just as firm. "Jules, come closer," she told him. And when he did so, she said, "Don't blame yourself unnecessarily, you hear? It wasn't your fault. That vicious bastard was more than a match for us."

"Of course it was my fault." Jules met her eye for the first time. "I didn't search him. I'll never forgive myself."

"Rubbish," she said gently. "No more of that. It upsets me. If you want to exacerbate my condition, carry on. Otherwise, give it a rest." Having won yet another verbal duel, she turned to Lucie. "You're looking great, angel."

"I can't say the same for you. You look like a plucked chicken. You should sue your hairstylist for damages."

"Charming. Still, I'm glad you've recovered so well from your unpleasant adventure. Any word from my grandfather?"

"I've spoken with him, Rabea," said Lukas. "He's well. I'm to tell you he'll pray for you. He also asked me to give you a message. His exact words were, 'For many years now, I've been skipping a line in my morning prayer.'"

Rabea listened to this in surprise. Her drawn face broke into a faint smile. She knew what her grandfather meant. It was his way of telling her he'd been wrong.

Her thoughts went back to the day that had shaken her small but stable world to its foundations. She was ten years old and had already been living with her grandparents for several years. She could hardly remember her parents, who had been killed by a terrorist bomb in Jerusalem.

Several boys at her school often met after lessons to play football. Rabea, who loved football, usually joined in uninvited. The boys had never minded because she was small and elusive and scored the most goals, but this time it was different. A handsome, dark-haired boy who was new to the school pushed her over and proclaimed that Jewish girls didn't play football.

Rabea had already heard the girl argument, but what did being Jewish have to do with it? She scrambled nimbly to her feet and shouted, "My grandfather's a rabbi, and I'm going to be one too!"

The boy stared at her in surprise for a moment. Then he burst into derisive laughter. "Listen to that! She wants to become a rabbi! Listen, I'm Jewish myself. Jewish girls get married, have children, and look after their husbands—it's their only job in life. A girl can't become a rabbi, because women are inferior creatures. Why do you think we grown-up Jewish men thank God we aren't women at prayers every morning? Go home!" And he turned on his heel.

Rabea refused to give up so easily. Seething with fury, she yelled, "You're just a dirty liar and a wannabe grown-up!"

The boy froze. Then he came striding back and gripped her roughly by the shoulders. "Never call me a liar again!" he shouted. "You're just a little girl, so I won't soil my hands by whipping a shrimp like you. Ask your grandfather the rabbi whether or not I'm a liar. And now shove off!"

"Just a little girl . . ." There had been so much contempt in his words that tears of rage sprang to her eyes. Hurrying home to fetch her grandfather right away, she stormed into his study and blurted out the lies the boy had told her. Instead of reaching for his jacket, however, he mystified her by sitting her down in his favorite armchair. "But Grandfather," she protested, "we must go back and tell him at once."

"Calm down, my girl. Here, have one." He pushed a plate of chocolate cookies toward Rabea and signaled to her grandmother, who had come hurrying out of the kitchen, to leave them alone together. "Well now, Rabea, er . . ." He cleared his throat and fished a freshly ironed handkerchief out of his pocket. Unfolding this with care, he noisily blew his nose. Then he found his suspenders needed adjusting.

Rabea shuffled around restlessly in the huge wing chair.

"Well, now, my girl. Of course women aren't inferior creatures." Despite his arthritis, he kneeled down in front of her and rested his scholarly hands on her frail shoulders. "It was absolutely wrong, the way that boy treated you. A man should treat a woman with respect at all times. But on one point I'm afraid he was right. It is, in fact, written that a woman cannot become a rabbi."

To his dismay, he watched his beloved granddaughter's face turn alarmingly pale in a heartbeat. He discerned a wide variety of emotions on it: first incredulity and then, when it dawned on her that the boy had not been entirely wrong, profound disappointment. Then the look in her eyes changed again, and the rabbi realized that the faith she'd placed in him was dying out in a green fire of despair. He knew it was his fault. He had underestimated her seriousness, her intelligence and willpower, and had thereby wounded her tender, childish soul. Now it was too late to repair the damage. For a small eternity, absolute silence reigned between the old man and the young girl.

He continued to wait for Rabea's reaction. It distressed him to find that the silence and the waiting upset him far more than if she'd fiercely attacked him. After what seemed like an age, she looked him in the eye. "Tell me just one thing, Grandfather. If women aren't inferior creatures, why do you thank your God you aren't a woman at prayers every morning?"

From that day on, their relationship changed. Its point of balance seemed to have shifted.

Where Rabea used to covet every minute alone in her grandfather's company, it was now the old rabbi's turn to court her favor. Although she continued to accord him due respect and love, she never asked him another question about Judaism. Overnight, her burning interest in the subject was extinguished. Never again did grandfather and granddaughter enjoy an intimate conversation in his study. Never again did she seek out and listen to his tales of long ago.

Since then, old Rosenthal had wondered if Rabea had deliberately or unconsciously found the most painful way of all to punish him for his betrayal: deprivation of his pleasure in their tête-à-têtes. Only her cruel little heart could have answered that question.

A few days later, she rushed into her grandfather's study and made an announcement: "I know what I'm going to be. I'm going to be a reporter. Reporters get at the truth."

Years later Rabea had learned that it was quite possible for a woman to become a rabbi, albeit with restricted rights, but their conversation had robbed her of all interest in the subject. She had been most hurt by the realization that his slavish adherence to tradition had prompted him to lie to his granddaughter. The message sent her via Lukas proved that he had changed his mind.

With a melancholy smile, Rabea returned to the present. Her grandfather had just presented her with a precious gift. Her heart opened wide and allowed her former love and esteem for him to flow back in. "Thank you, Lukas. My grandfather has made me so happy. His message is about the secret of life and the value of each individual, whether man or woman. Lukas . . ." Her hand tightened on his.

"Are you in pain?" he asked in dismay. "Shall I call the doctor?"

"No, no, I'm all right. Just a little tired, but I must tell you something wonderful. I've . . . I've found it at last, the truth I've been looking for all my life. It was among Bentivoglio's documents. Father Simone had started to translate one of them. It was a letter signed by a Joshua of Jerusalem . . . a long letter to two women both named Myriam. This Joshua . . . in his letter he describes his message to the world of the faithful and gives the women precise instructions on how to proclaim God's word and, above all, his love . . . He chose them to transmit his message of love." She was gazing intently into Lukas's face, her eyes shining like two green stars.

Lukas had been listening to her low, halting voice with deep emotion, never doubting the significance of her words for a moment. Overwhelmed, he sank to his knees beside her. "Oh my God," he murmured. "Oh my God."

"What's wrong?" Lucie broke in. "What does the letter mean and who was this Joshua?"

Rabea closed her eyes, a gentle smile lighting up her face.

Lukas raised his head and drew a deep breath as if gathering the inner strength he needed for what he was about to say. "It may mean that Rabea and Simone have discovered the most important manuscript in Christendom. Jesus was one of the most intelligent men that ever lived, but he didn't leave posterity a single word in writing, allegedly because he was illiterate. Everything we know about him was handed down by others. Jesus was a Jew. His Jewish name was Joshua, which the Romans rendered as Jesus. The two Myriams could be his mother Mary and Mary Magdalene, or Mary of Magdala. It sounds incredible, but if it's true, and a testament handwritten by Our Lord Jesus Christ exists, it would explain the lengths to which someone was prepared to go to gain possession of the document. It would be humanity's most precious manuscript—more valuable than any other relic in the world."

"It most certainly is true, Lukas. It's . . . it's the only genuine Holy Grail," Rabea whispered, clinging to his hand. "When I held that papyrus in my hand, the papyrus that *his* hands had held, and saw the words *he* had written, I felt that for the first time. I could feel his love and . . . I could also understand you and your faith. I always envied the fact that you could feel something special, while I . . . just felt empty inside. But the love his words conveyed was like . . . like a balm to my soul. That letter is genuine, Lukas; I know it is, and anyone who reads it will realize that too. Jesus bequeathed the world a gospel of love. He loved women and revered them. He knew their strength and their love . . . and their tenderheartedness. He knew how much women respected life, because God himself chose them to bring forth life from their loins. God and Jesus believed in the life-giving role of women—they created it themselves. The exegesis—the 'leading out' of the apostles—Jesus wanted the two Marys to lead it. He placed them at the head of the apostles and gave them the task of proclaiming love and faith in God. Knowing everything, he knew his disciples were weak. You must go and get his gospel, Lukas, and make it accessible to everyone. Because his real message is that all are equal regardless of gender or race or color. All that counts is love of one's neighbor and peaceful coexistence. Jesus had no wish to create a new religion. He wanted to teach people love. That was his vision of a new kingdom on earth. Jesus wanted peace . . . He condemned war and violence, lust for power and greed. I've found it at last, Lukas, the thing I've been looking for—the reason why I always envied you and Grandfather. I've found peace, and I'm happy because I know that Jesus's testament will make the world a better place."

"Of course, my sweet Rabea, but you mustn't overexert yourself."

Lucie reverted to her habitual, rather sardonic, pragmatism. "Far be it from me to spoil this moment of truth, but if the papers are as valuable as you say, perhaps Jules and I should go and get them right away."

"I was about to make the same suggestion," said Jules. "Father Simone is dead. It might be a good thing if the police looked around his brother's apartment in the course of their inquiries."

"Yes," said Rabea, "please go, but be careful. I'm not entirely sure because Simone had translated only about half of Bentivoglio's diary and I could only take a superficial look at everything, but it appears that the document was stolen from the Jesuits in 1773 with the intention of duplicating the true Gospel of Jesus and publishing it. The idea was to compel the established church to reform itself along Lutheran lines. The conspiracy was discovered, and everyone involved was killed. I think Bentivoglio was murdered because he also planned to . . . to make the documents accessible to all believers." Rabea coughed and an almost imperceptible look of pain crossed her face.

Lukas noticed it nonetheless.

Rabea felt her energies waning, but she needed to speak with him alone. "Get going, you two," she said.

Lucie and Jules kissed her on the forehead and left the room.

"Lukas—" she began, but he stopped her at once by laying his forefinger on her lips. His eyes conveyed all the years of love and longing pent up inside him.

"Hush, Rabea, you must conserve your strength. You know how much I love and have always loved you. I'm going to ask to be released from my vows, and then we'll make up for lost time. Everything we dreamed of as children will come true, I promise."

Rabea's eyes suddenly filled with tears.

The realization that something was amiss pierced his heart like a dagger. "What is it, Rabea? What's wrong?"

She turned her tear-stained face to his. Try as he might to resist it, her sadness invaded his soul.

"No, Lukas. It's too late for us. The Rabea you knew in the old days hasn't existed for a long time. I . . . My burden of guilt is too great . . . I was . . . selfish. I deprived a child of its father . . ." She was shaken again by a dry cough. Suddenly, Lukas was pierced to the core by a shrill bleep right beside him.

A nurse dashed into the room and pushed him aside. A doctor hurried in after her and banished him with an unceremonious "Out!"

As he lingered in the doorway for a moment, unable to tear himself away from the sight of Rabea, he heard her voice once more. Her last words were faint but audible: "Lukas, you must go to Urnäsch in Switzerland . . . Promise . . . And forgive me . . . I love you . . ."

The doctor spouted something about complications. Rabea's heart had already been damaged before the operation, he said, and some of her arteries were occluded by a superabundance of white blood cells. In the long term, this could have resulted in a heart attack even in the absence of a bullet wound. He asked Lukas if he knew whether Rabea had been depressed or under stress. When Lukas said that she was a journalist who had recently returned from Iraq, the doctor seemed to consider that a sufficient explanation. He murmured he would do everything humanly possible for her.

Lucie and Jules returned soon afterward to find Lukas beside himself. They bore more bad news: Simone's brother's apartment had been ransacked, and none of the neighbors had noticed a thing. Grassa, who had arrived soon after them, was furious.

So all these terrible events had come to nothing. Their efforts had been in vain. The sacred documents were gone, stolen. The Dutch woman had gotten there first.

WHEN GOD
SMILES...

It was a glorious day in late summer. There had been a brief but heavy shower of rain early that morning, but now everything was dry and the air smelled clean and tangy. Fresh from their bath, the birds were giving a concert. Rabea, who had loved living creatures of all kinds, would have enjoyed their merry twittering. It was the day of her funeral.

Old, bent, and leaning heavily on his cane, Grandfather Rosenthal stood beside Lukas von Stetten in front of the simple granite tombstone. Rabea had been laid to rest beside her beloved grandmother. The rabbi's lips moved in a silent prayer as a single tear overflowed his eye and trickled down his furrowed cheek. The handful of other mourners—Lucie, Heinrich and Evelyn von Stetten, Jules, a few old school friends, and several of Rabea's journalist colleagues—waited quietly for the prayer to end, some of them in silent communion with the dead. Lucie alone sobbed unrestrainedly, while her mother, who was standing beside her, plied her with tissues.

Lukas himself was immersed in prayer, but he couldn't really concentrate. For some days now, prayer had failed to bring him the comfort he'd always found in it. This was his second funeral in three days. He had arrived back only late last night from the island of Lampedusa, where he had conducted Father Simone's funeral at his parents' request. Rabea's funeral should have taken place before Simone's because Jews are customarily buried within twenty-four hours of death, but the Roman authorities had delayed releasing her remains because she was the victim of a crime of violence. Although Father Simone had also been the victim of a crime of violence, his body had been released at once.

Lukas's thoughts continued to stray, and he mulled over his conversation with Rabea's grandfather after he and Jules had accompanied her body back home in his father's executive jet.

As soon as they had delivered her sealed coffin to the director of the funeral home, Lukas had felt impelled to call on old Rabbi Rosenthal, and not merely because he had to discuss the formalities of Rabea's memorial. He was accompanied by Stellina, who had once belonged to the murdered contessa. The little shih tzu had not stirred from his side since Rabea's death.

The rabbi had greeted him with the words, "Shalom, Lukas, I was expecting you." Then he looked down at the dog. "Aha, and here, I suppose, is the last poor creature Rabea rescued. Come in, both of you." Having ushered Lukas into the cozy little living room, he disappeared into the kitchen, and Lukas heard him putting the kettle on. Tea and homemade chocolate cookies had always been produced on his visits in the old days.

It was years since he had been there, but time seemed to have stood still in the little house. The grandfather clock in the corner, however, seemed to deny this and was ticking as loudly as ever. The sound drilled into his ears, awakening painful memories.

Old Rosenthal returned with two steaming mugs. Lukas sat down on the sofa on which Lucie, Rabea, and he had so often sat and devoured whole mountains of chocolate cookies. There were no cookies this time.

After taking a cautious sip of tea, the rabbi said, "Thank you, Lukas, for bringing my Rabea home. I know what's troubling you: you think you're partly responsible for her death and could possibly have prevented it. You're wrong. Rabea was fated not to grow old. Her grandmother and I, we always had an inkling of it and prayed that we would die first. At least her grandmother was spared this sorrow. Rabea knew it too, Lukas. That's why she was so erratic—why she kept constantly on the move as though afraid to put down roots. She was never at home anywhere. Did you ever pay a visit to her apartment in Berlin?"

Lukas shook his head.

"I visited her there two years ago, shortly after her grandmother's death," Rosenthal went on. "It saddened me profoundly. I've never seen anything bleaker than that apartment. It was a distressing reflection of Rabea's personality—a motley assortment of unopened moving boxes and suitcases. Nothing personal, as if she rejected close ties and wanted to preserve no memories. She was lonely, Lukas. The Berlin apartment was a springboard on which she landed occasionally, but only to repack her bags for the next foreign assignment. She changed even more after her grandmother's death, becoming more reserved and visiting and writing less often. I longed to help her, but she had to conquer that inner restlessness herself. For a while, I hoped you two would be together. You were her anchor, Lukas. Perhaps she would have found the peace with you that she never found alone, but we all make decisions about ourselves and our lives that exclude other people. When I think of Rabea, I see a unique and wonderful blossom in the precious vase of life. Rabea loved the innocent—children and animals. Remember the many sick or injured creatures she used to bring home? She was so full of love and concern for the helpless. As a little girl she always said that God smiles when his animals are doing well."

At the recollection of Rabea's private zoo, which was perennially populated by birds, hedgehogs, rabbits, cats, and once even a little donkey, the old rabbi's wrinkled face broke into a sorrowful smile. "Rabea would have liked to save the whole world. Alas, she completely neglected to save herself. But there's one thing that will always console us both, Lukas. Even though the precious vase of Rabea's life has been smashed, our memory of the sweet scent of that purest of all blossoms will never leave us."

Someone touched his arm. "Lukas?"

He was so engrossed in his thoughts, he'd failed to notice that the old rabbi had concluded his prayers.

Rabea's former classmates rounded off the proceedings by playing an MP3 of Rabea's favorite song, which Lukas had suggested would make a suitable conclusion to this day of farewell. It came from the movie *River of No Return* and had once been sung by Marilyn Monroe: *Worn silver dollar, changing hearts, changing lives, changing hands.*

Once the last, plangent notes had died away, the mourners left the graveyard.

At the request of Lucie and Lukas, their mother had arranged a reception at the von Stetten residence. Although the guests numbered less than twenty, the Rosenthal house would still have been too small to accommodate them. Most of them lingered until the small hours, talking about Rabea, laughing and grieving and reminding each other of the many unforgettable times they'd spent together.

That night, Lukas made an irrevocable decision: he would keep his promise to Rabea. He would ask to be released from his vows and quit the Jesuit Order as soon as possible. How ironic it was that Rabea had died just as she had finally acknowledged what true faith really signified, what he felt, and why his faith had meant so much to him. True faith didn't steal love, as she had thought, but enriched it.

* * *

Lukas was finding the burden of grief unendurable. At night he tossed and turned in his bed, unable to sleep. Every minute seemed to last for hours, every hour for an eternity. *All wounds take time to heal*—how often had he uttered those words when comforting the bereaved. But what was he to do if time ceased to pass for him? Time was becoming his enemy. It was as if Rabea had left him imprisoned in a time loop devoid of anything but the darkness of a leaden present.

He mechanically did what had to be done: got up in the morning, showered, chatted with his parents. He ate and drank without tasting anything—his surroundings seemed universally gray, dismal, and dead. He was paying too high a price of grief for Uncle Franz, for his friend Simone, and for the loss of his beloved Rabea. If the kidnappers had done anything to Lucie, as well, he doubted he could have mustered the courage to go on living.

He had no plans mapped out for the future, although he knew he would soon have to figure out how to earn his keep as a private individual. He had no wish to be dependent on his family in any way. Perhaps he could be a teacher. Rabea had always thought he should put his talents at the service of humanity, not just the Christian God alone.

Although he still felt incapable of reaching a decision, he intended to fulfill Rabea's last, whispered request and drive to Urnäsch, which he had located on the map some twenty-five miles southwest of Saint Gallen in Switzerland. He had no idea what she had meant or what he was supposed to do there. Lucie's response when he asked her about it was, "I don't know what to advise you, but I know what your own advice would be: 'Put your faith in God.'"

Lukas had two more matters to settle after Urnäsch. The first was in Santo Stefano di Sessanio in Abruzzo, where he would ensure that the unknown man in the cave was finally laid to rest in consecrated ground. Secondly, having discussed the subject with his father, he would soon fly to South America to do what his ancestor Emanuele had intended more than 230 years ago: return the treasure map showing the secret location of Paititi to its true owners, the Peruvians. Both he and his father realized that this would be a tricky undertaking in need of careful planning and preparation.

Since Rabea's death, Lucie and Lukas's father had broken the surprising news that he would turn the family business into a foundation, and that most of its profits would also accrue to Peru. After all, he said, the von Stettens' wealth had originally been founded on the exploitation of the Incas' treasures. Lukas, who would never have thought his father capable of such a gesture, was utterly amazed. Although they still handled one another with kid gloves, their previously strained relationship had improved considerably. These tasks and obligations were all that prevented Lukas from sinking into a slough of black despair.

Unable to sleep yet again, Lukas went over to the window. It was a warm summer night. Propelled by a gentle, fitful breeze, some puffs of cloud released the moon from their embrace. Its soft rays stole into the room, picking out the small package that lay on his desk. It had been lying there for two days, forgotten until this moment.

Rabea's grandfather had given it to him during his visit, saying that it had arrived inside a parcel some days before. The old man had opened the parcel and found the package. It was inscribed, in Rabea's handwriting, with the words: *For Lukas. Personal. To be given to him when the time is right.*

This cryptic information had been typical of her. How was he to know when the time was right? Had she guessed that her own time was running out and not wanted to alarm him by writing, *To be opened in the event of my death*? Anyway, the rabbi had resigned himself to fate and decided to keep the package until something tipped him off. Sadly, that moment had come all too soon.

The contents of the package were a total mystery to Lukas, and he still hadn't brought himself to open it. To be honest, he was afraid of doing so. What if it contained Rabea's final thoughts, possibly a clue to her approaching end? It didn't really matter now. Rabea was dead and the sacred writings from Bentivoglio's safe-deposit box had vanished without trace, together with the Dutch woman. To avoid having to look at the package anymore, he stowed it away in the farthest corner of his clothes closet. He would open it sometime, but not tonight.

He got back into bed, but sleep still refused to come. He continued to drift on the dark waters of sorrow. His life was bereft of love and faith, laughter and color.

Nevertheless, the next morning the sun climbed into a turquoise sky and a cheerful voice on the radio announced that temperatures during that day would be in the mideighties. Sleepless night or no, Lukas had risen, showered, and dressed at dawn. He hadn't gone jogging since the morning he tripped over Rabea's red shoes—a lifetime ago, it seemed.

At half past six, accompanied by little Stellina, he set off to fulfill Rabea's last request: that he follow her mysterious parting words to Urnäsch.

He reached the small Swiss town after driving for several hours. The main street was flanked by picturesque, timber-framed houses with window boxes full of geraniums. In the center of town, he spotted a hotel with a large terrace on which some guests were enjoying their breakfast in the warm morning sunlight. The terrace afforded a good view of the marketplace and the main street, so Lukas decided to take Stellina for a walk and then have coffee there.

The dog had always come when called in the past, so he let her off the leash. She promptly made friends with an old waitress whose apron was deliciously redolent of the hotel kitchen, and she was rewarded with a little veal bone.

Stellina's artfulness made Lukas smile for the first time since Rabea's death. The little animal had clamped the bone between her forepaws and was gnawing it with gusto when her attention was distracted by something on the other side of the street.

Following the direction of her gaze, Lukas saw a group of nursery-school children walking along hand in hand, marshaled by two young female supervisors. Ahead of them trotted a small dog indistinguishable in appearance from Stellina. Without warning, Stellina sprang to her feet and, before Lukas knew it, she was scampering across the street.

His heart skipped a beat when he heard a car brake sharply. Jumping up too, he hurried across the street with the leash and managed to capture her and reattach it on the opposite sidewalk. While simultaneously cursing and petting her, relieved that she was unscathed, he heard a small boy's voice addressing him in Swiss German.

"It won't learn that way. If a dog's been naughty, you mustn't stroke it or it won't know what it's done wrong."

Lukas, who was kneeling beside Stellina, looked up. Standing roughly eye level with him was a flaxen-haired boy of around five. His hands were thrust deep into the pockets of his lederhosen. He had a snotty nose and a sizable smudge of dirt on his cheek. Behind him, the other children were whispering excitedly and giggling at the dogs, whose acquaintanceship had entered a new phase. Stellina's doppelgänger was clearly demonstrating his gender by trying to mount her.

Lukas rose and gave Stellina's leash a vigorous tug. Then, because this proved ineffective, he picked her up, whereupon her male counterpart excitedly sprang at his leg and tried to copulate with it. Highly embarrassed, he attempted to shake the dog off without hurting it while Stellina struggled in his arms, all to roars of laughter from the watching children.

The supervisor at the end of the line came hurrying up while her colleague tried to control their charges. Assessing the situation at a glance, she grabbed the male shih tzu by the scruff of the neck and firmly said, "Enough, Caruso! Naughty dog. Sit!" The dog sat, but not without regarding Stellina with a lustfully lolling tongue.

"You see? That's the way to do it. This is my mummy," the fair-haired boy told him triumphantly, pointing to the pretty young blonde beside him. She had crouched down to put Caruso on his leash. Now she straightened up, looked at Lukas for the first time, and froze.

So did he. All the blood drained from his cheeks.

After breaking Jules's nose in his fit of jealousy, Lukas had gone to see Uncle Franz and despairingly sought his advice. He had wanted to marry Rabea, and now his dream was shattered. Had the incident in Munich been an omen? Did God want him to dedicate his life to him?

Bishop Franz had grasped the nature of his spiritual dilemma and suggested two alternatives: he should either spend a few weeks in retreat at a monastery or completely let loose for the first time in his life. "Go away somewhere, Lukas. Let your hair down—just be your age and live a little. You're far too upset right now to decide on your future."

Lukas opted for a convent, but the silence and introspection failed to bring him peace. So after only a few days, he fled and impulsively bought an airplane ticket to Majorca. He spent several days roaming the island aimlessly, sitting on the beach at night and looking up at the stars. One night he heard someone sobbing softly nearby. A young blonde was also sitting forlornly on the beach like him, hugging her knees, and crying her heart out. Needless to say, he had to attempt to comfort her.

The girl had just suffered a bitter disappointment. She had flown to the island with her boyfriend to spend their first vacation together, but the swine had deserted her for another girl after only a day. Lukas invited her to join him at a nearby beach bar, where they drank enough sangria to make them both tipsy.

The warm summer night, the twinkling stars, and the murmur of waves breaking on a beach of velvety sand did the rest. At some stage, they ended up in Lukas's room and spent an ecstatic few hours of which he remembered little more than soft skin, silky blonde hair gently brushing his face, and the scent of wildflowers. Late that night, drunk on sangria and sex, he fell asleep. In the morning, she had disappeared.

He looked for her everywhere—he even postponed his departure for a day, but all he knew about her was her name, Magali, and that she was Swiss. Never having seen her in daylight, he couldn't even have said what color her eyes were.

Now he knew: they were blue as a field of cornflowers in summer. He stared at her. She stared back, and the silence dragged on until the little boy claimed their attention with a question that burst like a bomb: "Mummy, what's the matter?" he asked in his broad Swiss German. "Do you know this man? Is he my father?"

Lukas thought he must have misheard. He couldn't have known that the youngster was obsessed with finding his father and asked the same question about every man who happened to cross his mother's path. Twice in recent months he had run away to look for his father in the big, wide world—expeditions that had fortunately ended on the outskirts of town. Until now, his mother had always laughingly dismissed his question, smoothed down his refractory mop of fair hair with a motherly gesture, and said, "No, Matti, that isn't your father."

But this time was different. She said, "Yes, Matti, this is your father."

Lukas nearly fainted.

Matti was hunkered down on the landing of the small house where he and his mother lived. The two dogs, Stellina and Caruso, were quietly sitting beside him. The boy listened anxiously to the voices of the grown-ups in the living room. But things weren't going at all the way he'd imagined. He had thought that if he found his father at last, he and his mother would fall into each other's arms and live happily ever after, the way people did in the fairy tales his mother read him. Instead, they were shouting at each other.

"What did you think you were doing, turning up here with no notice, and upsetting my son?" his mother snarled.

"Me? I didn't say a thing. It was you that told him. I wonder if that was wise. Our son is far too young to digest a surprise like that. You should have broken it to him gently."

"What?" Magali snapped. "*Our* son? I must have misheard! Kindly don't tell me what *my* son can or cannot digest. You don't know him— you've never shown any interest in him. Just because you once sent me a whopping great child support check, don't imagine you've any say in his upbringing. Matti and I have managed perfectly well without you up till now, and we'll continue to do so. It'd be best if you turned around and went straight home."

She glared at him angrily. Though somewhat taller than Rabea and not as petite, she seemed no less temperamental. Lukas was just wondering if the memory of her gentleness had become somewhat transfigured in his mind when one of the words she'd hurled at him sank in. "Child support?" he repeated in astonishment. "But I never paid you any child support. I didn't even know that you—I mean, that we had a child. I came here only by chance . . ."

Suddenly his heart missed a beat, and the floor seemed to sway beneath him. The realization hit him with the force of a cannonball. Rabea! *She* had told him to go to Urnäsch. *She* had known the truth. Now at last he grasped the meaning of her burden of guilt, and the child whom she'd robbed of a father. Rabea had known about the boy all those years and never told him. It was *she* who had sent the money as a way of salving her conscience. But how had she known in the first place?

"Magali, sit down. I think we've got a lot to talk about."

When six years earlier Magali discovered she was pregnant, she had sent Lukas a letter to his home address in Nuremberg, which she was able to get from the hotel register. She felt the prospective father had a right to know, especially as she had been the one to disappear from his hotel room without a word. In the letter, she had emphasized that she wanted nothing for herself, only the legally prescribed child support for their child.

Two hours later, after Magali had cleared the supper table, Lukas had a novel experience: for the first time in his life, he put his blissfully happy son to bed with a good-night story.

When the boy had fallen asleep at last, he gently kissed the unruly mop of fair hair that so closely resembled his own. He continued to sit beside and gaze at his peacefully sleeping son for quite a while, still unable to absorb the happiness this little human miracle had brought him.

All at once, he felt a slight breeze. The fledgling father cast an anxious glance at the window—worried about the draft chilling his sleeping son—but it was shut. Strange, though. He could still feel that breath of wind caressing his cheek, soft and gentle as a kiss. At the same time, and for one brief moment, he was enfolded by a familiar, consoling scent, and the words of wise old Rabbi Rosenthal came back to him: even if the precious vase of life was smashed, his memory of the sweet scent of the lovely blossom it had once contained would endure forever.

ACKNOWLEDGMENTS

This book subsists on the tension between Rabea the atheist and Lukas the Catholic priest.

My worldly-wise husband has advised me to point out that the religious and political views expressed by my principal characters do not reflect those of the author.

Apropos of my husband, this book—which could not have been written without him and his understanding—is dedicated to him. Thanks are also due to my mother and sister and Heike and Myriam for their constant advice and criticism.

I should also like to thank my agent, Lianne Kolf, and her friend and editor Ingeborg Castell. Dear Frau Castell, I know you were fond of Father Simone, but he's doing fine: he's cooking in heaven now. And Rabea? Who knows?

Above all, though, I thank *you*, dear reader, for reading this book. I wrote it for you!

—*H. M., January 2013*

ABOUT THE AUTHOR

Photo © 2014 Fotostudio Dörr

Having always possessed a lively imagination, Hanni Münzer devoured every book she could lay her hands on starting at age six—not all of them suitable for young readers. With hundreds of thousands of copies sold, her dark, sexy thrillers mix historical intrigue, murder, and heated romance. After stops in Seattle, Stuttgart, and Rome, Hanni Münzer now lives with her husband and dog in Upper Bavaria, Germany.

ABOUT THE TRANSLATOR

Photo © Sherborne Photographic

Originally a classicist whose school diet from age eight included ancient Greek as well as Latin, John Brownjohn won a major scholarship to Oxford, whence he graduated with honors. Thereafter, partly because he hails from a ramified family whose members fought on both sides during World War II, he made the transition to modern languages and a career as a literary translator, which has earned him critical acclaim and many British and American awards. In addition to translating the better part of two hundred books, he has produced English versions of many German and French screenplays and cowritten several feature films with Roman Polanski.